"I'm a fun date. You'd have a good time. There's got to be somewhere in town you've always wanted to go but haven't gotten around to. Tell me what it is and I'll take you tonight."

Darcy was about to shut him down, but as she stood there looking at that half-playful, too tempting smile all she could think was how long it had been since she'd really had fun. Of all the things she'd told herself she'd get to some time but had never managed to do.

Now her time was up. She was leaving tomorrow.

Jeff was offering her a chance to— God, was she seriously considering this?

She never said yes. Never gave in and did the fun thing for fun's sake. Maybe tonight, after living the straight and narrow for so very long, just this once she could afford to break the rules without worrying about tomorrow.

"I'll think about it."

Dear Reader

It's no secret that I'm all about the Happily Ever After. I like my true loves and for evers big, beautiful and wrapped up with a gorgeous bow—preferably the kind that comes with a sparkly diamond ring or maybe even a baby on the way.

Now, normally I make my heroes and heroines work for those fairytale accompaniments. But for some reason when I started playing with the idea of best friends Connor Reed (WAKING UP MARRIED) and Jeff Norton (WAKING UP PREGNANT) I couldn't resist mixing things up by giving these guys the traditional happy endings at the beginning of their stories!

Of course a ring alone or even a baby on the way doesn't guarantee for ever... But with heroes as charismatic, determined and resourceful as these two you can bet they'll be pulling out all the stops to earn that hard-won Happily Ever After we dedicated romantics thrive on.

I hope you'll enjoy reading Jeff and Darcy's story as much as I enjoyed writing it.

All my best

Mira

PS If you haven't read WAKING UP MARRIED, no worries. While the stories are loosely tied together by one fateful evening in Vegas, they can most definitely stand alone.

WAKING UP PREGNANT

BY
MIRA LYN KELLY

MILLS & BOON

Published in Great Britain 2014
by Mills & Boon, an imprint of Harlequin (UK) Limited,
Eton House, 18-24 Paradise Road, Richmond, Surrey, TW9 1SR

© 2014 Mira Lyn Sperl

ISBN: 978 0 263 91223 4

Printed and bound in Spain
by Blackprint CPI, Barcelona

Mira Lyn Kelly grew up in the Chicago area and earned her degree in Fine Arts from Loyola University. She met the love of her life while studying abroad in Rome, Italy, only to discover he'd been living right around the corner from her for the previous two years. Having spent her twenties working and playing in the Windy City, she's now settled with her husband in rural Minnesota, where their four beautiful children provide an excess of action, adventure and entertainment.

With writing as her passion, and inspiration striking at the most unpredictable times, Mira can always be found with a notebook at the ready. (More than once the neighbours have caught her, covered in grass clippings, scribbling away atop the compost container!)

When she isn't reading, writing or running to keep up with the kids, she loves watching movies, blabbing with the girls and cooking with her husband and friends. Check out her website—www.miralynkelly.com—for the latest dish!

**This and other titles by Mira Lyn Kelly
are available in eBook format
from www.millsandboon.co.uk**

To Eleanor, Joyce, Jessica, Elizabeth and,
kicking off the fourth generation…Jacqueline

CHAPTER ONE

WITHIN THE FAST closing walls of his downtown L.A. executive office—a modern, stylized space reflective of his personal tastes, professional achievements and global priorities—Jeff Norton watched the limitless sky of his future crack and crumble as the woman in front of him doubled over, one arm clutching his trash can, while the other shot straight. Her hand alternating between a traffic cop's stop signal and a single finger indicating it was going to be a minute before she got to him.

"Not a problem, Darcy," he managed in a voice barely recognizable even to himself. "Really. Take all the time you need."

The sounds of distress emanating from the depths of his violated wastebasket ceased and the Vegas cocktail waitress he'd found too tempting to resist three months ago pinned him with a watery stare before rolling her *you-did-this-to-me* eyes in disgust.

Which was almost enough to pull a laugh from him, except, yeah, that look said it all. This was the end of days.

Probably.

Because while it wasn't any great mystery as to why this woman was seeking him out now, months after those fateful few hours they'd spent together that ended with him staring down in abject horror at what could best be described as an epic latex fail, whether the hormone-wreaking miracle behind this reunion was, in fact, his, or whether his portfolio simply made him the most obvious solution to a problem which might be laid at the feet of any number of other candidates, was still yet to be seen.

Though even as he thought it, something inside him rebelled at the idea.

Three months.

If she'd been here after one… Hell, if she'd still been there that first night when he came back from the bathroom…

He swallowed. Sucked a deep breath, only to realize what a monumental mistake he'd made when the smell permeating his office—his sanctuary, his power position, his godforsaken happy-place-no-more—had his stomach contracting in some kind of sympathetic reflex.

Darcy looked over the plastic liner at him and, seeming to catch the wayward direction of his stomach, tightened her hold in a move very obviously saying, *Get your own can, buddy.*

Nice.

His molars ground together. This was the mother of his child.

Maybe.

Crossing to his desk, he dialed his assistant's extension. "Charlie, I need a bottle of mouthwash, a toothbrush and paste and a dozen trash liners. And if you can get it all in here in the next five minutes I'll cut you a check for a thousand dollars today."

Darcy pinched her eyes shut a moment and when she looked back at him, it was with reluctant gratitude. "Thank you."

"Suppose it's the least I can do…." Considering what he'd *maybe, probably* done already.

He watched the rise and fall of her shoulders as she struggled for her composure.

"I'm sorry—"

He waved her off, but her eyes narrowed so he let her go on. "About springing…this on you. It must…be a shock."

More so now than it would have been two months ago.

"We can talk about it after you've had a minute to yourself. There's a private bathroom back this way. Charlie's freakishly efficient—"

As if underscoring his point, a knock sounded as the office door swung open for the fastest man in the West, who'd somehow managed to collect a tray of the requested items along with an unopened sleeve of saltine crackers in a matter of seconds. Considering Charlie normally coordinated international business meetings, spoke seven languages and had an MBA from the top school in the U.S., the toiletry run wasn't perhaps the best use of his time. But for Jeff, the guy had just come through in what ranked up there with a life-and-death emergency.

"Charlie Litsky, this is Darcy—" And there it was, the glaring reminder he didn't even know her last name. Right. Moving on. "Darcy, Charlie," he said, leading them back to the private bathroom in the far corner of the office.

"Why don't I take this?" he said, relieving a sallow-cheeked Darcy of the trash can at the door. "Before you leave today, I'll give you Charlie's contact information. If you need to get ahold of me, or anything else, he'll be able to help you."

But then Charlie produced a card of his own, already inked in with a private mobile number. The man was worth his weight in gold. Proven even more so, when they excused themselves to leave Darcy at the bathroom and Charlie eyed the trash Jeff was holding at arm's length.

"Can I take that for you?"

Jeff blew out a humorless laugh. More than anything he wanted to say yes. But whatever the actual protocol for vomit in the office was, Jeff couldn't stick this with someone else.

Holding out a hand for the liners instead, he shook his head. "This is my mess. Think I'd better be the one to clean it up."

Darcy Penn glared into the mirror in front of her, scrubbing the foul taste off her teeth and tongue with a vigor fueled by humiliation and outrage. One that wasn't going to get her anything but gums that wouldn't grow back if she didn't ease up a little.

The nerve.

He'd referred to her as "his mess." And offered *his assistant's* number in case she needed to get ahold of *him*.

What an ass.

And to think she'd been afraid of seeing him again. Worried she'd find herself susceptible to the same judgment-obliterating spell she'd fallen under that last night in Vegas when she'd found this guy so unbelievably compelling, she'd essentially broken every rule she had, just for a few hours with him. Anxious the man whose easy charm and demanding kisses infiltrated her dreams with nightmarish frequency would be as irresistible as she remembered him. And once again, he'd tempt her toward the kind of destructive fantasies she'd made it her life's mission to avoid.

Nope. Whatever freaky mojo he'd been working back in Vegas wasn't in play today.

Not even a little.

Well fine, maybe a little.

There'd been an instant when Jeff opened his office door and she'd seen something hot in his eyes—but that was before she'd lunged past him making a practiced grab for the nearest garbage. Before the horror replaced the heat. And all the walls she'd suspected were there from the start slammed into place.

Now not even a little.

Which was good. Because her plate was more than full enough with this serving-for-two fate had dished her without having to worry about some weird chemistry snaking through the air between them. It distracted her with a momentary feel-good buzz she was too much of a realist to think might actually last, when she needed to focus on working out the details that would impact not just the rest of her life, but her child's, as well.

Their child's.

Her frenetic brushing slowed and she spit the paste.

God, what was he going to want? The mess cleaning reference didn't exactly suggest an instant, joyfully embraced, paternal connection. And how she felt about that… she didn't know.

On the one hand, her child would be lucky to have the kind of emotional security afforded by two parents who wanted it. But on the other, did either she or her baby really need to be tied to some overgrown kid who, by all appearances, didn't know the meaning of the word *no?* The man had made a desk of some repurposed airplane wing and a conference table from a disassembled jukebox topped in glass, for crying out loud. Essentially turning his workspace into a playground filled with the toys of a boy's heart.

And, yes, that boyish, world-on-a-string mentality packaged within a rugged all-man's body may have held some appeal when she first encountered it in Vegas. He'd known how to laugh. How to grab life with both hands and live in the moment without overanalyzing every move he made, without weighing every decision. And for a few incredible hours he'd shown her how to do the same.

But now, as that same mentality applied to the father of her child and with her body as exhibit A as one of the consequences to that *just for fun* mindset?

She let out a slow breath. Reached for the mouthwash, went for a bracing swish and spit.

Not so much.

Darcy placed a hand over her still flat belly, her emotions caught in a tug-of-war between awe over the precious life within her and resentment directed at herself. Disappointment. Frustration.

She'd known better. She'd spent years saying no to every temptation, because she'd had no one to count on but herself. No net to fall back in. No desire to allow herself to be trapped the way her mother had been.

She'd always been so relentlessly careful.

So how was it, this time, this one night, *this guy*...she'd said yes?

CHAPTER TWO

Three months earlier...

AND HERE HE'D thought he might be bored.

Within the swank Vegas lounge, Jeff Norton folded his arms over the tabletop, leaning forward in what had turned out to be a ringside seat for the crash-and-burn All-Stars playing out before him as a table of guys tried to score on the leggy blonde who'd just served him his Scotch.

He couldn't believe the one kid was throwing her a line after the world-class freeze she'd laid on the last chump. And his *friends* were encouraging him. Forget that on the hot scale, this woman ranked so far out of the kid's league, they weren't even on the same planet, let alone page. But hadn't they seen her eyes? The flat, wholly uninviting, all-business expression leaving zero wiggle room for misinterpretation: not interested. Period.

Probably not. These guys had a just legal look about them, which, coupled with their collection of empties lined up like trophies on the table, and the frequent "Vegas, baby!" fist pumps suggested they hadn't made it past the admittedly dynamite body before their brains blew out.

Live and learn, boys.

Thirty seconds later, the kid was taking a round of conciliatory back slaps from his cohorts and Jeff was back to waiting for Connor. His best friend fresh off a broken engagement and the reason behind this "guys' weekend" in Sin City.

Where the hell was he anyway?

Checking his texts, Jeff cursed seeing it was going to be at least another hour.

Screw it. He wasn't interested in watching guys, age twenty-one to ninety-three line up to strike out while Connor wrapped his call with Hong Kong. Flagging another server, he handed her his still full drink then pulled out a few bills for the table.

He was halfway to the door when feminine laughter, rich and warm, spilled down the hall beside the bar. The full-bodied sound of it snared his senses and had him cranking his head around to catch a glimpse of the source.

He stopped dead, his eyes locking on the silky blond ponytail streaming over one shoulder. The legs. The hourglass curves, and finally the softest, warmest, twinkling gray eyes he'd ever seen, crinkled at the edges as *his cocktail waitress* peered up at the ceiling laughing at whatever it was the shorter, redheaded server adjusting her shoe had said.

Gone was that untouchable, unattainable, disinterested, cold set of attractive features. And in their place was this *woman*.

No way.

And no wonder she'd kept that laugh under wraps. She could barely make it across the lounge as it was without some bozo putting a move on her. If anyone saw her like this…

Well, hell, their thinking would probably follow the same as his.

How do I get her to laugh like that for me?

They'd never leave her alone.

The redhead sauntered deeper down the hall and the leggy blonde with the killer laugh straightened her apron and turned—pulling up short at the sight of Jeff standing there.

The warmth and light from her eyes blinked off as she schooled her features back into a mask of utter disinterest.

The one that probably would have been easier to take if it were utter contempt because at least then a guy would know he'd made her radar. Damn, she was good.

Yeah, Jeff wasn't going anywhere.

"Another Scotch when you get a minute," he said, flashing her a grin before starting back to his table.

It wasn't like he'd come to Vegas with some plan to score. He hadn't. Only now the part of him that couldn't resist a challenge, the part that got off on getting what no one else could have—the fastest time, the highest grade, the biggest trophy, the most successful company—that part wanted to stake a claim on the secret prize so effectively hidden away, he wouldn't have believed in its existence if he hadn't heard the seductive, tantalizing sound of it himself.

And as it happened, he had an hour to kill.

Whatever the deal was with the guy from table twelve, Darcy didn't have time for it.

To think she'd pegged him as harmless.

Not in general, no. He definitely had the whole devastating male magnetism thing happening with those roughed up looks and his buttoned-down suit. Every set of female eyes in the place and probably half the men had homed in on him the second he entered the bar. But he hadn't been on the make—and she'd clocked enough hours in this lounge over the past two years to be able to tell. So she hadn't paid him much mind. At least not until she turned around to find him watching her with some half-cocked gotcha grin, looking like he'd busted her with her hand in the cookie jar.

Because he'd caught her *laughing*.

Something she didn't let happen very often at work as it tended to give the male clientele the wrong idea about what kind of good time she might be interested in having.

But then, tonight of all nights, what did it really matter?

Leaning a hip against the bar, she waited for Mr. Not-So-Harmless-After-All at table twelve's fresh Scotch.

This was her last night on the job. Her last—she checked her watch and felt a surge of excitement—two hours. And then she was through.

Sheryl Crow echoed through her mind, singing about leaving Las Vegas, and it was all Darcy could do not to put a little swing in her step as she pushed off the bar. Two more hours of tables to turn, drinks to serve, tips to make. And then she'd move on to life's next adventure.

Though even as she thought it, the word seemed an off fit to the relentlessly conservative way she managed her life. *Adventure* implied risks and unknowns. Challenges. Excitement. That wasn't exactly how Darcy rolled. She couldn't afford to. Not after the steep price she'd paid to ensure her independence. She knew the suffocating experience of being at the wrong man's mercy and she'd been willing to sacrifice her education to facilitate that escape. Drop out of high school and get the job that set her free.

She'd sworn never to allow herself to be in a position of dependence again, which meant she took care of herself. She played it safe. Stayed in control. Lived within her means. And if the cost inherent to a life that felt safe was adventure of the tall, watered-down variety? She'd gladly pay it.

Stopping at table twelve, she leveled him with a flat stare. "Your Scotch, sir. Anything else?"

His speculative look had her wondering what this guy's game was exactly.

And then his focus lowered to her mouth, causing an unfamiliar dip and roll deep in her belly. One she met with a stern frown because oh, no, she was *not* going to be tempted by this guy. No way.

"Relax, Darcy. I get it. Not interested. Couldn't be more clear if you were wearing it on a T-shirt like the table of bridesmaids over there."

Her gaze shifted to the three women and the corner and

her mouth twitched, making something in his gut fire up. Though just as quickly she had the impulse tamped down.

"I'm not hitting on you," he assured. "This is about filling some hang time. You're my temporary hobby."

A slender brow pushed up. "How's that."

"I like the smile I saw. And I want one of my own."

That smooth hip of hers rocked out to one side. "You want a smile? I'll save you the hassle." She flashed him a grin barely a step above the flat business she doled out to every Tom, Dick and Harry who rolled through her section and Jeff shook his head, giving in to his own more sincere version.

"Nice try. But you're not going to put me off with some cheap imitation. I've seen the real thing, and now I want one for myself. An honest to goodness, hard-earned, full tilt smile. Bonus for the laugh. And no pity grins, either."

She opened her mouth to say something—probably another dismissive shutdown, but then pulled her mouth to the side as she studied him.

"So you want to work for it?" she asked.

And hot damn, was she actually going along? "I'm not into easy."

Her eyes were definitely on his now. Engaged in a way almost as satisfying as her elusive smile had been.

"Look—"

"Jeff," he supplied, without trying to take her hand because touching her would probably get him slammed up against an impenetrable wall of "no" faster than he could blink.

"Look, Jeff, you're interesting. Which is a nice change from the norm. But I'm working so I can't really hang out and be your *hobby* or anything else."

"Not a problem. I know you've got to work. So on average, how much time do you think you allot each customer outside of taking their actual drink order? I mean for the niceties: *Hello, how's your day? Good, yours? Good, know what you want?* Etcetera, etcetera, etcetera…"

"Fifteen seconds."

Nice try. "I'm talking the chatty ones."

"Forty-five."

"And if they're ordering, you'll give them the time?"

As if sensing a trap, she answered hesitantly, "Yes."

"Great. I'd like to send an order of white chocolate martinis to the bridesmaids over there. But tell them it's from the manager or something, not me."

When she just stared at him, he stared back. "I think our forty-five seconds are up. I mean, unless you'd like to sit down. You're welcome to stay for a drink. Take a break."

"This is because you're bored?" she asked, those steely gray eyes narrowing on him in a way that said he had her focus completely.

Had he really said he wasn't into easy? Because this was shaping up to be just that…and there wasn't a single molecule in his body or thought in his head, not totally into where it was going.

Jeff shrugged, raising his Scotch before taking a swallow. "I like to keep busy."

CHAPTER THREE

"CONSIDER IT A public service."

Darcy set the Scotch on a fresh napkin and, fighting her threatening smile with everything she had, slid it in front of Jeff. The guy who was making her last night in Vegas one she'd never forget. "Letting you take me out? Okay, let's hear it."

"Are you really going to make me say it?" he asked with a look all but begging her to make him do so.

She should walk away. She didn't date the customers and never gave into even this much interaction. But there was something about him. Something that wouldn't let her put him off the way she did with every other guy who crossed her path.

Even now, she could feel the corner of her mouth nearly betraying her as it threatened a smile. And Jeff knew it. He was watching, one brow raised. And then his eyes were locked back with hers. "Almost had you."

Yeah, it had been close.

"Okay, I give. How is my going out with you a public service?"

Satisfaction lit his smile.

"Because of my ego."

When she crossed her arms, he went on. "You've seen it. It's absurd. Honestly, the size is almost a handicap."

This was going to be good. Her brow pushed up, wanting more, but unwilling to open her mouth to ask for fear she'd break down laughing.

"If you crush this beast— Darcy, I'm not going to be able to drag it out of here."

"That big?"

"Like you really need to ask."

This guy was trouble. And exactly the kind of fun she deserved on her last night in Vegas. So long as it didn't go any further than a little flirtatious back-and-forth.

"I'm telling you, it'll be flailing around on the floor. Going boneless when I try to pick it up."

"Wow, almost like another person."

He offered a nod. "I call it Connor."

"An ego named Connor." Now she'd heard everything... and somehow it only made her want to hear more.

He let out a short laugh and rubbed a hand over his mouth as if trying to push the smile off his lips before going on. "And here's the problem. That ego's going to need some serious stroking to recover from your rejection."

Her eyes started to narrow, but he waved her off.

"It'll demand I hit on every female to cross my path. Forcing me to turn on the charm, we're talking full blast—"

"Like a fire hose?" she supplied, knowing she shouldn't have said it, but—well, she kind of couldn't help it.

Jeff's mouth was open, halfway to the next ridiculous part of his pitch when he froze. Cranked his eyes over to hers, the look in them one of amusement and warning.

"*Exactly* like a fire hose."

But for the way this guy was working her, there was something about him that seemed safe. Whatever it was, it was tempting her to push what she knew better than to play with. "So after you spray all these women down with your big hose. What happens then?"

"Widespread devastation. Women weeping everywhere. Broken hearts littering the streets. They're all going to fall in love with me, but all I'm really looking for is a date. Nothing serious. Just some fun."

Ahh, the circle back to her and suddenly eye contact

seemed more than she could handle. "And this is what happens every time a woman turns you down?"

Jeff shrugged, reaching for his Scotch. "Wouldn't know. It hasn't happened yet. Seriously, what kind of decent woman would want that kind of emotional carnage on her conscience?"

Darcy looked this guy up and down, taking in the details she'd glossed over before. The overly thick shock of dark hair with a mess of unruly cowlicks at total odds with the serious, straight cut of his classic suit.

But if the hair and suit were a working contradiction, they were nothing compared to his face. The heavy, squared-off jaw and single flashing dimple. The rough look of a nose that had seen a break or two and the ridiculously long fringe of dark lashes over eyes a soft, earthy hazel. On looks alone, this was a man who could keep a girl guessing. Add his confidence and charm to the mix and she imagined most women wouldn't mind playing Jeff's guessing game for as long as it was on offer.

Yeah, he was definitely more dangerous than she'd given him credit for.

Time to clear things up.

"Look, Jeff. I'm flattered, but I don't date customers. Ever."

"I noticed when I came in. I like it."

Mmm, and this she was definitely familiar with. "Because it makes me a challenge?"

"Yeah," he answered with an unrepentant grin and glint of mischief in his eyes.

And okay. Not so familiar after all. "Wow, and honest, too."

"It's the best policy. Eliminates the potential for all kinds of trouble. Ensures everyone is on the same page. But back to the issue at hand…I'm a fun date. You'd have a good time. There's got to be somewhere in town you've always wanted to go but haven't gotten around to. Tell me what it is and I'll take you tonight."

Darcy was about to shut him down, but as she stood there looking at that half-playful, too tempting smile all she could think was how many things she'd told herself she'd get to sometime, but never managed to do. And how long it had been since she'd really had fun.

Now her time was up. She was leaving tomorrow.

Jeff was offering her a chance to— God, was she seriously considering this?

She never said yes. Never gave in and did the fun thing for fun's sake. Maybe tonight, after living the straight and narrow for so very long, she could afford to break the rules without worrying about tomorrow.

"I'll think about it."

A few minutes later, Jeff was exchanging back claps with Connor Reed, whose call had been the typical success his buddy made of everything he set his mind to—the only glaring exception being a broken engagement from two weeks prior. One Connor wouldn't acknowledge any kind of emotional reaction to whatsoever. Hence, the *bromance* intervention in progress.

Because Jeff had been there. He knew what it was to be blindsided with the realization that the perfect romance you were about to bet your future on—not so perfect after all.

"No, I don't love him, Jeff. It's not about him. Or you. It's about me feeling trapped and doing something desperate to escape. I'm sorry."

Yeah, it sucked.

So, they'd done the gambling bit the night before, hit a few clubs and bonded in the manly way guys were most comfortable bonding. Thereby ensuring the whole guys' weekend spiel Jeff had lured Connor in with, wasn't a total snow job. But the grunts and knuckle bump portion of the weekend was at a close, and their friendship being what it was, Jeff made no bones about it.

Pushing the Scotch he'd ordered in front of Connor, he jut his chin at the drink. "You might want to get a head start on that."

Connor shot him the half smile he'd never quite figured out how to make whole. "Little old for drinking games, aren't we?"

"Time to put your big girl panties on, man. I brought you here to talk *feelings*. Deep emotional feelings. And because you know I'm your best friend *and always right,* you're going to sit there and take it like the man I know you can be."

The half smile was gone. "Jeff, I told you—"

"Don't bother. This is going to happen. But because I respect your stunted emotional intimacy boundaries, once I've said my piece we'll have a few minutes of smack talk, just to get back on comfortable ground and then I'm going to give you your space and take off. Most likely taking the blonde bombshell who happens to be our server with me. Deal?"

Connor picked up the glass in front of him and took a fortifying slug. Then cocking his jaw to the side, he leaned back in his chair and closed his eyes. "Okay. Let's have it. But make it fast."

Jeff caught Darcy watching him from over by the bar, a little furrow marring the otherwise flawless skin of her brow. He cast her a quick wink and then folded his arms over the table returning his attention to Connor.

"Your wish, my command. So, let me set the tone… I love you, man…."

A few dozen old adages, choice idioms, apt metaphors and select bits of fortune-cookie wisdom later, Jeff's work was done. There were things he'd needed the guy to hear, and things he needed to hear back. As it turned out, Connor hadn't been so bad off after all.

At least not in the way he'd imagined.

Emotionally stunted, however, didn't quite cover it as far

as the intimacy issues went. But that was a can of worms for another trip. Connor had given him his walking papers a few minutes ago and now Jeff leaned back against the bar, watching as Darcy worried her bottom lip.

No, she wasn't the unreachable, cold woman he thought at all.

"What about your friend? He looked really upset while you guys were talking."

Uncomfortable, yes. Upset, probably not. "Turns out the broken heart may have been more a case of dinged ego."

"You men and your egos. Does he name his, too?"

Jeff waved her in closer. "Guys don't tell other guys what they name their egos."

This time when he saw the little twitch at the corner of her mouth, he acted without thought and brought his thumb up to brush the vulnerable spot threatening to give him exactly what he'd been working for.

At the bare touch, her lips parted on a small gasp and their eyes met. Then quietly but firmly she said, "I won't go back to your room with you."

Jeff brushed that little corner of her mouth again and then withdrew his hand, parking it firmly in his pocket. "So when are we leaving?"

She searched his face as if looking for a reason to say no, and for one crushing instant when she ducked her head and glanced away, he thought he'd lost her. But she was just untying her apron. And when she looked back at him, it was with eyes that were confident, clear and determined. Excited. "As soon as I get out of this uniform."

"Does this count as sweeping you off your feet?" Jeff shouted, the laugh lines branching from his eyes, deeply creased, and the grin promising pure mayhem, gone full tilt.

"I'm totally carried away!" she gasped around the elated laughter she'd given herself over to.

The night breeze whipped at Darcy's hair as she careened

down to Freemont Street, gripping the security harness tight as she went and wondering if this rush of unadulterated exhilaration had more to do with the zip line or the man a few feet away.

Still decked out in his suit and rocking a very double-oh-seven vibe with the harness and wind and all, Jeff cocked his head in her direction. "Your turn to pick next, beautiful. I'm looking for some more local flavor. It better be good."

They'd been going back and forth for hours already, starting with a light dinner at one of the city's most coveted hot spots, where a twenty-second phone call from Jeff five minutes prior to their arrival scored them an immediate table complete with the VIP treatment and a breathtaking view. The restaurant had been her choice. One she'd only suggested because Jeff's cocky grin and wild assertion he could get them into any place she wanted to go had been a challenge she couldn't resist.

Turned out, there was more to the guy than talk.

Dinner, despite the upscale locale, had been casual and easy. The conversation varied and entertaining. Jeff was one of those men who seemed to know something about everything, and—whether the topic be movies, her wish list of travel destinations or the local economy—listened as much as he talked. And by the time they'd finished their coffees, Darcy had stopped second-guessing whether agreeing to go out with him had been a mistake, and was looking forward to finding out where they would go next.

From there they'd hit a rooftop roller coaster, stopped to get Jeff a snack at her favorite taco stand, driven out to the Neon Museum where the old signs of casinos past were put out to pasture, stopped to watch the choreographed fountains and then went on to walk the famous casino and hotel's gallery of fine art.

Along the way, Jeff seemed to make fast friends with everyone. He checked the score for big games with valets, and made small talk with old ladies when he held the door for them. He was the kind of smooth that normally had warning bells clanging in Darcy's head but for some reason, with Jeff, none of her typical knee-jerk reactions or default defenses were coming to the fore. In fact, she found herself letting go around him in a way she seldom did.

And the laugh he'd been working so hard to earn…well, once they'd left the casino, she'd given up the fight and had been paying with interest ever since. Laughing at his outrageous stories, at herself, at a last night in Sin City she never would have expected. A night she doubted she'd ever forget. Because not only was she experiencing a side of Vegas that had been previously unavailable to her, but thanks to Jeff's curiosity about her tastes, she had a last opportunity to relish those old favorites, by introducing them to him and explaining what made each a standout on her list.

It was a getting-to-know-you game. One she never would have played if she hadn't been leaving. But there was a safety in knowing this was just one night. No risk of expectations getting away from her. Darcy knew the score. This was about a few hours of fun. It was safe.

At least that's what she'd thought until the zip line ended and her feet touched the ground. Jeff walked over and, catching her hand in his, pulled her gently against him in a hold that really shouldn't have come across as anything but casual. Only with the heat of his body seeping into hers, the steady, deep thud of his heart beneath her hand and the warm rush of his breath teasing through the hair behind her ear as he asked in that low rough voice of his if she was having a good time—casual had never felt so intimate.

Tipping her head back to meet his eyes, she nodded, swallowing past a wordless reaction she wasn't accustomed to. A displaced sort of tug low in her belly made her feel as though she were flying and falling all at once. Jeff's gaze searched her own, drifted lower. Her thoughts went to the moment when he'd touched her mouth back at the bar. To the words she'd said.

...I won't go back to your room...

And the question of whether she still meant them.

"Let's go find someplace to get a drink and figure out what's next on our agenda," he said taking a step back as he let her go. The move was so unexpected, Darcy nearly stumbled at the absence of contact.

For an instant she'd been sure he would kiss her. Even now as he scanned the surrounding area in search of their next stop, she couldn't believe she hadn't felt the press of his lips against hers.

More, she couldn't believe she'd wanted to. Because what kind of madness would that be?

Jeff reached around her, resting his hand at the small of her back and asked, "What's the best bar in a three-block radius?"

The light contact felt good, even if for a crazy moment she'd thought she might want more. This was quality date stuff and she wasn't in any hurry to lose it. But a bar... "How about ice cream? There's a creamery just up the way here."

At Jeff's speculative look, she answered his unspoken question. "It's sort of a trust thing."

There was no judgment in his eyes when he asked, "You don't trust me? Or, and since you serve drinks for a living, I'm going to guess this isn't it, you don't trust yourself to stop?"

She laughed, leading the way as they walked. "The *only* person I trust is me. So don't take it personally. I like to stay sharp because I don't want to find out the hard way who I can or can't trust not to take advantage."

The easy smile Jeff had been sporting throughout the night slid from his lips and something dark and protective pushed into his eyes.

"Don't look at me like that," she said with a knowing shake of her head. "There's no horror story. At least not mine. In Vegas or probably any city, you hear things. I pay attention. And I'm just very…practical. I've always been like this."

Jeff's expression relaxed. "So you're risk adverse."

"Some would say to a fault."

"But not you?"

"But not me. If I thought I was doing something wrong, living in a way that didn't satisfy me or left me feeling like I was somehow missing out—I'd change it. Like I said, I'm pretty good at looking out for myself. I'm my number one priority. So I'm not really one to sit idle waiting for someone else to call out my problems or fix them for me."

"So you're a risk adverse woman of action, taking charge of your own destiny."

The corners of her mouth curled beneath his succinct categorization of her.

She'd been called a lot of things, by a lot of guys when they hadn't gotten their way with her. Cold, hard, icy. Names that indicated her lack of interest must stem from a shortcoming on her part rather than a simple lack of desire to pursue something with a guy making passes at her while she was at work.

She slanted Jeff a sidelong look. He was just that—a guy making passes at her while she was working. And yet something about him struck her as so wholly different. Different enough, that as she kept telling herself the reason she'd agreed to go with him was because it was her last night in Las Vegas, some small part of her wondered if she would have gone with him whether she'd been leaving or not.

No. She shook the thought off, casting an inward scowl at the idea she'd do something that went against her principles after she'd just explained how keen she was on self-preservation.

"Strong and independent. A woman who knows her own mind. I like that."

"Yeah?" she asked, turning around to walk backward as she looked at him. "And me?"

"I definitely like you." He raked those big hands through the mess of his hair as he scanned the sky above them and then met her eyes with a straightforward stare. "I like the way you surprise me. That I didn't have you figured out within thirty seconds, or hell, even now, hours later."

Her steps slowed and Jeff closed the distance between them, resting his hand over the curve of her hip. "And I like that I can make you laugh, because the sound of it—"

He shook his head, still holding her gaze. "When you give into it for me—" his fingers tightened against her hips in a brief possessive grip "—all I can think about is how I'm going to get you to do it again."

"Jeff."

If he'd thought her laugh knocked him flat, hell, it was nothing compared to the breathy sound of her voice when she said his name like that. Like maybe she wanted the very thing he'd been about killing himself not to press for.

Sure once he'd made up his mind about getting her to go out with him back at the lounge, he'd assumed the natural progression of the evening would lead to a physical conclusion. They were both adults and there'd been a chemistry between them.

And he wanted it.

Hell, yeah, he did.

But something kept holding him back through each of those crossroad moments where the opportunity to change the tone of the night presented itself. The conflict in her eyes was like none he'd seen before. And it spurred some deeply instinctual need in him to protect her.

This woman he'd thought had ice in her veins and could level a man with one look alone was vulnerable and for some reason, tonight, she'd trusted him to take her out, show her the good time she all too rarely got and give her the night she deserved without whatever had her worrying that lush bottom lip of hers between her teeth. They could be the simple, uncomplicated, good time the other remembered in the years to come.

He smiled, thinking Darcy would get a kick out of that bit of fire-hose-flexing ego.

Who the hell knew if she'd remember him next week, let alone next year. But he hoped she would. Because he'd remember her.

What was she doing, looking into this guy's eyes like she couldn't physically make herself look away.

She didn't make the reckless choice. Not ever.

She didn't give in to the feel-good moment.

She liked control. In her work, in her life, in her heart and mind.

But somehow Jeff with all his ego talk, comfort in his own skin, confidence in his actions…his going after anything and everything he wanted like it never occurred to him he couldn't have it, was tempting her to behavior she didn't indulge in.

Making her want something she knew she shouldn't take. The experience of surrendering to a feeling. The chemistry tingling across her skin, batting around in her belly and whispering temptations through her mind since the first moment their eyes locked, and she realized this guy had just seen something she didn't show to anyone. And he'd liked it.

Her belly knotted tight at the idea of stepping so far out of her comfort zone. She'd already made too many exceptions. Starting with the conversation at his table and ending with the two of them standing here looking into each other's eyes.

Because Jeff was like a desert mirage. The kind of fantasy that could drive a woman to lose herself in the futile hope of finding shelter within a cool oasis that was never really within her grasp in the first place. Jeff was here for a single night. A few hours of fun.

She couldn't afford to lose sight of that because her pride wouldn't allow her to be one of those women who pinned all their hopes on the wealthy, jet-setting billionaire realizing the "good time" he picked up in Vegas—the city whose tourist industry had made a slogan of the promise that what happened in Vegas stayed in Vegas—was actually the woman he'd been waiting for his whole life.

No. The only way she could give in on any level, was if it was on her terms. With her eyes open and her expectations clear.

There was no tomorrow with this man.

"A lot of questions in those eyes tonight, Darcy." Jeff said, brushing her cheek with a single knuckle. "But there doesn't have to be. Tell me you're ready to call it a night and I'll take you home and thank you for an evening I won't soon forget. Or we can keep doing what we've been doing, without taking it any further at all. Stay up until morning. Watch the sun rise."

His eyes held hers as he asked, "What would you like to do next?"

Her heart raced. He was giving her a clear out. The easy goodbye.

She could tell him good-night. Take a cab home to her packed-up apartment. Sleep snug in the knowledge she'd cut things off before they'd gone too far. Before she gave in to the risks that pushed her beyond the boundaries of safe.

Or she could answer with the truth. That something about being with him made her ache for things she never wanted. Made her body shiver and heat. And most of all, want to grab hold of this moment and just give in to it. Surrender.

She reached for the open neck of his shirt and, letting two fingers curve into the gap between the button and plain white T-shirt beneath, pushed to her toes to meet his mouth with her own.

It was the barest of kisses. The lightest brush. Separated from a friendly peck only by a quiet, lingering beat promising what she hadn't found the words to say. Words she didn't need, based on the satisfaction in the eyes meeting hers as she stepped back into her own space. The wolfish smile as Jeff shook his head and, taking her hand, tugged her back against him.

"I've been telling myself no all night, Darcy," he murmured gruffly into her ear, rubbing his cheek against her hair. "If you're saying yes, that little kiss isn't going to be enough to tide me over until we get back to my room."

Her words were barely more than a trembling whisper. "Then you better take what you need now."

When he kissed her again, there was nothing tentative about it. Nothing friendly. It was firm and commanding. A decadent back-and-forth press of his lips against her own, deepening with every pass until she'd opened to him completely.

He licked into her mouth, his tongue gliding over hers in a wet velvet rub that had her fingers tightening in his shirt and a helpless whimper betraying her desire.

Her knees must have given out because he was holding her against him, supporting her in his powerful arms as he kissed her like she'd never been kissed before.

Senseless.

Breathless.

Taking her with the firm thrust of his tongue and—oh, that was so good—then again and again, until every part of her turned liquid and hot.

Needy.

Alive.

Another deep thrust and her belly twisted with a sensual hunger threatening to make her its slave. She'd been starved for this.

Jeff's arms snaked tight around her, one hand running the length of her back until it covered her bottom, firmed over her, pulled her in closer as he bent her back so she could feel him against her, and oh, yes, yes—

Abruptly Jeff broke from the kiss, setting her back a step even as he continued to support her. No!

"That was enough?" she asked, panting, her lips tender in a way that made her desperate for more.

"Not even close." He rubbed a hand over his mouth, the look on his face one of pure bewilderment. "But based on that kiss, I don't think either one of us wants to risk what will happen if I get my hands on you in public again."

Darcy wasn't so sure. For more of what she'd just had, she might be willing to risk anything.

CHAPTER FOUR

Somehow they'd made it back to Jeff's suite. Barely. And when the door snicked closed, it was with Darcy against it. Jeff's hands braced above her head as he devoured the lush mouth he'd gotten only the cruelest taste of back on the strip.

She was so hot and wet and soft, and how they made it back without him pulling her across his lap in the cab or taking her against one of those mirrored walls in the elevator, he had no idea. Because once he saw the indecision gone from her eyes, and got his first taste of the heat she'd been keeping as much a secret as everything else—God help him, all he could think was *more*.

He rocked into her, nearly losing it at the sound of those desperate little noises she kept making. The humming and moaning. Catching her breath when he hiked her legs at either side of his hips and ground against her. Purring when, after she locked her ankles at his back and urged him on, he did it again and again and again—driving them both mad with the contact that wouldn't be enough until the clothes were gone and he was thrusting hard and deep inside her.

"Jeff, please," she whimpered against his jaw, her body taut as he pushed her closer toward the peak she'd be visiting about a half dozen times over the next few hours if he had his way.

"Like this, baby?" he asked, canting his hips so the hard shaft of his erection rolled over her sweet spot.

Another desperate cry and her fingers knotted in his hair. He'd take that as a yes.

"Jeff!" she gasped a second before her body arched and her lips parted on a silent cry that held and held and held but never found its voice. One that invited him to take advantage, licking and nipping as he carried her through the last waves of pleasure. And then she was kissing him back, her lax body a satisfying contrast to his. Her eyes, heavy-lidded and soft like he hadn't seen them yet.

So gorgeous.

So damn sweet.

And for tonight, his.

Though even as he thought it, he realized one night wouldn't be enough. Hell, he'd known before she kissed him he'd be back.

"Darcy," he started, his mouth moving against the slender column of her neck. "This, tonight—"

Her fingers tightened in his hair as she urged him back to her mouth. "I know. It's perfect. Everything I didn't think I wanted."

She kissed him again, distracting him with the slide of her tongue playing over his and the wiggle of her hips as she unlocked her ankles and went back to her feet. Her delicate hand smoothing down the front of his shirt, over his chest and stomach, and down the jutting ridge of his erection still contained behind the confines of his suit pants. He pushed into her palm, groaning at the feel of her stroking him through the fabric and then curling her fingers into his belt and, walking backward, tugged him toward the bedroom.

Perfect.

It was the single thought in his head, reverberating with each step as he let her lead him toward the only salvation he wanted.

They pulled at each other's clothes, reveling in each new stretch of bared skin, tumbling onto the bed in a frenzied, desperate tangle of limbs. Darcy grabbed the condom he'd tossed up by the pillow and tore open the foil.

"I can't wait," she panted, her hands trembling as she began rolling the latex down his more than ready shaft.

"No more waiting," he agreed, positioning himself between her legs so he was notched at her slick opening.

Their eyes met, and he pushed inside her with the first shallow thrust. It nearly killed him to pull back, but he wasn't a small man and Darcy—heaven help him, she was so very tight. So he went slowly, carefully, penetrating by degrees until sweat beaded over his brow and his jaw clenched and finally he took her the way he needed to. Completely.

And then he was sliding full-length in and out of Darcy's tight, wet heat, letting her soft moans and broken breath lead him down the decadent path to her pleasure, answering the needy clutch of her body when he touched her just right, reveling in the helpless surrender of her eyes when he held her at the brink—

"Tell me what you want."

"Please, Jeff," she gasped, her heels digging at the back of his thigh as she urged him toward the contact he wouldn't give her until she gave him what he wanted first.

"Say it. Tell me and I'll give you anything."

Looking into his eyes, she gave up her fight for control, let her knees slide farther up his ribs and whispered, "Make me come."

And then firmly he pushed her into oblivion...making sure not to follow himself. He wasn't close to done with this woman.

Breathless. Boneless. Stunned and sated, Darcy lay within the damp sheets blinking at the ceiling as her body and mind worked in frantic concert to pull all the shattered bits of her back into some semblance of their previous working order. This wasn't the way she was supposed to feel. Like something monumental had occurred. Like there'd been a sudden unexpected shift in her life. Like she'd had her first taste of *incredible* and from that point forward, nothing again would compare.

Because this was a one-night stand.

A date gone past midnight with a man who most definitely wasn't her Prince Charming.

It was a one-off.

A last fling, because Jeff might be gorgeous, fun and devastating in bed…but he wasn't offering her more than a good time.

They'd spent hours laughing and talking and working up to this last brash act, and for all the chemistry between them, for each glint in his eye that told her he was having as much fun as she was, there was another opportunity left untaken when he might have suggested the possibility of more. Asked about another date. Implied he was even considering something beyond a single night of simply killing time together.

The man was smooth. Slick. And just because he had the ability to make *her* act out of character didn't mean tonight was anything out of the norm for him. For all she knew, Jeff hit a new bar each week, making his Friday night special the most hard-to-get girl in the place.

"Darcy, Darcy, Darcy." Her name, rumbling against her neck like pebbled kisses, pushed all thoughts from her mind but one. It didn't matter what Jeff did every other Friday night. This one he'd shared with her had been perfect.

Jeff lifted his head, pushing up on his arms to ease the weight of his body over hers—a weight she hadn't been ready to give up and felt the immediate loss of as cool air slipped between the growing space between them.

Backing off the bed, he got sidetracked by her breast, which he stopped to kiss once at the side, then again on her nipple before casting her a wicked grin as he finished his retreat. "Give me a minute, sweetheart. Don't go anywhere."

She watched him walk to the bathroom and close the door behind him. Heard the muffled sound of the running tap and waited as the seconds ticked past.

Alone in the bed, she glanced around at the suite, noting the luxurious accommodations for the first time. It seemed extravagant. Frivolous.

Sure it wasn't like he had sixteen rooms, but a suite, for one man through two nights?

The moments stretched by. The water was still running.

Beginning to feel somewhat self-conscious she reached for the sheet at the side of the bed, but came back with a handful of blouse instead.

Don't go anywhere...

She looked at the sliver of light breaking beneath the door and then at the shirt in her grasp.

Don't go anywhere...

Five minutes ago she wouldn't even have considered it. She would have flopped back on the bed relishing the full-body fatigue that was the result of Jeff's thorough attention.

Obviously, she wouldn't have planned to stay forever. But she wouldn't have considered up and leaving while he was in the other room, either.

Except then he'd gone and said it, and a thousand and one thoughts started pushing into her mind. They'd had sex. It was over. And though Jeff might not want her to run off that second, it was obvious from his words he expected her to go shortly. Which made perfect sense, this being what it was. A little meaningless fun.

But as she sat in the middle of his big bed, the heat of their intimacy dissipated into the air around her, what had happened between them still fresh and tender in her mind—so good—she wanted to protect the memory of it. This night had been a gift to herself. And she didn't want to risk the simple perfection of it being lessened by Jeff's inevitable dismissal.

Chances were, he'd be as adept at a goodbye as he'd been with everything else. And yet rather than wait, she found herself pulling on her shirt. Dragging the sheet off the bed with her as she sifted through the blast radius of discarded

clothing, darting glances at the bathroom door as
continued to run.

She didn't want to be the one clinging to their last m.
together. The one waiting to be excused.

She'd known what she was getting with Jeff from the
start. A few hours of fun. He'd made sure she understood
back at the bar.

Another look at the clock.

It's why he'd chosen her in the first place. Because he'd
recognized she had the sense not to get ideas where they
didn't belong.

Jeff gripped the marble countertop, staring at his reflection
as he tried pull himself together and figure out what to say.

Damn it, he *always* knew what to say. But he'd been off
his game since about minute one with Darcy. Closing his
mouth around a tongue inexplicably tied up over a girl he
couldn't quite figure out. And hadn't had nearly enough of.

That's where his head had been when he dragged himself out of bed, walked into the bathroom with the intent to
clean up and then come back with an offer of…*something*.

Something more than the cursory "thanks for the great
time, have a nice life" that generally came as standard with
the kind of night they'd just indulged in.

He liked her. Liked the way she made him laugh and her
unique perspective on—well, hell—everything. Sure she
lived in Vegas, and this wasn't exactly a typical stopover
for him. But if she was receptive, he'd been thinking about
making it one. Or better yet, swinging by to pick her up and
bring her down to L.A. once in a while. For an overnight or
maybe even a weekend.

That's where his head had been until he looked down
to discover the condom he'd been using had failed in a no-
maybe-about-it kind of way.

Now? He was trying to figure out how to break the news
to Darcy, rolling through the scenarios, imagining what he

was going to see on her face when he told her. Accusation, fear, dread.

The idea he would cause her any of those things was like a blow to the gut. He wasn't *that guy*. Not to anyone.

Not after Margo, his girlfriend through most of high school and college, and the woman he'd assumed, like everyone else, he would marry. At least until the day she'd come to him red-eyed and blotchy-cheeked with the confession she'd slept with another guy. She'd felt claustrophobic, trapped by all the expectations of their too serious, too neat, too well-planned relationship. She'd wanted out and, though a phone call would have been less traumatic to all involved, she'd found her escape in the bed of some frat guy with a coke habit.

As a result of that lesson, Jeff had all but perfected the no-hold relationship. He was a safe guy. A good time. The lover who always remained a friend after, because the romance never went too deep to come back from.

He kept his finger on the pulse of his affairs, making communication a priority. It was why he'd gotten his reputation as "Mr. Sensitive"—which was fine by him if it meant avoiding another blindside like the one he'd taken with Margo. Hell, yes, he'd talk about feelings. And the added benefit of that open dialogue? Nothing got too serious. No one got the wrong idea.

He was *not* the guy who put panic into someone's eyes. But that's what was about to happen. Because if ever there was a way to make a woman feel trapped, this was it.

Pulling it together, he reminded himself while this was the first time it had happened to him, it certainly wasn't the first time a condom had broken in history. Both he and Darcy were adults who understood prophylactics weren't 100 percent. Accidents happened. And this was an accepted risk inherent to sex.

They'd talk. He'd assure her he was compulsive about using protection and he was clean. She'd tell him that while she didn't generally go home with guys she just met, she was on birth control and also clean. They'd exchange contact information and stay in touch.

But whatever fantasies Jeff had been entertaining about going forward with a casual relationship had pretty well shriveled under the icy splash of reality offered in the form of a blown-out rubber. And now all he was thinking was he'd be damn lucky to make a clean getaway.

Tightening the towel wrapped around his hips, he headed out of the bathroom and froze with one hand midrub at the back of his skull, his mouth open and all thoughts of what he'd been about to say gone—just like the woman he'd been inside of less than ten minutes before.

CHAPTER FIVE

Present day...

MOMENTS LATER THE bathroom door swung open and the mother of what was presumably his child emerged.

The cool steely gray of her eyes met with his. Eyes he remembered warming through the course of those hours they spent together. Eyes he'd watched go soft beneath him, and had made him wonder if a single night was going to be enough. Eyes that had haunted him for weeks after he'd been back in L.A., until he'd forced himself to put them out of his head. Get a new game plan and move on.

Which is exactly what he'd done.

Olivia.

Pinching the bridge of his nose, he gave his head a stern shake. *One thing at a time.*

Darcy took a nervous breath and then cleared her throat. "So, maybe we should start by getting a few things straight up front."

Jeff nodded, checking the legal pad he'd started making a list on. "Agreed."

Validate paternity.
Confirm/upgrade health care.
Establish child support.
Hire nurse.
Buy house with yard and security.

Start screening for nanny.
Private preschools (*gifted and talented programs?).
Top five universities in country.
Quality playgroups.
Safety reports *family vehicles.

"I don't want to marry you," she said abruptly, wincing almost as soon as the words left her mouth.

Jeff blinked.

Wait. *She* didn't want to marry *him?*

He blew out a measured breath while mentally talking his ego down from the ledge. Because seriously, after slinking out of his bed without so much as a "thanks for the good time, sport," *that's* how she wanted to kick this conversation off?

"Not that I remember asking," he said evenly. "But good to know we're on the same page."

Or maybe not quite so evenly after all, considering the slender brow arched in his direction, topping off an all too familiar look that did something to him not entirely bad, but not exactly welcome, either.

Their eyes held a beat before she glanced away. "And I'm not interested in picking things up where we left off."

"Something the woman I'm seeing will appreciate, I'm sure."

Yeah, and best to get that out there right away, even though he was fairly certain there wasn't one thing about this Olivia was going to appreciate.

Especially if she ever got a look at Darcy. Because even having just spent twenty minutes losing her lunch, she was still a knockout. So far as he could see the pregnancy hadn't done much to her body yet.

Before he realized where that thought was taking him, his attention was doing a slow crawl south of her neckline, roaming over the full curves and narrowing tucks of a figure that—

"That's great about your girlfriend, but I'm not here to option my baby, either, so…" Her fingers came into his line of sight which happened to have stalled out around the navel he'd dipped his tongue into, snapping twice and then veering into the universal *eyes up here mister* flag. "…so whatever you're thinking with that look on your face? Stop."

"*Optioning* your baby?" he choked out. "Excuse me?"

Her shoulders squared up.

"Well, you were staring," she shot back with an accusing jut of her chin. Then seeming to lose a bit of her bravado, she more quietly added, "With a sort of greedy, speculative look on your face. How am I supposed to know what you're thinking?"

Jeff shook his head, opened his mouth once and then simply closed it again, because…

Really?

And then it was like the tension that had been accumulating since she'd first lunged past him…just snapped. And suddenly, all he could do was laugh. Which probably didn't do much to alleviate the whole greedy, speculative vibe he'd been putting off, but oh, well. Apparently there wasn't much lower he could sink to in Darcy's eyes.

So instead, he simply rubbed his palms over his cheeks and looked across at the woman who'd turned his life upside down in a single night, and just when he thought he'd put it back to rights, showed up and sent him into a tailspin.

One he needed to pull out of and fast.

"Relax. I got distracted by your body. It doesn't look like it's changed much." And at the risk of coming across like a jerk, he added the truth. "You look good, Darcy."

"Oh." Then after a moment she rolled her eyes as if making some painful, grudging acknowledgment herself. "Thank you. You look good, too. Even though it doesn't matter."

He couldn't help the grin, but as it turned out, she didn't seem to mind, answering with one of her own.

It caught him off guard, but he recovered quickly, suggesting they sit down and talk.

Darcy stepped away from the door and crossed over to the couch where Jeff set an empty can on the floor, out of the way but still within reach.

She looked down and her eyes fluttered through a few wet blinks. "You got a fresh can for me?"

She was looking at him like he'd just handed over the keys to a new Mercedes.

"I didn't want you to have to put your face in the old one."

Her hand moved to what was still the flat plane of her belly and she gave him a watery half smile he didn't quite understand, but sensed meant something important to her. "You're a thoughtful guy, Jeff."

And there it was. Reassurance. Because she had to be scared out of her mind right now, coming to him when he was virtually a stranger.

Reaching for her hand, Jeff gave it a brief squeeze and looked her in the eyes. "Hey, this is all going to work out fine. Don't be nervous." He sat back, legal pad in hand. "So, where should we start—after, you're pregnant, of course."

She winced almost as if hearing the words was still new and shocking to her. But then maybe that was the best place. "When did you find out?"

"I didn't know until a week ago. Which is late, but…" She offered a frustrated little shrug. "My cycle is irregular enough so I don't really wait around for it and, normally I don't have any reason to anyway. But the past few months… I've been running pretty much nonstop. I thought the stomach upset was nerves. Then it got worse and I thought I must have caught the flu everyone was talking about, except it didn't get better."

He was following her words, but a part of him was still stuck on this news being nearly as new to Darcy as it was to him. "Have you been to a doctor yet?"

"For the blood test." She opened her purse, retrieved the

printout she'd gotten from the lab and handed it over. "But my first appointment isn't until next week."

Jeff scanned the paperwork before setting it on the small table beside his chair. "So, if you don't want to get married, or pick things up from where we left off…I think it makes sense to ask, what do you want?"

"I'd like you to agree to a paternity test."

Darcy could see the wheels turning in his head, the man stepping back from the prospect of fatherhood with the idea maybe this child wasn't his.

"Jeff," she said as gently as she could. "You should understand, I'm only asking for the test for your benefit because I don't expect you to take the word of some woman you knew for a handful of hours three months ago. But there are no other options. This baby *is* yours. Once you have the confirmation from a lab, the decision you need to make is whether you want to be a father to it. That's what I need to find out."

Jeff was watching her closely, his eyes so intense she had to fight the urge to squirm under his scrutiny. For a guy who could do irreverent like she'd never seen it done before, there was another, more serious, side to Jeff to balance it. And in this moment, the balance was a comfort.

"No other *options?* You're telling me you haven't slept with anyone else since we were together."

She took a bracing breath, not insulted by his request for clarification. "I realize I haven't given you much reason to believe this, but I don't make a habit of going home with guys I just met. Or at all, really. There wasn't anyone else."

Jeff drew a long slow breath, his eyes still on her, but his focus seemingly directed inward. He nodded.

"Okay. So the test is basically a formality. I'll have Legal look into it and set something up. In the meantime, I'm going to be a father. I may need to get used to the idea, but as to whether I'm up to the responsibility, there's no deliberation necessary." He pushed to his feet and walked back to his desk. "So how are we going to do this?"

"Could we start with the paternity test and go from there?" she asked. "This is still so new to me, too. I wanted to get in touch with you right away, but I haven't worked out exactly how *I feel* about everything. I guess I just wanted to know where you stood before I started making too many decisions about a future you might want a say in."

He let out a contemplative breath. "Okay. I can respect that. And I appreciate it. So we'll take this one step at a time. Start with the test. You could think about whether moving is something you'd consider and we'll set something up to talk in a week?"

She nodded, relieved by his easy accommodation and perhaps by the distance he'd established between them with that last parting comment. It would be an appointment. Because they were going to handle this like business.

Exactly the way she wanted them to.

CHAPTER SIX

WITH HIS AFTERNOON cleared, there was nothing Jeff would have rather done than call Connor. Tell his best friend he wasn't the only one to pick up a souvenir in Vegas. Talk out the changes ahead of him and have the guy—the only guy on the planet who knew him as well as he knew himself—tell him he had his back.

But Connor had just reconciled with his wife—a woman he'd married within hours of meeting that same night Jeff met Darcy—and even if Jeff thought he could live with himself for interrupting them…he was fairly certain the two lovebirds were still off the grid.

Just as well.

There was someone else who deserved to know what was happening first.

Olivia. The woman he'd started a relationship with five weeks ago. The *something* Jeff had found to fill the empty spot in his life he'd only become aware of after Vegas.

Jogging across the marble-and-glass atrium, Jeff caught the elevator to Olivia's top floor office.

How the hell was he going to explain this? And how would she take it?

Things had been going well with them. They'd been a smart fit from the start. Comfortable together, compatible.

She was open and pleasant. Harvard educated. Business savvy. Connected.

Two hours ago, he would have given it six months at the outside before he popped the question. And only because it seemed like an appropriate time to wait. In Olivia he'd found a woman who was all the things he'd known he wanted for a partner in life from as far back as he could remember— from the first time he looked across the table at his parents and thought to himself, *someday, I want that.*

The business journal over morning coffee. The dinners at the club. The shared interests for their shared lifestyle. The sparkling hostess championing the charities and foundations they supported.

It sounded shallow as he itemized it in his head, but it wasn't.

He wanted the kind of good match that meant a lifetime of companionable, easy happiness. What his parents had up until the day five years ago when a heart attack took his father. The best man he'd ever know. The example Jeff had always hoped to live up to. Hell, he wished he was around to talk to about this.

Riding up to Olivia's, he couldn't help question what she would think when she looked at the woman he'd been with before her. The one who'd been his wake-up call about putting an end to the screwing around with women who weren't right for him and thinking about getting serious with one who was. Settling down. Starting a family.

Olivia would see everything she wasn't when she looked at Darcy.

And it would make her wonder.

Darcy had been a good time he hadn't seen coming. And the only reason she'd gotten under his skin the way she had was because of the way she'd left.

So the chemistry between them had been hot enough that even months later, he could feel the lingering burn of it, so what? That was sex. Not exactly a foundation to build a solid forever on. But neither was it something he could, in good conscience, ignore when it came to a relationship with another woman.

"Hey, Mel. She in?" he asked, when he got to her office.

"She's on a call. Should I interrupt?"

"No. I'll wait."

This was news he needed to tell her today and in person.

Sometime later, Jeff was searching stages of pregnancy on his phone, checking them against his calendar and travel commitments when Olivia's office door swung open and she walked out to greet him with a welcoming smile.

"Jeffrey, what a wonderful surprise!"

"Got a few minutes for me?" he asked, unfolding from the deep sofa to lead her back into the office. And once there, he closed the door behind them. "Is it private in here?"

Olivia's brow crumpled a bit at the question as she looked at the closed door behind him and then her neatly organized desk loaded with her current projects. "I was thinking you might be here to take me to lunch." Her nose crinkled before reluctantly meeting his eyes again. "But are you here for something…else?"

A bark of laughter escaped him as he realized the direction of her thoughts. She'd thought he was here for some kind of afternoon desktop quickie. Yeah, now he got her confusion. It wasn't exactly like that between them.

Shaking his head, he crossed to the cluster of club chairs across her office and held a hand out asking her to join him. "No, Olivia, I'm sorry. Something…unexpected has come up. We need to talk."

A little furrow had cut between her delicate brows as she lowered herself into the chair across from him. "You're worrying me, Jeffrey. What's happened?"

Looking at her guileless face and earnest eyes, he wished there was some way to sugarcoat the bitter news he was about to give her. But it wouldn't help either of them. "A couple of months before we met, I spent the night with a woman who came to my office today. She's pregnant."

Olivia sat stone still, her eyes gone wide. "Was there something between you?"

He opened his mouth to say no, but said instead, "It was one night."

"Who is she? Would I know her? Is she the type to keep quiet? What does she want from you?"

"I doubt very much you know her, unless you've spent more time in Vegas than you let on."

"She's a *stripper*. Oh, God, Jeffrey, please tell me she isn't a prostitute."

"No!" He raked a hand back through his hair. "No, she was the waitress at a bar I was stuck at waiting for Connor the night he met Megan. I was killing time and one thing led to another."

He didn't like the sound of his explanation, but the deeper, expanded version of the truth wasn't something Olivia needed to hear.

"You just found out? So, there hasn't been any time for conclusive paternity testing, then. This baby might not even be yours. I mean, Jeffrey, one night with some *Vegas cocktail girl* three months ago. We don't know anything yet."

A part of him wanted to agree. Tell her she was probably right and to give him a few weeks to sort it out. Only she deserved the whole truth. "We'll have the DNA testing done, but I already know this baby is mine."

She didn't ask for details but he could see the understanding in her eyes. The way the hope shifted toward disappointment.

She swallowed, withdrawing her hands from his to tuck them around her waist. "Are you going to marry her?"

Darcy's emphatic pre-proposal rejection came to mind, pushing a wry smile to his mouth. "No."

"Okay," she said, nodding slowly before meeting his eyes with a steel he hadn't encountered in hers before. "Then cut her a check."

He stared hard at the woman seated across from him, the one he'd thought might be able to share his life. "To what, go away? Disappear?" He couldn't even voice the next alternative he hoped to hell she wasn't suggesting.

Something roared inside him, as a protective instinct churned hot in his gut. "It's *my child*."

"And we'll raise it as ours," she said quickly, taking his hands. "We'll get married. Have a private adoption. We'll craft an explanation to suit us both."

Adoption. Of course, that's where Olivia's head would have gone first. Adoption and marriage. A neat package, except for the part where she'd completely discounted Darcy as a part of the equation beyond a dollar amount on a check.

"Jeffrey, we have something here. Something I've been waiting to find for a very long time. We could make this work."

Offering Olivia's hand a quick squeeze, he pushed up from his chair.

He needed to cut Olivia some slack. She'd jumped to the wrong conclusion, probably because the few details he'd parceled out pointed that way. She was trying to come up with a solution to a problem he'd dropped in front of them. It just wasn't the right one.

Walking over to the bank of windows, he rubbed his hand over his jaw. Darcy was right. They all needed a little time to get their heads around this new development.

"Darcy doesn't want to give the baby up. She was offering me an opportunity to be a part of its life. Not to…option it off. You don't know her."

Olivia sat back, watching him the way he watched guys from across the conference table. Reading their tells and all the things their faces and bodies said without their mouths having to. "And you do?"

"Only enough to say, she wasn't here to give her child up."

"Okay. Then we'll take it from there." She followed him across the office, laying her hand gently over his arm.

"Olivia, I don't know what this next year is going to bring. I think it might be better for everyone if we—"

"No. I'm not going to give up on us because things aren't exactly the way I thought they would be." She met his eyes. "We're so well suited. So right. All I'm asking is you give us a chance before making any decisions. Please."

Jeff wrapped an arm around her shoulders. She felt stiff against him. Like an off fit in a way he'd never noticed before.

Which he supposed made sense, considering he'd just put something between them neither of them knew exactly how to deal with. Now the least he could do was grant her request and give them a chance.

CHAPTER SEVEN

"YOU GOT THE *waitress* pregnant?" Connor shook his head, rocking back on his bar stool as though the news had physically blown him over. "You're sure? I mean, all the question marks…?"

Jeff nodded. "Had a DNA test pushed through, but even if I hadn't—I'm sure."

"A baby. How in the hell?"

At Jeff's raised brow, the other man held up a staying hand.

"Don't. I know how. Your dad did a bang-up job with the 'talk' back in high school. I just can't believe—you—like this—now." Then shooting him a concerned look, he asked, "Someone mentioned you were seeing Olivia Deveraux. That you two might be serious."

"Before Darcy showed up at my office, I would have put money on a future with Olivia. But now." Now, even two weeks later, he wasn't any closer to knowing what their future held. Olivia hadn't changed. "She wants it to work. Offered to marry me and adopt the baby."

"Generous."

"If Darcy were considering giving it up. But not for even a single second."

He thought about her busting him looking at her narrow waist, and accusing him of trying to option her baby. Once again giving in to the reoccurring grin that stomped all over his face every time he thought about her outraged, accusing look, he held up his hands. "She's going to be an amazing mother. You can see it."

"Olivia?"

Jeff caught Connor's stare and the subtle, unspoken question behind it. "*Darcy*. But, yeah, I'm sure Olivia would, too."

Connor pushed his drink around in a neat square on the bar. "But you don't *see it* with her?"

Worse, he wasn't even sure he'd looked. Olivia had asked him to give them a chance and so far he hadn't made the time to actually do it.

"I've been so focused on Darcy, there hasn't been a lot of time for anyone or anything else. She's living in San Francisco and I've been trying to talk her into moving down here. But she's…stubborn. I think she intends to move, but not until the baby comes. She's got a job and—" He shook his head. "And the job thing is a really big deal to her. But I'm not giving up. I want her here, like yesterday."

"Am I missing something about the waiting tables thing? What the hell kind of job does she have that *you* can't compete with it?"

Jeff rocked back in his chair and expelled a frustrated breath. "One she got for herself."

Understanding lit Connor's eyes. "She does know who you are, right?"

"She doesn't *care* who I am." He raked a hand through his hair. "She won't take any money until the baby comes. And, damn it, she's just very independent…and stubborn."

Connor's brows pulled together and his jaw cocked to one side.

Jeff scowled at him. "It's not like that. Even if Olivia weren't in the picture. We've already agreed, in no uncertain terms, neither of us is interested in picking things up from where we left them. What Darcy is to me is the most important person in the life of the most important person in mine. Our relationship is going to be about this kid and it's got to work forever. Which means there's too much at stake to risk any potential friction over some affair gone bad."

And he knew from experience what the fallout from a failed relationship could cost.

Connor took a swallow of his drink. "Right. Definitely not worth the risk for an affair."

Jeff stared at him. "I'm serious."

A nod. "Okay."

Oh, that burned. "Bite me."

Connor grinned and flagged the bartender for the tab. "Sorry, my friend. Megan doesn't share."

The elevator doors opened at the eleventh floor and Jeff followed Olivia down the hall toward her apartment.

She cast a bright smile over her shoulder at him, her efficient steps eating up the distance to her door. "Thank you for dinner tonight. I know how busy you've been."

That was Olivia. Not raking him over the coals. Sensitive to the situation he was in while letting him know she still enjoyed seeing him when the opportunity arose. He hadn't meant for their relationship to fall by the wayside, but he'd been neglecting her for weeks. Working long hours and even through the couple of times he'd taken her out, he'd been distracted. There, but not *really* there. Because being with Olivia wasn't enough to keep his mind from visiting all the places he didn't want it to go. To Darcy.

To the space he was trying to give her, and how hard he was trying not to hate the space she already had. To wondering what she'd do if he pushed too hard.

It wasn't fair. But Olivia had been so accommodating. Assuring him she understood. He shouldn't put her off. He shouldn't be able to.

And yet, as he walked behind her his mind kept drifting to another woman. How she was feeling? If anyone was making her laugh? If her belly was starting to show?

"You're coming in?" Olivia asked at her door, putting the

breaks on a train of thought threatening to go off the rails and pulling him back to the woman who ought to be holding his attention for the few hours they had together.

She was watching him expectantly. As if she knew, mentally he'd already dropped her at her door and was halfway back to the office. Where he'd have a fighting chance of losing himself in work.

"Olivia," he started, catching her chin in the crook of his finger. "I've got a call scheduled with Hong Kong in three hours."

She leaned a shoulder against the frame of the door and looked him over assessingly.

"Then you've got two and a half to spend with me." Her fingers wrapped around his tie to tug him closer. "I know you've been waiting, not pushing the physical element of our relationship out of respect for me, but it's time. You need a distraction, Jeff. Let me help you forget for a while."

Respect. Maybe that was part of what had been holding him back. But to really respect her meant acknowledging that not taking the next physical step in their relationship had been far too easy. She deserved better than to be used as a distraction. And far, far better than a distraction he already knew wouldn't work.

He'd tried to tell himself this was the woman for him. The perfect fit he'd imagined her to be when they first started seeing each other. Because she'd been so different from the one who'd walked away... But once Darcy stepped back into the picture he'd started making comparisons.

"Jeff, you said you'd give us a try. Can't you please, come in and let me show you how it could be between us, if you let it?"

He hated the pleading in her eyes, hated knowing it was about to turn to hurt. But it was, because his hands had already moved to her shoulders, gently putting the space back between them. "I'm sorry, Olivia."

Oh, no, not again.

Darcy sat at the folding table in the suddenly too warm

back room of the party coordinating business where she'd been hired to inventory catering supplies, stuff envelopes, assemble favors, scoop birdseed satchels and anything else the overbooked business needed assistance with during their seasonal rush.

The pay wasn't great, but she'd been lucky the manager of the restaurant where she'd been working had put in a good word with the owner to get her the temporary position. And at least she was maintaining an income, if somewhat reduced.

A few more weeks and the nausea would ease because it couldn't get any worse. And once her stomach was back under control—

As if on cue, her belly lurched again.

"You okay?" her boss asked from the open doorway.

Darcy pushed to her feet, lifting a hand to let the older woman know she was fine. Except the shrinking edges of the room hazing into sepia tones warned she wasn't.

She tried to get a hand back to the table, but too quickly everything went loose and dark and down until there was only one thought left in her head...and that was the silent plea that her baby be okay.

Darcy woke slowly, her senses coming back online one at a time as she registered the hard mattress of the hospital bed beneath her, the dimmed overhead light and the deep rumble of a voice she hadn't been expecting. One which shouldn't have been coming from anywhere near her.

Jeff.

"...Dehydration, fatigue, low blood pressure, weight loss... No, they say both she and the baby will be all right, but there's no way in hell I'm leaving without—"

She shifted in the bed, remembering too late about the needle threaded into her vein and letting out a short gasp when she put weight on it.

Whatever Jeff had been about to say, she missed and now

the conversation was over. Jeff was suddenly in her room, filling up the small space with his enormous presence. Dropping his phone into the inside pocket of his suit jacket, he crossed to her bed like he was going to slide into the open chair beside her. But instead, he reached for the call button and signaled the nurse before taking a step back. Fixing her with a serious look. "Do you need anything? How are you feeling?"

"Tired still, but, Jeff, you didn't need to come. I told Charlie, they just wanted me to get some fluids and an antinaus—"

"You told me *you were fine*." It wasn't exactly accusation she was getting off him, but the intensity was like a palpable thing. "I spoke to your doctor already and *hyperemesis gravidarum* can be dangerous and severe. You are *not* fine, Darcy."

Guilt washed over her in a wave. She'd thought it was just morning sickness in an all-day, extended package, which she'd heard was normal, too. Though she'd planned to speak to her doctor at her next checkup about the extremity of it, she'd had no idea her body had begun turning against her, threatening what she'd been struggling to protect.

"I didn't know it had gotten so bad. I don't own a scale so I didn't know how much weight I'd lost. My clothes fit a little differently, loose, but I'd heard lots of people lose weight early on." She felt a burning pressure at the backs of her eyes and blinked to defend against the emotions trying to slip free.

She was supposed to be the one who took her responsibilities seriously and made the right decisions. She was supposed to be able to count on herself. Her child's life depended on it.

She swallowed and looked up at Jeff.

The man who was all laughter and easy good times hadn't shown up at her bedside. This Jeff was serious. No-nonsense. And he was here because the woman responsible for protecting his child hadn't even realized she was at risk of failing.

This Jeff had every reason for making an appearance. If the tables were turned, she'd be looking at him the same way.

"Jeff, I'm sorry."

He nodded, but the look in his eyes was hard. "Here's the deal, Darcy. I know you're tough and I know you're independent. But I'm uncomfortable with you alone like this. From what I understand, it was a fluke your boss happened to be walking by when you passed out. You work in isolation for hours at a stretch. Take public transportation home alone to the apartment you don't share with anyone else. You don't have anyone here looking out for you, so what I'm asking, is does it really make sense for you to still be up here?"

She looked down at her hands, at the plastic tube snaking its way up her arm, feeling more alone in that moment than she could ever remember feeling before.

"I've got a job here, Jeff."

He stepped closer to the bed, and after a pause, dropped into the chair beside her. His hand moved to her belly and rested there for a beat. "You've got *our baby* in here. And he's kicking your butt. Come back with me and I'll take care of you. We'll get through this together. You don't have to be on your own."

Darcy couldn't take her eyes off the sight of his hand against her stomach, couldn't think about anything but the heat radiating from his touch and how good it felt, when nothing had felt good, since the last time—the first time— he'd put his hands on her.

Which she couldn't think about. Not like this. Not with him touching her in a way that was so totally not about her at all, but about the child they shared together. About his concern.

Jeff cleared his throat. "We could get married."

Darcy stiffened. "We don't even know each other."

"I don't mean permanently. Just until the baby is born, so he'd be legitimate."

The breath leaked from her lungs, as she shook her head,

trying to ignore that pinch of disappointment there was no justification for. "Legitimacy isn't any reason to get married, Jeff."

"I know. Forget it." Jeff let out an impatient growl, pulled his hand away and then ran it through the mess of his hair going on as if he hadn't dropped that bomb. "You're determined to work?"

He couldn't understand, but he needed to accept it. "Yes."

"Fine." He stood, stared down at the spot where his hand had been and nodded.

Then heading for the door, he looked back with a frown. "I actually know of a position that might be the perfect fit."

CHAPTER EIGHT

"YOU LOW-DOWN, DIRTY *liar,*" Darcy accused, her color looking better than Jeff had seen it since Vegas.

Catching the finger she was jabbing into his chest with a gentle hand, he eased her back into the deep leather seat of the limo and clarified. "I never lied."

Omitted, evaded and manipulated? Yes.

Definitely.

But he'd taken one look at her lying in that hospital bed, and decided the moral hit was one he'd gladly take to ensure he got Darcy out of San Francisco and down to L.A. where he could make certain she was getting what she needed.

"False pretenses, Jeff," she hissed, her head working like a spindle as she shot nervous looks out one window after another as they rolled through the immaculately manicured upscale neighborhood of Beverly Hills.

"I told you, it was a part-time position as a personal assistant—"

"Oh, you told me all right," she snapped. "Flexible hours, excellent benefits including room and board, assisting an elderly widow with her social and charitable obligations—"

Her words cut off with a squeak as they turned into a private community where security waved them through.

"Hey, I never said *elderly.* I said *older.* Which is true." That's all he needed. The wrath of both his pregnant non-girlfriend combined with the wrath of his—

"Your *mother,* Jeff!"

The key here was to remain calm. Not to reach over and

haul Darcy into his lap and yell into her face about all the things *he* didn't like about their situation. About his lack of say. And her stubborn mule streak and the fact that she wasn't going to need a damn job for the rest of her damned life and why the hell wouldn't she just take one of the damn checks he kept trying to give her.

So instead, he blew out a controlled breath and met her enraged stare. Turned up his palms and shrugged. "She needed an assistant."

Okay, so his mother hadn't actually needed the assistant until Jeff called her and told her she did. But then, she'd rather desperately started needing one. Had been downright giddy about it, truth be told.

"Oh, does she? Your mother is so very busy, so lonely and desperate for help, she needs a woman she doesn't know moving into her home with her. A high school dropout, Jeff, who grew up in a beat-down trailer on the wrong side of the park. A Vegas cocktail waitress who went home with a virtual stranger, got knocked up and then—surprise!—showed up three months later. You think that's the woman your mother needs assisting her with her charitable endeavors?"

Jeff stared, wondering who was in this car with him. Because the woman he'd met in Vegas, the one who'd shown up at his office, and he'd been talking to every few nights for the past few weeks knew her own worth and would never in a million years let anyone undervalue her the way she'd just undervalued herself.

He understood pregnancy hadn't been a part of her plan, and he expected the loss of control for a woman who'd been all about the ironclad of it, had been a tough pill to swallow. He was certain it had shaken her confidence. But the words that had just come out of her mouth angered him.

"I don't know who to be offended for first, my mother, myself, my kid or you. Look, I don't come from a family of snobs. Yeah, we've got money and have had for a long time. But it doesn't mean we don't know the value of hard work, or respect people who've had to overcome challenges different than the ones we've faced. And here's something else. My mother respects me. That I took you home the night I met you will tell her something about you, too."

Darcy let out bitter laugh. "My measurements?"

"What the hell is wrong with you, Darcy? If it was just about your body——" And then he was right where he shouldn't be. Inches from Darcy's face, his eyes searching hers for any sign of the understanding he couldn't believe wasn't there. "Damn it, you *know* that wasn't how it was. *I wanted you!*"

As soon as the words left his mouth he cursed himself for saying them. Going forward as they intended would be easier without the acknowledgment of an attraction that was more than physical driving the hot pursuit he hadn't been able to shut down their first night together. But listening to Darcy sell herself short, he hadn't been able to stop himself.

Only now, as he saw the surprise in her eyes—the flash of hurt or remorse, maybe?—he realized she didn't know. Or at least hadn't been sure.

How could she have missed it? Why hadn't she believed him?

And what the hell difference did it make now? *None.*

Except perhaps to underscore yet another way in which he'd misperceived their initial connection. As much as he sometimes sensed that they were, he and Darcy weren't on the same page. He needed to remember that.

Jeff cleared his throat and sat back.

What mattered now was getting Darcy to agree to getting out of this car when they arrived, moving into his mother's house and if she was going to be bullheaded about the damn job thing, accepting the make-believe position of his mother's assistant.

Which meant getting her to settle down in the next thirty seconds before they reached the turnoff for his house.

"Couple things we need to get straight, Darcy. Here's what

I know. You've got your G.E.D., have a clean credit history, no criminal record, pay your own rent on time every time and until the past three months when you ran into some unexpected health issues, have had an exemplary work record. You don't fool around with customers…except that once, and you don't appear to do much dating. None of which is going to matter to my mother at all. The only thing she cares about is you are going to have her grandchild. That and someone else is going to be confirming the floral arrangements for her luncheon next week."

When she just stared at him, he stared right back. "You're the mother of my child. So yeah, I did a web search on you."

"All that came up?" she asked quietly, her brows inching up in a way that had the corners of his mouth twitching.

"No. It didn't. Now, stop putting yourself down. I don't like it."

The car pulled to a stop at the foot of the flared stone stairs leading to the front door.

Darcy shot a tentative look toward the house. "It's not like that's the way I see myself," she said quietly. "But I just don't know how someone who hasn't even met me yet could see anything else. And I don't want— If I'm living under the same roof—"

Jeff reached across the car and took her hand. "It won't be."

And the reason why, had just flung open the front door.

Darcy's heart began to thump, as Mrs. Norton, decked out in formfitting yoga gear and a disheveled ponytail, jogged down the stairs with a beaming smile and wide wave.

"Older?" she asked Jeff incredulously, wondering whether his father should have served time for taking a child bride. The woman couldn't be fifty.

Helping her out of the car, he answered, "She's older than we are."

"Jeffrey! Darling, it's so good to see you," Mrs. Norton

said, opening her arms wide to pull her six-foot-something son into her diminutive embrace. Then just as quickly as she'd pulled him in, she pushed him back, redirecting her focus on Darcy. Eyes that were the same warm hazel as Jeff's met hers as she held out a hand in welcome. "Darcy, thank God you've agreed to help me. This couldn't be more ideal. I was absolutely desperate and now we have the perfect opportunity to get to know each other. Ooh, I want to throw my arms around you, but Jeff would probably dive between us to protect you from my overzealous embrace. He's twitchy about you. If you haven't figured it out already."

Darcy shot a surprised look over at Jeff, standing there, hands hooked into his pockets, totally at ease in this bizarre situation.

"Mrs. Norton, thank you very much for opening up your home to me." She wanted to stress she wouldn't be staying long, but there was something in the open, welcoming smile on her face that made Darcy feel to do so would somehow be an insult.

"Oh, please, not Mrs. Norton. It's Gail. Believe me, five years from now when you're hearing Mrs. Norton every time one of this little guy's friends looks up at you, you'll know what I mean."

Darcy blanched at the reference to nuptials, but it was Jeff who jumped in to make the clarification. "Not *Mrs. Norton,* Mom. Ms. Penn."

Gail's cheeks went pink and her eyes squinched shut, but then she just laughed. "Oh, hell."

With a deep breath she waved her hand about dismissively. "I know. It's just the idea of having a little grandbaby— And as to Ms. Penn?" She shook her head conspiratorially. "In five years. Not a chance."

"Mom." This time Jeff's voice was more serious. "Don't—"

"Don't worry, darling I won't be pushing anyone in front of her until I've gotten to know her better. Why waste time with bad matches. Okay, come along now, kids. We'll get Darcy settled and then after a bit of rest, give her the tour."

"Honestly, Mrs. Nor—"

The arch look sailing over Jeff's mother's shoulder had her in place in a beat.

"*Gail.* You don't need to go to any trouble for me."

"Thank you, dear. But it's no trouble at all. Honestly, I couldn't be happier to have you here and just want you settled and comfortable as soon as possible."

"All right. Then thank you."

Gail nodded, her brisk steps taking her up the wide curving stairs to the still open front door. "I'm putting her in Connor's old room."

Darcy coughed, her eyes going wide as she looked over at Jeff. "Wow, *Connor* had a room to himself, huh."

Jeff was walking beside her, the strap of one bag slung across his chest. The handles from the other duffel hanging from his hand. "He spent a lot of time here when we had breaks from school." He answered distractedly, looking a bit tense all of the sudden. Was he having second thoughts about her being here? Or more likely he simply didn't remember the line he'd used to pick her up. The joke about his ego named Connor. But in truth, it was probably better there not be some collection of inside jokes between them.

The connection she felt to this man was dangerous enough without the added intimacy.

CHAPTER NINE

UP IN CONNOR'S old room, a space Jeff knew nearly as well as his own, he looked around wondering at what Darcy would make of it. The walls were still sage-green. The trim the same white that ran through the rest of the house. But somehow every bit of lingering high school boy and college man had been stripped from the space within the past day. The shelves emptied of all but a few items—and those last few he was certain remained just to ensure Darcy didn't walk into a space that felt barren and stark.

A gesture he appreciated after seeing how few belongings she actually owned.

He set the bags on the bed Darcy would be sleeping in. He'd never paid much attention before, but now, couldn't help but notice it was king-size. Huge for a single woman sleeping alone.

Which despite his mother's apparent desire to marry her off to someone—Darcy would be.

Mrs. Norton.

Not going to happen. Slip of the tongue or Freudian slip… His mother had been completely off base with that.

Darcy Norton.

He didn't know her middle name.

He blinked. What the hell was he thinking? He didn't need her middle name. Didn't want to know it.

Because even if there was some lingering bit of attraction between them, it wasn't the stuff *Mrs. Nortons* were made of.

Yeah, she was beautiful, and fun, and having his baby.

But Darcy was one giant no trespassing sign. And not in some sexual sense—but, damn, he needed his head to stop going there, too.

She was just so unavailable. Different than he'd believed that first night.

"It's bigger than my apartment."

He turned to where Darcy stood in the doorway, her arms wrapped across her belly signaling her stomach wasn't doing well, but hadn't reached critical levels yet.

"And it comes furnished, too. You'll have this room. The bathroom connects through there and you've got a sitting room with desk and computer on the other side."

"Okay, so it's a lot bigger than my apartment."

"Think you'll feel okay staying here?" It was such a strange question to ask, after he'd all but railroaded her into making the concession, swearing up and down she'd be comfortable.

Only now that she was precisely where he'd wanted to get her—the idea of actually leaving her here unsettled him in a way he couldn't reconcile.

Darcy looked around. Crossed to the window and peered out over a view of the pool and tennis court. "Your mom is kind of a firecracker."

"Yeah, she is. Make you uncomfortable?"

"No. It's nice. She's so…excited and welcoming. And it's a relief, but still sort of a surprise."

"Not what you were expecting." He knew, from those last moments in the car.

Darcy turned to him, a tentative smile on her lips. He could see how overwhelmed she was. And tired. And then before he could stop to think about whether it was a good idea or not, he'd crossed the room and pulled her into his arms. It didn't matter that they were strangers with this intimate past between them and uncertain future ahead. She was alone and he was there, and there wasn't anyone else on hand to give her the hug she needed.

For an instant she stiffened within his hold, and he thought she might pull away. But then she simply gave herself over to it. Bowing her head into his chest with her arms tucked up between them at either side, she let him hold her.

"It's going to be fine, Darcy. Give it a little time and all this is going to work out."

She nodded and took one deep breath after another, melting further into him with each pass of his hand over her back.

"I know," she whispered. "I'm just not used to being out of control."

Jeff let out a quiet laugh. "If it makes you feel any better, I'm not much of a fan of it myself."

"I've been taking care of myself since I was sixteen. I don't like...help. I don't like...needing things from other people. It makes me feel...*trapped*."

Her voice broke the smallest extent on that last word, twisting something deep in his chest.

Leaning back just far enough to catch the side of her face and bring it up so she was looking into his eyes, he promised, "Don't. Don't feel that way about this. About being here. About anything."

Their eyes were locked. Hers so vulnerable as she looked up at him, it made him ache to make it better. Made him ache to give her back all the things he'd seen in those eyes before. Steel, mirth, resolve, confidence...heat.

Hell.

Scratch that last. He didn't want to think about what she'd looked like when it was heat filling her eyes. Desire. Need.

Not when she was standing within the circle of his arms as he told her everything was going to be fine. When she needed reassurance. Not the muscle memory of some residual attraction she wouldn't be able to ignore springing to life between them.

But, she was so soft and warm and lush and...all the things he didn't want to notice. Shouldn't remember about the last time he felt her against his body, beneath his fingertips.

Setting her back a step, he walked to the door, not meeting her eyes as he spoke over his shoulder. "Why don't you take a few minutes and then meet us downstairs? Get that tour underway."

It wasn't as though Darcy had thought Jeff would be moving in, too. She'd known he was simply dropping her off and then returning to the life he led in the city. They weren't together. They weren't a team. They weren't going to get through all this together.

They were two people, who were going to be sharing a child.

She understood it and had every intention of adhering to those mutually agreed upon limits.

It was just that in a day filled with so much uncertainty and upheaval, he'd made her feel safe. A little less alone.

And for a few minutes, she'd clung to that.

But now, Jeff was leaning in to kiss his mother's cheek. He'd already made certain Darcy had a list of two dozen phone numbers to use in case of emergency. And after a moment's hesitation when he didn't seem sure of whether to hug her or pat her arm, he leaned in and kissed her cheek, too. And then he left.

And Darcy stood staring at the closed door he'd walked out of, next to a woman she didn't know, in a house she didn't belong in.

Gail rested a hand at her elbow, offering a sympathetic look. "Are you all right with Jeffery gone?"

"I'll be fine. Honestly." It was so difficult to know what to say, circumstances being what they were. But meeting Gail's eyes she got the sense Jeff's mother was someone who appreciated the truth. "We hardly know each other."

Gail looked toward the door. "Give it time. You'll get to know each other, and figure out how exactly you fit into each other's lives."

The way the older woman said it, Darcy wondered if she

was holding out hope for a more traditional outcome for their relationship.

"Until then, you can take my totally unbiased opinion as gospel. Jeffrey is a wonderful man, who is going to make as wonderful a father as his was to him. And in case you haven't figured it out already, he'll do just about anything to make sure his child has a stable, happy home. You'll have everything you need. He'll see to it. And so will I. So…" She leaned in with a conspiratorial wink that was so very Jeff, Darcy almost did a double take. "Would it help even the playing field a bit if I started telling you stories about all the times Jeffery lost his lunch as a boy?"

"In what universe are we living that you, a guy who makes me look like a pauper, would move your pregnant non-girlfriend into your parents' spare room? You could buy the building next door to your office tomorrow. With cash. What the hell, man?"

Jeff gripped the wheel with fingers long gone white at the knuckles. "Give me a break, Connor. She's staying in your old room, so it's not like we're talking about some hole down in the basement with a moldy futon. She's got the entire west wing of the house to herself. She doesn't even have to use the same door."

"Glad to hear you aren't trying to smuggle her in and out through the basement window, but seriously, *your mom?*"

Connor chuckled from across the miles, his voice going muffled as he invariably filled in his new wife, Megan, on the details. Then he said, "Megan wants to know if your mom is making her pizza puffs on demand."

"Ha-ha. Megan's a laugh a minute."

"Man, I know it. She's great." Then quieter, as though there were a hand almost covering the phone, Connor said, "Come here, sweetheart… Great, see you in a few hours, gorgeous."

When Connor's attention was returned to the call, Jeff

let out a tight breath. "It was the first thing I thought of. She wasn't going to budge on the job thing. So I found her a job."

"Working for your mom? And Darcy's okay with it?"

"Not really. But for now, she's agreed. So it's a start."

"So what happens once she realizes Gail doesn't actually need any help with anything, from anyone—that if she wanted, she could probably add your job and mine to her mix of charitable foundations without breaking a sweat."

Jeff stared out the windshield, toward a sea of congested taillights. "I'm hoping Mom can keep her highly efficient tendencies under wraps for at least a couple of months. Long enough to give Darcy a chance to get some rest and me a chance to come up with my next game plan."

CHAPTER TEN

DARCY WOKE TO the unfamiliar and yet totally identifiable sound of lawn mowers from beyond her window. The sun shone in through the shades she'd neglected to close the night before, casting the room in a warm, golden glow she might have lingered in if not for her standing appointment with morning sickness.

Once taken care of, she showered, and then slipped into a pair of yoga pants and a thin, long sleeve T-shirt before heading downstairs. Gail had been gone when she woke up yesterday and only stopped in for a few minutes around late afternoon before disappearing through most of the evening, which had given Darcy the bulk of the day to familiarize herself with the house. She'd met the two housekeepers, Nancy and Viv, who had been incredibly warm and welcoming, right up to the minute she'd asked if she might help them out with anything. At which point those warm smiles had turned stern and she'd been pointed toward the couch and handed a glass of juice. Apparently, Jeff had spoken with them.

The break had been nice, but so much free time left her at loose ends, and she was looking forward to sitting down with Gail and finding out what her temporary position would entail and how quickly she could get her hands into something. Anything.

Stepping into the kitchen she found Gail standing at the farmhouse-style table a china cup in one hand, a tablet in the other. Stacks of folders spread out in front of her.

She looked up at Darcy's entrance and smiled her son's genuine smile. "Wonderful, you're up! Sleep okay?"

"I did, thank you. How about yourself?"

Gail nodded, quickly, then flapped her hand at the air as if to brush aside the morning pleasantries. "I'd like us to be friends, Darcy. Real friends."

"That would be nice," she answered.

"It would. So in the interest of friendship, I suggest we make a pact to be honest with each other. Truthful. Up-front. So we always know where we stand."

Nervous tension began to creep through her, because honesty had pretty much been the plan from the start. But maybe Gail wasn't as okay with having her here as she'd sounded when Jeff was around. "All right."

"Great! So I'll start. Now honestly, do you want to dive right into your made-up, fake job this morning or—" she clutched her hands in front of her, like she was making a plea "—go shopping for *baby clothes*."

Six hours later, Darcy was on the phone with the caterer, confirming Tuesday's menu modification when Gail walked into the small office Darcy had made of her sitting room. Setting three binders on the edge of the small desk, she dropped into the chair on the opposite side. When Darcy wrapped up the call, Gail scanned the desk.

"For a fake job, we've actually scrounged up quite a bit to keep you busy."

Darcy let out a short laugh. There'd been a candid discussion between them earlier about the motivation behind this manufactured position. Gail had asked Darcy to put a pin in her frustration toward Jeff and consider the opportunity before her. If Darcy was serious about continuing to work—and she was—this was an opportunity to expand her skill set and open up avenues in the employment market that wouldn't have otherwise been available.

It was an offer Darcy realized she would be crazy not to

take. And within the hour she'd been on the job with Gail only huffing the smallest amount over the decision not to go baby clothes shopping.

Darcy reached for the top binder, only to have her fingers swatted away.

"*Part-time,* fake job. You agreed to take it easy for a few weeks, so this one will have to wait. For now, Jeff's got a friend of his—a doctor—stopping over in about an hour to check on you. Which leaves you some time for a phone call if you were planning to make one."

Jeff stared down at the phone in his hand, not sure what shocked him most. That his mother—his supposed number one fan and most staunch supporter—had completely, unequivocally thrown him under the bus in favor of his pregnant non-girlfriend. Or that Darcy had thanked him for what he'd done.

Definitely the latter.

And she'd sounded genuine. Excited even. Enough so the piece of her mind she'd given him about scheduling a doctor's appointment without consulting her first hardly stung at all. And in truth, he'd meant to call her about it, but then had ended up speaking to his mother and passing the message along, which had probably sounded more like a dictate, than the *on condition she didn't object,* he'd assumed would be implied.

She was going to stay with his mom.

She was going to take it easy with the work thing.

And for the first time since he'd found out she was pregnant, Jeff breathed an almost easy breath.

CHAPTER ELEVEN

"IF YOU DON'T give me that file," Darcy warned, leaning over her small desk toward the pilfering grandmother-in-the-making/woman-of-steel who happened to be Jeff's mother, "I'm—I'm—I'm not going baby clothes shopping with you this weekend."

Gail looked down at the manila folder she'd swiped from Darcy's hold and then looked back. "You said fifteen more minutes. That was over an hour ago."

She had. But after two weeks of taking it easy, Darcy's energy was back up. She'd regained a few pounds. And she'd found a satisfaction and meaning in the work she was doing she'd never had before. So on days like today, when the hormones ran rampant and her mood was a bit off, the work was her best distraction. And she didn't want to give it up. Besides, there was a benefit coming up to raise funds for a series of summer programs for at-risk youth. She wasn't ready to call it a day. Which meant she'd have to play hardball with Gail. "That little boutique we drove by Sunday... with the Frog Prince–themed window... I know you know the one. I *know* you want to go."

Gail got a sort of fevered look in her eyes. Baby clothes were this Superwoman's Kryptonite, and while Darcy mostly didn't like to exploit the weakness...she knew Gail would respect her for it in the end.

The file flopped back onto her desk.

"Fine. You win. But I was hoping to talk you into joining me for dinner with the girls tonight."

The invitation wasn't totally unexpected. Gail had offered to include her in her plans more than a handful of times over the past few weeks, but Darcy had yet to take her up on it. And when she made her excuse tonight, Gail didn't push but left with her usual, friendly "next time, then."

By the time Darcy found a good stopping place and turned off her desk lamp, the house was empty, the sky beyond the window glass already dark. Picking at a dinner her stomach wasn't interested in, she finished her book on pregnancy and motherhood. She watched five minutes worth of drivel on TV before turning it off in an impatient huff and setting out to walk the halls of the house, again.

When she reached the second floor, she turned toward her rooms but stopped instead at the first door on the left. Jeff's room. Normally she kept walking but tonight, she was at a loose end. As always, the door was open. And as always she experienced a tug of curiosity about the space within, and what it might tell her about the man who'd called it his.

Scanning the room, her eyes snared on the built-in shelves behind a desk. The rows of trophies and medals: baseball, tennis, swimming, football, track. The evidence of Jeff's achievements. It made her smile to think what he must have been like as a kid.

Gail had told her he'd been into mischief almost as much as he'd been out of it, but never in a way that was hurtful or destructive. She'd called him a rule bender. A perpetual charmer.

Traits apparently carried over into adulthood.

And if ever there was a man who made a bit of trouble look like fun, it was Jeff.

Pushing back from the doorframe she returned to her room. But her ping-ponging thoughts wouldn't still. Would she have a little boy or a girl? Was Jeff hoping for one over the other? What would labor feel like? Would Jeff be there? Would he stay cool? Hold her hand? Tell her not to be scared?

One question after another, and they kept circling back to Jeff.

How often would she see him? What would he do if they disagreed?

What kind of father would he be? She thought about the trophies and ribbons, and how nothing short of first place earned a spot on his wall of fame. Would he be as successful in parenting as he was in what appeared to be every other area of his life? Would he go it alone or hire in help? *Marry* in help?

Not the woman he'd been dating when she first came to him. Gail had mentioned they'd broken the relationship off already. But a man like Jeff—she closed her eyes trying to stop her train of thought, but already her mind had found the deep rumble of his laugh, the heavy cut of his jaw and the feel of his untamed hair between her fingers.

The weight of his body over hers.

The heat of his kiss.

Her eyes popped open. Because closed, well, obviously that wasn't helping. And as tempting as it was to recall their night together in exacting, vivid detail—it was a mistake. When she thought about Jeff now, it should be in the context of his role as co-parent to their child. Nothing else.

Which was fine. She was realistic enough to understand the enormity of the gulf between their worlds. She was okay with it.

Like she'd be okay when Jeff found the next woman to get serious about. Mostly. Though even as she thought it, some little piece of her rejected the idea of him with another woman. Not because she wanted him for herself.

No.

Just because...well...well...an irritated growl left her throat. It didn't matter why and she didn't need to justify anything.

What was wrong with her today?

Turning to happier thoughts, she tried to imagine Jeff's

youth, wondering whether he would describe himself the same way his mother had? What he thought life would be like for their child—if he'd want to do things the way his parents had done with him, or if he'd like to see things happen differently for his own son or daughter.

She glanced at the phone and, experiencing a pull even greater than the one outside Jeff's room, wondered if they talked, if he'd make her laugh again, the way no one else seemed capable of doing.

Jeff met Charlie's knowing eyes across the table where the two of them had set up for the call in his office. It was time for a break.

"Why don't we take thirty so everyone can grab a bite," Jeff suggested, pushing back from the table himself. "And we'll pick up here when we get back."

Charlie went to grab a few files from his desk and Jeff was left in the quiet of his office alone. Shoulder propped at his favorite window, he was scrolling through his messages, rereading the one line updates from his mom when the little black-and-white, fifteen-week ultrasound image popped up on his screen signaling a call from the very woman all his extra hours at work were supposed to keep him from thinking about—but weren't.

"Hi, Jeff. I hope I'm not interrupting."

"Not at all. What's going on?" He closed his eyes. "Everything okay with the baby?"

His baby. *Their baby.*

The little troublemaker wreaking havoc on his mother's system and scaring the living hell out Jeff with the fragility of his existence alone.

"Oh, yes. Sorry, I should probably text before I call so you know not to worry," she said, the words sounding almost amused. Playful.

He liked it, and found himself relaxing.

"What's up?"

"I was just wondering if maybe you had time to talk awhile."

He scanned the conference table. "I'm heading back into a call here in the next few minutes."

"Oh, of course, it definitely doesn't need to be now. You know, just sometime. I could come by your office. Or meet you after work—you're so busy, the evening would probably be better. But maybe not, because it's late and you're still working and I don't want to—you know what? It doesn't matter. It's not hugely important or anything—"

"Darcy," he cut her off, her fluster in trying not to inconvenience him somehow pushing a smile to his mouth. "Of course I'll make time. What is it you wanted to talk about?"

A sigh filtered through the line, and the sultry quality of it curled around his senses, rubbing soft against the places he'd been trying to ignore.

"I was just thinking this little guy is going to have a very different experience growing up than I did. And, I don't know," she continued softly. "I was hoping maybe you'd tell me more about what it was like for you. What you'd like it to be like for him."

Right. More information exchange, because that was the only reason she'd be calling. The only reason he wanted her to call. They'd agreed and for good reason. So yeah.

"How about this," he said, clearing his throat. "I'll get in touch tomorrow to set up a block of time when we can talk. Also if there's anything in particular you've got questions about or have on your mind, you can email me and I'll try to get a response back to you by the next morning. Okay?"

"Um. Sure. Sounds great, Jeff," she answered simply, but something had changed in her tone. There was no emotional inflection evident whatsoever. "Have a good night."

"You, too." He stared at the phone, suddenly on alert. Because he'd heard that total absence of *anything* in her voice before. In Vegas. When her impassive facade was hiding something she didn't want seen.

Charlie walked back into the office and within a few keystrokes had a modified timeline up on the big screen. He glanced at Jeff. "Want to go over this before we pick up?"

Yellow. Box mix. Cake.

The mouthwatering revelation had struck Darcy like a lightning bolt shortly after talking to Jeff.

There'd been a heaviness in her chest after their call because, inexplicably, she'd gotten it in her head that talking to him might snap her out of this strange funk. But she didn't feel any better. If anything she'd hung up feeling more adrift than she had before.

But what did she really expect. While Jeff definitely made her health and well-being a priority, the guy was busy. He had a life. Commitments to his corporation, his friends and whatever it was he did to fill his time when he wasn't checking in to make sure her blood pressure was where it should be.

So she'd hung up and sat at the side of her bed, wishing she could muster some enthusiasm for anything. Hating the way she'd lost her appetite completely and how nothing sounded good to her. It had been a full-on pity party the likes of which she never indulged. And then, in a flash, inspiration.

Cake.

Followed by something even more shocking still.

Hunger... Craving.

Next thing, she'd been rifling through the pantry, nearly bursting into tears at the discovery of one single cardboard box in the very back, and the tub of fudge frosting beside it.

Some forty minutes later she was staring down two eight-inch rounds, fresh from the oven, mentally calculating how long before they'd be cool enough to frost and eat. Too long.

"God," she half moaned, recognizing the near breathless desperation in her own voice. "I want you *so bad*."

The sound of a throat clearing behind her had her jumping back, one hand moving instinctively toward her belly, the other going to her chest.

"Jeff," she gasped at seeing him in the doorway, tie askew, suit jacket flipped over one arm, shirt a perfect cut for his broad shoulders, looking rugged and powerful and thoroughly entertained with an amused smile tilting his lips. "I thought you had a call. What are you doing here?"

Rubbing a hand over the back of his neck, he nodded toward the counter. "Looking for some cake?"

CHAPTER TWELVE

SURROUNDED BY THE familiar dark wood cabinetry, heated stone floors and wide granite counters of the kitchen he'd spent a significant part of his youth hanging out in—it was with immense satisfaction that Jeff watched Darcy standing at the counter where she frosted the now-cooled cakes, her head tipped back as warm, full-bodied laugher bubbled past her lips.

"Traitor?" She teased, catching her breath. "She's *your* mother. And *you* were the one who finagled me into staying here and working with her. You had to know we'd find some middle ground."

"She sold out over a trip to some baby boutique? Come on."

He was crying foul, but seeing Darcy in person, his anxiety about her overdoing it was alleviated. Mostly anyway. And for all the noise he was making, he knew his mom wouldn't have skipped out for the night if she'd had even a moment's doubt about how Darcy was doing.

Darcy slid a fat slice of yellow cake layered with some kind of thick fudgy frosting onto a waiting plate.

Man, his mouth watered and he went to the counter, catching himself an instant before he leaned in to drop a kiss at her neck. Which was crazy, because it wasn't like this sort of domesticity was a habit. But seeing her there, laughing, chatting with him, looking so comfortable in her bare feet—it was like the scene flipped a switch in him and he'd forgotten exactly what they were doing and how it was between them.

Which was, not like *that*.

He slanted another look at her neck. Bare and long, and hell, with a tiny speck of cake batter along the side to match the few decorating her thin cotton hoodie.

She looked sweet. Tasty.

Because she was. He remembered running his tongue from her collarbone up behind her ear, and how the silky length of her hair had felt in his fingers as he gathered it out of his way.

"You okay?" Darcy asked, a wary look in her eyes.

Except for the way his entire body had gone online in the span of a few seconds, yeah, perfect. "Hungry. For cake."

Satisfied, she smiled and served him a slice. "Then here you go."

A *smaller* slice. Significantly.

"Really?" he asked with an arched brow.

Darcy flashed him a sassy grin and patted her flat stomach. "Eating for two. And since this is the only thing I've actually wanted in as long as I can remember." She looked down at her slice with a covetous intent and put on a growling brogue as she muttered, "Get in my belly."

Jeff blinked, not believing he'd just heard her quote an Austin Powers movie. He let out a hard laugh as she enthusiastically swept up her plate and went to the table, his little mama-in-the-making diving in without so much as a look his way.

Her lips closed around the fork and she gave up one of those unabashed moans that had his body reacting in a way where the best course of action seemed turning his back to her as he went to the fridge. "Think your belly's up for a glass of milk?"

Darcy was still sucking the frosting off her fork when he turned to look at her. Rather than just finish the bite, she continued to savor the cake and frosting, turning her fork upside down to suck the tines as she absently nodded at him.

He swallowed, gave himself a firm mental shake and then poured a couple of glasses.

They were drinking milk. And milk and hard-ons didn't go.

But even without the dairy, he shouldn't be thinking about Darcy like that. Because he wasn't ever going to *be with* Darcy that way again. Even if his head seemed to be making frequent sojourns to a time when he had, he had enough control to keep his body from following.

The pressure behind his fly told him he was lying to himself, but he threw a mental finger in that southern direction.

There was too much on the line with a child between them to risk emotions gone awry, which meant keeping it platonic.

He couldn't afford for things to end up the way they had with Margo. After all the years of friendship between them, in the end they could barely stand to be in the same room, let alone carry on a civilized conversation.

So resisting a few wayward urges shouldn't be too difficult considering it wasn't love they were fighting. Darcy was just so damned sexy, was all.

Yeah, their initial connection had been beyond the physical. But the part that *was* physical? He could still feel the embers from that blaze where they sizzled and burned in the back of his mind. Eventually though, he'd get past them.

Pulling it together, he slid into the chair across from hers. "So it's going well with my mom?"

Seeing Darcy was still working the damned fork, he shifted in his seat, adding tightly, "No rush to answer. Whenever you're finished molesting that fork with your tongue. By all means, take your time."

Her eyes widened, a satisfying rush of red tingeing her cheeks. It looked good on her.

Sliding the fork from between her lips in a way that didn't

do him any favors, she set the utensil at the side of her plate and neatly folded her arms in front of her.

"You mom is wonderful. I think she's one of the most generous people I've ever met."

Jeff smiled. "Did she try to buy you the house across the street—which incidentally is on the market if you like it. Smaller than this one but for the two of you—"

"No," she said waving him off with an annoyed glance. "She's very thoughtful. And observant. When I said generous, I meant with her time and her thoughts and feelings."

"She is, isn't she? I hoped she wouldn't overwhelm you. I know you like to be on your own."

Darcy shook her head, picking up the fork again and scraping at frosting left on her plate. Accumulating the smallest glob before bringing it to her mouth.

"We've struck a pretty good balance. We go for a walk each morning, sometimes just around the yard if my stomach is sketchy. We talk about interests and goals. And if ever I'm feeling embarrassed or something from having to rush away for my stomach, she always has some fantastic story about you to make me feel better."

Jeff's brow shot up, his ego taking a stretch and pulling him forward to hear more. "Yeah?"

"Yeah, like the time you got into the caterer's stash of dessert toppers and then got sick in the pool."

He slumped back. "No."

Not exactly the tales of heroism and maternal adoration he'd been banking on.

Darcy pointed the freshly cleaned tines at him. "Yeah. Her thinking is, it's only fair you share in the humiliation once in a while, too."

"I'm almost afraid to ask, but how often are you still getting sick."

There was a wicked glint in Darcy's eyes as she answered. "Often."

Jeff reached across the table and took her hand in his.

"Then I can say with the utmost sincerity, I hope you get past this soon."

She looked him up and down and then closed her eyes, laughing. "I'll bet you do."

She was so glad he'd come. Glad to the point where there was no choice but to acknowledge Jeff's little baby had been working her over good with the hormones.

Twice she'd felt the inexplicable push of tears at the back of her eyes. The first, when she realized halfway through her third slice of cake she was too full to eat any more, and the second when, at her request, Jeff had pulled his favorite trophy down and told her he had absolutely no idea why he favored it, and then after a shrug, stuck it back on the shelf.

Yes, the hormones were having their way with her for sure. Which was reassuring in that it gave her something to blame for other inexplicable reactions. Like every time she got within breathing distance of Jeff. All it took was the barest hint of his clean masculine scent and everything within her started to whir. He smelled better than box mix, but thankfully she'd exercised more restraint with the man than she had with the butter recipe.

As a result they'd been talking comfortably on the back terrace by the pool for more than an hour, Jeff answering whatever questions he could for her. Occasionally asking one himself—though in truth, Darcy didn't have very much to share about her own youth. If he asked whether she'd participated in some traditional all-American kind of activity, the answer was typically no. The explanation always the same. They hadn't had the money for team sports, camps or after school programs. Of course there had been more to it, but Jeff didn't need to know about those details. All that mattered was their child's life would be more like his than hers. This baby would be happy, loved and wanted.

They'd hit on the topic of school a few moments ago, and now Jeff leaned back in the terrace chair that looked more like it belonged in a showroom than outside by the pool. His long legs were extended out in front of him, his ankles crossed, hands folded behind his head as he stared up into the night sky.

"I don't know, Darcy. The boarding school thing was something both my parents agreed on. It's an experience I value. But with you barely halfway through the pregnancy, I don't really know whether it's something I'd want for him or her or not. To me this little guy's personality, drive and temperament will play pretty heavily into my position." His gaze locked with hers. "But whatever we decide, we'll decide together."

It had been the unofficial theme of their discussion for the night. That they were in this together. Not in a relationship way, but as far as working at keeping communication between them strong.

She nodded, letting him see the gratitude and appreciation in her eyes. "I believe you."

A breeze ruffled the leaves in the trees around the grounds and then caught a few loose strands of Darcy's hair, blowing them across her face. Tucking them behind her ear, she glanced up to find Jeff watching her with a look she couldn't read.

Suddenly self-conscious, she asked, "What?"

He waved her off.

"Nothing. It's late is all." He braced his hands on the armrests of his chair and pushed to stand. "You ought to get some rest and I've got to drive back."

Taking her hand, he helped her to her feet.

They walked back toward the house and, reaching the door, Jeff stopped. "I'll say good night here. Sleep in tomorrow, will you?"

At Darcy's rolled eyes, he flashed her one of those devastating grins that ought to require a special license the way he wielded it. "Come on, so I don't worry about you."

No question, this guy knew how to get what he wanted.
"I'll do my best."

Satisfied, he leaned in—probably to drop a kiss on her
cheek—only as he neared, the rich masculine scent that had
been playing with her senses and control all night caught her
off guard. Her eyes closed and her head turned toward him
as she drew a deep breath through her nose.

Whoa—what the heck was she doing?

Her eyes popped wide, and there was Jeff, inches away,
a darkening scowl underscoring his confusion.

Immediately, she took a step away to put more distance
between them, but caught a heel on the edge of the walk.

Jeff's hand was there in an instant, guiding her back the
way she'd come. Then closer. Until she was looking up into
his face, their bodies only a breath away from contact.

This close there was no getting away from how good he
smelled. Her heart was pounding, her breath coming too fast.

"Darcy?"

She shook her head. Trying to figure out exactly what
to say when the truth—that she'd lost control and he'd, yes,
just caught her going in for a whiff of him or whatever the
cheap-feel equivalent would be for smelling someone up.
This was so low.

"Honey?" His hold tightened as concern put an urgent
edge to his voice. "Are you okay?"

She blinked. Okay? And then realization…she had an out
here. Only her conscience pricked at the idea of passing off
blame on her baby for her moment of weakness.

No, on second thought, she could definitely live with herself.

Raising a hand to her temple, she offered a weak shrug.
"I think maybe I'm a little more worn out than I realized. A
little light-headed is all."

The muscles of Jeff's throat worked up and down…and
then before she realized what was happening, the man had
her scooped into his arms.

"Jeff!" she squeaked, gripping his shirt as he shouldered his way in through the terrace door.

"I'll get you into bed and call Grant to come over."

"Jeff, no," she started and he stopped midstride to look down at her.

"Is it bad?" But before she could answer his attention seemed to have shifted inward and then he turned around, ready to carry her back out the door they'd just come through. "We'll go straight to the hospital."

Oh, hell.

"Jeff, no. Stop a second. Jeff. *Jeff.*" She squirmed in his arms, trying to get a leg down, but the man wasn't having any of it, at least until she grabbed his collar in her fist and gave it a solid shake, demanding, "Set me down this minute, damn it."

And then her feet were on the ground but he was still holding her far too close for comfort, especially because it had become painfully clear, she was going to have to own up to her crimes, or take a ride to the E.R.

"Darcy, if something's wrong—"

"Listen." She squared her shoulders, and dug up a bit of the no-nonsense steel she used to find so readily on hand. "I lied."

CHAPTER THIRTEEN

"You what?" Jeff's chin pulled back, his brows crashing down. "Are you telling me—all night? Has this been going on, all night, with the— Damn it, Darcy, this is serious. What the hell am I going to have to do to get you to take it easy, tie you to the bed?"

Her lips parted, but before the words she'd had ready mere seconds before could get out, her mind short-circuited and her eyes locked with his.

He raked a hand through the dark shock of his hair, and took a step back. "The chair."

Then he took another step back and swore under his breath. "I'm not going to tie you up at all. But—"

This *so* wasn't getting any better.

"Jeff. I lied about being worn-out and light-headed. I—I—" She took a deep breath and let the truth spill out in one huge gush. "You were standing so close—and this supersensitive smell thing that's part of the pregnancy, kind of got the better of me for one minute before I realized what I was doing, and then I tried to back up, but I tripped, and you asked if I was okay, and I thought it would be better to avoid any misunderstandings about me wanting to smell you if I just lied and blamed the baby, which sounds really terrible when I say it, but now that I'm thinking about it, is pretty much the truth. Your baby is making me crazy. There."

She sucked a great lungful of air and then covered her

cheeks with her hands, knowing they had to be burning crimson.

Jeff's jaw cocked to one side, his eyes focused down around his shoes. "So…you were…smelling me."

She crossed her arms and stared at the ceiling. "You smell…really good. It was like with the cake."

His head snapped up. "Like the cake? I mean, what you did to that cake."

And there were about a million wrong ways he could interpret what she'd just said, and based on the rapidly morphing expressions crossing his face, he was hitting on each one of them.

"I don't mean you smell like a cake. And I wasn't saying… you made me—"

Something dark flashed in his eyes as he looked down at her mouth. "Hungry?"

She nodded, thinking the way the night was playing out, they were going to need a couple of neck braces. "Right. No. I mean, no, you didn't make me hungry. I just don't want you to think—"

"I don't. And I'm not thinking about tying you to the bed, either." Then he ran a wide hand over his mouth, and the eyes that met hers were filled with some twisted combination of apology, amusement and heat.

She gasped.

"Okay, okay," he answered with a distinctly unapologetic laugh. "I *am* thinking about it a little. Now. But normally I don't." He closed his eyes and held up a hand. "Not the tying up part at least. Sometimes I think about the rest. I mean, we did it. And it was good. But it doesn't mean I'm interested in an act two. It's just a guy thing."

Okay. She'd take him at his word. "So we'll forget this then," she offered, not meeting his eyes as she thrust out her hand.

"Deal," he said with a firm shake before turning to go without a backward glance. "Now, lock the door and go to bed."

* * *

So the forgetting thing hadn't worked out. Which meant Jeff really should have stayed away from her. But that wasn't happening, either.

Rolling past security with a wave, Jeff pulled up the winding drive and parked around the side of the house.

Initially he'd thought he wanted the distance between them. He'd thought keeping Darcy at arm's length while knowing she was being looked after would be enough for him. More than enough.

But after the other night...hell. He'd been back three times in the two weeks since.

The first, because he wanted to make sure everything was still cool between them. The second, because everything *was* cool. And talking with Darcy was so damned easy. And the third...yeah, that's where his moral compass began to spin like maybe he'd landed himself in the Bermuda Triangle. The third time, like tonight he'd gone back to have Darcy to himself.

In a strictly platonic, or at least nonphysical way.

He might not be able to control his thoughts hopping the express train to Dirty Town when Darcy did certain things. Like laugh or eat cake or succumb to one of those mysterious blushes he figured it was better not to ask about. But physically, well, he'd kept his hands to himself.

With a child between them, they couldn't afford to risk souring their relationship because of some affair gone bad. Not when they needed to maintain positive relations...well, for as long as they both shall live. Forget the sanctity of marriage. They had to peaceably share a child. They were in it for the long haul. And really, if he looked past the whole out-of-wedlock, non-girlfriend part of the pregnancy, he was pretty damned lucky to have Darcy be the mother of his child. She made him laugh. Got what he was saying. Connected with him in a way that made him believe they could really make this thing—this parenting thing—work.

He liked her.

A lot.

Which was why he was driving out again tonight after spending the entire day and the majority of last night telling himself he wouldn't—reminding himself not to think about the way Darcy's hair sometimes spilled over one shoulder, leaving the bare length of her neck exposed on the other side. Or the soft curve of her mouth when she'd just finished laughing. Yeah, he'd figured some distance wouldn't be the worst thing. Tried to talk himself into a solid week before he saw her again. But after barely four days he'd gotten in his car and driven out anyway.

Throwing the car in Park, he checked his phone for whatever messages had come through between leaving his office and pulling in the drive, wanting them out of the way before he was with Darcy.

Not *with* with her. Though, sure enough, now that he'd made the mental jump—

He blew out a harsh breath.

It would be fine. So long as Darcy did her part to keep it wholesome...well, he'd be good for his.

Half a dozen hangers clattered together as they hit the bed, their high-end couture spilling across the duvet in a spectrum of linens, crisp cottons and stunning raw silks.

"Gail, please, I can't borrow your clothes."

The older woman turned a cool smile on her. "If you'd let me take you shopping like I wanted, you wouldn't need to. But now we're being picked up in less than an hour, and you need a dress for dinner."

Dinner with Grant Mitchel. The doctor Jeff had gone to school with and then bullied into checking on her a couple times a week.

When Gail had sprung the plans on her earlier that afternoon, Darcy had tried to put her off with the usual excuses. Only tonight Gail was having none of it. She'd looked her straight in the eye, smiling a sort of frightening smile and said, "You're going."

She'd seriously considered faking sick again to get out of it, because as nice a guy as Grant was, she knew the score. Gail was doing what she'd basically promised to do from the start— Trying to find her a nice husband. But after the way her last fib had blown up in her face she wasn't about to lie again.

"With you barely beginning to show and the loose cut of the pieces I've pulled out, all of these will fit. And if you want my opinion the burnt-orange would be fabulous on you."

Darcy opened her mouth to voice another protest—but Gail cut her off with a look that brooked no argument and a hanger against her chest.

Five minutes later, an airy sheath the color of a setting sun was skimming over her hips and belly in a silky caress. It was gorgeous, light and flattered her exactly the way Gail had promised it would. And more than anything she wanted to take it off, hand it back with whatever apology or excuse it would take to get out of a dinner the mere thought of was making her stomach roil with nerves.

From beyond the bathroom door, Darcy could hear the rise and fall of Gail's animated voice, but not exactly what was being said. A second, deeper voice sounded, and she stilled as her heart skipped a beat.

Jeff.

She swung the door wide.

"Why the hell *wouldn't* I join you?" Jeff demanded as his mother scoffed at him.

"Don't be dense, honey. If Grant wanted to catch up with you, he'd have set up some rock climbing retreat." She cocked her head. "He's the climber isn't he? Keeping all you boys straight can—"

"Yes, he's the climber. But you can't seriously be suggesting this is a date? Now? *He's her doctor* and she's preg—"

His words cut off when, pointing in Darcy's direction, Jeff caught sight of her, stopped talking and straightened, his eyes going dark as he stared at her.

"Hello, Jeff," she offered lamely, not quite knowing what to make of the interaction she'd walked into. Particularly as she was the subject…and yet not really a participant.

Jeff cleared his throat and wiped his expression clear.

"Beautiful, Darcy," he said, offering a polite smile that didn't reach his eyes. His hands went into his pockets, and she could swear she saw them ball into fists beneath. "Looking forward to tonight?"

There was any number of different ways she could answer. Most of them began with the word *no.* But out of respect for Gail and Grant as well, she was having difficulty voicing even one of them.

Gail began to collect the rest of the outfits she'd brought for Darcy to try. "Of course she is. Grant is a lovely man, and I know how appreciative *we all are* for the way he's given up so much of his time to *personally* check on her."

Ugh. The guilt trip. Even seeing it for what it was, her resistance crumbled. She had to go.

Schooling her features the way she'd done at the bar, she offered a nod.

Jeff stared at her a moment, a question forming in his eyes before his brows pushed high and he turned to his mother. "Oh, no way are you *making* her go out with him."

Darcy opened her mouth to defend Gail—but in a blink Jeff and Gail were going head-to-head.

"Making her? Please—"

"This is about that whole Mrs. Someone-suitable business—"

"She's a gorgeous, vivacious, available woman—"

"—can't even wait until after the baby—"

"—any man would be lucky to have—"

"I know that!"

"And you've made it clear you aren't—"

"*She's* not interested—at least not tonight. So she's not going. Period."

The truth was, she was too beat to care that they were arguing over her life like she wasn't there. Which really made Jeff's next move—pulling out his phone and calling Grant himself—probably for the best.

"Sorry, man, she's exhausted…no, I don't think a quick exam is necessary. Just some rest… Right. Mmm-hmm… No, you and Mom should go and have a great time.… *I insist.* I'll make sure Darcy gets whatever she needs." He shot her a wink and mouthed the words *cake* and *pizza* and something inside of her gave an almost painful twist.

Gail let out an infuriated growl and stalked out of the room, leaving Darcy and Jeff alone.

"I think I love you." She sighed, using the words in a careless joking way to underscore their throwaway quality, so there was no misunderstanding what had to be a look of utter adoration on her face. Hero worship for the man who'd just rescued her night.

Jeff flashed her his crooked smile, tucking the phone away.

"First a baby, now you love me." Nodding toward the door, he set his hand lightly at the small of her back in that gentlemanly way he had about him. "So if I'm reading this right, this is my window to propose?"

"I don't know, Jeff. What kind of pizza are we talking? And I want to hear more about this cake."

He leaned in close, so his voice was a low rumble just above her ear, so seductive she almost missed what he actually said. "I've got a yellow box mix in the car."

CHAPTER FOURTEEN

His mother wasn't speaking to him when Grant arrived. And, considering she'd been trying to set his pregnant non-girlfriend up with one of his oldest friends he could totally live with that.

It wasn't like he wanted Darcy for himself. He'd spent the past two months making sure everyone who crossed their paths understood he didn't. But did he want to see her set up with the guy who'd earned the nickname "Homer" in undergrad for all the "home runs" he scored on the female student body and a fair number of the faculty, as well? Sure Grant had grown up since then. Jeff had even set him up with a friend or two over the years.

But Darcy?

The mother of his child?

No.

The guy had been cool about it, too, shooting him a brief nod of understanding before ushering Jeff's mom out for the evening, and leaving Jeff and Darcy with the house to themselves.

He'd gotten her a pizza, and even made her the cake as they talked about movies and food, the work she'd been doing for his mother. They joked about Vegas and he told her about Connor and the wife he'd met and married all in one night, sharing a few of the more colorful highlights of their romantic journey.

Darcy laughed until she cried listening to his account of moving heaven and earth to keep a monumentally intoxicated Connor from taking the classic "drunk dial" to plane-hopping extremes in his quest to win Megan back after a particularly rough patch. And like always, the sound of her laughter got to him like nothing else. It did something to the space in the center of his chest he wasn't even aware of when he wasn't with her. Made him wonder if there was anything he wouldn't do to ensure he got to keep hearing it.

Darcy snuggled into the corner of the couch, her feet tucked up against the buttery leather as the last of her laughter subsided. "Honestly, Jeff, after all that I hope they name their firstborn after you."

"Firstborn, hmm?" He stretched back himself, feeling the tension ease from his muscles. "You do that more now, too? Find yourself making reference to babies when you never did before? My V.P. suggested making it a drinking game, everyone taking a shot of espresso each time I drop the *B* word."

And there was the little twitch at the corner of her mouth. The telling precursor to the smile she didn't try to keep from him any longer.

"I guess maybe I do." She met his eyes. "But it makes me happy to know I'm not the only one with baby brain."

"I told you. We're in it together."

"Glad to hear you're volunteering to share in the labor and delivery."

He ran a hand through his hair, watching Darcy as a comfortable silence fell over them. Labor and delivery. It was hard to think that far ahead when she was hardly showing.

That dress she'd had on earlier—hell, it had been so damn sexy. Hugging the curves of her breasts, sliding around her hips and thighs, and there for the first time, he'd seen the barest curve of her belly. He'd wanted to put his hand over the little swell, rub his face against the silky fabric and whisper to the child they were sharing between them.

The possessive impulse stabbing through him had been sharp and deep, and he'd nearly blown a gasket at the thought she looked like that for another man.

But then the craziest thing had happened. She'd given him one of her placid smiles, the kind so bland, it wasn't supposed to reveal a single thing about the thought process taking place behind it…and he'd seen exactly what she was thinking.

She didn't want to go. She'd wanted to stay with him, like he wanted to stay with her. Because they were becoming friends, and the lure of this mutual interest that went deeper than any he'd known before, was almost impossible to resist.

Darcy's eyes closed, her features falling into a gentle expression so soft and beautiful, Jeff couldn't look away, couldn't stop the words that came from his mouth next because he hadn't even realized he was thinking them.

"Why did you go?"

Those gray eyes blinked open at him, so unguarded he knew right then she hadn't understood what he was asking.

He had the chance to take it back. Pretend at asking something other than the question haunting him for five months already. But he wanted to know. Somehow, he needed to, despite the fact it wouldn't change anything.

"In Vegas. Why did you leave the way you did?"

Like he knew it would, the soft smile hovering over her lips evaporated into the air along with the ease and comfort that had been between them.

Darcy's arms crossed over the small swell of her belly. Defensive. Guarded.

"I had to go. I shouldn't have been there in the first place."

Damn it, he didn't get it. "Why not? We met. We had fun. We had chemistry. What was so horrible about one night of giving in to it? It wasn't like you made it a biweekly habit."

The look she gave him held shades of hurt he didn't understand. "I know for you, one night is no big deal. You meet someone, have some fun, decide you want to take it back to your room for the night…and you go for it. You're good with a few hours of giving in because you won't walk away bruised. You won't get caught up in feelings you don't want to have. You won't start building fantasies about a reality that has an expiration date of a couple hours from then. But it's not like that for me. I've spent the past ten years being the only person looking out for me. So I've been careful. About my job. My time. My life. But then there you were, offering me a night to do a few of the things I'd never done. Tempting me to break the rules and live up Vegas like it was my last night to do it."

"And because it actually was your last night, you agreed."

"After all the years of saying no and doing the right thing, I couldn't resist. I thought I had it all figured out. I was done with work. I wasn't going to be around for any unwanted attention. You seemed safe enough—plus you seemed smart enough not to dump me in a ditch after six hundred video cameras captured us leaving the casino together."

The way her brain worked. He both loved and hated it.

"So I figured, what was the harm? It seemed safe. No risk. Just a night of fun."

Her mouth pulled to the side and her eyes went to some faraway place it made him feel good to think he might be with her in.

"It *was* fun. It was great," he said, appreciative for what she was sharing, but still not any closer to understanding why she'd taken off without so much as a goodbye.

"When I fell into bed with you, I thought I could handle it. We were both adults. You made me feel things I never feel. And I wanted more of it."

The next breath she took was unsteady.

"I wanted more of your eyes on me, looking like you couldn't look away." She peered back at him and lifted one shoulder. "I know that wasn't really the way it was. What we were doing was about a physical release. It was about sex. And I was okay with it. It's just—I don't know, it had been so long since I'd been intimate with someone—I wasn't prepared for how it would make me feel. And I knew the kinds of things running through my head didn't belong there."

He shouldn't ask. But, hell, he wanted to know. "What things?"

Darcy turned to the window, hiding her eyes from his, but not the pink stain infusing her cheeks.

"That being in your arms made me feel like I never wanted to leave. It was something I could get used to too fast. Something I might hope for more of."

"Then why the hell did you leave?"

This time the laughter that passed her lips had a bitter sound to it. A sharp edge to warn him from getting too close.

"Because that's not what either of us had been looking for. You didn't pick me up looking for a new girlfriend or someone to settle down with. You picked me up looking for the kind of good time that happens in Vegas and stays in Vegas. A few hours of fun, remember? No broken hearts in the street. But the time we shared meant something to me, and I wasn't willing to risk tainting the memory of it with some awkward dismissal where you handed me my panties and thanked me for the great time."

"You didn't know it was going to go that way."

"I didn't. But that's the point, Jeff. I couldn't stand the idea of waiting around to find out. I didn't want to be the cocktail waitress tucked into your bed hoping you weren't going to kick her out before morning."

So she'd bolted. Taken the drastic, undoable action before he'd even had a chance to give her another alternative. It wasn't the same as what happened with Margo. Not even close to the betrayal he'd never seen coming. And yet that sense of somehow being cheated lingered in the back of his mind, prompting him to come back with the different ways it could have gone.

"You could have gotten dressed and waited for me to come back. You could have been the one to say goodbye."

"Except then I'd still have been standing there hoping." The vulnerability in her eyes was like a blow to the chest, momentarily knocking the wind from his lungs.

What kind of life had she had that a little hope was such a bad thing?

He caught her chin in the crook of his finger. "I wanted to see you again. I wanted—" He broke off and shook his head. "Before I realized our protection failed, I was going to tell you I wanted to see you again."

But then the moment he saw what had happened everything changed. If Darcy had been there when he'd come out of the bathroom, yes, he'd have been able to explain about the protection. They'd have exchanged information. He'd have promised to get in touch within a few weeks. But he wouldn't have asked her to stay. He wouldn't have tried to convince her to give him the next day or night or anything else. Because he'd have been too worried about the rest of his life.

Only now the worst-case scenario that had eaten at his gut for months was a reality and it didn't feel like the worst of anything. It was just...not what he'd expected. Yes, it had turned his life upside down. Disrupted plans for the both of them. But he wouldn't take it back. He was going to be a father. With months yet before he would be able to lay eyes on his child, the connection was already there.

"I know I shouldn't have left, Jeff. And I'm sorry. But I was out of my depth. And the truth is, even if everything had been different, if you'd asked me for more than a single night, I still wouldn't have been able to take you up on it. I was moving. That day."

"I have a helicopter, cars, money. I could have met you. Anywhere."

What was he doing, trying to convince her of the possibility of a scenario he knew wouldn't have come to fruition? Unless, what he wanted was for her to start believing in the potential of what might have been—because he wanted her to believe in what still could be.

Her head tipped back, and Jeff found his eyes drifting over the slender extended column of her neck, the soft spill of blond down her back and the small smile playing across her lips. Hell, was that what he was doing there? Had he started to believe?

Darcy, closed her eyes. "Hmm. You would have buzzed over to San Francisco for a night out on the Wharf with your Vegas cocktail waitress?"

"Probably would have skipped the Wharf unless it was where *the woman I met in Vegas* wanted to go." There was no missing the emphasis on his clarification or the hard look he gave her when he made it. But then the amusement was back as he leaned in conspiratorially closer.

"I would have booked the first trip around business. Made it look like I was playing it cool. Like meeting up just happened to work out."

What if? was a dangerous game to play. One Darcy had made it a life habit to avoid. But as with so many things, all Jeff had to do was flash a dimple and there she was, playing along. Flirting around a road not taken.

If things had gone like this...which they didn't...it could have been like that.

And why not? It wouldn't lead anywhere.

"Just look that way?" she teased.

But then Jeff was looking into her eyes, the small concentrated furrow between his brows giving her pause, drawing her attention to the way that *invisible thing* she could feel but couldn't see shifted in the air between them.

To a slow spreading warmth skimming the surface of her skin.

To one beat of time blending into another, until Jeff answered, "Yes."

With Jeff's eyes locked on hers and his make-believe admission still hovering in the air between them, suddenly giving in to this flirtation once removed seemed far from harmless. Like it had become a dangerous thing with the potential to destroy something important to her.

And Darcy wasn't going to let that happen.

So clearing her throat, she made a show of screwing up her face and pushing a wry note into her voice. "Hmm, sounds nice. But if you really want to know, I have an aversion to *Pretty Woman* fantasies." Then quickly added, "Not that I see myself as a prostitute."

Jeff laughed. "Geez, Darcy, what kind of childhood did you have? Cinderella ring a bell? Hardworking-maiden, working her fingers to the bone serving the wealthy-but-cruel stepsisters, sneaks off to meet a hot prince who doesn't want to let her go and then moves heaven and earth to find her."

The slender arch of her brow pushed high. "Truth?"

"Always."

Well he'd asked for it. "I've never seen Cinderella. Of course, I know the gist of the story. It's the one with the shoe where the prince sends some lackey out to do his dirty work because he can't be bothered and doesn't even remember the face of the woman he's decided he wants to spend his life with. I'm way more familiar with Julia Roberts being pulled out of her low income life by the wealthy, romantic Richard Gere. It was my mom's favorite. We had it on VHS and at the end, it was so worn the thing would barely play anymore."

For a moment she could feel the oppressive heat and stale air within the old trailer coating her skin. "I used to hate seeing my mother's rapt expression as she stared at the screen, that same infuriating combination of hope and hopelessness in her eyes.

"The thing is, Jeff, I was never really into the idea of some Charming sweeping in to rescue me from my life. My fantasy, from as far back as I can remember, has always been to take care of myself. To be dependent on no one." She sighed, giving him one of those lopsided little grins that did things to him he wasn't used to. "So much for fantasies, huh?"

"What's wrong with letting someone with the means and desire take care of you? I know your independence is important to you…but, Darcy, we made this baby together. You're giving it your body, your very lifeblood. At this stage the only thing I have to give is support to you in whatever form you need. Emotional. Financial."

Darcy looked at the man who had been nothing but generous with her from the start and wondered if she'd ever trust him enough to explain. If she could make herself vulnerable enough to share why she was the way she was. If coming from this life of love and privilege, he could even begin to comprehend what it had been like to feel hungry, trapped, afraid. Hopeless. To have such a keen awareness of how precarious the only existence you knew was. To watch the man between you and a fate too terrifying to contemplate, count out one bill after another with his grimy hands, wondering if, when he was done with the sick game he played, he would give up a bill to her mother to buy food, or if he'd make them wait another day. Or more.

She could still hear her mother's nervous pleading. *"Earl, don't make me beg."*

And the answering sneer, *"Why not? Why the hell should I give you anything? Or that brat of yours."*

Then those yellowed eyes searching her out across the cramped space, and her mother's sudden desperate agreement. The sight of her mother on her knees, laughing like it was all a game, but the humiliation and desperation evident in every forced breath.

"Hey," Jeff asked, his brows drawn together. "What's wrong?"

"Nothing," she answered quickly. "Nothing's wrong. I know how lucky I am in all this. And I'm very grateful for your support."

Jeff stared at her a moment more, but whatever he was thinking she couldn't quite tell. And then, "I don't want your gratitude, Darcy. I want you to feel secure."

CHAPTER FIFTEEN

WITHIN THE WALLS of his modern L.A. apartment, Jeff pinched the bridge of his nose with one hand and tried not to crush the phone at his ear with the other. Only Jim Huang wasn't doing anything more than delivering the news that the two weeks Jeff had just spent in Melbourne nailing down a new deal with Lexington Construction had been a success. The contracts were in hand and everything was a go. But after fourteen fifteen-hour days, a seventeen-hour international flight, customs, a trip home only to shower and change, then a four-hour meeting at the L.A. office, Jeff was shot. And this verbal confirmation of what he'd already ascertained through email was his limit.

"Jim, that's fantastic news. Get in touch if anything critical comes up. Otherwise, I'll talk to you guys Monday. Round of drinks on me tonight."

Disconnecting, he looked at the clean lines and open space of his apartment and let the silence settle over him. A half-eaten microwave dinner sat in front of him. The beer he'd cracked, down a single swallow. It was only seven, but for the number of hours he'd been running, it was definitely late enough to go to bed.

Only he kept thinking about Darcy.

He'd talked to her a handful of times while he'd been gone, and texted daily. But after having gotten in the habit of heading over to the house a couple of times a week, going this long without seeing her was making him itch.

He'd checked in with her earlier. Said he'd drive out tomorrow after he'd gotten some sleep and might make company worth having. But now…

Hell. He ought to just go to bed. In fact, forget the bed.

He flopped back on the couch and stretched completely out for the first time in he couldn't remember. Felt the ache and creak of a body running on fumes.

And didn't go to sleep.

Because he couldn't stop thinking about her.

His arm slung out from the couch, fumbling across the coffee table until he found his phone.

He'd just check in. And then he'd be able to sleep.

Punching in a few numbers, he waited for the line to pick up. "I need a car."

The house was mostly dark by the time Jeff arrived, the downstairs deserted, no sounds of activity filtering through from the floors above. Maybe he should have called ahead, but he hadn't wanted to risk Darcy telling him to stay put and get some sleep…because he hadn't wanted to explain he didn't think he'd be able to until he saw her. Only, yeah, looked like that's how it was going to have to go.

At least he'd see her first thing tomorrow.

On leaden legs he took the first flight of stairs, his brain zeroing in on the bed a few yards away. Except then he heard it. A noise from Darcy's end of the hall.

She was awake. Shaking off his fatigue he strode toward her room, his heart starting to pound at the sliver of light leaking out from beneath her door. Raising a hand to knock, he stopped short at the sound of a muffled sniff from within.

Then another, followed by some kind of low growl.

What the hell?

He rapped twice. "Darcy?"

A thud.

Then a squeaked, "Jeff?"

"Yeah, you okay?"

Some shuffling sounded and he waited for the door to

open. Then more shuffling, this time farther from the door. And finally she answered.

"I'm really tired tonight. How about we talk in the morning, okay?"

He stared at the door, his hand already on the knob. Because, no, it wasn't okay. He could hear in her voice something was wrong.

"I'm coming in," he said giving her a second's warning to cover up if she needed to before turning the knob and stepping into the room.

"Aww hell, Darce," he said, crossing to the little heap of a woman crumpled at the edge of her bed, like the hundred or so tissues littering the end table and spilling onto the floor. "What happened?"

"It's hormones," she sniffed, trying to pull herself together as she waved him off with one hand. "I'll be fine tomorrow. Go to bed. Please."

Right. Not happening. Instead he gathered her up against him, so her head rested at his chest and his arms closed around her.

"Talk to me, honey. Tell me what's going on."

For a moment he thought she wouldn't answer. But he waited her out, stroking a palm over that soft spill of blond down her back, giving in to the impulse to let his fingers play at the ends. And then it was as if the fight and resistance simply drained away as a ragged sob escaped her.

"I'm so tired," she admitted in a defeated, broken voice. "I'm t-tired of getting sick. I'm tired of f-feeling like every minute my body becomes a little less m-my own. I'm tired of being d-disgusting and weepy and wiped out and confused. I keep telling myself to hang in there, that things will turn around and I'm going to feel better, but I don't. I feel worse. I'm still sick. Instead of my body getting round, i-it's lumpy. And—and—I don't have *anything* to wear."

That last one she finished on a sob so tragic it was like a knife to Jeff's gut. "Wait, what? Anything to wear where?"

"Anywhere. Nothing fits me. Everything is—" she broke off with another wretched sob.

Okay, he was tired. Really tired. But something didn't compute.

"Honey, why didn't you get some new clothes?"

She had a credit card and an account his mother had finally gotten her to let him fund. There was *plenty* of money.

"These fit fine two days ago! And today I didn't feel well, and I didn't want to ask your mom because I figured I'd just go tomorrow.... Only now, everything I put on is all bunchy and rough and tight and scratching and—" the face she made was utter, tortured frustration "—*I can't stand* the feel of it touching my stomach. *Not. For. One. More. Second.*"

Her last words were punctuated by her hands fumbling around at the closures, jerking at the offending garments as she—holy hell—started stripping them off.

Jeff looked behind him at the door, then back at the woman in front of him who was huffing and puffing with outraged indignation over the way her clothes were touching her.

Hormones.

That's what she'd said.

He'd heard tales about the havoc they wreaked. The kind of lows they'd brought men to when trying to appease the women caught in their violent, unpredictable sway.

Hell one of his buddies' wives had actually called a divorce lawyer at his suggestion they stop for something healthier than fast food when she was in her eighth month of pregnancy. The guy had laughed when his wife told the story, but there'd been a haunted look in his eyes that said the fear never truly went away.

Which meant the decisions he made in the next critical moments could be the difference between his simply knowing to fear and respect the hormones and being left with that haunted look himself.

Darcy already had the skirt she'd been wearing unzipped and halfway down her hips, a blue streak he wouldn't have credited her with flying from her lips.

Tread carefully.

He backed to the door and, catching the handle, swung it shut and locked it without ever taking his eyes off Darcy.

Yeah. The gentlemanly thing to do might have been to look away. But instinct was telling him hormones were like the sea. Something he didn't want to turn his back on.

The skirt was balled up in her hands now, only to be thrown on the floor in spectacular tantrum fashion.

He shouldn't be registering anything beyond compassion, he knew. But that his being there wasn't incentive enough for her to shut it down, made him want to puff out his chest like he had something to crow about. Like after all the polite, and nice and thoughtful they had going on for the sake of the little life growing inside her…there was trust between them, too. Enough that she was willing to *let him see* what she was really feeling.

Which was enraged.

The buttons down the front of her blouse, which were definitely straining under each ragged breath, went next.

"I can't stand it!" She cried her temper boiling over to next level proportions.

And yeah, he was ready for her.

His hands went to his tie, loosening the knot with a couple tugs. Then the buttons and links at his wrists.

CHAPTER SIXTEEN

DARCY FUMBLED THE slim disk again and that was it. Her hands bunched into the fabric at either side of the row of delicate mother-of-pearl buttons she'd loved so much when she saw them in the store, ready to rip the damn shirt into rags before she'd tolerate one more prickly seam cutting into her chest and stomach.

Two big hands closed gently around her wrists, the warmth of them radiating down her arms as a soft "Shhh," penetrated the fog of her harried mind.

Her eyes blinked open and—

Jeff was standing in front of her, his tie undone, shirt open to his waist.

"Jeff." She swallowed past the humiliation-sized knot lodged in her throat and peered up at him. "This isn't what I—I don't even know what I was thinking."

Those earthy hazel eyes met hers as he shrugged first one shoulder and then the other from his suit shirt, dropping it behind him. He tugged the soft cotton of his undershirt free at his waist before pulling it overhead, and Darcy was left staring at the broad bare expanse of Jeff's hard-cut upper body.

And wow.

"You were thinking you were tired of being uncomfortable," he started. "That the morning sickness isn't something you can control but *this*—clothes rubbing too tight—is. After months of how you've been feeling, no one could blame you for having had enough. You've been pushed to the edge by circumstances beyond your control. You hit your limit and needed to blow off a bit of steam."

Her throat tightened as emotion different from the frustration, the bitterness, the humiliation began to work its way to the surface. Blinking back a fresh rush of tears, she nodded unable to voice the gratitude for his simple understanding in any other way.

The seconds ticked past and Jeff stood holding her gaze with his own. Letting her see the compassion in his eyes. The lack of judgment over actions that would have had most men backing away slowly—hands in the air, eyes on the ceiling, too uncomfortable with the messy fallout of emotions gone off the chain to do anything more than leave. But not Jeff.

He was giving her all the time she needed. Letting her know he'd seen what she was going through. And it wasn't running him off.

Drawing her balled hands from where they rested at her own chest, Jeff brushed his thumbs in circles over her clenched fists and the sensitive skin at her wrists. "Open up, honey. Let go and try to relax a minute."

His touch was light, a graze, and yet the barely there quality of it drew her focus completely. It felt good, those slow, soft circles a balm to her battered soul.

Her fingers unfurled, leaving her palms open to his touch.

To the same slow, soft circling attention pulling the tension from the farthest reaches of her body. Her toes and calves, the backs of her knees, deep in her belly and down the length of her spine.

Then he was resting her palms against his chest, pressing his hands over hers for a single beat before moving on, following the line of her arms up to her shoulders and then—

Her lips parted on a stunned breath at the feel of his knuckles brushing the sensitive skin between her breasts, at the cool air spilling over the deepening V of skin exposed as his long fingers deftly worked each delicate disk free from its catch.

She shouldn't be letting him do this, only she couldn't find the words to tell him to stop. She didn't want to.

His gaze skimmed slowly up her body and, meeting with hers, held as he helped her out of the shirt and gently set it aside.

It was so intimate. Standing there in nothing but a bra and panties, the only changes to her body since the last time Jeff had seen her bare were the ones he'd caused. Her breasts were swollen, her belly thickening in a soft and mushy way that wasn't yet round enough to be beautiful for what it was.

While Jeff was *everything* he'd been from the very first. His body displaying the kind of clean chiseled perfection his too-rugged face lacked. Tall and broad, tapered and taut, it made her want to step closer and take shelter against him. From the solitude. The cool night air. The exposure of her changed body.

From being alone for so very long.

Because this man could make her feel good. Like no one else ever had.

Her gaze drifted to where her hands rested against the banded terrain of his abdomen and then slowly, it drifted up, her fingers following.

"Here, let's get this on you," Jeff said in a tight voice, holding up the white T-shirt he'd stripped off to pull over her head. The cotton was soft, still carrying his body heat, and once it billowed around her thighs like a dress, he took a step back to remove himself from the intimate little bubble of insanity that surrounded her.

What was she thinking? While she'd been eating up the expanse of his body with her eyes, he'd been offering a public service by helping her out of her shirt. He hadn't even looked below her chin.

Because that's not what it had been about for him.

Jeff had been rescuing her. Talking her down from the ledge and resolving the most immediate problem at hand. A scratchy stitch in her shirt.

And resolve it he had, because nothing in all her years had ever felt better against her skin than the T-shirt she was currently draped in.

But, holy cow, she was pathetic.

"Thank you for this," she muttered, barely able to meet Jeff's eyes.

"Welcome," he answered, sweeping his discarded suit shirt up from the floor as he headed for the door. "See you in the morning, Darcy."

Jeff stalked to his room, every muscle in his body working against him, kicking and screaming, and trying to drag him back the way he'd come. To the lush warm woman wrapped up in his T-shirt looking like the kind of Sunday morning fantasy he desperately wanted to get back in his bed.

It wasn't supposed to be like that with her. She didn't want it. Hell, he didn't want it, either. Fine. He *wanted* it. But he knew there was a good reason he wasn't supposed to. And still, he'd unwrapped her like the present he'd been waiting for all year.

Yeah, his intentions may have been pure when he'd started. At least as pure as they ever got around Darcy. She was suffering and he hated it. After months of persistent nausea, the complete upset to her life, her loss of autonomy and every other consequence she bore the burden of—the guilt was eating him alive. Because all of it, everything she was going through, could be laid at his feet.

So he'd seen an opportunity to make something better—and he'd charged in like some nut job white-knight-wannabe with delusions of good intentions as he shucked his shirt and went to town on hers.

The only thing he had going for him was the fact that he hadn't looked once he got her peeled out of a blouse that had definitely been snug in all the right places. The fabric pulling against the swell of her breasts, and fitted to perfection across a belly only just beginning to soften in the most temptingly touchable way.

Not that he'd gotten more than the barest taste of it.

He'd been trying to help, not cop a feel.

Yeah, keep telling yourself that, chump.

Truth, the intentions had started out good. But when he'd rested her delicate hands against his chest—those pure intentions had hopped the express freight straight to hell. The feel of her fingers brushing his bare skin had flipped every switch he had and it was nothing short of divine intervention he'd been able to keep that sudden and intense *want* from shining like a beacon. But he'd shut down the visual tells. Ruthlessly. With extreme prejudice. Because this was the mother of his child. And aside from the fact that he couldn't afford to screw it up with her—she damn well deserved better from him.

Darcy stared out the long-vacated door to her room, a sinking, horrible feeling deep in the pit of her stomach as her actions flashed though her mind like a slideshow of shame.

She'd *stripped* in front of Jeff.

And then when he'd done the only thing he could think of to help her out—literally giving her the shirt off his back—she'd gone and eyed him like some freaking piece of man candy she couldn't wait to wrap her lips around.

She wanted to tell herself it couldn't get worse. But it was about to. Because there was no way they were going to be able to quietly ignore what just happened, chalk it up to hormones and sweep it under the rug to forget.

No way.

She had to apologize. And she had to make sure Jeff knew that brief disconnect with her sanity wasn't a regular or long sustained thing.

Hands clasped at her chest, she forced one foot in front of the other until she'd made it to Jeff's door—where she found him stretched out across his floor in a hard plank position, those powerful shoulders and arms working his body in one relentless cycle of up and down after another.

His eyes were closed. The muscles along his arms and back shifting and rolling, standing out in sharp relief as his skin incrementally darkened with each set.

"Don't do it," he muttered under his breath, dropping a savage expletive before shifting the position of his hands from flat against the wood to fists. "Don't even think about going back in there."

Back? To her room, or to something else?

"Jeff." Her voice was hoarse, little more than a nervous whisper but enough that he heard her. Because suddenly, he stopped. All motion arrested, as though someone had hit Pause on the remote to his life, freezing him in place halfway between up and down.

Then slowly he straightened his arms and turned his head to look at her. Starting at her feet and moving up the length of her bare legs and over the expanse of his T-shirt before dropping his head back between his shoulders.

"Go back to your room, Darcy."

He didn't even want to look at her. This was so bad.

"I want to apologize for what happened. I—"

"I accept." Jeff pushed slowly to his feet, still not meeting her eyes. "Darcy, I've been awake for somewhere around forty-eight hours, and as far as good judgment and restraint go, I'm about tapped out. The last of my reserves having gone toward walking out your door just a few minutes ago."

Forty-eight hours? She'd known he was traveling, had been thrilled at the prospect of seeing him again, but by the time he'd arrived she'd been too far gone to register much of anything beyond her intense discomfort and frustration, and then the overwhelming and incredible relief the man before her had provided. But now as she looked closer, the evidence of fatigue cutting deep lines around his eyes, the shadows beneath and the weary stance were unmistakable.

He dealt with her the best he could and then used the last

of his resources to drag himself out of her little circle of hell...only to have her follow him back to his room. Nice.

Only, something was off. If he was so exhausted...

"Why are you doing push-ups?"

"Damn it, Darcy, I don't think you get how close I am to losing it here." Letting out a harsh laugh, he shoved his big hands through his hair. "Do us both a favor and, before I do something we'll both regret, go."

"I won't regret it. Whatever you have to say, just say it. I can take it." They'd clear the air and tomorrow it would be a new day. "Jeff, please, would you look at me?"

A second passed and then another. Jeff's shoulders and chest rose and fell with one ragged breath after another. And then he looked at her—and everything stopped.

The eyes that met hers weren't the eyes of the amicable man Jeff had been these past two months. They weren't harmless. They weren't benign.

They were dark, intense and hungry. They were the eyes of a man who'd left restraint behind.

And then he was closing the distance between them, all signs of fatigue thrown off as he caught the back of her head in the cradle of one palm and her hip with the other. "Damn it, Darcy, I warned you."

CHAPTER SEVENTEEN

HE'D LIED. NOTHING could have warned Darcy or prepared her for the kiss Jeff delivered. Because this kiss was like no other. Like nothing she'd experienced before. Not even with him.

This kiss was a crushing, urgent demand. An almost angry claim. A brutal stamp against her mouth so searingly hot and unexpected it terminated all thought, all reason, all response beyond the most base, primal instinct within her.

To take more.

More of him. His kiss. The heat surging through her veins. The high charge current coursing over her skin in search of an outlet.

She needed it with a desperation she'd never known. And when her mouth fell open beneath his in welcoming surrender and his tongue drove between her parted lips it was as if the circuit closed and this hot, shared, sensual energy overtook them both.

Her fingers were in his hair, tight and pulling him closer into more demanding contact. Her body arching into a firm press of breasts, and belly, and thighs to meet the hard bow of his. Oh, God, it was good.

All that heat against her sensitive, so long neglected body.

All that contact and promise.

All that *want*.

She was drowning in it. Lost in the desire ratcheting higher with each thrust of Jeff's tongue. Begging him with every needy gasp and tug to take her deeper. Give her more. Make it last.

And it did, until the dizzying need for air had them breaking away, but only to move on in their greedy exploration. Hands roaming a restless path across her back and bottom, into her hair and over her arms, Jeff devoured her neck—each wicked pull of his mouth, firm stroke of his tongue and gentle scrape of his teeth acting as the trigger to another sensual detonation within her.

"It's got to be you, Darcy," he growled between deft flicks of his tongue into the shallow behind her ear, the palm of one hand finding her heavy breast. "If this needs to stop…"

He pulled back, his eyes burning down the length of her body before meeting hers. "I can't make myself do it."

She shook her head, hating the scant inches between them and the cool air threatening to carry *reason* back into the mix. "Don't stop. I don't want to stop. Just this once. Tonight. I don't want you to stop."

"Just this once." His thumb swept across the soft cotton at her breast, and again when it pebbled tight against the confines of her bra. "And then we put it behind us."

Nodding frantically, she asked, "Can you do that? Can we agree?"

"Right now I'd agree to anything." His eyes dropped to the straining bud of her nipple. Went darker as he gently pinched it through the layers of fabric making her breath catch and stutter at the pleasure piercing her core, the molten heat spilling through her center. "But yes, I can do that."

At the next decadent circle of this thumb, she moaned, pressing into his touch. "Jeff, please."

His eyes blinked closed in an expression that bordered on pained. "You don't know…Darcy, how many nights…I've replayed those two words in my head."

This time, Darcy was the one to still. The sharp ache in her heart, clearing the sensual fog surrounding her in one stab. He'd admitted to thinking about them being together in the past. But always in the context of some emotionally barren, throwaway comment, underscoring the lack of meaning behind it. But this time, tonight, there was nothing throwaway in his tone. Only they'd just agreed—

Before she could think too much about it though, his hands were on the hem of her borrowed T-shirt and he was stripping it from her with the same efficiency he'd pulled it off himself.

And then his eyes were on her, reverent, filled with an awe that made her feel beautiful rather than self-conscious about the way her shape had changed.

"You're so gorgeous," he said in a voice so gruff, she felt the deep vibration of it down to her bones.

Catching her behind the knees and back, he carried her to the bed and followed her down, their mouths fused in a decadent, promising kiss that had Darcy's hands coasting over the hard planes of Jeff's chest, working down his abs, and then fumbling with his belt.

At her frustrated whimper, he brushed her fingers aside and backed off the bed. His skin was flushed with a combination of exertion, restraint and arousal. His defined musculature flexed with every motion.

He ran his palm over his mouth and from beneath, she thought she heard the word *fantasy*.

But then he was back at his belt. Never in her life had she seen anything so sexy as when, inside of two tugs, he had the belt loose and his fly open. Her eyes followed the neat line of hair arrowing south of his waist and—

Oh, yes, please.

His fully engorged shaft was thick and dark and jutting out from his body at an angle that defied gravity. And though she'd seen him like this before—had intimate knowledge of how he fit within her—the sight of him was shocking.

Arousing. Incredibly, unbearably arousing.

Making every part of her achy and swollen. Needy. Desperate.

So she did the only thing she could think of, banking on it garnering the same powerful response it had the first time. Breathless and trembling, she whispered, "Jeff, please."

It worked, because before she could draw her next breath, he'd kicked off his pants and shorts, returned to the bed and, body half covering hers, was kissing her senseless.

Supported on one arm, he stroked her greedily with the other, running a possessive hot touch up and down her thigh, catching the back of her knee in one hand so he could pull it alongside his hip and make hard contact with the soft need-ful place she wanted him to be.

Only she was still in her bra and panties. Too many lay-ers between them.

She was about to complain when Jeff rocked against her just right, and her breath caught and her mind blanked of anything beyond the pressing, immediate need for him to do it again.

Her hips tilted in wanton invitation. Her hands running from his shoulders down his spine as far as she could reach, her heels sliding up the backs of his hard thighs to just be-neath his butt as the steely length of him rolled across the wet strip of thin cotton covering her sex.

"Yes!"

Dipping into the cups of her bra, he carefully worked the lace beneath her breasts and sat back, eyes locked on the erotic display he'd made of her.

"Darcy—"

But whatever he'd meant to say was lost when he low-ered his head and flicked his tongue against the turgid peak.

The fleeting contact wasn't enough. Not when he blew a warm breath across the tip, either, and especially not when he brushed his lips in a wicked back and forth tease that on every other pass or so allowed the achingly tight bud to slide between.

More.

"Please, Jeff," she whimpered. "In your mouth. Please."

He groaned and closed over one nipple, drawing with a sweet suction as he slid a hand into her panties and cupped her tender flesh.

His touch.

She'd tried not to think about it after that first night, but there was something so incredible about the way he'd handled her. Like he knew exactly what to do, what would feel the best, how she liked to be stroked, when to tease and when to give her what she was desperate for. So in those weak moments when her thoughts strayed, they'd strayed to this.

His fingers pressing between her slick folds, playing over her cleft. One thick digit working slowly inside her swollen, slick channel, then a second, stretching and filling her in a way that was so good, it made her beg for more, open her legs wider and tip her hips into his touch.

"Yes," she gasped, head tossing against the pillow as pleasure rocketed through her center with each gentle thrust. The tremor of need built fast, gathering strength with each guttural bit of praise, encouragement and promise of more.

He drew her nipple into the wet heat of his mouth, suckling in a rhythm that matched the slow stroke of what then became three fingers.

"Oh, God! Jeff, please," she panted. "Please! I need. I—"

Her pleas cut off as his thumb settled firmly at the top of her sex and—

"Come for me, Darcy."

—her world came apart, sensation and tension from every extremity surging, together, crashing through her in wave after wave of pleasure that was sharp and sweet and hot and, as was so often the case with Jeff, like nothing she'd known before.

Holy. Hell.

Darcy was coming against his hand, the pleasure he wrung from her body more satisfying than if he was the one finding his release.

An hour ago, he'd been about ready to sell his soul to get some sleep, but now? He'd forgo sleep for the rest of his life if it meant more of the silky sound of Darcy moaning his name. Only the rest of his life wasn't an option. What he had was tonight, and he wanted to make it last. Draw it out as long as possible. Give her what she wanted first. Then start in on what she needed. And after that, what he needed to give her.

One night.

Hell, the dull edge of that thought was nearly enough to yank him out of this perfect moment. But with so few precious hours available, he wasn't going to waste them dwelling on the things he couldn't have.

When the last of her tremors subsided and her body melted back into the mattress beneath her, Jeff backed down the bed, peeling her panties off in the process. Then coming back up, he pressed a kiss against her sex, earning himself another pleasured gasp and Darcy's full attention.

Pushing to her elbows, she stared down the length of her body at him. And damn, he'd never seen anything like it before. The silk of her long blond hair hung in a sexy tumble around her face and past her shoulders. Her eyes were all bedroom, slumberous and sated while somehow asking for more. Her lips parted and kiss swollen in a way that had him fighting about a dozen depraved impulses at once. Her belly softly rounded. And her breasts—

God help him, he should have finished what he started in taking off her bra, but some primal part of him was seriously getting off on the tight, peaked bounty of ripe flesh, overflowing the lace constraint he'd only managed to pull partially out of his way.

Darcy seemed to have noticed where his attention had been snared, too, because she glanced down at herself and then arched a questioning brow at him.

"I look—"

"Like a goddess," he said, reaching for her and helping her to her knees.

He unhooked the back clasp of the bra that had served his purposes more than hers for the past minutes, and brushed the straps down her arms before ducking aside to retrieve a condom from the wallet he'd tossed on his nightstand. Then circling behind her, he pulled her against him so they were kneeling upright together and whispered in her ear, "Not of this world, you're so incomparably sexy."

The little noise she made suggested she didn't entirely believe him, but it was true.

She'd been gorgeous that first night in Vegas, but now he couldn't look at her without being blown away by the absolute lush perfection of her.

And tonight she was giving herself to him.

His erection was throbbing painfully with need where it rested between the press of their bodies. He had to get inside of her. Had to have what he'd been ruthlessly denying himself.

Pulling back he ripped open the condom—and Darcy turned, looking over her shoulder first at the condom and then at him.

Her eyes skated away and she quietly asked, "Do we need that?"

Which was when it dawned on him. She was pregnant. He couldn't get her any more so.

But that wasn't what she was asking.

Pressing his forehead against her shoulder, he told her the truth. "I haven't slept with anyone since we were together."

She stiffened. "Olivia?"

Her doubt made sense. Everyone had known it was serious with Olivia from the start. But in that moment, Jeff realized his need to make a connection might have been more a result of the one he hadn't been able to keep with the woman finally in his arms, than the woman he'd found to replace her.

"We didn't—we never had sex. I don't know why, but I just—" He'd found and manufactured one excuse after another for them not to, somehow managing to convince them both it wasn't about him. But it had been. Or more likely, about Darcy—whose breath had left her in a rush, though which emotion was behind that forceful push he didn't know.

"The condom, it's an ingrained habit. I wasn't even thinking about it, but whatever you're comfortable with. I can wear it."

She looked back at him again, meeting his eyes over her shoulder and looking almost shy. "I want to *feel you*. Inside of me. Only you."

His heart began to thump to a savage rhythm as some possessive part of him roared to life.

Only him.

He couldn't wait another second.

Adjusting his knees, he positioned his shaft between Darcy's legs. Groaning at the slick heat he found there, the skin on skin sensation that was only about to get better, he ran the length of himself through the spread of her folds.

"Lean forward, baby. I'll go slow."

God help him, the sight of her when she did was almost too much to bear.

Taking himself in hand, he notched the head at her opening, and at her eager plea for more, carefully fed the length of himself, inch by painstaking inch, into her tight, clenching sheath.

Heaven.

Bliss.

Nirvana.

Her bottom was pressed into his groin, the inner walls of her sex hugging him as he was as close to her as he'd ever been to another person. A part of him wanted to hold on to the connection forever, but another instinct-driven part urged him to move.

To draw back through all that snug, wet friction and then watch his uncovered length sink deep again, while Darcy's fractured, needy cries stroked all the places within him her body couldn't touch.

But he wanted more. Wanted to give her more.

Buried deep, he urged her upright. Thrusting slow and steady, he kneaded her breast with one hand, while letting the other ride the hills and valleys of her body to where she was slippery and wet for him. To the hot, swollen bud that made her inner walls clench like a fist every time he grazed it.

Made her mindless and wild and, for however briefly, *his*.

"Jeff, oh, yes, yes, like that," she panted, pushing back into his groin even as her knees widened in a plea for more of his fingers on that secret place.

He circled, the slick orbits closing ever tighter until at last, she gave him what he needed. Another throaty cry of release as she came around his thrusting shaft and against the stroke of his fingers.

And while she lost herself in pleasured delirium, the hand he'd had at her breast coasted lower until he was cradling the place that was theirs together, and he gave in to the fantasy that for those few moments, everything he wanted was within his hold.

CHAPTER EIGHTEEN

THAT WAS—
    She'd never—
    There weren't—
    How had he—?
    Wow.
Darcy blinked, shook her head and contemplated a hard pinch on her arm, just to make sure she hadn't actually been dreaming. Only if she was, forget the pinch—with Jeff still dropping slow sensual kisses around her hips, thighs and belly—this was a dream she never wanted to wake from.

Of course thinking like that was enough for her to give herself a hard mental shake and remind herself this was about one night. About the both of them burning off the last of a lingering attraction while it still wouldn't get in the way. While they had the chance.

Only as she lay in this bed that was Jeff's, and yet not really, soaking in the attention of a man with a gift for spoiling her, she had to admit, at least to herself, her attraction wasn't going anywhere. So maybe tonight was more about the chance to act on something she wanted but knew better than to try and keep.

And tonight what Jeff had given her was an experience incredible enough to keep her in fantasies through the months and most likely years to come.

Eventually there would be someone else—another man in her life. Maybe. If Gail had anything to say about it, anyway. But it would have to be a very long time off. Long enough for the memory of what being with Jeff was like to dull and fade. Because this, tonight—she already felt like he'd ruined her for all other men. And based on the glint in his eyes, he'd only just gotten started.

Crawling over her, he positioned himself between her legs, careful not to allow his weight to rest on her, but still somehow maintaining a contact between them in too many places to count. "Marry me."

Darcy blinked up at him, her heart freezing until she caught the playful mirth in Jeff's eyes and relaxed back into the bed. "Okay, but only for tonight. And only if you do that thing again."

Gathering her close, Jeff kissed her long and slow and sweet as if he too wanted to draw out the night between them.

"God, you feel so good," she whispered, awed by how true it was. "It's been so long since I didn't feel *bad,* I didn't even remember what this was like."

"It's only been five months, baby, and you've already forgotten? My ego demands I make a more lasting impression this time."

"Your ego again. Hasn't he gotten us into enough trouble already?" Her hand smoothed over his chest, her knees sliding up against the outsides of his solid thighs.

It was so intimate.

The eye contact. The touch. The press of his hard sex against the wet softness of hers.

They wouldn't have this again and she trusted him, so she told him what she'd meant.

"Besides, I'm not talking about the sex. What I'm feeling right now is more than that." Then realizing how he might take her words, she quickly amended, "Don't worry, I don't mean *love* or anything crazy. It's just…for once I'm not worrying, or sick, or uncomfortable or any of the other things. When I'm with you like this, I feel like everything is going to be okay. I feel…safe."

There weren't any questions. There wasn't any risk.

Braced on his powerful arms above her, he searched her eyes, a slight furrow forming between his own. "Then maybe you should stay in my arms."

Darcy stilled, not wanting to read…*anything* into his words.

He meant tonight. Right now. For a few more minutes.

His gaze darkened as he stroked her ear, down her neck and over her breast, where he circled her nipple with the tip of a single finger. "Maybe I shouldn't let you go—"

His words cut off at the quiet thud of the door closing downstairs.

And suddenly Darcy's heart was pounding for a different reason altogether than it had mere seconds before.

"Your mom!" she choked, trying to wiggle out from beneath Jeff, whose chin had pulled back and seemed to be eyeing her with equal parts amusement and irritation. Okay, and the lust was still there, too.

She shoved at his shoulders and he backed off the bed, muttering something about the joys of being a teenager again, and Darcy wondered just how many times he'd been caught in his parents' house.

Then getting back on track, she realized the only thing that mattered was that *this would not be one of them.*

Jeff already had his pants on, and tossed Darcy her bra and his borrowed T-shirt. Then ducked, coming back up with her panties.

"Relax, I'll head my mother off downstairs. Tell her not to bother you tonight."

Darcy coughed. "What? No! Jeff, you look like…"

He pulled his T-shirt on over his head, thankfully covering the skin she'd marked.

"…well, like you've been doing exactly what we've been doing in here. I didn't think it was possible, but even your hair makes you look guilty."

Jeff stopped and, one arm in his dress shirt, craned to catch his reflection in the mirror. "Geez, you're right."

Yanking the T-shirt on as fast as she could, she looked around. Though they'd never actually made it underneath the covers, the duvet was a crumpled heap and the pillows scattered clear across the room. One was even in the doorway to the bathroom.

"She doesn't still check on you before going to bed at night, does she?"

Jeff looked at her like she'd gone mad, and he thought it was adorable. Which was so *not* the response she was after right then.

"This is bad," she stated, dread settling deep in her belly.

"No, it's not."

"Your mother opened her home to me. And the second she walks out the door, I'm treating it like—"

Jeff was in her face, then cutting her off with a hard kiss before pulling away to meet her eyes. "I know for a fact she's left the house since you moved in."

"That's not the point and you know it. Button your shirt," she said, desperately.

"Yours is inside out," he returned, flashing a grin when she gasped.

"How can you be so blasé about this? It's your mother. In her house—"

"Technically, it's my house. But I know what you mean."

She blinked at him, then yanked her shirt off and quickly pulled it back on.

Jeff held up a hand, squinting. "Do you hear her? Because I don't. And for reasons I prefer not to get into, I'm pretty adept at sounding out my mother's tread on the steps."

Darcy arched an amused brow at him. "I can only imagine."

And then her betraying mind was doing just that and it must have showed because suddenly Jeff pulled her in close, tsking at her ear. "Mmm, naughty. I've mentioned how much I like that, right?"

Flustered she pushed back, trying to make her scowl stick.

"I don't hear her. So I'm going to make a break for it. Good night, Jeff."

He shook his head, catching her hand and threading their fingers together. "She must have gone up the south stairs. Stay."

Darcy looked down at where their hands were joined, felt the overwhelming pull of *yes* from the very deepest part of her.

She peered up at him, again seeing the fatigue he'd shaken off while they were together, but now seemed etched in every line and shadow on his face.

It made her want to wrap her arms around him, kiss away the tension and— No.

"Better to end it like this I think."

Because suddenly she didn't feel so very safe at all.

Watching Darcy walk out his door, Jeff was struck with the thought that at least this time he'd seen her go. It wasn't the blindside of Vegas, not even close.

Only witnessing the actual departure didn't feel a whole hell of a lot better than it had the first time.

Which was nuts considering the panic and urgency he'd faced that night, while tonight he'd agreed to the limitations up front. So what was his problem?

Maybe it was the fatigue which, admittedly, had reached critical levels. He wasn't thinking clearly was all. Once he'd caught a few hours of sleep, he'd have his head back on straight and his expectations as they applied to Darcy back in line.

CHAPTER NINETEEN

PERCHED AT THE edge of her kitchen chair, heat from the mug tucked against her chest warming the skin beneath, Darcy tried for a calming breath. Chances were good she wouldn't see Jeff today. The low rumble of an engine had pulled her from a restless sleep around three, and when she'd walked past his room on her way downstairs a half hour before, the bed was more or less made up, the room empty.

Just as well.

"Stay..."

With echoes of the night before still whispering through her head, some distance couldn't hurt. In fact, the idea of Jeff in the city, figuring he'd wait a few more days, or maybe a week before coming back did more to ease the tension within her than all the chamomile-infused air she been gulping for the past ten minutes.

"...Maybe you should stay in my arms..."

Who knew, maybe he'd need to go back to Australia and it would be weeks before he had an opportunity to see her again. Even better.

"...Maybe I shouldn't let you go—"

It would give her time to stop wondering about whatever had been hovering on his lips when they'd realized his mother had returned home and the thought was cut off. Whether he'd been about to say *tonight, at all* or *for a few more minutes.*

It would give her time to remember it didn't matter what

qualifier he'd been about to apply. The man couldn't be held to anything he said after two days without sleep.

"...*I warned you...*"

A shiver ran through her at the memory of the heat those words had caused and all that had happened after.

Yes, it would be good if Jeff got very, very busy and she didn't have to see him again for a long, long—

"Are you interested in dating any of the guys my mother's getting lined up for you?"

Darcy jumped at the gruff voice she'd mentally relocated to downtown L.A., sloshing tea over the lip of her mug. "Jeff! You scared the life out of me. I—I thought you'd left last night. Your room was empty.... Wait, what?"

Jeff stood in the doorway to the kitchen wearing a contemplative scowl and a sleeveless white runner's tank with navy shorts. His skin was sweaty and dark from exertion, his hair standing in a sexy mess of damp spikes.

"Because she's not going to let it drop." He stared at her, a dark look in his eyes. "Hell, you've met her. She's tenacious. And these guys aren't going to be the usual fare of tail-chasing chumps you've spent the past few years deflecting. If you decided you wanted one of them..."

Darcy pushed back from the table and went to get a dish towel to wipe up her spill.

How could he even ask after what happened last night? It hurt—but it shouldn't. She shouldn't give him so much power over her. Steeling herself, she kept it simple.

"No." And then because she couldn't stand the sight of the scowl he was wearing, she added lightly, "I shudder to think how *your ego* would take it."

His mouth kicked up, and Jeff walked into the room, going straight to the coffee machine. "Hmm, I like how susceptible you are to his plight. With that in mind, what do you think about packing your things and coming back with me?"

"*What?*" She most definitely couldn't have heard him right. Not with the way Jeff was standing there casually brewing himself a mug of coffee while he basically blew everything they'd agreed upon last night straight to hell.

"Turns out I'm the jealous sort. As it applies to you, anyway."

Jealous. Where was this coming from? After her near-date with Grant?

"If my mom's parading Southern California's most eligible bachelors in front of you every now and then..." He shook his head, again running that wide palm over the scrub of his solid jaw. "Yeah, I'm losing it a little thinking about one of them catching your attention. Because you'll catch theirs. Every one, Darcy. So, self-serving bastard that I am, I'm going to be driving out here seven days a week with the straight-up intention of sabotaging her efforts."

"Jeff," she tried again, needing to inject some reason where suddenly there seemed to be none. "I'm a high school dropout. They aren't—"

"Going to care. Mom wouldn't let some stuck-up prick with a hard-on for credentials within ten thousand feet of you. But the men who would appreciate how easy it is to carry on a conversation with you about virtually anything— the ones who would respect that you've been steadily working your way through my old textbooks since you got here and read two newspapers a day. The ones who earn that laugh of yours—" Breaking off, he looked away muttering a coarse expletive.

"So yeah, even after I run the lot of these great guys off, the ego you keep indulging is still going to have something to prove. Which means...I'm going to be pulling out every dirty, low-down trick I can think of to seduce you back into my bed. And, Darcy?"

The dark look in Jeff's eyes did things to her she didn't want to think about. Didn't want to acknowledge.

Didn't want to stop. "What?"

He stepped behind her and, gathering her hair in a loose twist over one shoulder, ran his lips and then the stubble rough edge of his jaw along the sensitive exposed length of her neck in a way that made her breath catch and a needy ache stir low in her belly.

"I've got a lot of tricks. And I already know several that work on you."

"So what are you saying?" she asked, fighting the purr and moan trying to slip out with her words. "If I move in with you, you won't be compelled to seduce me?"

His hands slid down the length of her arms, then slowly back up as the low rumble of his laugh vibrated against her back. "No. I'll seduce you either way. But for a change, once I get you into my bed, I'd like to wake up to you still there the next morning."

A weight settled in her chest.

"Jeff, we talked about this. We agreed *last night*."

"You can't hold me to anything I said last night. I hadn't slept in days. This morning, though, I'm seeing things clearly. I know you're worried about complicating a relationship we need to sustain for our child's sake. But it doesn't need to get complicated. What's between us—"

"Is sex," she stated evenly, though inside everything felt turbulent and chaotic.

"Yeah, really, really incredible sex. But there's friendship and caring and respect, too. And the truth is what I'm suggesting makes sense. You're pregnant with my child. I don't want you to be alone. And while you most definitely *could* stay out here with my mother…there's a very big part of me asking why you would, when we could be making the most of this time we've got before our little guy comes. We could take care of each other."

It was those last words that caught her, the balance suggested in *taking care of each other* that gave her pause.

"And what happens if one of us realizes they want more than the other? If one of us suddenly wants less? What happens if it gets messy?"

"It won't. We can keep it simple. You move in with me,

I make you feel good in ways that get you to give up those breathless little cries on a frequent basis, my ego gets regular feedings and we take all the guesswork out of it by putting a natural stop date on the fun and games when Junior comes—if we're open and honest about the limits of where this can go, no one gets hurt. We know what we're getting into."

He made it sound so easy, but it wouldn't be. Not for her. And yet what he was offering held an unmistakable appeal. It was the ready excuse to take more of this man she wanted so badly. The handy justification she needed to give in to the *want* without hating herself for being weak, for all but inviting the hurt and vulnerability some open-ended go at a relationship would involve.

If she agreed to what Jeff was suggesting, even if her emotions did get away from her, she wouldn't be waiting around for a happily ever after. She'd know there was a limit on the relationship and, having been a part of establishing those boundaries, wouldn't feel as though she'd betrayed herself by giving in. She'd have made the conscious, informed decision to grab hold of this pleasure for the time it was available.

And when it was over, she'd be able to look at herself in the mirror without seeing some pathetic victim with her hand out waiting for whatever emotional scraps were available and her breath held for some fantasy that would never come true.

She turned to face him, searching his eyes. "So you're talking about a sort of extended friends-with-benefits arrangement?"

Jeff winced as though he didn't like the sound of it, but then seemed to reconsider. "I suppose that would be accurate."

She wouldn't be his girlfriend. It wouldn't be a relationship.

It would be an affair with a bittersweet but predetermined end date. Something she could live with.

"What would we tell your mother?" she asked. "What would you tell everyone?"

Because people would talk. How could they not? She remembered some of the stories about Connor and Megan and knew the talk they'd had to contend with was nothing compared to the gossip and speculation that would surround her. Not that there wasn't plenty already, but if she moved in with Jeff...and then moved out.

"Nothing. It's no one's business but ours." His arms snaked around her back in an unmistakably possessive hold. "You're not going to regret this."

This close she couldn't think, at least not about anything beyond how good it felt to have him touch her. How much closer she wanted to get. Pressing her palms into his chest she pushed, trying to keep the action from turning into a shameless feel.

"Jeff, wait, I haven't decided yet."

The corner of his mouth kicked up. "Yes, you have."

And when he ducked his head to catch her mouth with his, there was no denying he was right.

For long moments he kissed her, slowly, deeply, thoroughly—the languid sweep of his tongue between her lips serving both to seal the deal as well as remind her they could take as much time as they liked.

And then from the hall beyond came the rattle of keys and Darcy jerked back, only to have Jeff catch her before she could put more than a few inches between them.

"Not done with you yet," he murmured at her ear as Gail's sing-songy chatter—a little more clipped than usual, spilled around the corner.

"Running late...Pilates...lots of errands...back later."

Jeff's brow arched and they both looked toward the doorway leading to the back door in time to see Gail buzz past with a hasty wave and barely a backward glance.

Darcy glanced up at Jeff. "She knows."

Jeff wagged his head. "Probably. On the upside, she won't be surprised when we tell her you're moving out."

CHAPTER TWENTY

THE UNIVERSE WAS conspiring against him. There wasn't any other explanation for why three times Jeff had gotten Darcy into his bed, and three times he'd woken up alone.

Rubbing the sleep from his eyes, he rolled onto his back and stretched across an expanse of sheets better suited to two than one.

He'd get up earlier tomorrow because he was determined to have Darcy in his bed, every way possible. He hadn't thought it could get any better than having her coming apart for him in this space that was his alone. But after the passion had been sated and they lay together with Darcy tucked into the shelter of his body—for once not going anywhere… the rhythm of her breath slowing until she was asleep in his arms, his hand resting over the small swell of her belly— yeah, that was a satisfaction, a rightness beyond expectation.

It made him want more.

Starting with the sleep-softened morning version of her lazing between his sheets. Warming beneath his unhurried touch. Giving up those little pleasured sounds he couldn't get enough of.

Pushing out of bed, Jeff groaned thinking how gorgeous she'd be in the morning with nothing but sunshine blanketing her lush body, making all that silky hair shine like spilled gold across his pillow.

Maybe he'd coax her back into bed, he thought, about to swing the bathroom door open—when Darcy beat him to it emerging from the other side, hair pulled back into a snarled knot, the skin beneath her eyes looking like an old bruise and her complexion in general making the slate-gray of his sheets look downright rosy.

"Darcy, are you okay?" he asked, wrapping an arm around her shoulders, ready to swing her into his arms and jog over to the E.R. She looked like death warmed over and suddenly a part of him was sincerely wishing Grant was the man she'd spent the night with so he could help her. But even as the thought skirted through his mind, a highly possessive part of him roared. Definitely no Grant.

"I will be," she half moaned then, looking down at her watch, added, "in about five minutes. It never lasts past eight-thirty these days."

Holy hell. This was the morning sickness she still endured a few times a week. Which meant it wasn't the universe conspiring against him after all. Just his little baby in the making.

"Do you want to get back into bed? I can bring you some crackers, ginger ale, tea, eggs or a cake—do you want more cake?"

She waved a frenzied hand in front of him, her lips pinching together as her cheeks puffed out, effectively conveying her "No thank you" in somewhat less polite but more effective nonverbal means.

Which left him standing there looking down at her with a sense of impotence he didn't dig at all.

"Darce, is there anything I can do for you?"

Shaking her head, she muttered, "Just give me a couple of minutes. Alone."

Alone.

Why did she always want to go it alone? And damn it, why did it bother him so much that she did?

Giving her hand a parting squeeze, he headed out to the kitchen figuring he'd make some tea for when she was ready.

She couldn't catch a break. Darcy flattened her hands on the solid marble counter and stared into the mirror in front of her. One morning. That's really all she'd wanted. Just the one to get accustomed to being with Jeff on an extended basis without her stomach rolling out the welcome mat for this new phase of their relationship. Temporary phase. For their non-relationship.

She let out a deep sigh. It was supposed to be *based on sex*. And morning sickness, hers in particular, was so totally not sexy. Not even close.

Her belly gave a twist of the more traditional dread-filled variety as she geared up to leave the sanctuary of Jeff's sleek master bath. If she was going to find regret in Jeff's eyes or discomfort or whatever else, she wanted to see it now.

She'd be able to handle it, too. Because there wasn't any part of her that had gotten attached to the idea of being here.

No, she was fine.

She was tough. Practical. And resilient.

A last glance in the mirror told her she was also about as put together as she was going to get. Freshly showered, teeth cleaned, hair blown out smooth and neat. Sure the blouse was a little tight and she didn't love the feel of it, but she was banking on the snug fit to give her an edge in the coming exchange.

Walking down the hall, her bare feet quiet over the blond hardwood, she took in the modern clean lines of the place—the open layout, high ceilings and stark-white walls—all contrasting with the repurposed hunks of heavy steel.

The apartment was so Jeff she couldn't help but love it on sight.

And she'd only just gotten there.

It didn't matter.

In the kitchen, Jeff was on the phone, issuing one word replies between brief pauses as he cracked some eggs, single-handed into a bowl with shredded cheese. He hadn't bothered to pull on a shirt and was still sporting those superthin drawstring plaid pajama bottoms with bare feet. His hair looked the same as always—messy in a tempting but touch-me-at-your-own-peril way. And the look was hot enough to nullify any advantage her too-tight blouse might have earned her.

This was the man who'd pleasured her senseless the night before. And then this morning—

Don't think about it.

Darcy slid onto a stool that looked like some kind of industrial spring with a leather padded seat top, and watched the play of muscles across his broad shoulders and down his arm as he used a fork to whip through the mix.

"Yep…Uh-huh…That's great…In about an hour, then… Excellent." Jeff thumbed off the phone and catching sight of her over his shoulder turned. "Hey, you feeling better?"

"Completely, thanks." That was the thing about the morning sickness, once it was gone, it was really gone. Well, until it came back. But the interim…she felt like a million bucks.

Darcy nodded toward the phone in his hand. "Do you have an appointment?"

"Oh, no. Well, yes. It's for you. Charlie got the name of a maternity boutique and coordinated the delivery of a selection of clothes this morning. No more itchy seams…you know…touching you."

Maternity clothes. Delivered. So she wouldn't have to go out in clothes that bothered her.

This man was thoughtful in ways most people would never think of.

"Thanks, Jeff." Then forcing herself to bring up what she really wanted to forget, she started, "About when you woke up…"

Jeff set the phone down on the counter behind him. "I knew you still got sick. But I haven't really seen the way it affects you for a while."

"Not exactly what you had in mind, I'm guessing." Not after all the seductive promises and racy talk.

A short breath. "Not exactly."

How could it be?

Jeff crossed to the counter where Darcy was seated and braced on his forearms. A muscle in his jaw started to jump.

Darcy forced herself not to shift on the stool, not to look away from his remorse-filled eyes when he said, "I'm sorry."

This was it. He was going to tell her it was a mistake. He shouldn't have asked her to come.

She'd agree, and look relieved while she said it, even if it killed her. Because she'd known better. And because what mattered was keeping their relationship amicable. For their baby and themselves.

"Don't be. Neither of us was thinking straight," she offered, backing up her words with a lightness she didn't feel. "Seriously, let's chalk it up to lack of sleep and pheromone overdose and—"

"Darcy, what the hell are you talking about?" Jeff demanded, whatever guilt there'd been in his eyes now replaced with a sharp accusation. Then, "Forget I asked. I've got it, but clearly you don't. I'm not sorry my morning sex kitten fantasy got rained out by a little reality. What I'm sorry about is you going through this alone. I'm sorry I haven't been there every morning and through whatever part of the rest of the day this sickness occupies from the start. I'm sorry you're so used to being on your own, that even now when I'm right here, you're more comfortable sending me away. Darcy, I'm just sorry it hasn't been easier for you."

"Jeff—"

"And you aren't moving out, so don't even start about it. I just got you here. And damn it, you're going to let me take care of you and you're going to like it." Catching the back of her neck with one hand and her stool with the other, Jeff planted a firm kiss on her, stepping between her legs as they softened together.

"You brushed right?" he asked, a mirthful smile quirking his lips until he looked down between them, apparently noticing the swell of her breasts within the too-tight blouse for the first time. "Never mind. I don't care."

He kissed her again. Deeper. Longer.

Darcy broke away, threading her hands between them to link around his neck. "I brushed," she murmured, leaning into the heat of his bare chest where she pressed her own soft openmouthed kiss at the center. "And flossed."

The next kiss landed at the tight bead of his masculine nipple, and was followed by a flick of her tongue and Jeff's rumbling groan.

"Baby, I love it when you talk oral hygiene to me."

Darcy couldn't help her laugh, even as her body turned hot and needy. Looking up at him from beneath her lashes, she purred, "I rinsed, Jeff. Mouthwash. A full sixty seconds."

His hands caught her hips, and without so much as a strained breath, he lifted her onto the counter, positioning himself between her legs, so they touched in all the most critical ways.

Jeff looked down into her eyes and let the humor fall away. "Darcy, let me be here for you."

And like that, the part of her she'd steeled against this man crumbled. Because when he looked into her eyes like he was, when he let her see how badly he needed her to let him in, there was no defense against it.

And so long as she remembered that no matter how good it felt to give in to Jeff, this was temporary…she'd be okay.

CHAPTER TWENTY-ONE

DARCY STARED INTO the half-fogged mirror, admiring the round swell of her belly as she turned from one side to the other. The swirling wisps of warm steam pinwheeled through the air as the bathroom door opened and then Jeff's reflection joined her an instant before his hands became solid, gathering the wet tendrils of her hair so it twisted to hang down her chest.

"Talk about an incentive to come home early," he murmured in her ear, their eyes locked in the reflection before them. Her, a naked bounty of soft and round and ripe, and him, a devastating contrast of disheveled and immaculate as always.

"Only in your world is seven early, Jeff."

His hands smoothed down the length of her back, his thumbs working gentle circles into the muscles strained from carrying the weight of two bodies in one. And then they slid forward over the hard swell of her belly, coasting in that reverent caress of here and there before succumbing to the temptation he could never resist. He cupped her breasts, gently taking their weight in his palms.

"Used to be your world, too."

"Yeah, but I wasn't at the office at six-thirty in the morning, either."

Those wicked thumbs made their first pass across her nipples and her breath rushed out in a shuddery gasp as she grabbed for the marble vanity in front of her.

She wanted to wrap her arms around his neck and bury

her face in the front of his shirt. Breathe in the masculine scent of him, but that would mean she couldn't watch.

Satisfaction gleamed in the eyes still holding hers as Jeff now brought his mouth to the curve of her neck, wetting that decadent spot with the slide of his tongue that had her body reacting in ways she couldn't control.

Her hips pushing back into the strong thighs braced behind her. Her lips parting on a ragged breath.

"God, I love coming home to this."

To this.

Not to her.

He loved this heightened, ever ready state of semi-arousal that had been the hormonal flip side to all those months of nausea. It wasn't news. And it wasn't a blow.

It was a reality she'd accepted and made peace with a month ago. Embraced. Because with his mouth moving against her skin, his thumbs making one slow circling pass over her nipples after another—she was so sensitive—his erection thickening long and hard against her bottom, she loved it, too.

She loved the release. Loved how sexy he made her feel. Loved the hot look he was giving her now.

And more than that, she loved the way this man never stopped surprising her. She loved the spontaneous unstoppable side of him that, last week, had him pulling her out of her seat at the tapas bar they frequented and spiriting her off for a night flight over L.A. in his helicopter. She loved that low growl rumbling against her neck every time he put his arms around her and the way, just before he fell asleep, he always pulled her that much closer.

She loved that he held her hand when they walked along the beach and, no matter where they found themselves, a gallery, the symphony or local market, the insatiable man always had something decadent and outrageously wicked to whisper in her ear.

And she loved that he knew it drove her wild.

It was so good. Like nothing she'd dreamed could be possible.

Not enough.

The words whispered through her mind, unwelcome, but not entirely unfamiliar.

Only she wasn't supposed to want more. She knew better.

But how was she going to give this up? How was she going to give him up when she'd already fallen—

"What's the matter?" Jeff asked, a furrow between his brows, his hands on her breasts still.

She shook her head. "Don't stop."

He stared at her through another beat, those too-perceptive eyes searching until she bit into her bottom lip, drawing his focus back to the need between them both. Then, "Please."

Their time was limited. She didn't want to waste a second.

The balmy night air surrounded them as Jeff watched Darcy suck and lick her last spoonful of brownie batter ice cream, if not totally immune to what she was doing to that spoon, at least in a place where he could control his physical reaction to the pleasured moans accompanying it. Though possibly his newfound control had more to do with knowing an hour before, he'd been the reason for Darcy's moans, and they'd put this paltry ice cream business to shame.

Still. He leaned close to Darcy's ear as they walked. "You know my ego's working itself into a snit right now."

Darcy slanted him a questioning look, her lips still wrapped around the spoon.

"With all that moaning, he's going to have something to prove in a serious way when we get home."

Her brows pulled together in some sort of faux apologetic look totally belied by the deliberate way she then slid the spoon in and out between her lips, adding a sultry little moan wholly different from the unconscious ones she'd been delivering moments before and Jeff's head shot around looking to see if anyone on the street was watching. But thankfully no one seemed aware, and then Darcy was just laughing, filling the street around them with that easy gorgeous sound he couldn't get enough of as she tossed her empty dish into a trash.

She was so relaxed now. Untroubled. Different from when they'd been making love and suddenly she wasn't in the same sensual place they'd been sharing the moment before. He'd let her put him off, but now he wanted to understand.

"Earlier tonight, Darcy, where did you go?"

She knew what he was talking about. He could see it in the instant of deliberation flashing through her eyes before she made the decision to trust him with the truth.

"I never realized what I was missing before," she answered, staring down the street ahead of them. "I mean I saw couples together, saw them having fun, but I always wondered what happened when they went home and no one was around to see, whether those bright smiles turned to fear."

Jeff's stomach turned to lead, and he pulled Darcy to a stop. "Did someone make you afraid?"

She seemed to consider, almost as if she didn't know the answer. In the end, though, she found her way to it. "Not a boyfriend of my own. I didn't really let guys get that close. But yes. My mom wasn't so discriminating and some of the guys who took us in—they made me scared."

He couldn't breathe. Couldn't do anything but take her hand because he needed to hold it, and wait for her to tell him the rest.

"Some of them had tempers that could get physical. And some of them would look at me in ways they shouldn't. And some of them just liked to play the kind of control games that might mean going hungry or not being able to go to school or to sleep."

"How the hell could she have let you live like that?" he asked, sickened and enraged by the actions of a woman he knew to have died in a car accident years before.

Darcy wouldn't meet his eyes. And when she answered, the hollow sound of her voice was like a blade to his heart.

"She said she didn't have a choice and we'd starve without someone to take care of us. She told me she couldn't risk leaving me alone with them to get a job, that we couldn't leave until she found someone else. Someone better. But that was a joke. The guys she found…" She shook her head. "I don't know what was wrong with her. But the guys she gravitated to were all just different shades of the same sick. And the worst of it was, I actually believed she didn't have a choice. I thought she was trapped the same way I was. I didn't know there were programs to help us. I didn't know she was actually choosing to live that way, to make me live that way until I got the full-time job that let me pay rent. Now that I'm going to be a mother and the need to protect this baby is so strong within me, it's like a tangible thing—more than ever I want to know why. But it's too late to ask, and I don't think I could have believed anything she said anyway."

Jeff pulled her into his arms, stroking her hair as a part of him died inside thinking of those beautiful gray eyes he'd seen so many ways filled with fear, their innocence draining away years too soon.

"Baby, I'm so sorry."

Now he got it. This was why she'd dropped out of school.

Why she'd been afraid to trust him enough to let him take care of her.

Why with all the money and resources at his disposal, he'd never be able to give her the thing she wanted most in her life. To be totally independent. And worse, that hard-won freedom she'd sacrificed so much for? He was the reason she'd lost it. He'd taken it away.

And when he looked at the round swell of her belly, he couldn't even regret it.

All he could do was show her there was another way. Prove that he never wanted to hold her back or hem her in or take away the opportunities available to her. He'd make certain she never felt trapped because of him again. She'd never need to escape.

Cradling her jaw in his hands he met her eyes.

"I know you don't believe in the fairy-tale rescues and you've already saved yourself, Darcy, but I'm behind you now, too. Nothing will ever be like that again. Not for you. Not for our baby. I swear it."

Blinking back tears, Darcy nodded and said the most amazing thing. "I already know."

"Locker-room talk?" Connor scoffed, his voice oozing the kind of censure only a best friend could muster. "I thought you were above all that."

Jeff paused in the act of relocating the stacks of papers and files from his desk to a mirror position on the conference table at the other end of the office.

"It's not like I'm starting a daily blog." He looked at the half-cleared desk, and then at the clock, his heart kicking up. "But *holy hell,* man—"

"Yeah, I've got it. The hormones. They're like the sea. And the tide's turned or whatever."

"She was at the door. Waiting, Connor. *At the door.* I didn't make it past the coat stand. *For. An. Hour.*"

Connor made an indifferent noise that had Jeff shaking his head in stunned disbelief.

"Good to hear she's feeling better. So what's Gail think about the move?"

"Yeah, yeah, Darcy's feeling much better. Aside from the mornings, she hasn't been sick for about two weeks. And my mom—she's not pressing. I told her I was more comfortable with Darcy staying with me. Didn't want to miss out on anything, yada, yada, yada. But forget about my mom and pay attention. About the hormones, because seriously, you and Megan might want to—"

"Enough. I get it. The sex with your pregnant non-girlfriend lover—"

"Darcy."

"Okay, sex with Darcy is insane. But I'm starting to feel a shade dirty, hearing about it."

Jeff stalled where he was. Yeah, truth was, he didn't want Connor thinking about Darcy like that, either. He wasn't nuts about the few details he'd been subjected to about Megan. There was just something different about being subjected to details about a guy's wife.

Not that Darcy was his wife.

The intercom from his desk sounded. "Ms. Penn here to see you."

With a quick goodbye for Connor, Jeff started to return the phone to his pants pocket, then thinking better of it, tossed it onto a chair. In one sweep, he had the rest of his desk cleared and the stack dumped in a heap on the conference table. And then he was striding to the door, swinging it open with a welcome greeting that didn't make it past his lips once he saw Darcy waiting for him in a shirt he knew for a fact she'd decided was too tight the week before. His eyes went momentarily unfocused as his tongue all but rolled out of his mouth.

"Hi, Jeff," she said. And he was sure it sounded completely innocuous to anyone who hadn't heard all the incredibly, fantastically naughty things coming out of her mouth when she'd called him thirty minutes before.

"Darcy, glad you could come. By. To talk." He coughed into his hand, mentally giving himself a violent shake. "Come on in."

Her gauzy layered skirt swung around her calves, showing off the slender turn of her ankles and hinting at the sexy length of what hid beneath.

Pulling his door closed behind them, he ducked back out offering a quick, "Hold my calls."

And then Darcy had hold of his tie and was pulling him deeper into his office. Tugging at him with hands that were everywhere at once.

"I don't know what's wrong with me," she gasped, when he jerked his tie loose and was halfway down the buttons of his shirt. "Faster."

"Wrong with you? Not one damn thing," he assured, wishing he had four hands instead of two so he could get them both naked in the next six point two seconds. Because now that she was here, he needed to make good on the promise she'd breathlessly reminded him of from the backseat of her car.

"You said you'd take care of me."

Apparently she'd been at the organic market shopping for dinner when she'd started feeling *restless* as she'd explained it. And then she'd started thinking about his desk. The high shine airplane wing that was the prize in his collection. With him *on it.*

Jeff freed the last button and started in on his fly, at which point he realized Darcy's eyes had glazed with lust and she'd only gotten her blouse half open before abandoning the task, in lieu of watching him strip.

Which reminded him of the night at his mother's house…

Slowing it down, Jeff methodically unbuckled his belt and then pulled it free of the loops.

"What—what are you doing?" Darcy asked, the breathless tremble in her words sending blood pounding toward his groin.

"Making you wait." He rolled the belt and set it on the desk chair. And shrugged one shoulder out of his shirt and then the other. "Letting you watch."

Darcy blinked in rapid repetition, her throat making some effort at words that didn't get past a few clicks.

Crossing his arms to reach for opposite sides of his T-shirt, he eased it up, getting hotter and harder with every grueling second that passed of watching Darcy watch him. Yeah, slow was definitely better than fast. This time.

He pulled the T-shirt overhead and Darcy let out a little sigh, spurring him on. His hands went to his pants, to the top button, the tab of his zipper, then lower as it traveled down, the teeth straining against his hard-on. He leaned back against his desk, shirtless, his pants open, his erection beyond the point of containment as it pushed past the top of his boxer briefs.

"Your body," she murmured, those smoky, soft gray eyes flitting to his for a moment of contact. "Is my very favorite plaything."

Shoving the briefs beneath his sac, he took himself in hand. "And you said we had nothing in common."

Darcy sucked a harsh breath, as he firmed his grip and rode up and down the length of his shaft with a few slow, sure strokes.

"Oh, God," she whimpered, wetting her lips with the sexy pink tip of her tongue. "I—I— You— I'm so—"

"Yeah," he groaned, "me, too. Take off your blouse for me, gorgeous."

Without taking her eyes off the up and down cycle of his hand, she undid her shirt, slipping out of it and letting it flutter to the ground, as her hands found the soft, ripe mounds of breasts that seemed to be growing in proportion to her belly.

"Like this?" she asked, the flush of excitement pinkening her skin as she ran her shaking open palms against the stiff points of her nipples.

"Yes." Immediately he eased up on his grip, because, holy hell, add Darcy touching herself while she watched him? A man knew his limits. "Your skirt, too."

Catching her bottom lip in the clasp of her teeth she gingerly stepped over to his desk chair and sat down. He stalled, wondering what—but then she was inching the filmy layers of her skirt up one teasing inch at a time, until he could see what she was most deliberately showing him.

And the world ceased to spin.

"Panties?" he choked out.

"Didn't think I was going to need them," she said with

that mind-blowing mix of shy minx as she reached between her legs.

He couldn't be seeing what he thought he was seeing. Even if he'd started this game and she seemed to like it a lot, she'd been shy about it. So this couldn't—

"Letting you watch," she moaned, reading the question in his eyes. "Making you wait."

One slender brow arched his way and suddenly, his gorgeous girl was in the power position. And he was all for letting her have it. For the next few minutes anyway.

"Don't stop, Jeff."

He resumed his stroke, fighting for control as he watched Darcy's fingers play at the place he desperately wanted to visit. She was slick and swollen, panting and ready, and getting close to the peak he wanted to take her to himself.

Needed to take her to himself.

This game had gone on long enough.

Going to his knees, he caught Darcy by the backs of hers and wheeled the chair closer.

A moment more and their discarded shirts were tucked behind her back, her hips were at the edge of the chair and her legs trembled atop his shoulders as he licked and kissed and teased her.

And then slowly, so slowly, so she wouldn't miss a second of what was happening, and he wouldn't miss a second of her response, he made a firm point of his tongue and sank into her waiting center.

"Jeff!"

His name hit with the first clench of her sex because all it had taken was one slow thrust and she'd come apart around his tongue. And because he wasn't ready to give up even one second he could have of this, he continued to lap and kiss and stroke her until he'd coaxed the very last shudder from her body.

Rocking back on his heels, he looked into her gorgeous,

pleasure-sated face. He'd never get tired of seeing her look at him that way.

Her smoky eyes tracked over him. "I knew I could count on you."

He let out a gruff laugh. "I aim to please."

"Good," she hummed, easing out of the office chair with Jeff's help. When she was up, she flashed him another sultry smile. "Up on the desk. You promised."

Hell, yes.

CHAPTER TWENTY-TWO

"You didn't actually say that," Darcy giggled, her head tipping back as she gave in to the laughter Jeff had a knack for spurring.

The strong hands massaging her right foot stilled. "You *dare* doubt me?"

Sensing her foot rub might be at stake, Darcy offered her best winsome smile and promised, "Never."

At seven-and-a-half months, her feet were feeling the strain of all the baby her body was carrying around, and there wasn't a whole lot she wouldn't do or say to ensure this heavenly attention continued.

Fortunately for her, Jeff had developed the unconscious habit of pulling her feet into his lap every time he dropped onto the couch beside her to talk. And they talked a lot. About whichever project was occupying center stage in her work with his mother, the latest developments at Jeff's company, the psychological thriller they'd watched in bed the night before or their preference of one ethnic cuisine over another and whether they ought to try cooking it or just hit the place around the corner instead.

They talked about the house Jeff had picked out a half mile from his mom's place, and whether Darcy wanted to move in right after the baby was born or whether she wanted to wait a month or so.

And they talked about the baby. Speculating on whether it was a boy or girl and which combination of traits from either of them would be the equivalent of winning the genetics jackpot.

Jeff's take was their kid would be better off with her looks and hair in particular, regardless of whether it was a boy or girl. His singing voice—which was nuts. Her aptitude for quick learning and problem solving. And his brute strength—especially if it was a girl because if she looked like her mother, he wanted her to be able to protect herself like her dad.

Darcy's picks were different. If they got a boy, she wanted him to look like Jeff and a girl she wanted to look like Gail— the fine-boned, feminine version of her son. Beautiful and refined rather than built with too many curves and looks that tended to attract the wrong attention. She wanted their child to have Jeff's sense of humor, drive and generosity. And most of all she wanted this baby to grow up knowing the same kind of love and support that had fostered the happy, confident man across from her.

Jeff grinned, gently rolling her ankle and squeezing her heel. "That's what I thought. Seriously though, Darce, I know it was a work thing, but you should have come with me. Garry's a piece of work, but you would have enjoyed Denise. She's got a six-month-old daughter and a sense of humor like yours and, you know what, they're actually going to be at my table for the benefit next week."

Pushing up against the cushions behind her, Darcy didn't realize she'd begun to pull her foot into her body until Jeff drew it back to his lap.

"Don't pull away," he chided, losing some of the lightness in his expression. "I just thought you might enjoy meeting a few people. Maybe making some friends."

"We've talked about this. I'll make plenty of friends once the baby is born. I just don't want to do it now, as *your date*. I don't want to have to figure out how to explain how we're together and how we aren't, and I know you're not naive enough to think it wouldn't come up. I mean, honestly, Jeff, how would you even introduce me?"

He met her eyes with a hard stare, betraying a frustration that went deeper than this one night. "I'd say 'This is Darcy Penn.'"

"And when they looked at my stomach, or asked how we met, or waited until you were caught up in some discussion about employment trends and then asked me about our relationship?"

"You say we're friends. You say, your house won't be ready to move into for another couple months. You say whatever you're comfortable with."

"That's the thing, Jeff. I'm not comfortable with any of it. Not now. In six months, when your mother is throwing some garden party, and I'm living in my own place and you want us to go together? I'll be fine. You'll be able to introduce me as your son's or daughter's mother. I'll be on my own, actually living the life I'm going to have and not caught in some fairy-tale place I don't want to have to explain the temporary nature of."

He looked like he wanted to argue, but then their in-vitro soccer player took a hard shot at her belly and she flinched, still stunned by the force of those kicks.

Her hand covered the spot and Jeff's attention was immediately fixed on the little world contained within her belly.

"Active?" Abandoning her foot, he shifted closer so he could rest his palms across the hard swell of her stomach.

"I think he liked the roast chicken your mother brought over earlier."

Another kick landed just below Jeff's hand, and Darcy watched his face light with awe and enough tender joy she could feel it in her own chest.

Leaning down, he dropped a kiss against the spot where his hand had been and then turned so his cheek rested lightly there. Darcy stroked his hair, focusing on the bliss of that moment, trying to remember every detail. The warm wash of breath against her skin. The fullness of her belly and her heart.

She wouldn't hope for it to last forever. Only that she remember it when it was gone.

Standing in the doorway of the master bath, Jeff straightened his tie and secured his links. Across the bedroom, Darcy lay half covered with the blanket she couldn't commit to and preferred to keep balled up against her chest, with one leg covered and the other thrown over the top.

She'd finally gotten past the morning sickness, but contrary to how his fantasies had played out, morning was still not her friend. She slept later every day, probably because she was up several times a night thanks to Baby Norton sleeping with one foot on her bladder. And when she woke—

Don't make Hulk angry.

—it was definitely better to give her a few minutes before trying to strike up a conversation.

He'd been seeing her less and less before he left for work. And then thinking about her more and more through those hours they were apart...ultimately leaving the office earlier than his workload required.

Which brought him to his current system. Glancing at the clock, he saw it was four-fourteen. He'd be at his desk by quarter to five and then home a dozen hours later. Which left him as many hours as Darcy had in her in the evenings.

It worked for him.

He was there to see her every day. Be a part of all the doctor visits. The quirky moods and quiet reflections. And around all that—whether she was purring like a kitten or snoring just that side of delicately—she was in his bed. Exactly where he wanted her to be.

Problem was, in just over a month Darcy was going to leave his apartment to have their baby. And when the hospital released her, she wouldn't be coming back. She wanted to move into her own space. No blurry lines regarding the end of their affair.

That's what they'd agreed on.

It had seemed like the easy means of giving Darcy whatever emotional space she needed so she'd still be comfortable sharing physical space with him. So she wouldn't feel trapped or hemmed in. Now that he better understood her past, he was more cognizant than ever of that need to tread carefully.

Only sometime over the past few months, that clear plan with the easy exit strategy had stopped working for him and a new one had begun to take shape. A plan that involved more than blurring the lines.

Leaning down at the edge of the bed, Jeff dropped a light kiss at Darcy's protruding belly and then moved up to do the same at her crown. "Have a good day, gorgeous."

He was going to erase those lines all together. He knew he could. He'd make a success of this unconventional arrangement the way he did with everything else he wanted. Because now that he'd had a taste of what it could be like between them, no way was he going to give that up.

"I thought you said we were going to your mother's?"

Darcy adjusted the pillow at the small of her back watching as Jeff navigated the roads of Bel Air, the look of supreme satisfaction on his face suggesting he was about to burst over *something*.

They were only about a mile from Jeff's mother's house, two from the "little" place Jeff had bought for her and the baby, and headed in the opposite direction. The mystery surrounding their destination making her wonder if he or, more likely, Gail had orchestrated a shower for her despite her protests.

She hoped not, but if that's what it was, she'd be grateful and appreciative because she knew their hearts were in the right place.

"What's this?" she asked when they pulled up to a security gate at a private drive.

Jeff rolled the window down. "Morning, Phil."

The guard offered a quick wave activating the gate, which rolled silently open.

Darcy's eyes landed on the for sale sign posted out front and then looked back at Jeff, nerves kicking up hard in the belly she'd been slowly rubbing.

"Jeff?"

"Wait and see." He flashed her a dazzling grin and her heart started to pound.

A moment later they were parked in front of a breathtaking Spanish Colonial. Jeff hopped out of the car and circled around, that grin going full tilt as he helped her maneuver out of the front seat. Holding her hand, he led her to the open front door.

He didn't knock.

Didn't call a greeting of any sort, just walked a few steps ahead of her, pointing out the soaring ceilings, the wrought iron detail, the oversize formal dining room, the sprawling family room and the top of the line kitchen.

"Did you make an offer on this place?" she asked, afraid to hear the answer. Afraid to find out what they were doing there and why. Afraid to trust the heart that had begun to race dangerously ahead of her mind.

Jeff cocked a brow at her so full of mischief that even in her anxious state, she couldn't help but answer with a laugh.

"Jeff, it's beautiful. Incredible." Enormous. "Are you thinking of making it an investment property?"

"I was thinking it reminded me of all those Spanish-style homes you're always sighing over when we drive around. Only this place was better. Bigger. Eight bedrooms and ten baths…"

He'd been thinking of her.

"…I was thinking it's a house that has everything but the family that belongs in it…"

Oh, God.

Her legs began to shake and she reached for the wall to steady herself, but then Jeff was there, taking her hand and holding it in his.

"…I was thinking we couldn't fill this place yet, but we've got a good start with our little bundle here. And maybe, if you were interested, in another year or so we could think about a brother or sister."

"Jeff," she whispered, her eyes filling with tears, because it couldn't be real and suddenly she knew she wanted it to be with everything she had. It couldn't be—except Jeff was going down on one knee in front of her. Holding her hand in the warm clasp of his, looking at her with eyes filled with expectation, excitement. Happiness.

She'd told herself not to hope for this. Not to let herself believe this was even a possibility, but as she stared down at the man she'd fallen helplessly in love with, she recognized the truth. She'd been a fool to think her heart would end up anywhere but here.

"Darcy, I know this isn't what we talked about. But these past few months, it's been so right having you with me. And as the days get closer to a time when you won't be…I don't even want to think about it. I can't stand the idea of whole days going by when I don't see our child. Of missing every other weekend and every other Christmas morning, when I don't want to miss anything at all. And I know you don't, either."

That thundering heart ground to a halt as Jeff's words hit her. What he was saying. What he wasn't.

He was talking about not wanting to miss out on being a full-time parent. And it was wonderful to know he cared so deeply for their child, but…

Maybe he wasn't done. Maybe as with everything else that happened between them, he was simply using their child as the starting point. Maybe there was more.

Only even as she thought it, disgusting words filled her mind.

You're a fool.

"I know it's not a fairy tale, Darcy, but you said yourself, you weren't interested in one. We get along. We've got chemistry in spades. Sure it's not exactly what either of us imagined our marriage would be, but people make sacrifices for the sake of their children all the time, and I can think of about a million reasons for getting married worse than making a full-time family."

The air felt thin entering her lungs, the edges of her vision starting to haze.

Her throat tightened around all the protests and pleas suddenly desperate to escape. Words she'd never give voice to, because in that moment of sudden grueling clarity, she realized she'd already betrayed herself in all the ways she'd sworn she wouldn't.

"No, it's not the worst reason." The truth was, Darcy hadn't spent a lot of time imagining herself getting married at all. Her fantasies had always been independence-based. But the longer she was with Jeff, the more those fantasies most every other girl had in grade school seemed to flesh out.

The more she started to ache for something they didn't have. "But, Jeff, for me, it's not the right reason, either. I'm sorry, but I can't do this."

CHAPTER TWENTY-THREE

I'M SORRY. THE words hit him like a battering ram to the gut.

The way she'd been looking at him. The way it had been with them the past week. The past months. He'd been sure.

Even now, as he looked into the eyes that had been staring up at him the night before like he was…everything, he couldn't believe it.

He wouldn't.

"Darcy, let's talk about this."

"No, Jeff," she said, pulling her hand from his to hold it trembling against the exaggerated rise and fall of her chest. "Not this time. We agreed."

She was panicking, her eyes darting around like she was searching for escape.

"Okay, slow down, sweetheart. Relax. Yeah, this isn't what we'd agreed on, but I think if we sit a minute and talk it through, you'll see—"

"What will I see? How quickly you can work your magic again?" she asked with a short laugh as the tears he didn't understand began to leak from the corners of her eyes. "How quickly you can figure out some way to tell me just exactly what I need to hear to justify another exception, to get me to bend my rules one more time, to convince me I won't regret it? Here's the problem, Jeff." She jerked back from him, nearly losing her balance and, when he reached to steady her, pushing at his hand. "*I keep believing you.* Through one mistake after another. And now my regrets? I'm trapped behind a wall of them piled so high, I can't even see the life I could have had anymore. The life I *wanted*. And the worst of it is I only have myself to blame…because I knew better!"

They'd driven back to Jeff's apartment in silence. Both absorbing what the other had said. Both wishing, Darcy was certain, they could have taken back their words before they'd been spoken. Taken back the other's, as well.

But if there was one lesson she'd learned, it was there were no take backs.

Once something was done, it couldn't be undone.

All she could do was move forward from there. And her first step, a sorely needed apology.

Jeff was in the living room, his laptop open though he didn't seem to be working on it when she sat opposite him on the couch.

"I shouldn't have said those things to you, Jeff. All you've done from the minute you found out about this baby was try to make things better for me. For us. You've been generous beyond belief. You've been supportive. You've been more than anyone could hope for."

"Don't apologize. You were right. Every time you gave me an inch, I've taken a mile. It wasn't what we agreed to and—hell, I don't know, as the delivery gets closer, I just thought maybe there was a way to make this work."

She shook her head. "It's not you, Jeff."

"No?" He let out a short laugh. "I got the feeling it was."

How could he not. She'd been angry. But more at herself than him. She'd finally seen through all the lies she'd been telling herself about what was happening between them. About how she felt about it and what she could handle. She'd fallen in love. And worse, she'd started to believe Jeff could give her the fairy tale she'd never expected to want.

But the depth of her feelings for him wasn't something she could share. It was information with the power to disrupt their future relationship—one of critical importance. So she would try to tell him the truth, make him understand, without revealing exactly how much he'd taken over her heart.

"You mentioned fairy tales earlier. How I wasn't interested in one anyway. And, for the most part that's been true. As far as destinies went, I wasn't interested in having mine tied to anyone else's. I'd gotten into the habit of looking out for myself. Being on my own. And it worked for me, mostly. But I started seeing things differently after being a part of your family, hearing about what it was like growing up in a home filled with love and respect and caring—the kind of home I'd never known. Not being alone to face every challenge. Having someone there—"

She stopped herself before giving too much away. Shook her head and started again. "I feel like I've been selling myself short my whole life, Jeff. When we met, I'd been on my own for so long, taking care of myself the only way I knew how. Avoiding risks. I'd already started to realize what all my avoidance and caution was costing me. That I was missing out on life, which is why I couldn't resist your offer that first night. I just wanted to live *a little*. But in the months since I've been in L.A.—living with your mom and then with you—I've had a taste of being a part of something bigger. Of something that isn't destructive or about giving things up. Something that makes me feel like *more* instead of less. And it's made me see the possibility of what's out there. What love might be like. You're an incredible man, Jeff. And any woman would be beyond lucky to have you in her life. But we both agree, you and I aren't the fairy tale, and I'm just not ready to resign myself to giving up on finding it yet. I feel like I owe it to myself and to our baby and to you, too, not to let any of us settle for less than we deserve."

And they all deserved so much more than a family founded on sacrifice.

Their child deserved a mother who made a better role model than she'd had herself. Who taught lessons with smiles instead of tears, strength instead of weakness. Bravery instead of fear.

Jeff deserved the kind of marriage his parents had. A wife he saw as a partner, an equal, the other half to make them whole. He deserved to marry someone he loved.

And she deserved more than a lifetime of imbalance in every regard. Loving a man who saw his marriage to her as the sacrifice he'd been willing to make for a "whole" family. She deserved to be able to hope that someday she'd meet someone who made her feel all the things Jeff made her feel, and who would want her for her. Not because a relationship with her would facilitate the full-time parenting package he was really after.

At some point during her explanation, Jeff had moved closer, taking her hand in his own. Now he met her eyes with the kind of understanding that made her wish for all the things she couldn't have with him.

"You're right, Darcy. I promise, no more proposals. Our original agreement stands." Offering a quick grin, he qualified, "Our amended agreement."

She swallowed past this new layer of regret. "I appreciate that. I really do." She tried to shift into a more comfortable position, only this time it wasn't her belly getting in her way. It was her conscience. "But, Jeff, maybe it would be better for both of us, if rather than waiting until the baby comes, I moved out now."

Something dark flashed through his eyes, and she thought he might argue. But instead he simply nodded and with a last gentle squeeze, released her hand. "I'll make some calls and we'll get it done tomorrow."

Darcy stared at the bedroom wall of her new home, telling herself she'd done the right thing.

Jeff had asked her to marry him. Offered to make her his family. To take care of her.

He'd proven time and again, though he didn't love her, he

would treat her like a queen—even going so far as to surprise her with a castle and the crown jewels.

He was beyond generous. Attentive. Caring.

Beautiful in the most rugged way.

Fun and intelligent.

Honest.

Strip away his wealth, and he was still everything she could want in a man. Except for the part about him not feeling quite the same way.

There was no doubt he found her attractive or that he cared for her in a very deep, very real way. But when Jeff had gone looking for a relationship…he'd looked for someone far different from her.

A part of her knew she was crazy to turn him down. But a greater part of her knew she couldn't stand to live like that.

She thought back to all the promises she'd made to herself and knew she'd broken every one…starting the night she'd gone back to Jeff's room. She'd justified and rationalized, for the feel-good of being with a man she'd known from the start wasn't for her. A man who'd warned her he wasn't interested in a relationship, just a few hours of fun. And yeah, later he'd said he'd thought about wanting more. An affair maybe. But for marriage, he'd been looking to Olivia with her social connections, business acumen and impeccable pedigree.

How could she marry a man she knew was settling for her? Making a concession.

She couldn't. She'd done the right thing.

But as the next tear rolled down her cheek, she wondered how she was going to live without him…especially when circumstance assured she'd never be able to get far enough away to forget him.

Jeff stood at his open refrigerator, staring at the second shelf where half a yellow-box-mix cake with fudge frosting sat, abandoned.

He'd bet money Darcy had probably come within a hair's breadth of tears when she realized she'd left it behind. And he'd bet, that had been at about eight-fifteen the evening before.

If he'd been home rather than working through the night at the office, he'd have noticed it there and probably done the same thing he was doing right now. Stood in front of the fridge debating whether he ought to drop it by her place for her.

But somehow the excuse seemed thin, even to him.

Besides if he knew Darcy at all—and despite the failure of his proposal and her subsequent exodus from his apartment as a result, he did—she'd already have taken care of whatever box mix needs she'd had on her own.

Just the way she liked it.

Pulling the phone from his pocket, he checked to see if she'd texted. Even set to near Richter-five vibration with a ringtone to match, it was possible he'd missed her call or text.

Only he hadn't.

He opened the fridge again. Laughed a little when he noticed the suspicious marks from fork tines in the frosting—but then the sound of his laughing alone in a space that had been filled with Darcy just two days before made his chest ache and all the humor evaporated into the still silent air around him.

He could *just call* and see if she wanted him to bring the cake. Maybe she hadn't thought to put a box mix on the list for the housekeeper he'd hired to shop and do all the things eight-months-pregnant women weren't comfortable doing. Sure there was a driver on call for her 24/7. And if she'd been up for going to his mother's today, she might have found a box there…but what if she hadn't.

What if she was hungry?

What if the only reason she wasn't calling to ask about the cake was because she felt like she shouldn't after moving out? What if she thought *he* didn't want to hear from *her?*

Okay, and what if he never got a grip again.

If Darcy wanted to talk to him, she'd call. If she wanted cake, she'd make one.

If she wanted him…hell. She'd still be here. In his arms. In his bed. In his life in a way that wasn't simply about waiting for their child to be born so they could share it like civilized adults.

And she wasn't.

CHAPTER TWENTY-FOUR

"DARCY, DON'T YOU make me take that file from you. It's nearly seven."

Hand flat on the top of the file in question, Darcy shook her head. "You even think about taking this from me, and you can kiss your 'Nana Gail' fantasies goodbye. I'll have this baby calling you Gammy Gigi for years."

Jeff's mother flinched, but apparently tonight she wasn't backing down. Slipping her phone from her pocket, she made a show of starting to text. "Hold on, dear. Let's talk about this in a moment. After I tell Jeff about how you aren't eating and you look so very pale."

"What?" she gasped, grabbing the plate with the remains of her organic burrito…the second burrito, because there wasn't even a single crumb left to show for the first. "This is my third, no, fourth meal today. Since I've been here!"

Gail didn't look up as she sighed. "We old people get so easily confused. The file, Darcy."

Old. At fifty-five, Gail was hardly material for the old folks' home, especially since she had the physique and attitude of a woman closer to forty. Add another item to her ever-growing "Why I want to be like Gail when I grow up" list.

Darcy looked down. She knew it had been a long day, but the truth was, being at home was difficult. It was beautiful and comfortable and all, but a week into living there, she still found herself watching the clock for the part of her day that had become her favorite, waiting for an event that wasn't going to come.

Reminding herself that Jeff wouldn't be swinging through the door at any moment.

It was just her. Alone. With nothing to wait for or anticipate at the day's end because she'd had to go and make the smart decision for herself. And it stunk.

She used to thrive on living by herself. But that was before she'd had a taste of what it felt like to share a home. Before Jeff.

"I wonder what he'll do when he hears how sad and thin and worn-out you look?"

Darcy narrowed her eyes. She did not look thin. The rest, possibly. But certainly not enough to report to Jeff. Gail was bluffing.

And if she wasn't...

No, she tamped down that insidious little hopeful part of her looking for any excuse or justification to see him. Anything to ease this hollow aching part of her that had opened up the day she moved out and secured his promise to give her some space as they adjusted to the new phase of their relationship. They'd be seeing each other soon enough once the baby arrived.

But Gail *was* bluffing because no matter what Darcy and Jeff had respectively told her about Darcy's move to her new place, Gail wasn't stupid. She wasn't blind. And she wasn't one to manipulate her son for sport. So no worries. That text wasn't going anywhere.

Still this was the most entertainment she'd had since ripping her heart in half when she moved out of Jeff's place. Maybe she wasn't ready to give it up just yet.

"You do that, and I'll tell him…I'll tell him…" What lie she'd never actually tell could she threaten Gail with—ha! She had it. "I'll tell him Grant put a move on *you!* You'll have that promising young doctor's blood all over your hands. So how about them apples, Gail?"

Darcy waited for the gasp, the cough, the laugh or the escalated threat, anticipating whatever the response with glee.

Ready for whatever her friend had to lob back at her. But all she got was Gail staring at her, wide-eyed and stock-still.

The seconds stretched, and Darcy's brows began to creep skyward. "No. Way."

Gail blinked, looked down at the floor where she made a small circle with the toe of her shoe. Finally she shrugged. "Give me the file and I'll tell you about it."

Three things ran through her mind at once.

First, Grant didn't value his life the way she would have expected him to.

Second, Wow. No wonder Jeff didn't know how to lose.

And third, rename her list as "Why Gail is my hero" and add this as the top line item.

Handing over the file, she tried not to think about what ran through her mind next. How relieved she was not to have to be heading back to her lonely house. How grateful she was for what would probably be the only distraction powerful enough to keep her mind off the man she couldn't stop missing.

The door swung open and Connor squinted out at him. "Not that I'm not happy to see you. But it's four in the morning, Jeff. What are you doing here?"

Yeah, what indeed. Trying to keep himself from making a seriously monumental mistake. And calling in a favor to do it.

"Needed to get out of the apartment for a while. So I went for a drive. Ended up in the neighborhood. Thought I'd stop in."

"Two hundred miles is a bit of a drive."

"Yeah."

"You look like hell."

Jeff gave Connor a once-over, taking in the bedhead that put the other man's hair on par with his own, the wrinkle running across his cheek and the unfocused look in general. "Coming from you, that's saying something."

"Ha. So you want to come in, or was this just a drive-by?"

"I need you to take my phone. Darcy asked me to give her some space. And I'm trying. Really, really hard. But I haven't seen her in two weeks. And even though I've talked to my mom and Grant and they both say she's doing great, I haven't seen her. Not being able to—hell, the only reason I'm not knocking on her door right now is because I forced myself to turn left instead of right…and keep going. And the only way I'm not going to call her and tell her that I can't stand another damn day like this…when I need to be able to stand a whole damn lifetime like it, is if you take the damn phone out of my damned hand. *Please*."

Connor looked down at the offending piece of technology and held out his hand for it.

"Thank you," he said as Connor waved him inside.

"I owed you one, right?"

Jeff was about to make the usual polite protest—even though it was the absolute truth—when he stopped at the sound of crunching plastic and metal.

Eyes bugging, he cranked his head around to where Connor was pulling the crushed phone from between the door and the frame, a sleepy half-cocked grin on his face as he handed back what had seconds before been a working phone, painstakingly programmed to accommodate every aspect of his life. At his stunned stare, Connor slapped the bits of phone into his palm and said, "Now we're even. And you're welcome."

Five minutes later, Connor set five bottles between them, then dropped into the kitchen chair, eyeing Jeff over the table. "Let's get this out of the way first. What kind of night are we having? Coffee?" he asked, holding a hand over the two bottles of caramel-and-cream flavored iced coffee, before moving to hover over the green glass of his favorite imports. "Beer?"

Then rubbing a hand over his mouth and the scrub of his jaw, Connor eyed the last bottle warily. "Or if it's really, really bad…and only for you…" He winced, look-ing away. "This."

A twenty-five-year-old Scotch Jeff was willing to bet Connor hadn't had a glass of since the night Jeff had had to run out of a meeting to head him off at the airport before Connor showed up drunk at his then-estranged wife's door.

"Wow. You really do love me," Jeff said, and grabbed the hard stuff as he pushed back from the table and set the bottle at the far counter. Looking back at Connor, he turned the bottle so the label wasn't staring him down like some school yard bully. "But I love you, too, and even if I didn't— do you honestly think I'm going to get plowed with my preg-nant non-girlfriend God only knows where? Doing God only knows what. With God only knows who."

"Isn't she with your mom?"

"No. She's at her new house. Probably sleeping. Alone." Of course alone. Definitely alone. For now.

And as soon as that thought hit him, the next certainty followed…. If she didn't want to be alone, she wouldn't have to be. He saw the way guys looked at her, eight months pregnant or not. Hell, he knew how he looked at her. How he wanted her.

How he missed her.

"I'll pass on the beer, too," he said, but scowled at the re-maining selection of iced coffee. "Caramel?"

"Megan bought it. The machine is broken, just man up and drink what's on offer. It's actually pretty good."

Reluctantly, Jeff grabbed his own and tried it. Smacked his lips. "Like liquid candy."

Connor gave him an I-told-you-so look and settled back in his chair with a bottle of the iced coffee. "Okay. So now that we've got the beverage portion of the evening—err, morning—out of the way. Let's have it. What's going on?"

"I asked Darcy to marry me." At Connor's raised brows, he added, "She declined."

"Aw hell, I'm sorry, Jeff. I didn't realize it was like that with you two. Or at least that you'd realized it was—and I'm probably not helping, either. Okay, why'd she say no?"

Jeff ran a finger through the condensation on his bottle, wondering how it was possible to feel half numb and wholly horrible all at once. "The first time, because she didn't *care* about 'the whole legitimacy thing.'"

"Umm, out of curiosity, how many times did she turn you down?"

He shoved his hands through his hair. "A couple. Few maybe. Once because I asked like I was joking around. I know. Big surprise. And okay, then because I asked when she was throwing up."

"Dude," Connor gasped, pulling away in his chair even as he said it.

"Yeah, yeah." Jeff waved at the air. He'd been trying to cheer her up but, yeah. He knew. "And most recently, because she thinks she can do better."

The coffee clanked on the table as Connor threw up his hands, all what's-this-world-coming-to? "She thinks she can do better than *you?* What the hell is she looking for? You're generous, kind, almost as intelligent as I am, not quite as good-looking, but what you lack in pretty you make up in portfolio."

Jeff let out a short laugh, but the real thing seemed harder and harder to come by these days. "Connor, no matter how you sweet-talk me, I'm not getting in bed with you again. So don't even try."

"Someone's still smarting over me thinking he was Megan," Connor responded in a deep singsong voice that really should have made Jeff's day. "And nice dodge, but aside from the nose and hair, you're like every woman's idea of Mr. Right. I'm serious, man. What does she want?"

Jeff took his own drink, only the sugary concoction had turned sour on his tongue. "She wants to be in love with the guy she marries."

Connor rocked back in his seat. And who could blame

him. There wasn't much room for outrage with a defense like that.

"She said she doesn't love you?"

Jeff pinched the bridge of his nose, thinking about all the times Darcy had pushed him away. Walked out on him. Told him she didn't want what he was offering. He thought of that last conversation, the way she'd looked at him with such regret in her eyes as she told him she couldn't marry him because… "She didn't have to."

He cleared his throat and met Connor's concerned stare. "Which was fine. It wasn't like that with us."

Connor's brows pinched together, concern turning to calculation in a blink, as he drawled, "Oh, really?"

Jeff shifted uncomfortably. Whatever that look was, he didn't like being on the receiving end of it. "Knock it off, Connor."

"I don't know what you're talking about."

"I got her pregnant. I didn't fall in love with her. It was never about love. It was about making a family. I'm upset because it didn't work out like I'd hoped."

More of that look. "Sure."

"Damn it, Connor. This isn't like you and Megan."

"Didn't say it was."

"You're looking at me…with this infuriatingly…*smug* look. And it's making me want to mess up your perfect nose."

Totally unconcerned, Connor reached across the table, his crooked smile smug and secure as he rubbed his hand over the top of Jeff's head.

Condescension and delight mixing in his voice, he said, "I love you, man. But come on, I can't believe you don't see what I've been hearing in your voice for months. In every mention of her. Every frustration, every funny story, every TMI account you can't seem to contain. And if you can't hear it in your own words, then maybe it's time you take a good look at why exactly you are so hell-bent on getting this woman to marry you. You keep asking her for everything, but I'm not sure you're seeing all you've got to give in return. Which means maybe she's not seeing it, either."

No. Connor was just reading his own happy ending into Jeff's story. But it wasn't that way. They'd agreed up front about the limits so no one would get the wrong idea. It had worked with every other relationship he'd had since Margo. And granted none of those women had held a candle to Darcy. They'd been easy to say goodbye to in a way he couldn't even contemplate with Darcy…but still.

Jeff collapsed back in his chair, the weight on his chest one of unwilling recognition. "Hell."

Connor was right. But unfortunately, that didn't change a damn thing as far as Darcy wanting to marry him. Or live with him. Or see him. Or talk to him. Or laugh with him. Or any of the million other things Jeff wanted to do with her.

That was the heart of it. He wanted everything.

While she wanted to be friendly, independent co-parents to the child they would share for the rest of their lives…he wanted the fairy tale.

And he'd promised Darcy he wouldn't ask for it.

CHAPTER TWENTY-FIVE

THERE WAS SOMETHING distinctly unsatisfying about going for a drive to clear your head when you were stuck in the back-seat behind a paid driver. Who wouldn't give up the wheel, even for a pregnant woman threatening tears.

Why the hell had she turned down Jeff's offer to buy her a car.

Her throat tightened as she wondered, not for the first time and with disturbingly increasing frequency, why she'd turned him down for anything. She loved him. And he'd offered to marry her. But because she couldn't have everything *just exactly the way she wanted it,* because she was too spoiled, too greedy, too selfish…she'd said no.

And then to top it off, because it felt *too good* being in his arms, his bed and his home…she'd moved out.

Every day her body grew, filling her more with the child they'd made together. And every day she went without Jeff, she felt like a bigger piece of her was missing.

All the regrets she'd thrown in his face that horrible last day together…there was only one she could see now. And there was no one to blame for it but herself.

She let out a heavy sigh and then spoke to the driver. "Harvey, I know I said we weren't going today, but could you take me to Gail's, please."

For as much as she'd avoided discussing her relationship with Jeff out of respect for all of them, she needed some advice. Because staying away from him felt more wrong by the minute. And not just because of how much it hurt not to be with him, but because he'd wanted to be a part of her pregnancy and share in the experience. And asking him to stay away, to give her space so she could try to get over him wasn't fair. And more than that, it wasn't going to work.

The drive up from San Diego at rush hour had taken twice the time it took to drive down in the middle of the night, but time to think wasn't necessarily the worst thing and Jeff accepted whatever traffic holdups the highway gods had in store for him without question. That is until he'd gotten to his mother's neighborhood and watched an ambulance fly by him, lights flashing, siren going full blast.

Instinctively he reached for his phone, but only came back with a handful of broken technology and a choice expletive with Connor's name on it.

As soon as the emergency vehicle passed, he hit the gas, telling himself it was going to turn off before his mom's place. Either that or roll right past. Sure Darcy was getting close, but those lights weren't for her. It wasn't the baby. It wasn't the end of his world. It couldn't be.

Please, no.

Only as his mother's drive came into view and the ambulance was already disappearing down it, that kernel of dread in his gut became a cannonball and the fantasy it was just his world that would end if something happened to Darcy went up in smoke. It would be the end of his universe. A loss so great, the limits were beyond comprehension.

Hands gripping the wheel tight enough that they threatened to rip it off, Jeff focused on that final stretch of road. Pulling up the drive. Slamming the car into Park as his mother, looking wild and desperate, pulled one of the responders with her around the far side of the house.

And then Jeff was out of the car, running across the lawn, trying to make a throat seized with panic work so he could call out, demand to know what happened.

The small group was huddled together between the house and a flower bed. The EMTs kneeling beside—

"Really, I don't need an ambulance. It's just a sprain. *I'm a doctor.*"

Skidding to a stop, the air punched out of his lungs as Grant's voice sounded above the rest.

What the hell?

Only then whatever was happening with Grant became secondary, as one fact washed over him with tsunami force.

Not Darcy.

He saw her, struggling up from her knees where she'd been on the ground next to Grant. One hand supporting her belly as she found her balance and looked up, meeting his eyes as he took those last desperate steps and caught her against him.

"Darcy." Her name was gravel-rough when he managed to get it past his throat. "You're okay."

"Jeff, look at your face." And he could see from the look on hers, that his must be reflecting exactly the soul-deep horror he'd been experiencing. "The baby's fine. I swear, we're okay."

He nodded, trying not to hold her too tightly, but having her in his arms after weeks without, finding her safe after seeing that ambulance—it was all he could do not to crush her against him and make her swear she'd never leave his arms again. Only that wasn't what he'd come for, and based on the scene around him, circumstances might not allow for him to make any kind of claim at all.

His eye shifted to Grant who, despite the fact there was an ambulance there for him, seemed to be doing okay.

But what was he doing there at ten in the morning mid-week? He hadn't needed to check on Darcy since she'd started seeing her regular doctor months ago. But then maybe the reason Grant was here wasn't professional. Maybe he'd found out Darcy had moved into her own place and decided to make his move before any of the other vultures swooped in.

Smart. But it made Jeff wish the guy looked a little worse off than he actually seemed to be.

"What happened?" he asked as Darcy buried her head against his chest.

"It's my fault," she started. "I'd told your mother I didn't think I'd be in this morning, but then I came over anyway. And when I closed the door—"

"Calm down, Gail," Grant urged, his voice overriding Darcy's whisper. "I know you're worried, but I'm telling you, it's a sprained knee and—"

"Don't you, 'Calm down, Gail,' me. You're the damned fool who decided to climb out the window and fell. A second-story window, Grant. I already lost one man I loved and I'm not about to let your dinged-up pride cause me to lose you, too."

Jeff choked on the breath he'd been taking, sure beyond any reason he hadn't just heard that right.

"Mom?"

His mother's head snapped around suggesting she'd only just realized he was there. For an instant her eyes registered the kind of shock and nerves one would expect—but then this was his mother. And in the next instant, those eyes flashed steel. "Not now, honey."

Jeff felt the span of Darcy's hands pressing into his chest, as though she meant to hold him back, which was adorable in itself. But unnecessary. He wasn't going anywhere.

"Grant and my mom?" he asked. All those times the guy mentioned how limber she seemed… He'd assumed Grant's mind was on osteoporosis. But apparently not.

"I guess he's had a thing for her…forever. The night he was going to take us out, really had been about spending more time with Gail. And I guess it worked." Darcy looked uneasy. "This morning Connor called asking if you'd arrived. When they heard the door downstairs a minute later, assuming it was you rather than me, Grant decided the window seemed like his best chance for survival."

Jeff took a deep breath, savoring the feminine scent of Darcy's shampoo and lotion and the woman beneath.

"Okay."

"Okay?" she asked, sounding skeptical.

"Darcy, I'm not going to attack the guy on his way into the ambulance." When she looked at him seemingly unconvinced, he added, "My mother would kill me."

And after all the weeks, he got what he'd missed the most. A flash of the gorgeous smile that started it all. The one he'd never get over. The one he still wanted to earn.

Grant grudgingly agreed to let the ambulance take him to the hospital to get checked out and Gail went along with him, leaving Jeff and Darcy at the house alone.

Since getting her into his arms, Jeff hadn't been able to let go. And Darcy seemed to understand, settling against him.

Damn, it felt so good to be standing beside her. To have his hands on her.

But as the ambulance disappeared down the drive, Darcy took the hand anchoring his arm across her chest and, with a light squeeze, extracted herself from his hold.

"Want to go inside?" she asked, looking more nervous now that the emergency had passed and it was back to just the two of them.

Jeff gave her a stiff nod, then looked back to his car, half parked on the grass, the door gaping wide from when he'd bolted out for the house.

"Let me pull around back. And I'll meet you there."

Darcy started to go, then paused and turned back, asking, "Are you okay?"

Not even a little bit. Not yet. "Give me a few minutes and I will be."

By the time Darcy made it back to the kitchen, Jeff had parked and was bringing in a breathtaking vase of flowers and a white pastry box, both of which looked as though they'd taken a hit during their stint in Jeff's car.

Still, Gail would be touched by the thoughtful gesture when she got back from the hospital.

Jeff, looking as weary and worn and sexy and compelling as he had that night after his return from Australia, set his load on the counter, and kept walking toward her.

"I know you wanted space and I know I just let you go, but, Darcy— I need— I thought— I'm so glad—"

She went to him, understanding the kind of fear he must have been feeling. Wanting to offer him whatever comfort she could.

Reaching for his hands she pulled them to the round swell of her belly, pressing them flat. "He's fine," she promised. And when a swift little kick met the warm spot covered by Jeff's open palm, she laughed—all the relief that Jeff was here, all the love and all the nerves bubbling up inside her at once. Finding release in that short moment.

Jeff stared down at the spot he was now rubbing in a soft circle. He gave her belly one last pat.

"Darcy, I'm relieved our baby is safe. Of course I am... but—" his voice broke, and shaking his head he cupped her jaw, and then met her eyes with a tortured look "—when I thought something might have happened to *you,* my God, I couldn't breathe. I couldn't think."

The way he was looking at her—what he was saying. It wasn't the way it sounded. She was seeing what she wanted to see, hearing what she wanted to hear, reading meaning that didn't exist again.

This time she knew better.

She offered the back of his hand a gentle stroke, wanting to remember the feel of it forever, and then stepped back.

Instead of letting her heart run away from her, she held firm to the reality she knew to be true.

Jeff cared about her. Of that there had never been a doubt. And if ever there was a moment she had the chance to secure the same offer he'd made to her three weeks before—to make her his wife, make them a family—this was it. He'd been afraid of losing them and knowing Jeff, right now the man would probably do anything—say anything—promise anything to make that feeling go away.

Which was why right now wasn't the time to talk to him about the possibility of them being together in some capacity. Of finding out what kind of arrangement would give them all what they wanted. Or as close to it as was possible.

She'd done it again. Pulled away from him. Given him another obvious cue she didn't want what he was offering.

The right thing to do would be to leave her be. But damn it, doing the "right thing" with Darcy always felt so wrong.

He'd been curbing his impulses from the word *go*. Trying to find compromise by taking more than he should without going after all that he wanted. By lying to both of them about what would be enough.

Letting Darcy down every step of the way.

He'd thought he'd been honest with her.

Thought he'd been fair. But the truth was, with every concession he'd made, some secret dark part of him had known he'd be going back for more.

That time was over.

"How have you been?" It seemed trite, but Jeff hadn't seen her in weeks. They hadn't been talking. And he wanted to know.

Darcy went to the sink and started filling a kettle. "We've been doing pretty well. Getting used to the new house. Settled in. How about you?"

Jeff pulled out a kitchen chair and sat down at it, watching as Darcy made tea. "I've been lonely. Missing you. Wishing I'd done about a thousand things differently and wondering if any of them would have gotten me an outcome other than this."

The kettle clattered against the stove top and Darcy grabbed the counter behind her.

Every part of Jeff wanted to go to her, usher her into a seat or, better, his lap. But he'd been taking what he wanted with Darcy from the start, pushing for his end goal without giving her the chance to decide what she wanted. He had to stop, for both of them. He wanted Darcy confident in the choices she made so they didn't end up feeling like regrets trapping her in a place she didn't want to be. So despite every instinct trying to drag him across the kitchen to go to her, hold her, use his body along with his words to get what he wanted…he made himself stay.

There was only one thing he could give her right now, and that was the truth.

"I've been working eighteen-hour days trying to keep myself distracted enough so I won't start formulating my next plan to get you back, plotting what I can say to convince you to bend your rules just a little to suit my needs. I'm exhausted. I'm miserable. And I'm thinking if I want any chance at the happiness I know we can have together, I need to start figuring out how to be the man you deserve. The one you can trust and count on. Who makes you laugh. Makes you feel safe. And most of all, makes you want to stay instead of leave."

"Jeff, when we talked last time—" She looked at him like she was terrified, her hands gripping the countertops at either side of her like they were the only things holding her upright. "Maybe today isn't the day to talk about this."

He wanted to be what she leaned on. The support she never doubted. Always.

"Don't worry. I'm not asking you to marry me again."

She nodded tightly, looking miserable and confused. And it was so damned hard not to go to her that very second.

"I promised you I wouldn't, and I'm going to be a man you can count on to keep his word." He cleared his throat then and met her eyes. "But I *am* going to ask you what I came here to ask today. If you'd give me a chance to take you out on a date."

Darcy blinked, not sure she'd heard right. "A date?" Her heart started to speed because he'd said a *date* and there weren't a lot of ways to misinterpret that word. And still she was using every bit of her rapidly diminishing self-control to hold herself in check, not to sail into his arms if he meant something else.

He was talking about missing her. About wishing things were different. But the way he'd said it didn't sound so very different from when he'd asked her to marry him the last time when it was all about wanting to be together for the sake of their child.

At least it hadn't sounded different until he'd gotten to the part where he asked for a date.

Which was…different. "A date, date? Or *just* a date…or maybe a date that doesn't mean what I think it means but—"

"A date, like I want to make you fall in love with me, date," Jeff answered, his voice steady even as he stared at his hands. "And okay, so that's maybe a lot of pressure up front, but I'm through telling you all I want is one thing, when the truth is I want everything. I want you to marry me, but I get—"

"Why? So you can be with our child each night?" The words burst past her lips, not in accusation but because she just needed to know. "It's okay if that's why…."

He met her eyes and what she saw in his stole her breath, made her grip the counter tighter still. Not to hold herself back—but to hold herself up. Because what she saw when he looked at her like that was enough to floor her completely.

"Because *I love you*."

Her lips parted, but whatever words she'd thought to say or breath she'd meant to take didn't come. All she could do was stare, wait for whatever he had to say next. Because she couldn't believe him yet. She was terrified and yet some part of her must have made the decision to do just that, because suddenly she wasn't holding on to the counter anymore. She was crossing the kitchen to the man who was staring at her like he'd just witnessed a miracle.

And then she was standing in the V of his legs, her hands were in the gorgeous unruly mess of his hair, her breath coming in broken little gasps.

"You love me?"

He swallowed and offered her a nod. "I think I have from the very first night, Darcy, I just couldn't let myself admit it. When I realized you were gone in Vegas—it rocked me. But I tried to tell myself it was no big deal. It couldn't be. We'd just met. I'd forget about you. Only instead of forgetting, I kept thinking about you. Wondering how I could have misjudged what was going on between us so badly."

"I'm so sorry," she started, wishing again she could go back, wondering how differently things would have gone if she'd stayed. If they'd kept in touch. "I was afraid of what you made me feel after we'd agreed to what kind of night it would be."

"I know, sweetheart. But at the time, and even after we were together again, I kept thinking this is a woman who leaves. A woman who keeps putting her hand up and telling me not to get any closer. And even though it didn't keep me from pushing past those boundaries we kept agreeing to... it was enough for me to use as an excuse to keep from owning up to the truth. That first night with you changed something in me, made me want more than I'd been settling for in my relationships."

"And you found Olivia."

"She seemed like such a smart fit...except for the part where she wasn't you."

Darcy buried her head against Jeff's shoulder, holding on to him so tight. "Everything I heard about her, she was different from me. And everyone said you two were serious.

Perfect for each other. That it was just a matter of time. And all I could think was she was everything I wasn't. I couldn't see myself as anything but a sacrifice so you could make your family work."

"*No.* I shouldn't have said it. I shouldn't have tried to make either of us believe it."

She wrapped her arms around his neck and stared into his eyes.

"So you really love me?"

"I really do."

"That's good. Because I've been falling for you from the start, and no matter how I've tried to stop it…nothing could. I love you, too."

Jeff kissed her then. Slow and tender and sweet and perfect. When they broke away, half breathless with desire, Darcy asked, "So what do we do now?"

Jeff nodded toward the counter. "I give you those flowers I brought for you, and woo you into letting me take you out by bribing you with that yellow-box-mix cake I made for you at Connor's, and then I romance you until you beg me to marry you."

Darcy laughed, her brows high. "I'm supposed to ask you?"

Very seriously, Jeff kissed her again. Then answered, "I'm a man you can count on. I promised you I wouldn't ask again. But——" He leaned closer and whispered in her ear, "I'm a sure thing. So whenever you feel safe. Whenever you feel solid about it. Tell me and——"

"Marry me, Jeff."

He blinked at her, the corner of his mouth kicking up into a sexy grin that was all mayhem and mischief. "Why?"

She gasped. "You just told me you'd say yes!"

"Oh, you better believe I'm going to say yes. But you asked why. So I'm asking."

Laying her hand over his heart and taking his to rest over their growing baby, she nodded. "Because I love you.

And you make me believe in happily ever afters. So say yes, please."

"Yes."

Two weeks later.

Her body heavy with fatigue, Darcy opened her eyes in the dim light of her hospital room to the most precious sight of her life. Her husband, leaning over eight-pound-one-ounce Garrison Jeffrey Norton as he affixed the tiny diaper in place, straightened the little hospital shirt and then, cradling him close, moved into the chair by the bed.

Arranging their son so Darcy could see him clearly, he took off the tiny knit cap revealing a dark brown shock of hair so wild, it made even his daddy's look tame. "Just look at what we made, Darcy. Can you believe it?"

"Our family," she murmured, her heart overflowing with love for this precious gift they'd been granted. For the man looking between her and their child with such unabashed adoration, such love, it took her breath away. Reaching out to stroke that silky fuzz, she smiled. "Our beautiful Happily Ever After."

Jeff looked down at his boy with pride and then shot her his most devastating grin, made even more so by the utter fatigue showing over every inch of him. "Our first one. What do you say we see about trying for a girl with your hair next."

* * * * *

'You're *dumping* me?'

Dan shifted his eyes briefly from the road to glance across at her, a mock grin on his face. Because of course this was some kind of joke, right?

Emma simply looked back at him, her brown eyes serious.

'Well, technically, no,' she said. 'Because we'd have to be in a *proper* relationship for me to do that, and ours is a fake one.' She put her head on one side. 'If it's actually one at all. To be honest, it's more of an arrangement, isn't it? A plus-one agreement.'

He'd never been dumped before. It was an odd novelty. And certainly not by a real girlfriend. It seemed being dumped by a fake one was no less of a shock to the system.

'It's been good while it lasted,' she was saying. 'Mutually beneficial for both of us. You got a professional plus-one for your work engagements and I got my parents off my back. But the fact is—'

'It's not you, it's me?' he joked, still not convinced she wasn't messing around.

Dear Reader

Doesn't time fly? I can't believe this is my fourth book. I'm as excited as ever to be writing for this fabulously fun, modern and flirty series, and I'm still pinching myself to make sure I'm not dreaming!

Talking of flirty... We've all had times when the dating game seems more trouble than it's worth—I know I have. In that kind of situation wouldn't it be great if you had a person on the end of the phone who could fit the bill as your date, no matter what the occasion? Someone who would always step up to the plate, make the right impression and never let you down or show you up? Wouldn't that make life easier?

Just as long as you don't fall in love with your perfect platonic plus-one, of course. Imagine the mayhem *that* could cause. Especially at a big family occasion where good impressions really count.

I've had so much fun playing around with these ideas while writing this story, and I hope you will have a lovely time reading it too.

Love

Charlotte x

THE PLUS-ONE AGREEMENT

BY
CHARLOTTE PHILLIPS

Published in Great Britain 2014
by Mills & Boon, an imprint of Harlequin (UK) Limited,
Eton House, 18-24 Paradise Road, Richmond, Surrey, TW9 1SR

© 2014 Charlotte Phillips

ISBN: 978 0 263 91223 4

Harlequin (UK) Limited's policy is to use papers that are natural,
renewable and recyclable products and made from wood grown in
sustainable forests. The logging and manufacturing processes conform
to the legal environmental regulations of the country of origin.

Printed and bound in Spain
by Blackprint CPI, Barcelona

Charlotte Phillips has been reading romantic fiction since her teens, and she adores upbeat stories with happy endings. Writing them for Mills & Boon is her dream job. She combines writing with looking after her fabulous husband, two teenagers, a four-year-old and a dachshund. When something has to give, it's usually housework. She lives in Wiltshire.

This and other books by Charlotte Phillips are available in eBook format from www.millsandboon.co.uk

For Gemma, who makes my day every day.
With all my love always.

CHAPTER ONE

Q: How do you tell your fake boyfriend that you've met a real one and you don't need him any more?

A: However you like. If he's not a real boyfriend, it's not a real break-up. Hardly likely that he'll start declaring undying love for you, is it?

CHANCE WOULD HAVE been a fine thing.

This Aston Martin might fly before arm candy addict Dan Morgan developed anything more than a fake attraction for someone as sensible and boring as Emma Burney, and it wasn't as if she hadn't given it time. Getting on for a year in his company, watching an endless string of short-term flings pout their way through his private life, had convinced her she was never going to be blonde enough, curvy enough or vacuous enough to qualify. In fact she was pretty much the opposite of all his conquests, even dressed up to the nines for her brother's art exhibition.

She glanced down at herself in the plain black boat-neck frock and nude heels she'd chosen, teamed as usual with her minimal make-up and straight-up-and-down figure. Romance need not apply.

She did, however, possess all the qualities Dan wanted in a supportive friend and social ally. As he did for her. Hence the fake part of their agreement.

An agreement which she reminded herself she no longer needed.

Not if she wanted to move forward from the suspended animation that had been her life this last year. Any residual hope that what was counterfeit between them might somehow turn genuine if she just gave it enough time had been squashed in these last few amazing weeks as she'd been swept off her feet by a whirlwind of intimate, luxurious dinners, expensive gifts and exciting plans. What was between her and Dan was now nothing more than a rut that needed climbing out of.

She watched him quietly for a moment from the passenger seat of his car, looking like an aftershave model in his dark suit and white shirt. His dark hair was so thick there was always a hint of spike about it, a light shadow of stubble lined his jaw, and his ice-blue eyes and slow smile had the ability to charm the entire female species. It had certainly worked on her mother, whose ongoing mission in life was to get Emma and Dan married off and raising a tribe of kids like some Fifties cupcake couple.

Perpetuating her gene pool was the last thing Emma wanted—a lifetime in the midst of her insane family had seen to that. Having Dan as her pretend boyfriend at family events had proved to be the perfect fob-off.

But now she had the real thing and the pretending was holding her back. All that remained was to explain that fact to Dan. She gathered herself together and took a deep breath.

'This has to stop,' she said.

* * *

'You're dumping me?'

Dan shifted his eyes briefly from the road to glance across at her, a mock grin on his face. Because of course this was some kind of joke, right? She simply looked back at him, her brown eyes serious.

'Well, technically, no,' she said. 'Because we'd have to be in a *proper* relationship for me to do that, and ours is a fake one.' She put her head on one side. 'If it's actually one at all. To be honest, it's more of an agreement, isn't it? A plus-one agreement.'

He'd never seen fit to give it a name before. It had simply been an extension of their work dealings into a mutually beneficial social arrangement. There had been no conscious decision or drawing up of terms. It had just grown organically from one simple work success.

Twelve months ago Emma, in her capacity as his lawyer, had attended a meeting with Dan and a potential client for his management consultancy. A potentially huge client. The meeting had overrun into dinner, she had proved a formidable ally and his winning of the contract had been smoothed along perfectly by their double act. She had seemed to bounce off him effortlessly, predicting where he was taking the conversation, backing him up where he needed it. He'd ended the evening with a new client, a new respect for Emma and the beginnings of a connection.

After that she'd become his go-to ally for social engagements—a purely platonic date that he could count on for intelligent conversation and professional behaviour. She'd become a trusted contact. And in return he'd accompanied her to family dinners and events like this one today, sympathising with her exasperation at her slightly crazy family while not really understanding it.

Surely better to have a slightly crazy family than no family at all?

He'd never been dumped before. It was an odd novelty. And certainly not by a real girlfriend. It seemed being dumped by a fake one was no less of a shock to the system.

'It's been good while it lasted,' she was saying. 'Mutually beneficial for both of us. You got a professional plus-one for your work engagements and I got my parents off my back. But the fact is—'

'It's not you, it's me?' he joked, still not convinced she wasn't messing around.

'I've met someone,' she said, not smiling.

'Someone?' he said, shaking his head lightly and reaching for the air-conditioning controls. For some reason it was suddenly boiling in the car. 'A work someone?'

'No, not a work someone!' Her tone was exasperated. 'Despite what you might think, I do have a life, you know—outside work.'

'I never said you didn't.'

He glanced across at her indignant expression just as it melted into a smile of triumph.

'Dan, I've *met* someone.'

She held his gaze for a second before he looked back at the road, her eyebrows slightly raised, waiting for him to catch on. He tried to keep a grin in place when for some reason his face wanted to fold in on itself. In the months he'd known her she'd been on maybe two or three dates, to his knowledge, and none of the men involved had ever been important enough to her to earn the description 'someone'.

He sat back in his seat and concentrated hard on driv-

ing the car through the London evening traffic. He supposed she was waiting for some kind of congratulatory
comment and he groped for one.

'Good for you,' he said eventually. 'Who is he?'

'He was involved in some legal work I was doing.'

So she *had* met him through her job as a lawyer, then.
Of course she had. When did she ever do anything that
wasn't somehow linked to work? Even their own friendship was based in work. It had started with work and
had grown with their mutual ambition.

'We've been on a few dates and it's going really well.'
She took a breath. 'And that's why I need to end things
with you.'

Things? For some reason he disliked the vagueness
of the term, as if it meant nothing.

'You don't date,' he pointed out.

'Exactly,' she said, jabbing a finger at him. 'And do
you know *why* I don't date?'

'Because no man could possibly match up to me?'

'Despite what you might think is appealing to women,
I don't relish the prospect of a couple of nights sharing
your bed only to be kicked out of it the moment you
get bored.'

'No need to make it sound so brutal. They all go into
it with their eyes open, you know. I don't make any false
promises that it will ever be more than a bit of fun.'

'None of them ever believe that. They all think they'll
be the one to change you. But you'll never change because you don't need to. You've got me for the times
when you need to be serious, so you can keep the rest
of your girlies just for fun.'

She looked down at her hands, folded in her lap.

'The thing is, Dan, passing you off as my boyfriend

might keep my family off my back, and it stops the swipes about me being single and the comments about my biological clock, but it doesn't actually solve anything. I didn't realise until now that I'm in a rut. I haven't dated for months. All I do is work. It's so easy to rely on you if I have to go anywhere I need a date that I've quit looking for anyone else.'

'What are you saying?'

She sighed.

'Just that meeting Alistair has opened my eyes to what I've been missing. And I really think our agreement is holding us both back.'

'Alistair?'

'His name is Alistair Woods.'

He easily dismissed the image that zipped into his brain of the blond ex-international cycling star, because it had to be a coincidence. Emma didn't know anyone like *that*. He would know if she did. Except she was waiting, lips slightly parted, eyebrows slightly raised. Everything about her expression told him she was waiting for him to catch on.

'Not *the* Alistair Woods?' he said, because she so obviously wanted him to.

He stole a glance across at her and the smile that lit up her face caused a sorry twist somewhere deep in his stomach. It was a smile he couldn't remember seeing for the longest time—not since they'd first met.

The glance turned into a look for as long as safe driving would allow, during which he saw her with an unusually objective eye, noticing details that had passed him by before. The hint of colour touching the smooth high cheekbones, the soft fullness of her lower lip, the way tendrils of her dark hair curled softly against the creamy skin of her shoulders in the boat-neck dress. She looked absolutely radiant and his stomach gave a slow and unmistakable flip, adding to his sense of unreality.

'Exactly,' she said with a touch of triumph. 'The cyclist. Well, ex-cyclist. He's in TV now—he does presenting and commentating.'

Of course he did. His face had been a permanent media fixture during the last big sports event in the UK. Dan felt a sudden irrational aversion to the man, whom he'd never met.

'*You're* dating Alistair Woods?'

He failed to keep the incredulity out of his voice and it earned him a flash of anger that replaced her bubbling excitement like a flood of cold water.

'No need to make it sound so unbelievable,' she snapped. 'You might only see me as some power suit, great for taking on the difficult dates when one of your five-minute conquests won't make the right impression, but I do actually have a dual existence. As a woman.'

'How long have you been seeing him?' he said.

'What are you? My father?' she said. 'We've been out a few times.'

'How many is a few?'

'Half a dozen, maybe.'

'You're ending our agreement on the strength of half a dozen dates?'

'Yes, well, they weren't dates in the way you think of them. He hasn't just invited me out for an impressive dinner as a preamble to taking me to bed. You can actually get to know someone really well in half a dozen dates if you approach them in a more...*serious* way.'

The thinly veiled dig didn't escape him and indignation sharpened his voice.

'OK, then, if he's so bloody marvellous, and you're so bloody smitten, why the hell isn't *he* on his way to look at your brother's wacky paintings and meet the parents? Couldn't you have dumped me on the phone and saved me a load of time and hassle?'

He pulled the car to a standstill outside the gallery steps and turned off the engine.

'I'm not dumping you! How many times? It's a *fake* relationship!'

A uniformed attendant opened Emma's car door and she got out. Dan threw his keys to the parking valet and joined her on the steps.

'So you keep saying,' he said, keeping his voice low. 'I could have spent this evening working.'

'Like you don't spend enough of your life doing that.' She led the way through the high arched doorway into the gallery. 'You can easily afford an evening. Alistair's out of the country until next week, and I need this opportunity to draw a thick, black and irreversible line under the two of us for my parents' eyes and undo the tissue of fibs I've told them.'

They walked slowly down the red-carpeted hallway, his hand pressed softly at the small of her back—the perfect escort as always.

'I really don't see why I need to be there for you to do that,' he said, smiling politely at other guests as they passed, maintaining the perfect impression. 'Especially since it's only a *fake* relationship.'

Even as he piled heavy sarcasm on the word *fake* he wondered why the hell he was turning this into such a big deal. Why should he care? It had simply been a handy arrangement, nothing more.

'Because the problem with it being a fake relationship

is that it was a pretty damn perfect one,' she snapped. 'And so now I need a fake break-up.'

She outlined her suggestion as they walked down the hall and it sounded so insane that his mind had trouble processing it.

'You can't possibly be serious. You want to fake an argument in front of your family so you can make some kind of a righteous point by dumping me?'

'Exactly! Shouldn't be too hard. I'll choose a moment, start picking on you, and then you just play along.'

'Why can't you just tell them we broke up? That things didn't work out?' He ran an exasperated hand through his hair. 'Why do I need to be here at all?'

'Because I've spent the last year building you up as Mr Perfect, bigging you up at every opportunity. You've no idea what it was like before we started helping each other out. The constant questions about why I was still single, the hassle about my body clock careering towards a standstill, the negativity about my career. Introducing you as my boyfriend stopped all that like magic. They think you're the son-in-law of their dreams—a rich businessman who adores me, good-looking, charming, not remotely fazed by my mother. They'll never just take my word for it that we broke up amicably. I'd spend the rest of my days being questioned about what I did to drive you away. You'd be forever name-dropped as the one that got away. No man I bring home would ever live up to your perfect memory.'

'You don't think you're going a bit overboard?'

'Are you really asking me that? You've met my mother. You know what she's like.'

He had to concede that Emma's mother was without a doubt the most interfering person he'd ever come across, with an opinion about everything that was never wrong. Her relationship with Emma seemed to bring out the critic in both of them. Mutual exasperated affection was probably the nearest he could get to describing it.

'This way your fabulous reputation will be ruined, by the time Alistair and I finish our trip to the States you'll be a distant memory, and they'll be ready to accept him as my new man.' She shrugged. 'Once I've...you know... *briefed* him on what they can be like.'

Trip to the States? His hands felt clammy. He stopped outside the main gallery and pulled her to one side before they could get swept into the room by the crowd.

'You're going on holiday?'

She looked at him impatiently.

'In a few weeks' time, yes. I'm going to meet some of his friends and family. And then after that I'm going to travel with him in Europe while he covers an international cycling race for American TV. I'm taking a sabbatical from work. I might not even come back.'

'What?' His mind reeled. 'You're giving up your life as you know it on the strength of a few dates? Are you mad?'

'That's exactly it! When do I *ever* do anything impetuous? It isn't as if sensible planning has worked out so well for me, is it? I work all hours and I have no social life to speak of beyond filling in for you. What exactly have I got to lose?'

'What about your family?'

'I'm hardly going to be missed, am I? My parents are so busy following Adam's ascent to celebrity status with his art that they're not going to start showing an interest in my life.'

She leaned in towards him and lowered her voice, treating him to the dizzying scent of her vanilla perfume.

'One of his pictures went for five figures last month, you know. Some anonymous buyer, apparently. But two words about *my* work and they start to glaze over.'

She leaned back again and took a small mirror from her clutch bag.

'And you'll be fine, of course,' she went on, opening the mirror and checking her face in it, oblivious to his floundering brain. 'You must have a whole little black book of girls who'd fall over themselves to step into my shoes. You're hardly going to be stuck for a date.'

True enough. He might, however, be stuck for a date who made the right kind of impression. Wasn't that how this whole agreement of theirs had started? He didn't go in for dating with a serious slant—not any more. Not since Maggie and...

He clenched his fists. Even after all these years thoughts of her and their failed plans occasionally filtered into his mind, despite the effort he put into forgetting them. There was no place for those memories in his life. These days for him it was all about keeping full control. Easy fun, then moving on. Unfortunately the girls who fitted that kind of mould didn't have the right fit in work circles. Emma had filled that void neatly, meaning he could bed whoever the hell he liked because he had her for the serious stuff—the stuff where impressions counted.

It occurred to him for the first time that she wouldn't just be across London if he needed her. He felt oddly unsettled as she tugged at his arm and walked towards the main door.

'You've had some mad ideas in your time, but this...' he said.

* * *

As they entered the main gallery Emma paused to take in the enormity of what her brother had achieved. The vast room had a spectacular landing running above it, from which the buzzing exhibition could be viewed. It had been divided into groupings by display screens, on which Adam's paintings—some of them taller than her—were picked out in pools of perfect clear lighting. A crowd of murmuring spectators surrounded the nearest one, which depicted an enormous eyeball with tiny cavorting people in the centre of it. His work might not be her cup of tea, but it certainly commanded attention and evoked strong opinions. Just the way he always had done.

She took two crystal flutes of champagne from the silver tray of a pretty blonde attendant, who looked straight through her to smile warmly at Dan. For heaven's sake, was no woman immune? Emma handed him one of the flutes and he immediately raised it to the blonde girl.

'Thanks very much…' He leaned in close so he could read the name tag conveniently pinned next to a cleavage Emma could only ever dream of owning. 'Hannah…'

He returned the girl's smile. Emma dragged him away. Why was she even surprised? Didn't she know him well enough by now? No woman was safe.

Correction: no curvy blonde arm candy was safe.

'For Pete's sake, pay attention,' she said in a stage whisper. 'You're meant to be here with me, not eyeing up the staff.'

She linked her arm through his so she could propel him through the crowd to find her parents. It wasn't difficult. Her mother had for some insane reason chosen to wear a wide flowing scarf wrapped around her head and tied to one side. Emma headed through the crowd, aiming for it—aqua silk with a feather pin stuck in it on one side. As her parents fell into possible earshot she pasted on a smile and talked through her beaming teeth.

'They'll never just take my word for it that we've just gone our separate ways. Not without a massive inquest. And I can't be doing with that. Trust me, it'll work better this way. It's cleaner. Just go with everything I say.'

She speeded up the end of the sentence as her mother approached.

'And you don't need to worry,' she added from the corner of her mouth. 'I'll pay for the dry-cleaning.'

'You'll what? What the hell is *that* supposed to mean?'

He turned his face towards her, a puzzled frown lightly creasing his forehead, and his eyes followed her hand as she raised her flute of champagne, ready to tip the contents over his head. She saw his blue eyes widen in sudden understanding and realised far too late that she'd totally underestimated his reflexes.

Dan's hand shot out instantly to divert hers, knocking it to one side in a single lightning movement. And instead of providing the explosive beginning to her staged *we're finished* argument, the glass jerked sharply sideways and emptied itself in a huge splash down the front of her mother's aquamarine jumpsuit. She stared in horror as champagne soaked into the fabric, lending it a translucent quality that revealed an undergarment not unlike a parachute harness.

She'd inadvertently turned her mother into Miss Wet T-Shirt, London. And if she'd been a disappointing daughter before, this bumped things up to a whole new level.

CHAPTER TWO

'Aaaaargh!'

The ensuing squawk from Emma's mother easily out-did the gallery's classy background music, and Dan was dimly aware of the room falling silent around them as people turned from the paintings to watch.

'An accident—it was an accident...' Emma gabbled, fumbling with a pack of tissues from her tiny clutch bag and making a futile attempt at mopping up the mess.

As her father shook a handkerchief from his pocket and joined in, her mother slapped his hand away in exasperation.

'It'll take more than a few tissues,' she snarled furiously at him, and then turned on Emma. 'Do you know how much this outfit *cost*? How am I meant to stand next to your brother in the publicity photos now? I've never known anyone so *clumsy*.'

Emma's face was the colour of beetroot, but any sympathy Dan might have felt was rather undermined by the revelation that she'd intended, without so much as a word of warning, to make a fool of him in front of the cream of London's social scene. *That* was her plan? *That?* Dumping him publicly by humiliating him? If he hadn't caught on in time it would have been him standing there dripping Veuve Clicquot while she no doubt laid into him with a ludicrous fake argument.

No one dumped him. *Ever*.

'An accident?' he said pointedly.

She glanced towards him, her red face one enormous fluster. He raised furious eyebrows and mouthed the word *dry-cleaning* at her. She widened her eyes back at him in an apologetic please-stick-to-the-plan gesture.

Emma's brother, Adam, pushed his way through the crowd, turning perfectly coiffed heads as he went, dandyish as ever in a plum velvet jacket with a frothy lace shirt underneath. There was concern in his eyes behind his statement glasses.

'What's going on, people?' he said, staring in surprise at his mother as she shrugged her way into her husband's jacket and fastened the buttons grimly to hide the stain.

'Your sister has just flung champagne *all over me*,' she snapped dramatically, then raised both hands as Adam opened his mouth to speak. 'No, no, don't you go worrying about it, I'm not going anywhere. I wouldn't *hear* of it. This is your night. I'm not going to let the fact that my outfit is *decimated* ruin that. I'll soldier on, just like I always do.'

'I've said I'm sorry. I'll pay for the dry-cleaning,' Emma said desperately.

Dan's anger slipped a notch as he picked up on her discomfort. Only a notch, mind you. OK, so maybe he wouldn't have it out with her in public, but he would most certainly be dealing with her later.

Emma closed her eyes briefly. When did it end? Would everything she ever did in life, good or bad, be somehow referenced by Adam's success? Then again, since her mother was already furious with her, she might as well press ahead with the planned mock break-up. Maybe then at least the evening wouldn't be a total write-off.

She drew Dan aside by the elbow as Adam drifted away again, back to his adoring public.

'We can still do it,' she said. 'We can still stage the break-up.'

He stared at her incredulously.

'Are you having some kind of a laugh?' he snapped. 'When you said you needed a fake break-up I wasn't expecting it to involve my public humiliation. You were going to lob that drink over *me,* for heaven's sake, and now you think I'll just agree to a rerun?'

She opened her mouth to respond and he cut her off.

'There are people I *know* in here,' he said in a furious stage whisper, nodding around them at the crowd. 'What kind of impression do you think that would have given them?'

'I didn't expect things to get so out of hand,' she said. 'I just thought we'd have a quick mock row in front of my parents and that would be it.'

'You didn't even warn me!'

'I didn't want to lose the element of surprise. I wanted to make it look, you know, *authentic.*'

He stared at her in disbelief.

There was the squeal of whiny microphone feedback and Adam appeared on the landing above the gallery. Emma looked up towards her brother, picked out in a pool of light in front of a billboard with his own name on it in six-foot-tall violet letters. She felt overshadowed, as always, by his brilliance. Just as she had done at school. But now it was on a much more glamorous level. No wonder her legal career seemed drab in comparison.

No wonder her parents were expecting her to give it all up at any moment to get married and give them grand-children. Adam was far too good for such normal, bor-ing life plans.

His voice began to boom over the audio system, thanking everyone for coming and crediting a list of people she'd never heard of with his success.

'I can't believe you'd make a scene like that without considering what effect it might have on me,' Dan said, anger still lacing his voice.

The blonde champagne waitress chose that moment to walk past them. Emma watched as Dan's gaze flickered away from her to follow the woman's progress and the grovelling apology she'd been about to give screeched to a halt on the tip of her tongue. Just who the hell did he think he was, moaning about being dumped, when *his* relationship principles were pretty much in the gutter? OK, so they might not have actually *been* a couple, but she'd seen the trail of broken hearts he left in his wake. He had no relationship scruples whatsoever. One girl fol-lowed another. And as soon as he'd got what he wanted he lost interest and dumped them. As far as she knew he'd never suffered a moment's comeback as a result.

Maybe this new improved Emma, with her stupid un-requited girlie crush on Dan well and truly in the past, had a duty to press that point on behalf of womankind.

'Oh, get over yourself,' she said, before she could change her mind. 'I'd say a public dumping was prob-ably long overdue. It's just that none of your conquests have had the nous or the self-respect to do it before. There's probably a harem of curvy blonde waitresses and models who've thought about lobbing a drink over you when you've chucked them just because you're bored.

And I didn't actually spill a drop on you, so let's just move on, shall we?'

Adam smiled and laughed his way back through the crowd towards them, and she seized the opportunity as he neared her proudly beaming parents.

'Same plan as before, minus the champagne. I'll start picking on you and...'

The words trailed away in her mouth as Adam clamped one arm around Dan's shoulders and one around her own.

'Got some news for you all—gather round, gather round,' he said.

As her parents moved in closer, questioning expressions on their faces, he raised both hands in a gesture of triumph above his head.

'Be happy for me, people!'

He performed a jokey pirouette and finished with a manic grin and jazz hands.

'Ernie and I are getting married!'

Beaming at them, he slid his velvet-sleeved arm around his boyfriend and pulled him into a hot kiss.

Her mother's gasp of shock was audible above the cheers. And any plans Emma might have had of staging a limelight-stealing break-up went straight back to the drawing board.

Emma watched the buzzing crowd of people now surrounding Adam and Ernie, showering them with congratulations, vaguely relieved that she hadn't managed to dispense with Dan after all. From the tense look on her parents' faces, as they stood well away from the throng, dealing with the fallout from Adam's announcement wasn't going to be easy. And despite the fact that it was a setback in her plans to introduce Alistair, there was no doubt that her mother was much easier to handle when she had Dan in her corner.

Dealing with her parents without him was something she hadn't had to do in so long that she hadn't realised how she'd come to rely on his calming presence. They might have only been helping each other out, but Dan had had her back where her family were concerned. And he'd never been remotely fazed by her overbearing mother and downtrodden father.

She wondered for the first time with a spike of doubt whether Alistair would be as supportive as that. Or would he let her family cloud his judgement of her? What was that saying? *Look at the mother if you want to see your future wife.* If that theory held up she might as well join a nunnery. Alistair would be out of her life before she could blink.

She couldn't let herself think like that.

Calling a halt with Dan was clearly the right thing to do if she was so ridiculously dependent on him that she could no longer handle her family on her own. But she couldn't ruin Adam's excitement. Not tonight. She'd simply have to reschedule things.

And in the meantime at least she wasn't handling her mother's shock by herself. She took a new flute of champagne gratefully from Dan and braced herself with a big sip.

'I'm sure it must just be a publicity stunt,' her mother was saying.

Denial. Her mother's stock reaction to news she didn't want to hear.

'It's not a publicity stunt,' Adam said. 'We're getting married.'

He beamed at Ernie, standing beside him in a slim-cut electric blue suit. He certainly *looked* the perfect match for Adam.

Her mother's jaw didn't even really drop. Disbelief was so ingrained in her.

'Don't be ridiculous, darling,' she said, flicking an invisible speck of dirt from Adam's lapel. 'Of course you're not.'

Adam's face took on the stoic expression of one who knew he would need to press the point more than once in order to be heard. Possibly a few hundred times.

'It's the next logical step,' he said.

'In what?' Her mother flapped a dismissive hand. 'It's just a phase. You'll soon snap out of it once the right girl comes along. Bit like Emma with her vegetarian thing back in the day.' She nodded at Emma. 'Soon went back to normal after a couple of weeks when she fancied a bacon sandwich.'

'Mum,' Adam said patiently, 'Emma was thirteen. I'm twenty-nine. Ernie and I have been together for nearly a year.'

'I know. Sharing a flat. Couple of lads. No need to turn it into more than it is.'

Emma stared as Adam finally raised his voice enough to make her mother stop talking.

'Mum, you're in denial!'

As she stopped her protests and looked at him he took a deep breath and lowered his voice, speaking with the tired patience of someone who'd covered the same ground many times, only to end up where he'd started.

'I've been out since I was eighteen. I know you've never wanted to accept it, but the right girl for me *doesn't exist.* We're having a civil partnership ceremony in six weeks' time and I want you all to be there and be happy for me.'

'I'm happy for you,' Emma said, smiling tentatively.

Happiness she could do. Unfortunately being at the wedding might be a bit trickier. Her plans with Alistair lurked at the edge of her mind. She'd been so excited about going away with him. He'd showered her with gifts and attention, and for the first time in her life she was being blown away by being the sole focus of another person. And not just any person. Alistair Woods had to be one of the most eligible bachelors in the universe, with an army of female fans, and he had chosen to be with *her*. She still couldn't quite believe her luck. Their trip was planned to the hilt. She would have to make Adam understand somehow.

He leaned in and gave her a hug. 'Thanks, Em.'

She had grown up feeling overshadowed by Adam's achievements. Just the look of him was attention-grabbing, with his perfectly chiselled features and foppish dress sense. And that was just now. She couldn't forget the school years, where for every one of Emma's hard-earned A grades there had been a matching two or three showered effortlessly on Adam. His flamboyant, outgoing personality charmed everyone he came into contact with, and her mother never ceased championing his successes to anyone who would listen.

It hadn't been easy being her parents' Plan B. Competing for their interest with someone as dazzling as Adam was an impossible, cold task.

'I blame you for this, Donald,' her mother snapped at her father. 'Indulging his ridiculous obsession with musical theatre when he was in his teens.'

Sometimes Emma forgot that being her parents' Plan A was probably no picnic either.

Adam held up his hands.

'Please, Mum. It's not up for discussion. It's happening with or without your approval. Can't you just be pleased for us?'

There was an extremely long pause and then her mother gave an enormous grudging sigh.

'Well, I can kiss goodbye to grandchildren, I suppose,' she grumbled. 'We'll have to count on you for that now, Emma. *If* you can ever manage to find a man who'll commit.'

She glared pointedly at Dan, who totally ignored the jibe. Emma had been wondering how long it would be before her biological clock got a mention. Terrific. So now Adam could carve out the life he wanted without bearing the brunt of her parents' wrath because they had Emma lined up as their biological backup plan to carry on their insane gene pool.

Going away with Alistair was beginning to feel like a lucky escape. She just needed to get her plans back on track.

Dan scanned an e-mail for the third time and realised he still hadn't properly taken it in. His mind had been all over the place this last day or two.

Since the night of Adam's exhibition, to be exact.

There was a gnawing feeling deep in his gut that work didn't seem to be suppressing, and he finally threw in the towel on distracting himself, took his mind off work and applied it to the problem instead.

He was piqued because Emma had ended things with him. OK, so her plans to dump him publicly hadn't come off, thankfully, but the end result was the same. She'd drawn a line under their relationship without so much as a moment's pause and he hadn't heard from her since. No discussion, no input from him.

He was even more piqued because now it was over with he really shouldn't give a damn. They were friends, work colleagues, and that was all there was to it. Their romantic attachment existed only in the impression they'd given to the outside world, to work contacts and her family. It had always been a front.

His pique had absolutely nothing to do with any sudden realisation that Emma was attractive. He'd always *known* she was attractive. Dan Morgan wouldn't be seen dating a moose, even for business reasons. That didn't mean she was his type, though——not with her dark hair and minimal make-up, and her conservative taste in clothes. And that in turn had made it easy to pigeonhole her as friend. A proper relationship with someone like Emma would be complex, would need commitment, compromise, emotional investment. All things he wasn't prepared to give another woman. Tried, tested and failed. Dan Morgan learned from his mistakes and never repeated his failures.

It had quickly become clear that Emma was far more useful to him in the role of friend than love interest, and all thoughts of attraction had been relegated from that moment onwards. It had been so long now that not noticing the way she looked was second nature.

But the gnawing feeling in his gut was there nonetheless. Their romantic relationship might have been counterfeit, but some element of it had obviously been real enough to make the dumping feel extremely uncomfortable.

He'd never been dumped before. *He* was the one who did the backing off. That was the way he played it. A couple of dinner dates somewhere nice, the second one generally ending up in his bed, a couple more dates and then, when the girl started to show signs of getting comfortable—maybe she'd start leaving belongings in his flat, or perhaps she'd suggest he meet her family—he'd simply go into backing-off mode. It wasn't as if he lied to them about his intentions. He was careful always to make it clear from the outset that he wasn't in the market for anything serious. He was in absolute control at all times—just as he was in every aspect of his life. That was the way he wanted it. The way he *needed* it.

He was amazed at how affronted he felt by the apparent ease with which Emma had dispensed with him. Not an ounce of concern for how *he* might feel as she'd planned to trounce him spectacularly in front of all those people. His irritation at her unbelievable fake break-up plan was surpassed only by his anger with himself for actually giving a damn.

Feeling low at being dumped meant you had feelings for the person dumping you. Didn't it?

Unease flared in his gut at that needling thought, because Dan Morgan didn't *do* deep feelings. That slippery slope led to dark places he had no intention of revisiting. He did fun, easy, no-strings flings. Feelings need not apply. Surely hurt feelings should only apply where a relationship was bona fide. Fake relationships should mean fake feelings, and fake feelings couldn't be hurt.

That sensation of spinning back in time made him feel faintly nauseous. Here it was again—like an irritating old acquaintance you think you've cut out of your life who then pops back up unexpectedly for a visit.

That reeling loss of control he'd felt in the hideous few months after Maggie had left, walking away with apparent ease from the ruins of their relationship. He'd made sure he retained the upper hand in all dealings with women since. These days every situation worked for *him*. No emotion involved. No risk. His relationships were orchestrated by *him,* no one else. That way he could be sure of every outcome.

But not this time. Their agreement had lasted— what?—a year? And in that time she'd never once refused a date with him. Even when he'd needed an escort at the last minute she'd changed her schedule to accommodate him. He'd relied on her because he'd learned that he *could* rely on her.

And so he hadn't seen it coming. That was why it gnawed at him like this.

You don't like losing her. You thought you had her on your own terms. You took her for granted and now you don't like the feeling that she's calling the shots.

He gritted his teeth. This smacked a bit too much of the past for comfort. It resurrected old feelings that he had absolutely no desire to recall, and he apparently couldn't let it slide. What he needed to do now was get this thing back under his own control.

Well, she hadn't gone yet. And he didn't have to just *take* her decision. If this agreement was going to end it would be when *he* chose—not on some whim of hers. He could talk her round if he wanted to. It wouldn't be hard. And then *he* would decide where their partnership went.

If it went anywhere at all.

He pulled his chair back close to the desk and pressed a few buttons, bringing up his calendar for the next couple of weeks with a stab of exasperation. Had she no idea of the inconvenience she'd thrust upon him?

Not only had Emma dumped him, she'd really picked a great moment to do it. *Not.* The black tie charity dinner a week away hadn't crossed his mind the other evening when she had dropped her bombshell. It hadn't needed to. Since he'd met Emma planning for events like that had been a thing of the past. He simply called her up, sometimes at no more than a moment's notice, and he could count on the perfect companion on his arm— perfect respect for the dress code, perfect intelligent conversation, an all-round perfect professional impression. There was some serious networking to be had at such an event, the tickets had cost a fortune, and now he was dateless.

He reached for the phone.

It rang for so long that he was on the brink of hanging up when she answered.

'Hello?' Her slightly husky voice sounded breathless, as if she'd just finished laughing at something, and he could hear music and buzzing talk in the background, as if she were in a crowded bar or restaurant.

From nowhere three unheard-of things flashed through his mind in quick succession. Emma never socialised on a work night unless she was with him; she never let her phone ring for long when he called her, as if she was eager to talk to him; and in the time that he'd known her she had never sounded this bubblingly happy.

'What are you doing a week from Friday?' he said, cutting to the chase.

'Hang on.'

A brief pause on the end of the phone and the blaring music was muted a little. He imagined her leaving the bar or the restaurant she was in for a quiet spot, perhaps in the lobby. He sensed triumph already, knowing that she was leaving whoever she was with to make time to speak with *him*.

'Tying up loose ends at work, probably. And packing.'

So she was storming ahead with her plans, then. The need for control spiked again in his gut. He went in with the big guns.

'I've got a charity ball in Mayfair. Black tie. Major league. Tickets like hen's teeth. It promises to be a fabulous night.'

He actually heard her sigh. With impatience, or with longing at the thought of attending the ball with him? He decided it was definitely the latter. She'd made no secret of the fact she enjoyed the wonderful opulence of nights like that, and he knew she'd networked a good few new clients for herself in the past while she was accompanying him—another perk of their plus-one agreement.

For Pete's sake, she had him giving it that ludicrous name now.

Their usual dates consisted of restaurant dinners with his clients. Pleasant, but hardly exciting. Except for Dan's own company, of course. Luxury events like this only came up occasionally. He waited for her to tear his arm off in her eagerness to accept.

'What part of "it's over" did you not understand, Dan?' she said. 'Did you not hear any of what I said the other night?'

It took a moment to process what she'd said because he had been so convinced of her acceptance.

'What I heard was some insane plan to desert your whole life as you know it for some guy you've known five minutes,' he heard himself say. 'You're talking about leaving your friends and family, walking out of a job you've worked your arse off for, all to follow some celebrity.'

'It would be a sabbatical from work,' she said. 'I'm not burning my bridges there. Not yet. And you make me sound like some crazy stalker. We're in a relationship. A proper grown-up one, not a five-minute fling.'

He didn't miss the obvious dig at his own love life, and it made his response more cutting than he intended.

'On the strength of—what was it?—*half a dozen dates?*' he said. 'I always thought you were one of the most grounded people I know. You're the last person in the world I'd have expected to be star-struck.'

He knew from the freezing silence on the end of the phone that he'd sunk his foot into his own mouth up to the ankle.

'How dare you?' she said, and a light tremble laced her voice, which was pure frost. 'It was obviously too much to hope that you might actually be *pleased* for me. Yes, Alistair is in the public eye, but that has *nothing* to do with why I've agreed to go away with him. Has it occurred to you that I might actually like him because he's interested in *me* for a change? As opposed to the grandchildren I might bear him or the fact I might be his carer when he's old and decrepit. Or...' she added pointedly '...the fact that I might boost his profile at some damned work dinner so he can extend his client list a bit further because he never quite feels he's rich or successful enough.'

She paused.

'You're saying no, then?' he said. 'To the all-expenses-paid top-notch Mayfair ball?'

He heard her draw in a huge breath and then she let

it out in a rude, exasperated noise. He held the phone briefly away from his ear. When he put it back her voice was Arctic.

'Dan,' she was saying slowly, as if he had a problem understanding plain English, 'I'm saying no to the Mayfair ball. I'm through with posing as your professional romantic interest so you can impress your damned client list while you date airhead models for a week at a time.'

Had he really thought this would be easy? It occurred to him that in reality she couldn't be further from one of his usual conquests, of which currently there were two or three, any of whom would drop everything else at a moment's notice if he deigned to call them up and suggest getting together.

You didn't get as far up the legal career ladder as she had by being a 'yes' girl. But her easy refusal bothered the hell out of him. He'd expected her to agree to resurrect their agreement without even needing persuasion. Had expected her to thank him, in fact.

The need to win back control rose another notch with her unexpected refusal of his offer, and also her apparent indifference to it. It put his teeth on edge and gnawed at him deep inside.

'How about helping me out with this one last time, then?' he pressed, confident that in an evening he could quickly turn the situation around. Reinstate their agreement and then decide what he wanted to do with it. End it, change the terms—whatever happened it would be up to him to decide, *not* her.

'Dan, you don't need my help,' she said patiently. 'I'm in the middle of dinner and I haven't got time to discuss this now. It's not as if you're short of dates. Grab your little black book and pick one of your girlies from there. I'm sure any one of them would love to go with you.'

There was a soft click on the end of the phone as she hung up.

That went well. *Not*.

CHAPTER THREE

'LET ME JUST recap. You're in a relationship with Alistair Woods—*the* Alistair Woods, the man who looks a dream in Lycra—and you're not planning on mentioning it to Mum and Dad?'

Adam's eyebrows practically disappeared into his sleek quiff hairstyle and Emma took a defensive sip of coffee. The fantasy she'd had of disappearing around the world on Alistair's arm and calling up her parents from Cannes/LA/somewhere else that screamed kudos, to tell them she would be featuring in next month's celebrity magazine, had turned out to be just that. A fantasy.

Because Adam was getting married.

Her big brother, Adam—who never failed to make her laugh, and who was so bright and sharp and funny that she'd never for a moment questioned her role in family life as the forgettable backing act to his flamboyant scene-stealer. Of *course* she had paled into insignificance in her family's eyes next to Adam—not to mention in the eyes of schoolteachers, friends, neighbours… But only in the way that everyone else had faded into the background next to him in her own eyes. He was simply someone who commanded success and attention without needing to put in any effort.

She couldn't exit her life without telling Adam, and she'd asked him to meet her for coffee to do exactly that. She'd even tried to sweeten the news by buying him an enormous cream bun, which now sat between them untouched. If she'd thought he'd simply scoff the bun and wave her off without so much as a question, she'd been deluded.

'You're not going yet, though, right? You're at least waiting until after the wedding?'

'Erm…'

He threw his arms up theatrically.

'Em! You can't be serious! How the hell am I going to keep Mum under control without you? I can't get married without my wingman!'

'Woman,' she corrected.

He flapped both hands at her madly.

'Whatever. You saw what Mum was like the other night. The wedding is in Ernie's home village. He's got a massive family, they're all fabulously supportive, and if you don't come along our family's big impression on them will be Mum telling everyone I'll get over it when I get bored with musical theatre and meet the right girl.'

'Dad will be there,' she ventured. 'Maybe you could talk to him beforehand, get him to keep Mum on a short leash.'

'He'd be as much use as a chocolate teapot. We both know he's been beaten into submission over the years. Since when has Mum ever listened to him? She just talks over him. I *need* you there.'

His voice had taken on a pleading tone.

'It's not as simple as that. Alistair's covering another cycling race in a few weeks' time. We're meant to be having a break before it starts because it's pretty full-on. I'm flying out to the States, meeting some of his friends and family, relaxing for a couple of weeks. It's all been arranged.'

She looked down at her coffee cup because she couldn't bear the disappointment on Adam's face.

Adam had never made her feel insignificant. Any inability to measure up was her failing, not his. And she was the one who let it bother her.

'Then there's no problem! Bring Alistair to the wedding,' Adam said, clapping his hands together excitedly. 'You've already said he's got time off from work. The guy's probably got a private jet. You could zoom in and zoom out on the same day if you had to.' He made a soaring aeroplane motion in the air with his hand.

She suppressed a mirthless laugh.

'You mean introduce him to Mum and Dad? A whole new person for Mum to drive insane?' She narrowed suspicious eyes at him. 'It would certainly take the heat off you and Ernie.'

He held his hands up.

'You'll have to introduce him at some point anyway. OK, so you might travel with him for a while, maybe even settle in the States with him, but you'll have to come home to visit, won't you?'

She didn't answer. Visiting wasn't something she'd thought about much in her excitement about getting away. It hadn't crossed her mind that she'd be missed that much.

'Bloody hell, Em.'

She sighed. She couldn't say no to Adam any more than the rest of the world could. He just had that gift.

'It'll be a nightmare if I bring Alistair,' she said. 'Mum will be all over him like a rash, demanding marriage and grandchildren and mentioning my biological clock. He's a free spirit. He'll run a bloody mile.'

Adam was on the comment like a shot.

'Then you definitely *should* bring him. You're talking about leaving your whole life behind to be with him— don't you think he ought to prove himself a bit before you take that kind of plunge? If he's really the guy you think he is—if he's really going to put you first above everything else in his life—then he'll love you no matter what crazy relative you introduce him to, right?'

She couldn't help latching on to that thought—that desire for a level of regard where she would come absolutely first with someone for a change. Was that what this was really about? Was she afraid to bring Alistair to the wedding because of some stupid subconscious conviction that he might see through her? Might see that she really was a plain and inferior mousy girl, despite all the years she'd put in on breaking away from that persona?

'He does love me,' she insisted, mainly to bat away the prickle of unease that had begun in her stomach. It was all Adam's fault for questioning her perfectly laid plans.

'Great. Then put your man where your mouth is. Introduce him to Mum and watch him prove it.'

Dan clicked his phone off with ill-suppressed irritation.

Cancelling a working lunch at a moment's notice was extremely bad form. Focused to a pinpoint on work performance himself, he found it difficult to tolerate lateness or bad planning in others. Especially when it meant he'd interrupted his day to turn up at a restaurant when he could have eaten lunch on the run or at his desk.

He gave the menu an uninterested glance and was on

the point of calling for the bill for the two drinks he'd ordered while waiting for the no-show client when he saw Emma cross the restaurant. A waiter showed her to a table by the window and she sat down alone, so engrossed in scrolling through her phone that she didn't even notice he was in the room.

The news that she was leaving seemed to have given him a new heightened perspective, and he picked up on tiny details about her that had simply passed him by before. He saw her objectively for once, as someone else might. Alistair Woods, for example. This time his gaze skimmed over her usual business dress when previously it would have stopped at observing the sharply cut grey suit. Instead he now noticed how slender she was. How had he never picked up before on the striking contrast of her double cream skin with her dark hair? The ripe fullness of her lower lip? When you had reason to look past the sensible work image she was unexpectedly cute. He'd been so busy taking her presence for granted he'd failed to notice any of those things.

Maybe this lunchtime wouldn't be a total waste of time after all. Dealing with her on the phone had been a bad choice. A face-to-face meeting might be a better approach to talking sense into her.

He picked up his drink and crossed the room towards her. His stomach gave a sudden flutter that made him pause briefly en route to the table—then he remembered that it was lunchtime. He was obviously just hungry, and since he was here maybe he should take the chance to grab a sandwich as well as a drink and a smoothing-over session with her. Not that his appetite had been up to much this last week or so.

'Dan!'

Her eyes widened in surprise as he slid into the seat opposite her and put his drink down on the table. She glanced quickly around the restaurant, presumably for a waiter.

'Really glad I bumped into you,' he said. 'Just wanted to say no hard feelings about the other night.'

A smile touched the corner of her lips, drawing his eyes there. She was wearing a light pink lipstick that gave them a delectable soft sheen.

'The other night?' she said.

'The charity ball.'

'I hadn't realised there *could* be hard feelings,' she said, toying with her water glass. 'It was just a work arrangement we had after all, right? Not like I broke off a date, is it?'

She held his gaze steadily and for the first time it occurred to him that it might take a bit more than sweet-talking for him to regain the advantage between them. His own fault, of course. He was judging her by the standards of his usual dates, who seemed to fall over themselves to hang on his every word. Emma was a different ball game altogether. Taking her for granted had been a mistake.

He gestured to the waiter for a menu.

'How did it go, then?' she said.

'How did what go?' he evaded.

'The charity ball?' she said. 'No-expenses-spared Mayfair hotel, wasn't it? Who did you take?'

'Eloise,' he said shortly.

She had to bring it up, didn't she? When what he'd really like would be to erase the entire evening from history.

'Which one's that?'

She cranked her hand in a come-on gesture and looked at him expectantly until he elaborated.

'She's a leg model,' he said. 'You know—tights, stockings, that kind of thing.'

The woman had the best legs in the business. Unfortunately she was entirely defined by that one physical feature. Tact, sense and reliability didn't come into it.

'Did you make any new contacts?' Emma said. 'Normally charity bashes are great for networking, aren't they? Perfect opportunity for a shared goal, loads of rich businessmen?'

'Normally they are,' he said. 'But normally I have you with me, oozing tact and diplomacy and class.'

It had been kind of hard to hold a professional conversation with Eloise's arms wound constantly around his neck like a long-legged monkey. The one time he had begun to make headway with a potential client she'd returned from the bar with two flutes of pink champagne and positioned herself between them by sitting on his lap.

He watched Emma carefully, to see if his compliment had hit its mark, and was rewarded with the lightest of rosy blushes touching her high cheekbones. Hah! Not so easily dismissed after all. A proper in-depth talk about her whirlwind plans and he was confident he could sow a few seeds of doubt. From there it would be a short step to convincing her to stay put, reinstating their working agreement, getting things back to normal.

He was giving her a quick follow-up smile when he realised her eyes were actually focused somewhere over his shoulder and the blush had nothing to do with him. A wide smile lit up her face and suddenly she was on her feet, being drawn into a kiss by a tall blond man with a

deep golden tan and perfect white teeth. No matter that
he was wearing a sharply cut designer suit and an open-
necked silk shirt instead of clinging Lycra cycling shorts
and a helmet. He was instantly recognisable—by Dan
and by the room at large.

Alistair Woods was on the premises.

The surrounding tables suddenly appeared to be filled
with rubberneckers. Clearly basking in the attention, he
offered a wave and a nod of greeting to the tables either
side of them before sitting down—as if he was a film
star instead of a has-been athlete. Dan felt an irrational
lurch of dislike for the guy, whom he'd never met before but who clearly made Emma brim with happiness.

Jealous? his mind whispered.

He dismissed the thought out of hand. This wasn't
about jealousy. Emma was clearly star-struck and on
the brink of making a rash decision that could ruin her
working life and her personal life before you could say
yellow jersey. If anything, he would be doing her a favour by bringing her back down to earth.

'Alistair, this is Dan,' Emma said, taking her seat
again, her hand entwined in Alistair's. 'Dan, this is
Alistair Woods.'

She glanced pointedly at Dan.

'Dan happened to be here meeting someone,' she said.
'He just came over to say hello.'

She didn't want him to join them. It couldn't be
clearer.

'Heard a lot about you, friend,' Alistair said in a
strong American accent, stretching in his seat. 'You're
the platonic plus-one, right?'

Of all the qualities he possessed that Emma could
choose to reference him by she'd chosen that. Just *great*.

'Did you get my phone message?' Emma asked Alistair eagerly. 'I know it means rejigging our plans a little, but I just can't let my brother down. It's his wedding day. And it'll be a good chance for you to meet my family.'

She was taking Alistair to Adam's civil partnership ceremony?

Dan felt a deep and lurching stab of misplaced envy at the thought of this guy slotting neatly into his recently vacated place—fake though it might have been—in regard to Emma's family. OK, so they were opinionated and mouthy, and in her mother's case that translated as being downright bigoted at times, but he'd never felt anything but welcomed by them, and their simple mad chaos had been something he'd enjoyed.

An unhappy flash of his own childhood rose in his mind. His mother, hardly more than a child herself. No father—at least not in any way that mattered to a kid. Plenty of 'uncles', though. He hadn't been short of those. And plenty of random babysitters—friends of his mother's, neighbours, hardly the same person twice. What he wouldn't have given for an interfering nosy mother at the age of thirteen, when babysitters had no longer been required and he'd been considered old enough to be left home alone.

He dismissed the thought. Things were different now. He'd learned to rely only on himself, without influence from anyone else. Maggie had been the one time he'd deviated from that course, and it had turned out to be an agonising mistake that he had no intention of repeating. He had no need for family. Past or future.

'Got your message, baby, but there's no way we're going to be able to make the gay wedding,' Alistair said.

Dan watched Emma's smile falter and suppressed an unexpected urge to grab Woods by the scruff of the neck.

'Why not?' she said. 'I can't miss Adam's wedding. I promised him.'

Dan recognised her tone as carefully neutral. She was upset and trying to cover it up. Did this Alistair know her well enough to pick up that little nuance? *Hardly.*

Emma took a sip of her coffee in an effort to hide her disappointment. Had she really thought it would be that simple? That he would just agree to her every whim?

'We're spending that weekend in the Hamptons,' Alistair was saying. 'I've been in talks to land a movie role and one of the producers is having a garden party. Can't miss it. Lots riding on it. I'm sure Arnold will understand. Career first, right?' He leaned in towards her with a winning expression and squeezed her hand. 'We agreed.'

His career first.

'Adam,' Emma corrected. She could hear the disappointment, cold and heavy, in her own voice. 'His name is Adam. And I really *can't* miss his wedding.'

Alistair sat back and released her hand, leaving it lying abandoned in the middle of the white tablecloth. His irritation was instant and palpable, and all the more of a shock because he'd never been anything but sweetness and light so far. But then, she hadn't demanded anything from him so far, had she? She'd been only too eager to go along for the ride. *His* ride.

'You do whatever you have to do, baby,' he said dismissively. 'You can fly out and join me afterwards.'

'But I really wanted you to be there, to meet my family.'

'Sorry, honey, no can do.'

Alistair turned to the waiter to order a drink. She noticed that Dan was looking at her with sympathy and she looked away. Everything was unravelling and it was a million times worse because he was here to witness it. She tried to muster up an attitude that might smother the churning disappointment in her stomach as her high hopes plummeted.

From the moment she'd met Alistair he had made her feel special, as if nothing was too much trouble for him. But it occurred to her that it had only related to peripheral things, like flowers and restaurants and which hotel they might stay in. Now it had come down to something that was truly important to her he hadn't delivered the goods. It wasn't even up for discussion. Because it clashed with his own plans.

Disappointment mingled hideously with exasperated disbelief. She felt like crashing her head down despairingly on the table. Would she ever, at any point in her life, meet someone who might actually put her first on their agenda? Or was this her lot? To make her way through life as some lower down priority?

'Look, I don't want to interfere,' Dan said suddenly, leaning forward. 'But how about I step in?'

'What do you mean, step in?' she asked, eyes narrowed.

Suspicion. Not a good sign, Dan thought. On the other hand Alistair was looking more than open to the suggestion.

Dispensing with Alistair to some swanky party on a different continent was far too good an opportunity to pass up. All he needed to do was step into Alistair's shoes as Emma's date and he'd have a whole weekend to make her rethink her actions and to get the situation working for him again.

'I got my invitation to the wedding this morning,' he said, thinking of the gaudy card that had arrived in the post, with *'Groom & Groom!'* plastered across the front in bright yellow, very much in keeping with Adam's usual in-your-face style.

'You've been invited?' she asked with obvious surprise, as if their interaction had been so fake that all the connections he'd made with her family were counterfeit, too. But he genuinely liked Adam—they'd always had a laugh.

'Yes,' he said. 'So if Alistair is away working I can fill in if you like—escort you. It's not as if I haven't done it before. What do you think?'

She stared at him.

'For old times' sake?' he pressed. 'I'm sure Alistair won't mind.'

He glanced at the ex-cyclist, who held his hands up.

'Great idea!' he said. 'Problem solved.'

Emma's face was inscrutable.

'That won't be necessary,' she snapped. 'And actually, Dan, if you don't mind, we could do with a bit of time to talk this over.'

She looked at him expectantly and when he didn't move raised impatient eyebrows and nodded her head imperceptibly towards the door.

All was no longer peachy with her and Mr Perfect and that meant opportunity. He should be ecstatic. All he needed to do was leave them be and let the idiot drive a wedge between them, because one thing he knew about Emma was that her parents might drive her up the pole but Adam meant the world to her. Yet his triumph was somehow diluted by a surge of protectiveness towards Emma at Alistair's easy dismissal of her. He had to force himself not to give the smug idiot a piece of his mind.

He made himself stand up and excused himself from the table.

Give the guy enough leeway and he would alienate Emma all by himself. Dan could call her up later in the role of concerned friend and reinstate their agreement on his own terms.

Bumped to make room for Alistair's career?

Her mind insisted on recycling Adam's comments from the day before. *'Don't you think he ought to prove himself before you take that kind of plunge?'* Was it really so much to ask?

The insistent 'case closed' way Alistair had refused her suggestion told her far more about him than just his words alone, and it occurred to her in a crushing blow of clarity. How had she ever thought she would come first with someone who had an ego the size of Alistair's? An ego which was still growing, by the sound of it, if he was trying to break into the movies.

The waiter brought their food and she watched as Alistair tucked in with gusto to an enormous steak and side salad, oblivious to the fact that there was anything wrong between them. He'd got his own way. For him it was business as usual. His whole attitude now irked her. It was as if she should be somehow grateful for being invited along for the ride. She'd been too busy being swept away by the excitement of someone like him actually taking an interest in her to comprehend that being with him would mean giving up her life in favour of his. Where the hell did she come first in all of that?

It dawned on her that he'd have a lot of contractual issues coming his way with his broadening career. Was that what made her attractive to him? The way she dealt so efficiently with legal red tape on his behalf? Had he earmarked her as his own live-in source of legal advice?

This wasn't a relationship; it was an *agreement*. All she'd done was swap one for another. She could be Dan's platonic plus-one or Alistair's live-in lawyer. Where the hell was the place for what *she* wanted in any of that?

'It's all off, Alistair,' she said dully. It felt as if her voice was coming from somewhere else.

He peered at her hardly touched plate of food.

'What is, honey? The fish?'

He looked around for a waiter while she marvelled at his self-assurance that her sentence couldn't possibly relate to their relationship. Not in *his* universe. Alistair probably had a queue of women desperate to date him, all of them a zillion times more attractive than Emma. He had international travel, a beach home in Malibu, a little getaway in the Balearics, his own restaurant and a glittering media career in his corner. What the hell did she have that could compete with that? Interfering parents and a tiny flat in Putney? Why the hell would he think she might want to back out?

'Us,' she said. 'You and me. It's not going to work out.'

He gaped at her.

'Is this because I won't come to your gay brother's wedding? Honey, have you any idea how much is riding on this new contract? This is the next stage of my career we're talking about.' He shook his head at her in a gesture of amazement. 'The effort that's gone into lining up this meeting. I'm not cancelling that so you can show me off to your relatives at some small-town pink wedding. And it's not as if I'm stopping you going. That Neanderthal platonic pal of yours has said he'll step up to the plate.'

She was vaguely aware of people staring with interest from the surrounding tables. His slight about Dan irked her. Neanderthal? Hardly. He looked like an Adonis, and he was smart, sharp and funny. She clenched her teeth defensively on his behalf.

'I want *you* to come with me. I want you to meet my family.'

'And I will, honey. When the time's right.'

'It's a family wedding. Everyone who knows me will be in one place for the first time in years. When could the time possibly be more right than that?'

His face changed. Subtly but instantly. Like the turning of a switch. The easy, open look that had really taken her in when she'd first met him, the way he'd listened to her as if she mattered and showed her real, genuine interest, was gone. That look was now replaced by a sulky, petulant frown.

'Because it's all about *you,* of course,' he said. 'No regard for *my* career. You have to make these opportunities, Emma, and then follow them up. You don't mess people like this about, because there are no second chances. I can't believe you're being so selfish.'

For a moment the Emma she'd grown up to be actually questioned her own judgement on the strength of that last comment of his. The insecure Emma, whom she'd begun to push out of her life when she'd at last moved away from home and gone to university—a place where she had finally been accepted without reference to Adam or anyone else. With her own successes not watered down but recognised. After university she'd moved to London instead of going home to the West Country, in case that old, pessimistic Emma was somehow still there, lurking, ready to take over.

No way was she going back to *that* mindset now.

She pushed her plate to one side and leaned down to pick up her bag and take out her purse. She took enough money to cover her own meal and put it down on the table. She didn't throw it down. She wasn't going to resort to stupid tantrum gestures—she was a professional.

'I'm sorry, Alistair.' She shook her head at him. 'I don't know what I was thinking. I thought there would be more to us than being driven by your career. You want me to travel with you so I can iron out your legal issues, don't you? Maybe draw up the odd contract, or just hand out advice where you need it?'

He didn't say anything.

'Come on—be honest with me. Is that what this has really been about?'

A long pause.

'Well, you can't deny it's an advantage,' he said eventually. 'But only in the same way as if you were a hair-dresser or a stylist.'

'I thought we were having a relationship. I didn't realise I was joining your entourage,' she snapped. 'I should never have let myself get swept away by this. Have a nice trip back to the States.'

She left the table and aimed her shaky feet at the exit, determined not to look back. When she did, inevitably, she saw that he was signing autographs for the people at an adjacent table. No attempt to follow her or talk her round. But why would he? He undoubtedly had a queue of people waiting to take her place.

She pressed her teeth hard together and concentrated on them to take her mind off the ache in her heart and the even worse heat of stupidity in her face.

She'd bigged up her relationship with him beyond all reason. How could she have been such a fool?

Now she had to face the climb down.

CHAPTER FOUR

EMMA GLANCED AROUND the half-empty office, grateful that her colleagues had finally drifted out for lunch. She'd informed HR first thing that her new, glamorous life as the jet-set girlfriend of Alistair 'White Lightning' Woods was no longer happening and the news had quickly filtered through the staff. At least she hadn't jacked her job in completely. That would have made things a whole lot worse. And it was best to get the humiliation over with, right?

Except that she wasn't sure how many more sympathetic stares she could take.

Her phone blared into life and she looked down at the display screen.

Dan. Again.

She pressed her hot forehead with the heel of one hand, as if it might help her think clearly. There'd been rather a lack of clear thinking around her lately.

What the hell had possessed her to let Alistair Woods sweep her off her feet? She was a sensible professional. She knew her own mind and she never took risks. Was she so bogged down in a stupid teen inferiority complex, in a lifetime of failed one-upmanship with Adam, that she'd momentarily lost all common sense? She'd built a life here in London, where she blended in. She'd excelled at not being noticeable and her professional life had flourished. And now, the one time she'd ventured out of that safe box, the same old outcome had happened. Her judgement had been rubbish, she hadn't measured up and it had all come crashing down around her ears. Why had she ever thought things would be different with Alistair?

Defensive heat rose in her cheeks even as she picked up the phone. By extreme bad luck Dan had been there in the restaurant to see that her romance with Alistair wasn't such a bed of roses after all. The thought of filling him in on all the details made a wave of nausea rise in her throat and her eyes water.

'Hello.' She shaped her voice into the most neutral tone she could muster.

'Hey.'

His voice was warm, deep and full of concern, and her heart gave a little flutter because as a rule Dan Morgan didn't do concern. He did sharply professional business demands, he did high expectations, he did arm's length.

'Just checking that you're OK.'

I blabbed to everyone who knows me in London that I was on the point of eloping with the most desirable man in sport. I've made the biggest fool of myself and now I have to tell everyone that, actually, he's an arse and it's not going ahead. So, yes, thanks, I'm just peachy.

Climbing down in front of Dan was somehow worst of all. And not just because she was embarrassed at her own poor judgement when she should have known better. There was a tiny part of her mind that was busy pointing out that for the first time ever Dan was showing interest and support for her beyond what she could do for him and his work. Had he suddenly realised he valued her as more than just a handy plus-one? How many missed calls from him had she had since lunchtime? Five? Wasn't that a bit excessive?

'Why wouldn't I be?' she said.

'Things just seemed a little tense at lunch yesterday.' *As if you could cut the atmosphere with a chainsaw.* 'Did you get everything sorted with Alistair?'

A rush of bitterness pelted through her as she answered. 'Oh, yes. I *definitely* got everything sorted with him.'

'He's changed his plans, then? He's coming to the civil partnership?'

Oh, bloody hell, the civil partnership.

An unsettling wave of trepidation turned her stomach over. The biggest Burney family get-together in years and she no longer had a date. Could her crushed and battered ego survive a whole weekend of jibes from her mother about the race for grandchildren being hampered by her inability to keep a man?

'Not exactly,' she said.

'How do you mean?'

There was a sharp over-interested edge to his voice that she recognised from the many work dinners she'd accompanied him to. This was how he sounded when he was on the brink of nailing a new client—as if nothing could distract him from his goal. *Five missed calls and now he was hanging on her every word.*

Oh, hell.

She leaned forward over the desk in exasperation and pressed her hot forehead against its cold wooden surface.

'Alistair and I are off,' she blurted out. 'He's a total *arse*. He wouldn't even talk about making it to the wedding.'

'You broke up because he won't come to your brother's wedding?'

'Pretty much, yes,' she said.

She couldn't bring herself to tell him the truth—that Alistair had only treated her like a princess because he'd wanted a live-in lawyer. Her cheeks burned just at the thought of it.

'I couldn't let Adam down and he just couldn't see that. It made me realise that work will always come first for him.'

'Sorry to hear that.'

Was there a twist of cool I-told-you-so about his voice? She pulled her head from the desk and narrowed her eyes, trying to decide. He was probably glad it was all off. Wasn't that exactly what he'd wanted? For things to get back to normal? Then again, at least he wasn't saying it out loud.

She tightened her grip on the phone.

Wallowing in self-pity was one thing, but it didn't change the fact that in a week's time she had to keep her parents in check while surrounded by Ernie's family. Knowing Adam, it would be the most stuffed-with-people event of the year. She'd become so used to relying on Dan at family get-togethers that the prospect of coping with that by herself filled her with dread.

With her dreams in tatters there was a warm tug of temptation just to scuttle back to the way things had been. And wasn't that exactly what Dan had been angling for all along? Why not resurrect the old plus-one agreement? That nice, safe social buffer that had stood between her and humiliation until she'd stupidly given it up. Her reason for ending it was on its way back to the States right now. She'd dipped a toe in the murky waters of proper dating and it had turned into a train wreck.

She thought it through quickly. Dan was brilliant with her mother, never remotely fazed and the epitome of calm. Exactly what she needed to get her through that scary event. And maybe then she could begin to look forward, put Alistair behind her, make a fresh start.

'Actually, about the wedding…' she said.

'You want to reinstate the plus-one agreement?' He might as well give it its proper ludicrous name.

'Yes. I know it's a bit of a turnaround.'

Just a bit.

He couldn't quite believe his ears. So *now* she wanted him to step back in as her handy fake boyfriend, as if the last couple of weeks had never happened? What about her insane plan to dump him in public? And she hadn't done him the one-off favour of going with him to his Mayfair charity ball—oh, no. He'd had to spend the evening peeling Eloise off him. But *now* she needed *him* things were different.

And he wasn't about to make it easy for her.

'I thought having each other as a social backup was *holding us back?*' he said. 'Your words.'

A pause on the end of the phone, during which a hint of triumph coursed through him as he reclaimed the upper hand. He was back in control. How they proceeded from here would be *his* decision, not hers.

'I may have been a bit hasty.'

He didn't answer.

'Please, Dan. Ernie has a massive family and his father's a High Court Judge. Our family is me and my parents plus a few distant relatives that my mother's alienated over the years. I've promised Adam I'll keep my mum in check, and the thought of doing it on my own fills me with horror. *Please*. You're so good with them.'

She paused again, and when he didn't immediately leap in to agree, deployed the big guns of guilt.

'I thought this was what you wanted—everything back the way it was? I know I screwed up, and I'm sorry. But how many times have I helped *you* out at the last minute? What about that race meet where you landed your biggest client? You called me two hours before and I stepped in. Won't you even consider doing this one tiny event for me?'

He hesitated. She had a point about the race meet.

'Please, Dan. I want to make sure everything runs smoothly for Adam. You know how hard it is to please my mother.'

She'd lowered her voice now and a pang of sympathy twisted in his gut because he *did* know.

He could tell from her defeated tone that she thought he was going to refuse. This was his opportunity to bring things right back to where he wanted them. Their agreement had paid dividends—there was no denying that—but he'd let it run on far too long. He'd become complacent and let her become too important to drop easily. He couldn't have someone like that in his life, even if it *was* supposed to be under the heading of 'work'. She wanted a fake boyfriend for the wedding? He'd be the best fake boyfriend in the world. For old times' sake. And then he'd dump their agreement without looking back for a second.

'OK,' he said.

Emma took a deep breath as sweet relief flooded her. It had absolutely nothing to do with the prospect of Dan's company of course. She was way past that. It was just the thought of having an ally in what was bound to be a social minefield.

'Really?' she said. 'I wasn't sure you'd agree after I said no to your charity thing. Thank you *so* much. And you know I'm happy to step in next time you need someone—'

'Please let me finish,' he cut in. 'I'll do it. But this is the last time. I'll stand in for you in acknowledgement of all the times you've stepped in for me at the last minute. But when we head back to London after the wedding, that's it. Our agreement is over. I'll manage my own socialising going forward, and you can carry on as before.'

Emma took a sharp breath, because for some reason that hurt in a way that the Alistair debacle hadn't. He didn't sound inclined even to retain a friendship between them. They would revert to being Mr Morgan and Ms Burney, businessman and lawyer, nothing more. Had she really meant so little to him?

It was a stupid, stupid pang of disappointment because she'd already *dealt* with the idea that nothing would ever happen between her and Dan. Her ridiculous crush on him was a thing of the past. She'd been planning to travel the world with Alistair, for Pete's sake, never looking back.

It had somehow been much easier to deal with when *she'd* been the one making that choice.

Emma glanced around the lobby of the Cotswolds hotel that Adam and Ernie had chosen as their wedding venue, surprised at the stunning old-world charm of the place.

Huge vases of spring flowers softened the dark wood panelling of the walls. Beautifully upholstered chairs and sofas stood in cosy groupings around the fireplace, which was taller than she was.

She would have expected Adam to want to make his vows somewhere screamingly modern in the midst of the buzz of London. Apparently Ernie's family were a lot more old-school than that. They'd lived here in this honey-coloured stone village for generations. She felt a stab of envy at the give and take in her brother's relationship. It seemed *Adam* didn't have a problem putting his partner's family first.

On the other hand it might have been less nerve-racking if the wedding *was* taking place on home ground. Here they would be surrounded by Ernie's nearest and dearest, all eagerly awaiting the impression the Burney family would make. Her stomach gave a churn of unease at the thought.

'What name is it?'

The blonde receptionist ran a manicured fingernail down her computer screen.

'Burney,' Emma said. 'I'm part of the Burney-Harford wedding party.'

Adam had made a block reservation.

Dan strode through the door, fresh from parking the car. He rested one hand on the desk and ran the other through his dark hair, spiking it more than ever. His blue eyes crinkled as he smiled his gorgeous lopsided smile—the one that had melted half the female hearts in London.

The manicured fingernail came to an instant standstill and the receptionist's jaw practically fell open as she gazed at him.

'Mr and Mrs Burney?' she asked.

Emma sighed.

'No, that would be my parents.' Mercifully they weren't here yet. 'It will be under Miss.'

The girl handed over keys—proper old-fashioned ones—and a wad of check-in paperwork.

Emma gave Dan an expectant look.

He smiled at her.

'Great venue.'

'What about you?' she said.

'What *about* me?'

'Your booking,' she whispered.

In her peripheral vision she picked up the interested change in the receptionist's posture. She'd seen it a hundred times before. She took in her appearance. Blonde hair—*check*. Sleekly made-up face—*check*. Eager smile—*check*. She knew exactly what would come next.

She waited for Dan to confirm loudly that he had a separate booking—ergo, he was free and single, and in possession of a hotel room and a shedload of charm. Instead he held her own gaze steadily, as if his radar no longer picked up pretty blondes. Not a hint of a flirt or smoulder. Not so much as a glance in the girl's direction.

'Didn't make one,' he said cheerfully.

Emma stared at him incredulously for a moment, before realising that the receptionist was watching them with an interest that was way beyond polite. She walked away into the corner and when he didn't immediately follow gave him an impatient come-on beckoning gesture. He sauntered over. The receptionist made a poor attempt not to watch the laconic grace of his movements.

'What do you mean, you didn't make a booking? You had your invitation—where did you think you were going to sleep? On the lawn?'

He shrugged. 'I never got round to booking a room and then, when you asked me to step in as your date, I didn't need to. I'll be staying in your room, won't I?' He put an arm around her shoulders and gave her a squeeze. 'All part of the façade, right?'

She was rendered momentarily speechless by a wave of spicy aftershave and the sudden closeness of him, and then his assumption about their sleeping arrangements slammed into her brain.

'You can't stay in *my* room,' she squeaked.

'The whole weekend takes place at this hotel. It's hardly going to give a loved-up impression if we sneak off to separate rooms at the end of the night, is it?'

'In the Burney family we'd fit right in,' she said, thinking of her parents, who'd had separate bedrooms since she was in her late teens.

He ignored her and turned his head sideways to read the number on the key fob in her hand.

'Eighteen,' he said, heading for the stairs. 'First floor.'

She stumbled after him, her mind reeling. The thought of their sleeping arrangements hadn't entered her head. This was the first time they'd faked their relationship for longer than a couple of hours. She'd simply *assumed* he would have a separate booking.

An image of her vanity case full of embarrassing toiletries danced through her mind, swiftly followed by the fact that her hair looked like a fright wig when she woke up. She gave herself a fast mental slap, because she absolutely did *not* care whether she looked attractive or not, and any attempt to make herself look good was *not* for the benefit of Dan Morgan.

She made a grab for his arm and he turned round on

the landing and looked at her, an expression of amusement on his face.

'I don't see what the problem is,' he said. 'This is a professional arrangement, right? We'll treat it as such. Or were you thinking that I might take advantage of the situation and jump your bones?'

His ice-blue eyes crinkled at the corners as he grinned at her and a flare of heat crept upwards from her neck.

'What am I supposed to think?' she snapped defensively. 'I know what you're like with your five-minute flings. So don't be getting the wrong idea. I am most definitely *not* interested in any shallow no-strings fling. If I'd wanted that I would have stuck with Alistair.'

'I wouldn't *dream* of suggesting one,' he said, holding his hands up. 'The thought never even occurred to me. You're perfectly safe with me.'

Her face burned hotter than ever, because if that wasn't a knock-back she didn't know what was. He was basically telling her she was arrogant for assuming he would *want* to hit on her. Of course he wouldn't. He'd had a year's worth of chances and he'd passed them all up. Her toes curled and she turned away, because her face undoubtedly looked like a tomato right now.

'Look, it's no big deal,' he said. 'We can just shelve the idea. I'll head back to London and you can go it alone.'

A sudden bolt of dread made her stomach lurch as a familiar bugling voice drifted through from Reception.

'Booking for Burney. It'll be one of the higher-end suites—parents of the groom.' A pause. 'The *real* groom, that is…'

Her parents were on the premises and her mother

was obviously on her usual form. Poor Adam. He was relying on her.

She glanced back at Dan. He spread his hands questioningly.

'Your call. Do you need a plus-one or not?'

'This is gorgeous, isn't it?' She sighed as she turned the huge key in the lock and walked ahead of him through the door.

Their cases and bags stood waiting for them at one side of the room, efficiently delivered by the porter. It was everything that a country house hotel bedroom should be. The floorboards were suitably creaky, the dark wood panelling of the walls gleamed, the bed had four posts draped with a soft voile fabric, and there was a pile of squashy pillows and a floral bedspread that matched the silk curtains. Behind a door to one side was a luxurious *en-suite* bathroom.

Dan had to bend slightly to avoid smacking his forehead on the doorjamb. He followed her into the room. She hovered awkwardly by the window, clearly still on edge at the whole room-sharing thing.

'Very nice,' he said and, unable to resist the tease, added, 'Nice, large bed.'

He found his gaze drawn to her face as she dropped her eyes and saw faint colour touch her pale cheekbones. Her obvious awkwardness was seriously cute. His usual dates were pretty full-on—a fast track to the physical. Shyness didn't come into it. It was an odd novelty to be sharing a bedroom with someone without bed actually being on the agenda.

He took pity on her and held his hands up.

'You don't need to worry. I'll take the couch.'

There was a squashy sofa to one side of the window, upholstered in a lavender floral fabric. It would be too short for him, but for a couple of nights it would do.

'We can take it in turns,' she said. 'You take the couch tonight. I'll take it tomorrow.'

Momentarily surprised at the counter-offer, he nodded. Not that he would let her.

'Deal.'

She clapped her hands together and took a business-like breath, as if she were about to start a work meeting.

'Right, then, let's get organised, shall we? This can be my space…' she moved one of the smaller pieces of her vast luggage collection onto a dark wood bureau with an ornate mirror '…and this can be yours.' She waved a hand at the antique desk. 'You get the desk and complimentary Wi-Fi. Should be right up your street. I can't imagine you needing much else.'

'You make me sound like some workaholic.'

'I hate to break it to you…' she said, nodding at his minimal luggage, which included a laptop bag. 'It's hardly a get-away-from-it-all minibreak, is it? You've brought your office with you!'

'Only out of habit,' he protested. 'I take the laptop everywhere. Doesn't mean I'm going to use it.'

She turned back to him and pulled a sceptical face. He held his hands up.

'And somewhere in here…' she shuffled through the wad of check-in bumph '…is the itinerary for the weekend. Might as well know what we're up against. Blimey, we'll hardly have time to draw breath.'

He took it from her—a piece of stiff white card decorated in eye-watering yellow. He was suddenly very aware as he looked at the packed agenda that he would be joined at the hip with her pretty much twenty-four-seven for the next couple of days—a situation he hadn't really considered properly when he'd made light of the room-sharing thing.

It all seemed a bit less amusing now they were actually in the room and she was talking him through their shared personal space and unpacking what seemed like endless belongings. He avoided guests at his flat as much as possible. One night was his limit, with sex the sole item on the agenda. Conversation and space-sharing didn't come into it. He simply didn't *do* the give and take required to cohabit. Not any more. He'd done it once and he had no inclination to be reminded of the lash-up he'd made of it.

Just a weekend. He latched on to that thought.

'Certainly not doing a small quickie wedding, are they?' he commented, speed-reading the itinerary.

Emma leaned in close to look at the card with him and he picked up a soft, sweet wave of the scent she always wore as she tucked a stray lock of hair behind her ear. His pulse stepped up a notch in response.

He wasn't used to her looking dressed down like this. That was all it was. Their usual encounters involved smart, polished business dress or the occasional evening gown for gala dinners and the like. Even then her outfits were always reserved, and he couldn't remember a time when he'd seen her in jeans or when she'd worn her hair down. Now it fell softly to her shoulders in waves, framing her heart-shaped face. When you took the time to look behind her uptight attitude, she was actually very pretty.

'When has Adam ever done anything on a small scale?' she said. 'It just wouldn't be him, would it?'

He refocused his attention on the itinerary.

'So, this evening there's welcome drinks on the terrace. Then tomorrow the wedding is here in the grounds, followed by a night of celebration. And then a slap-up cooked breakfast the morning after. That marquee must be for the wedding.' He nodded out of the window.

She followed his gaze, then moved away and sat down on the edge of the bed.

'Adam must be mad,' she said. She bounced up and down on the mattress approvingly.

Dan leaned against one of the posts at the foot of the bed, watching her. Diaphanous fabric softly draped over it—white with a tiny pale yellow flower print.

'Why? Because his wedding's the size of an elephant or just because there *is* a wedding?' he said.

She looked up at him, a tiny smile touching the corner of her lush mouth, and he had a sudden image of himself leaning her slowly back onto the floral quilt and finding out what she tasted like.

He stood up straight and gave himself a mental shake. What the hell was he thinking? This was a last-ditch platonic date—not one of his conquests. The fact that the venue involved a bedroom instead of a boardroom didn't change the fact that their relationship was work-based. It also didn't seem to stop the slow burn that had kicked in low in his abdomen.

'Both,' she said, and shrugged.

'Is that because of Alistair? I mean, you've got to admit he was a bit of a curveball. You *never* date. Not in all the time I've known you. And then suddenly in the space of a few weeks you're packing up and leaving.'

She didn't answer for a moment. There was a distant expression on her face, as if she was thinking it over.

'Partly because of Alistair,' she said at last. 'But really what happened with him was probably inevitable. Meeting the right person isn't something I've excelled at so far. He was so attentive and considerate that I thought for once I'd really cracked it. I really believed it was something special. But it was the same old story.'

She smiled at him, an I-don't-care smile that was just a bit too small to be convincing, and he felt a sudden spike of dislike for Alistair.

'Same old story?'

She sighed. 'Maybe you had a point when you said I was a bit star-struck—I don't know,' she said, picking at a loose thread on the floral quilt.

There was an air of defeat about her that made him want to kick Alistair's butt.

'I got a bit swept up in all the excitement of it. It wasn't so much him as the idea of *life* with him. It was exciting. It was glamorous. It was everything that I'm not.'

'It was two-dimensional Hollywood claptrap. Who wants to live in a shallow world like that? You can't be the first person to get sucked in, but you're the most grounded person I know. You'll soon get over that cardboard idiot.'

That made her smile, lighting her face. He liked her looking happy like that. He liked that he'd *caused* her to look like that.

'I won't be making the same mistake again,' she said. 'I'm going to put *myself* first from now on. But even if one day I do find the right person I won't be getting married with my parents in tow. *No way*. Nice plane trip to a beach somewhere with a couple of random witnesses.'

He grinned.

'What about you?' she said, wiping the smile right off his face.

'What *about* me?'

'Come on—surprise me. What kind of wedding would you have if you could choose?' She leaned back on her palms and narrowed her eyes at him. 'Some beach thing in the Maldives?' She flapped a hand. 'No, no, let me guess… It would be something small. You could probably do it in a lunch hour if you wanted to—take an hour or so out and nip to the registry office. Quick glass of champagne, handful of confetti, and then you could get back to work.'

'Very funny.'

Terrific. He should have seen that coming. The last thing he needed right now was a chat about marriage aspirations. He just wanted to get through this weekend and get on with his life. And he didn't even have his own hotel room to retreat to.

He moved away from the bed to look out of the window, his back to her.

'Of course you'd have to stick at a relationship for longer than a month, then, wouldn't you?' she teased.

He didn't look round. 'It has nothing to do with sticking at a relationship. I have to prioritise. The business is growing at a massive rate. I need to put all my energy into that.'

'Nobody needs to work twenty-four-seven,' she said. 'Not even you. Maybe you should think about slowing down, or at least taking a breather. I just don't get why you're so crazy for work. I've never known anyone so obsessed. And it's not like you've got anyone to share the rewards with. None of your girls last five minutes.'

He stared across the hotel lawn at the dense woodland right in the distance on the skyline. Stared at it but didn't see it.

Another image flashed through his mind in its place. *Sticking at relationships. Sharing the rewards. Maggie.* Dark-haired Maggie with her gentle smile and her kindness.

Maggie and—

He stamped hard and fast on that thought before it could multiply. What the hell was his stupid brain doing, dragging that old stuff up?

At the faint sound of voices and car doors slamming he glanced down onto the gravel drive as Adam emerged, beaming, from a yellow Rolls-Royce, quiff cemented in place, wearing dark glasses like a celebrity. Ernie was right by his side. A gang of porters staggered under a stack of luggage. Obviously overpacking ran in the family.

'Your brother's here,' he said, to distract her, because he couldn't imagine a time when he'd be keen to discuss his future wedding plans.

Emma scrambled off the bed and joined Dan at the window.

'We'd better get ready for the drinks party,' she said, turning to her heap of luggage and proceeding to unzip.

He checked his watch.

'But it's *hours* away.'

As if that mattered…

'I need to make a good impression,' she said. 'I hate being late. And you have to help me keep my parents in check.'

She looked up at him, suddenly feeling awkward,

with a bottle of pink shower gel in one hand and a loofah in the other.

'Do you want to use the bathroom first? I mean, perhaps we should work out some kind of rota.'

'For Pete's sake, we don't need a rota,' he said, his tone exasperated. 'It's two days. You take the bathroom first. You're bound to take longer.'

'What's that supposed to mean?' She made an indignant face. 'That you look great just the way you are but I'm some hag who needs work?'

He laughed out loud.

'No. It means I've never met a woman who takes less than half an hour to get ready.'

She turned towards the bathroom, her arms now full of toiletries.

'And you don't look like a hag,' he called after her. 'You never have.'

It was the nearest thing to a compliment he'd ever given her.

CHAPTER FIVE

DAN GAZED OUT of the open hotel room window and listened to the soft sound of falling water from the shower in the *en-suite* bathroom. It had kicked in five minutes after Emma had shut the door firmly and twisted the lock, as if she thought he might burst in on her.

The marquee was now bathed in early-evening golden sunshine. The sweeping lawns were perfectly manicured, and a lily pond lay on the far right of his view. If he leaned forward far enough he could see an ornate wrought-iron bench set to one side of it. He wondered how many brides' backsides had been plonked there over the years. It really was the perfect photo opportunity.

He was at the cream of wedding venues in the south of England and it was only natural that it might whip up a few passing thoughts of his one and only brush with marriage, right? Just fleeting thoughts... That was all.

Maggie and Blob.

The name filtered back into his mind before he could stop it.

Blob, he had called him—or her—after the fuzzy early scan which had been completely unintelligible to both of them except for the blob with the strong and speedy heartbeat. It had made Maggie laugh. An interim holding name while they bandied about proper full-on names. Andy or Emily. Sam or Molly. To delete as appropriate once they knew the gender, at a later date that had never arrived.

Four months hadn't been later enough.

Maggie and Blob.

An unexpected twist of long-suppressed dull pain flared in his chest—the blunt ache of an old injury. He wrenched his mind away forcibly. For Pete's sake, what was he *doing?* He did *not* need a pointless trip down memory lane right now.

He rationalised madly. He hadn't been near a wedding in donkey's years. Without a family to speak of, things like weddings didn't crop up all that often, and this place was Wedding Central. It was bound to stir things up. But that was all this was—just a momentary blip. He had dealt with Maggie and Blob. They were part of the past and he'd left them there with admirable efficiency. He'd dealt with it all and moved on.

Perhaps that was part of the problem. His life was drifting into predictability, leaving his mind free to wander where it shouldn't be going. He needed to up the stakes at work—perhaps a new business venture. Work had always been the solution before.

The shower splashed on and on, and judging by the enormous bag of toiletries Emma had heaved in there with her she wasn't going to be emerging any time soon. There was no time like the present when it came to refocusing your mind. He unzipped his laptop bag and sat down at the antique desk.

Emma gave her reflection one last glance in the steamy-edged mirror and paused to let her heart reconsider its decision to take a sprint. She knew she'd spent far too long rubbing in scented body lotion and blitzing body hair, telling herself it was because she wanted to make a good impression on Ernie's family. For Adam. It had absolutely nothing to do with the fact that Dan was on the other side of that door. He was fully rationalised. Whatever there was between them, it would always have terms. It would always be about work.

But he could easily have refused to accompany her here. I mean, really, what was in it for him? She knew she'd annoyed him with the public break-up thing, but he had no real understanding of how things were with her parents—how the pursuit of an easy life had become the norm for her. It was her defence mechanism against the endless nagging, and that was what Dan had been. Her route to an easy life. Shame it had all been fictional.

But still he was here.

And now there was that tiny nagging voice, whispering that he might just have come to his senses since she'd broken the news that she was leaving. He might have suddenly realised she meant more to him than a handy work date. Could that be why he now *wanted* the arrangement to end, despite his reluctance to let it go at first? Perhaps this weekend could lead to something more than a platonic agreement between them.

It was a *stupid* nagging voice. To listen to it, or even worse to act on it, would be to set herself up for humiliation. Was the Alistair debacle not enough evidence that she had warped judgement when it came to decoding male behaviour?

The twisty lurch of disappointment in her stomach when she opened the bathroom door told her she'd been stupid to read anything into his presence here.

He was still wearing the same jeans and T-shirt, he'd clearly made zero effort to unpack his minimal luggage, and worst of all he was leaning into his laptop where it stood open on the desk, surrounded by the usual scattering of work papers.

Had she actually thought for a moment that his presence here might have anything to do with an increased regard for her? What a fool she was. Nothing had changed between them at all. She was imagining the whole damn thing just because he'd shown her some support. Clearly she was desperate for attention now Alistair had humiliated her.

At best, Dan wanted to part on good terms—*that* was why he'd decided to accompany her to the wedding and help her out this last time. There was nothing more to it than that.

Undoubtedly the fact that the hotel had complimentary Wi-Fi had made the decision a whole lot easier for him.

Dan stared at her as she stood in the doorway, the deliciously sensual scent of her body lotion mingling with steam, epically failing to register the look of resigned disapproval on her face because of her transformation from office starch.

Her dark hair fell in damp tendrils, framing her heart-shaped face, and there was a pink hue to her usually pale skin. She was totally swamped by one of the enormous white his 'n' hers hotel bathrobes, and his mind immediately insisted on debating what she might or might not be wearing underneath.

He stared hard at the e-mail on his computer screen until his eyes watered, in the hope that his stupid body would realise that they might be sharing a bedroom and a bathroom but their interaction was limited to the professional—just the way it always was. For the third time he read it without taking a single word in.

'You're working,' she said with ill-hidden disappointment. 'Don't you ever take a break?'

He felt a surge of exasperation.

'What else was I meant to do? Take a stroll round the grounds? Sit and watch the bathroom door? It's just a couple of e-mails while I waited for you to be finished.'

'Well, there's no need to snap,' she said, crossing the room to the bureau and squeezing a handful of her hair with the corner of a towel. 'You could have gone first if you'd wanted to.'

Oh, for Pete's sake! He hadn't counted on the inconvenient need to be constantly polite that their space-sharing had caused. Without the shared goal of sleeping together it boiled down to a *you-go-first-no-you-I-insist* awkwardness about using the facilities.

With a monumental effort he curbed his irritation.

'I'm sorry,' he said. 'I'm just not really used to sharing my personal space, that's all. I'm used to doing what I like whenever I want to.'

She glanced at him and smiled.

'That's OK.'

She began combing her long hair out, looking at her reflection in the mirror.

'You have a different girlfriend every week,' she said. 'I'd have thought bedroom etiquette was your speciality.'

He watched as she sprayed perfume on her neck and pulse points. The intense scent of it made his senses reel.

'That's different.'

'I don't see how.'

He shrugged.

'There's no give and take needed. They stay over and the next morning they leave. There's no personal belongings cluttering up every surface.' He glanced at the bed, currently festooned with her clothes. 'There's no pussy-footing around each other over who's hogging the bathroom. It's done and dusted, with minimal disruption.'

And minimal emotional input. Which was exactly how he liked it.

'You make it sound *so* romantic,' she said sarcastically, dipping her finger in a pot of pink make-up and dabbing it gently over her mouth.

His eyes seemed to be glued to the tiny movements and to the delicious pink sheen it gave her luscious lower lip. She didn't notice, focusing on what she was doing in the mirror.

'It isn't *meant* to be romantic,' he said. 'It is what it is.'

A temporary and very enjoyable diversion, with no lasting repercussions.

'So it's fine for them to stay over until you get what you want, and then they're ejected from the premises at breakfast time? Is that it?'

'You make it sound callous,' he said, snapping his laptop shut and gathering up his work papers. 'When actually it's fun.' She threw him a sceptical glance and he couldn't resist adding, 'Hot, steamy, no-holds-barred fun,' just to see if he could make her blush again.

'You have no scruples,' she complained.

He saw the flush of pink creep softly along her cheek-bones, highlighting them prettily. Sparring with her was actually turning out to be enjoyable.

'I don't need scruples,' he said. 'We're all adults. I never make any promises that I don't keep. I'm honest with them about not wanting anything serious and they appreciate that.'

'No, they don't,' she said. 'They might say they're fine with it, but in reality they're hoping it will turn into more. It's not the same for women. Sleeping with someone isn't some throwaway thing. It's a big deal—an emotional investment. And, anyway, if you always put those limits in place when you meet someone you're cutting out the chance of ever having a proper relationship. You could meet the perfect person for you and she'd just slip through your fingers unnoticed.' She fluttered her fingers in the air to press her point. 'You'd never even know. You'll be perpetually single.'

'And that,' he said, grabbing his bag and making for the bathroom, 'is exactly the point.'

He smiled at the roll of her eyes as he closed the door.

Emma didn't usually go in for a second coat of mascara. Or a second squirt of perfume just to make sure it lasted the distance. But then she didn't usually go in for room-sharing. She wished someone would tell her stupid pulse rate that it was supposed to be platonic.

He had the speediest bathroom habits she'd ever come across, and as a result she was still balancing on one leg, one foot in her knickers and the other out, when the lock clicked and the bathroom door opened. Heart thundering, she thanked her lucky stars that she'd decided to keep the bathrobe on while dressing, and covered her fluster by whipping her panties on at breakneck speed, clamping the robe around her and then giving him a manic grin that probably bordered on cheesy.

Her entire consciousness immediately zeroed in on the fact that he had a fluffy white towel wrapped around his muscular hips and absolutely nothing else. The faint hint of a tan highlighted his broad chest and the most defined set of abs she'd ever seen outside a magazine. He rubbed a second towel over his hair, spiking it even beyond the usual.

She forced her eyes away, snatched the bathrobe more tightly around her and crossed to the bed.

'I think we should have a quick round-up of the ground rules for tonight,' she said, flipping through some of the clothes laid out on the bed, not really seeing them, just aiming to look busy.

'Did you just say "ground rules"?'

She glanced up and had to consciously drag her eyes upwards from his drum-tight torso. His amused grin told her that unfortunately he'd clocked her doing it, so she pressed the platonic angle hard to show him that they might be sharing a hotel room but she had no romantic interest in him whatsoever. None. Zilch.

'I did. We need to pull off being the perfect couple.'

He let out an amused breath. 'I think you can count on *me* to know how to do that,' he said.

She silently marvelled. He obviously thought a few posh dinners and hot sex was all it took.

'This is a whole different ball game. When you've been my date before it's mostly been an hour or two alone with my family in a restaurant. A trained chimp could probably pull that off. This is going to be a lot more full-on. The place is going to be stuffed with Ernie's family. We need to make a good impression for Adam. We have to look totally together but in an *über*-normal way, so we can counteract my parents' dysfunctional relationship.'

He looked briefly skyward. One hand rested on the

desk; the other was caught in his hair. By sheer will she didn't look at the towel, held up only by a single fold. Instead she fixed her eyes on his face.

'You're over-analysing,' he said. 'Trust me on this.'

He pulled a few items from his bag and headed back to the bathroom with them slung over his arm.

'I know how to pull off loved-up,' he called over his shoulder, with not a hint of trepidation at the evening ahead when *she* was a bag of nerves. 'Just like you know how to pull off professional couple. Just leave it to me.'

A couple of hours' work had certainly done the trick in terms of refocusing him. He'd fired off a ton of important e-mails, had a look through some figures, and if he needed any more of a distraction to stop his mind dredging up the past, looking at Emma as he emerged from the bathroom again was it.

Fully dressed now, she was wearing her hair long again, this time brushed to one side, so it lay gleaming over one shoulder of the soft green maxi-dress she wore. Her newly applied perfume made his pulse jump and she wore more make-up than usual, highlighting her wide brown eyes and the delectable softness of her lips.

Playing the part of boyfriend to *that* for the evening was hardly going to be a chore.

He could tell she was nervous just by the way she was behaving. Give her a room full of professionals and she could network her way around it with the best of them, holding her own no matter who he introduced her to. But with the prospect of a weekend with her own family she was reduced to a quivering shadow of her work self.

That very jumpiness seemed to heighten his awareness of her on some level, and it felt perfectly natural for him to lean in close to her on the way down the passage towards the stairs. He rested his hand lightly around her waist, conscious of her slenderness beneath the light flowing drape of her dress.

Emma was hotly aware of him next to her as he escorted her along the landing. As his arm curled around her waist she picked up the spicy scent of his aftershave on warm skin and her stomach gave a slow and far too delicious flip. Everything about him seemed to be overstepping the lines of her personal space in a way it never had before. The way he stood just a fraction closer to her than strictly necessary… The way he'd held her gaze a beat too long when he'd teased her about wanting ground rules.

'Er…there's no one actually here to see us,' she pointed out, glancing down at his hand, now resting softly on her hip. She looked up at him questioningly.

'Just getting into character,' he said easily, not moving his hand.

'I'm determined to inject a bit of tradition if it kills me, Donald,' she heard suddenly.

Her mother's distinctive tones drifted down the corridor from behind them and she froze next to Dan. And then they were getting louder.

'I think I'll have a word with Ernie's parents about top tables and speeches. It's a family occasion. They'll be expecting us to have some input.'

Emma's heart began to sink at the thought of her mother instigating a cosy chat about traditional wedding roles with Ernie's clearly far more liberal parents and she stopped at the top of the stairs, intending to intercept her and suggest a new approach of just enjoying the celebrations without actually *criticising* any of them.

The coherence of that thought dissolved into nothing as Dan suddenly curled his hand tighter around her waist and propelled her back against the nearest wall. Before she could so much as let out a squeak, he kissed her.

CHAPTER SIX

NIGH ON EIGHT months of conditioning herself that her attraction to him was just a stupid crush, and all it took to get every nerve-ending of attraction right back in action was one kiss. One kiss that made her toes curl and her stomach feel as if it might have turned into warm marshmallow.

He caught her lower lip perfectly between his own lips and sucked gently on it, his hand sliding lower to cup the curve of her bottom. The smooth wood panelling of the wall pressed against her back. She could feel every hard, muscular contour of his body against hers, and sparks danced down her spine and pooled deliciously between her legs.

Her eyes fluttered dreamily shut—and when she opened them she was staring right into the disapproving gaze of her mother, a vision in purple sequins, a few feet away over Dan's shoulder.

Reality clattered over her like a bucket of ice cubes and she wriggled away from him, the flat of her hand against the hardness of his chest, her heart racing. He made no effort to disengage whatsoever, so she added an extra pace's worth of space between them herself.

He was watching her steadily, the petrol-blue shirt he

was wearing making his eyes seem darker than usual, a grin playing about his lips. Her heart raced as if she'd just sprinted up and down the creaky stairs a few dozen times.

She tore her gaze away from his.

'Mum!' she gabbled.

'Hello, darling.' Her father leaned in to give her a kiss and shook Dan's hand.

Her mother glanced at him disapprovingly.

'Really, Emma,' she remarked. 'A little class would be good. *Anyone* could walk along this corridor and how do you think it would look to find you two in a clinch?' She radiated criticism, despite the fact that she was intending to steam in and openly re-evaluate the wedding plans. When it came to social etiquette she could be remarkably selective. 'You're not sixteen, you know. A little decorum would be good. Thank goodness Adam can rely on your father and me to make a good impression.'

She swept past them down the stairs.

Emma stared after her incredulously and then rounded on Dan.

'What the hell was that about?' she snapped. 'What did you think you were *doing?*'

'We've got an image to keep up,' he said, shrugging as if he'd done nothing wrong.

So he'd just been playing a part, while her knees had turned to jelly. There had been a moment back there when she'd thought she might simply fold into a hot puddle on the floor.

But he didn't need to know that, did he?

'I don't think we need to take things quite *that* far,' she said, trying to breathe normally.

'Are you complaining that my kisses are somehow

substandard?' he said, his gaze penetrating, a grin touching the edge of his mouth and crinkling his eyes.

Her blush felt as if it spread all the way from the roots of her hair to her toes, because as kisses went it had been utterly off-the-scale sublime.

'Of course I'm not saying that,' she snapped. 'It's just that when I said we were aiming for perfect couple I obviously should have specified that I didn't mean perfect couple at honeymoon stage.'

'What *were* you aiming for, then?' he said, blue eyes amused. He rubbed his lips thoughtfully with his fingers, as if he was savouring the taste of her.

She ran a hand self-consciously over her hair. Perhaps if she could smooth the muss out of it she could smooth the fluster out of the rest of her.

'I was thinking more comfortable in each other's company. You know the kind of thing. More the on-the-brink-of-settling-down stage.' She shrugged, her pulse returning to normal now. 'Then again, you're clearly drawing on your own experiences. When did you last have a relationship that made it past loved-up? You go from meet straight to dump. You miss out everything in between.'

He laughed, clearly amused by the whole affair.

'You gave it one hundred and ten per cent when you were staging our "break-up",' he pointed out, making sarcastic speech marks in the air with his fingers. 'Right the way down to the spectacular drink-throwing. What's the matter with that approach now?'

She could hardly say it made her knees unreliable, could she?

'Because the whole point of this is to stop my parents showing Adam up,' she said. 'And they've actually as good as just told *us* to get a room. I think we might have taken it a *teensy* bit too far.'

She led the way down the stairs

'Spoilsport,' he called after her, kick-starting her blush all over again.

As they walked out through wide-open double doors onto a stone-flagged terrace she was more aware than ever of his hand pressed softly in the hollow of her back. It seemed to generate sparks of heat that climbed tantalisingly up her spine. Her mind insisted on replaying his kiss on a loop, making her feel completely flustered.

Fortunately she had the reality check of Adam's flamboyant styling to smack her between the eyes. The terrace was softly lit by hurricane lamps on tables and pin-lights strung along the stone balustrade. A band were set up to one side, playing jaunty music to which none of the guests were dancing because they were all crowded around the centrepiece in the middle of the terrace.

For a moment she had to lean back and narrow her eyes while her brain processed exactly what it was.

Adam and Ernie had apparently commissioned a life-size ice sculpture of themselves. It gleamed in the floor-level spotlighting. It depicted Adam with one finger pressed against his temple in a thoughtful pose while Ernie looked on.

Her parents were standing to one side, and her mother's face was a stunned picture. On the bright side, at least it appeared to have rendered her speechless. As soon as she saw Emma and Dan she crossed to them, the beads on her purple evening dress shimmering as she walked. She wouldn't have looked out of place in a ballroom dance show.

The real Adam and Ernie joined them, wearing complementary head-to-toe designer suits, with a group of Ernie's relatives flanking them.

'Aren't they *fabulous?*' Adam was gushing, clasping his hands together in delight. 'And the best thing about having yourself carved is that you can tweak the way you look. So I made myself taller and we had a bit shaved off Ernie's nose.'

'Well, I've got to be honest, I'm not that impressed,' her mother sniffed, deploying her usual tactic: if it was outside her comfort zone then she was suspicious of it. She leaned backwards appraisingly. 'They've made your ears stick out,' she remarked to Adam. 'How much did you pay for them?'

'Mum, you can't ask things like that,' Emma said, smiling nervously at the group.

Her mother drew herself up to her full height and pursed her lips. 'Of course I can. Adam's my son. We're parents of the groom. I'm entitled to my opinion.'

'They were a gift,' Adam said, pink-cheeked. 'From Ernie's aunt. She's a sculptress. She spent *hours* working on them. In a freezer.'

There was an ensuing pin-drop silence, during which Emma's father took a canapé from a passing waiter and attempted to lever it into his mouth.

'No more of those tartlets, Donald,' her mother said, leaning in as if with a sixth sense. She expertly took the canapé out of his hand and his teeth closed over thin air. 'Cholesterol!' she snapped.

Ernie dragged a blushing Adam away to circulate, and Emma did her best to stand in as sounding board for her

mother's stream-of-consciousness opinions on every mi-
nuscule aspect of the proceedings. She was vaguely and
gratefully aware of Dan's calming presence at her side.

How would she manage at things like this in future,
without him watching her back? The thought of losing
that comfort gave her a needling sense of dread.

A couple of hours later she was worn out with smiling and small talk and her mother seemed to have re-
connected with a kindred spirit in the shape of Emma's
spinster aunt Mabel, last seen at a childhood Christmas
before moving up north. Emma watched them across the
terrace, their arms folded in matching poses, matching
critical expressions on their faces. Although her voice
was drowned out by the music, she saw her mother's
lips form the word *grandchildren* as the pair of them
looked her way.

She turned to see her father surreptitiously sliding
food from the buffet table onto an already heaped plate
while her mother was preoccupied.

'Your mother's got me on a diet,' he said when he saw
her disbelieving stare.

'Doesn't sound like much fun,' Dan said.

He shrugged.

'It's not so bad. I have a second lunch down at the golf
club most days. They do a fantastic pie and crinkle-cut
chips. What she doesn't know, and all that.'

Oh, for Pete's sake, she'd had just about enough of
this.

'I need a walk,' she said, heading for the steps down
from the terrace and onto the lawns.

'I'll come with you.'

Dan followed her away from the party, grabbing a
couple of champagne flutes from a passing waiter.

* * *

It was a beautiful clear summer night, the velvety cropped lawn silver in the moonlight. Strings of pearly pin-lights lent the trees a fairy-tale quality.

Emma walked on her toes at first, to stop her three-inch heels sinking into the grass, then gave up and took them off, walking barefoot, with the hem of her dress sweeping the grass. Dan was acutely aware of the change in their height difference. Now she seemed small and fragile as she walked next to him.

The faint sound of music and laughter drifted after them on the night air as the party carried on up on the terrace. The lawn swept gently downwards towards a small lake, molten metal in the moonlight. The fresh, sweet scent of dewy grass hung on the cool night air.

'And you wonder why marriage doesn't appeal to me,' she said as he fell into step beside her. 'If I ever found the right man why the hell would I marry him, if that's what it does to you? They lead separate lives. Separate rooms, separate friends. He spends his life trying to exist below her radar and she's got zero excitement in her own life so she makes up for it with gossip and by meddling in Adam's life and in mine. And yet they think they're presenting the image of joint marital solidarity.'

She warmed to her subject, flinging up an exasperated hand.

'Is that how I'll end up if I have kids? With them arguing over who *isn't* going to have the annoying old cow over at Christmas?'

He couldn't keep in a grin. She was so indignant.

'It's not all bad,' he said. 'At least they *are* interested in you.'

She sighed.

'On an interfering kind of a level, maybe.'

He shook his head.

'Maybe it comes across like that. OK, OK—it *does* come across like that,' he said as she gave him an incredulous look. 'But still you're lucky to be part of a family. I couldn't believe it when you said you were thinking about throwing it all away for some guy you'd known five minutes.'

Emma hid her fluster at his unexpected mention of Alistair by zeroing in on his other point. *Family* and *Dan* weren't really two words she thought of in the same sentence.

'That was part of the attraction,' she said. 'The idea of having some fun, for a change, with someone who put me first without criticising, without comparing me— who put me ahead of everything else. And with Alistair there was no prospect of settling into anything like my parents' take on domesticity. It would have been loads of travel and excitement, minimal chance of ending up in separate bedrooms living my life through my kids.'

'So the whole thing with Alistair was about you proving a point to your family? Why does it bother you so much what they think?'

Dan's comment made her feel as if she was being sloshed with cold water—especially as it was so astute. She *had* been blinded to Alistair by the desire to impress her parents.

'It had nothing to do with proving a point,' she lied. 'I'm a grown-up. What bothered me when I was a kid is just an exasperation now.'

She stopped to sit down on the bench he'd seen earlier from the bedroom window. He sat down next to her, the hard wrought-iron pressing cold through his shirt. He handed her one of the champagne flutes.

'Then what is it?' he said. 'You handle yourself brilliantly back in London. You're a real slick professional. You don't need to let anyone's criticism bother you.'

She stared across the silvery lawn. Faint laughter drifted across from the terrace.

'Ah, but that's exactly the point,' she said. 'When we see each other it's usually for some work reason or other. When it comes to work I know I can hold my own. I know what I'm talking about. I make sure I won't get caught out or make a slip-up.' She paused. 'It hasn't always been like that for me.'

'So what *was* it like, then?'

Emma looked at him, trying to gauge whether his interest was real or counterfeit. He'd never shown an interest in finding out more about her before—not unless it was related to work, of course. His blue eyes held hers steadily. She took a sip of her drink and smiled a little, remembering, letting the years fall away.

'Growing up, I was the clumsiest kid you can imagine,' she said. 'If anyone was going to make a fool of herself it was me. And it was even more difficult because Adam's always been such an overachiever. I started out at school trying to work hard, but it never seemed to matter how much effort I put in. I was never quite good enough to earn Adam's level of interest or praise. He was picking up A grades, winning competitions, excelling at everything. After a while I learned not to put myself in a position where people could notice I was falling short.'

A memory returned to her in all its cringeworthy glory.

'I had a part in the school musical once.' She looked

up at him. 'When I was thirteen. Can you imagine me doing that?'

He shrugged, a small smile on his face. A polite response.

'They used to do a musical every year. It was so popular. Everyone would come and watch—parents, locals. And that year they were doing *Grease*. Loads of singing and dancing. I was so excited by the whole idea. I just wanted to be part of it. It didn't occur to me that there could be a negative side, that things could go wrong. I was so naïve.'

'What happened?'

She put her head in her hands and pulled a cringing face.

'I forgot my lines. I stood on that stage and looked out at the hall, knowing it was packed, and I couldn't remember a word. And I don't mean I stumbled over my lines. I didn't just have a bit of a blip and then pick things up. My mind went completely blank. I froze. The lights were bright in my face, but I could still see the shadows of all the people. The music was so loud I could hardly think.'

'What did you do?'

'I ran off the stage and refused to go back on. They put the understudy on instead. My parents were in the audience and my mother gave me hell. She still brings it up now and then. I think in some part of her mind I'm still that nervy thirteen-year-old who had a public meltdown onstage and showed her up.'

She took a sip of her champagne, thinking back. The bright lights in her eyes. The cold horror rushing through her as she tried and failed to make her panicked brain work. The slick of sweat on her palms.

She looked across at Dan, easily pasting a smile on

her face. She'd had years of practice at doing it. She was an adult now, with her own life, and she didn't need to be defined by that awful feeling of failure—not any more. Yet on some level maybe it could never be erased.

'That's awful.'

She shrugged, smiling a little.

'It was at the time. I was mortified. And it never happened again—not to that extent. I never put myself out there again after that—not in any situation where I couldn't trust myself to get it right. I concentrated on academic stuff instead of the arts. Left all that to Adam. And, well, you can see how good *he* was at it. That's partly why I decided to study law. A lot of it is about bulk learning. If you know the rules you can apply them. If you put the work in you can build a career. It isn't left to the whim of anyone else liking what you do in order to secure your success.'

He watched her, looking down at her hands, her skin silvery pale in the moonlight, contrasting with her gleaming dark hair. The air of vulnerability about her made his heart turn over softly. He had an unexpected urge to sweep her into his arms and erase all that self-doubt, make her feel special.

'You care far too much what people think of you,' he said.

She frowned.

'Isn't that what everyone wants, though? Validation from everyone else? Or at least from the people you care about.'

'Maybe. But sometimes love doesn't show up as hugs and presents,' he said. 'Not everything is that in-your-face in life. Your mum, for example, shows she cares by—'

'By being the most interfering woman on the planet?

Maybe. But just a little…' she searched for the right word '…*positivity* might be nice now and then.'

She leaned back a little, surveying him with interest.

'I didn't think you had such strong feelings about family,' she said. 'It's not like I see you jumping through any hoops to see yours: You never seem to visit them—you never even mention them. They can't be any more of a nightmare than mine are, and even I do my duty and see them every few months.'

'Why?'

'What do you mean, *why?*'

'Why do you do your duty and see them? It's perfectly clear you don't relish spending time with them. Why don't you just cut them out of your life if they're that much of a chore?'

He made a slicing motion with his hand while she stared at him, momentarily speechless.

'I couldn't do that,' she said at last. 'They're my family.'

'You mean you care about them?'

'Of course I do. I've kind of got used to the criticism in a way. It's who they are. They might be a nightmare, but at least they're mine.'

'And there's your answer.'

She shook her head faintly at him.

'To what?'

'You were wondering why I never mention or see my family. There's your answer. That's the difference between you and me. I don't really have a family—not as such. And what I did have of one was never remotely interested in me, even in a critical way.'

She dropped her eyes from his.

'Look, I'm sorry…' she began.

He smiled at her.

'Don't be. I'm fine with it. It's always been that way. I don't *need* a family, Emma. What you don't have you don't miss. When I was a kid we didn't do overbearing parents or criticism or sibling rivalry.' He paused. 'We didn't actually *do* family.'

His mind waved the memory of Maggie before him again with a flourish and he clenched his teeth hard. Talking about family with Emma wasn't so difficult when it related to his mother. His feelings for her had progressed over the years to end up somewhere near contempt. But family as related to Maggie meant something completely different. That had been his hope. That had been their plan. Losing that planned future had somehow been so much worse than losing any excuse for a family he might have had in the past.

She was staring at him. He could feel it. He stood up, began walking back to the terrace, deliberately not looking at her.

'What do you mean, you didn't do family?' she said, catching him up, her long skirt caught in one hand.

He thought fleetingly about simply closing the conversation down, but found that on some level he didn't want to. When had he last talked his childhood over with anyone? His usual conquests were happy to go along with however much he told them about himself—or, more to the point, however little. There had never been any need to give much away. Dinner and a cocktail or two seemed to be all that was needed to get to first base, quickly followed by second and third.

'Exactly that,' he said. 'My upbringing wasn't in a nice suburban house with a mum and dad, siblings, pets. Out of all those things some of the time I had a mum.'

'What about your dad?'

'I've never known him.'

The look of sympathy on her face was immediate and he instantly brushed it away with a wave of his hand.

'I've never needed to know him. It's no big deal.'

It was a billion times easier to talk about the family he'd actually had than the one he'd wanted and lost. The two things were worlds apart in his mind.

'Yes, it is. That's awful.'

He shrugged.

'What about your mum, then? You must have been close if it was just the two of you.'

He could feel his lip trying to give a cynical curl.

'Not especially. She wasn't exactly Mother of the Year.' He caught sight of her wide-eyed look and qualified resignedly, 'Oh, hell, she was very young. It can't have been easy, raising a kid by herself. It just was what it was.'

Maggie flashed through his mind again. They'd been young, too, and totally unprepared for parenthood. But walking away had never been an option for him. He'd known that from the very first moment she'd told him about her pregnancy.

'She worked on and off,' he said. 'Bar work, mostly. When I was smaller I used to stay with a neighbour, or one or other of her friends. There was never any consistency to it. Then when I got older it was just me.'

He paused for a second, because that couple of sentences didn't really sum up what it had felt like in that house by himself. It had been cold, with a musty smell of damp that had never gone away, even in the summer. Never tidy. Ready meals and late-night movies because no one cared if he stayed up late or if he was getting enough sleep for school. Sometimes his mother had stayed out all night until he'd wondered if she'd return at all. What would happen to him then? Where would he go? The uncertainty of it all had made him constantly on edge.

'I'd never have known,' she said. 'You've done so well to get out from under all that.'

Emma felt a sudden stab of shame at her fussing about her own childhood. She must sound like some dreadful attention-seeker to him, with her comfortable middle-class upbringing, moaning that she'd never seemed able to please her family when he'd barely had one.

'Not especially. I think it did me a favour. I was so determined to find a way out of there, and when I went to college I found it. Not long after that I had the idea for my first business. It was a coffee kiosk. The cafeteria on campus really sucked. It was poorly run, and there was no facility for grabbing a coffee on the go. So I plugged the gap. It wasn't much more than a trolley at first, but I could see what worked and what didn't. I developed the business, ran it during my free periods, and pretty soon I was making good money. And that was when I *really* knew.'

'Knew what?'

He glanced across at her then, and the look in his eyes was intense in the moonlight, making her pulse flutter.

'That work can be your ticket out of anything,' he said. 'Anything at all.' He smiled at her, a half smile that was steely and determined. 'I just grabbed the coffee kiosk success and ran with it. Built it up, sold it, invested and started over. You can be in control of your own destiny through work. And that's why work will always come first with me.'

So that was why his relationships never amounted to anything. She saw now why their agreement had been of such use to him. She'd furthered his work. She'd provided a date so he didn't need to be distracted.

There had never been any prospect of him wanting more, then. She swallowed as she took that in.

'You'll meet someone one day who'll make you want to put work second,' she said. 'You won't know what you're missing until then.'

He shook his head.

'The moment someone becomes that important you start to lose focus. And things start to go wrong. I just don't need that kind of complication.'

She had the oddest feeling he wasn't just talking about overcoming his childhood.

'I think I'm going to turn in,' she said as they neared to the hotel. 'It's getting late now.'

The music continued on the terrace, more mellow now, and the crowd had dispersed a little. Adam stood to one side, mobile phone clamped to his ear, a stressed expression on his face.

That didn't come as any surprise to Dan. He could think of few things less stressful than getting married. Emma's parents were nowhere to be seen, but obviously just their presence on the premises was enough. In the centre of the terrace the ice sculpture continued its slow melt.

'I'll come with you,' he said.

The memory of kissing her danced slowly through his mind as they made their way inside. He'd known it might put her on edge—that had rather been the point...proof that he was calling the shots now. He hadn't thought it through any further than that. He hadn't counted on the way she would feel in his arms, all long limbs and fragile bone structure, such a contrast to the voluptuous curves that had always been his short-term fling diet. Or the way that satiny full lower lip would feel tugged between his own. There was a hotly curious part of him wondering how it might feel to take things further. He crushed that thought—hard.

His perception of her had changed. And not just because of the kiss but because of tonight. When had they ever discussed anything before that didn't have the ultimate goal of helping them in their jobs? It had been all insider tips from her. Who might be tendering for this contract, what their bid might be, who in her work circles might be looking for troubleshooting services. From him it had been handy introductions—name-dropping Emma to contacts who might want or need legal advice. All of it professional on one level or another.

This weekend was meant to be all about him taking charge, making the point that *he* was the one doing *her* the favour and then breaking off their arrangement the moment the wedding was over. The plan had seemed so easy in the wake of her insulting dumping of him—the perfect way to redress control and get rid of the gnawing feeling that he'd let her become indispensable in his life.

But the connection between them now felt more complex instead of more detached. The idea of walking away from it felt suddenly less gratifying. He'd been so busy taking what he could get from their agreement, manipulating it to suit his own ends so he could avoid close relationships, that he hadn't considered what might be in it for *her* beyond the shallow work reasons they both had.

For Emma it had been a way of making life easier.

Because to be 'good enough' she believed she had to fit a certain stereotype. He wasn't sure which was worse— using their agreement to escape past failures or using it to avoid any remote likelihood of ever having any.

As they walked up the stairs to their room Emma re-alised suddenly that he still had his arm loosely draped around her. There was no one around them to see it. No family members, no staff. Just what did that mean? Or did it mean anything at all?

She wondered if it felt as natural to him as it felt to her and gave herself a mental slap for even *thinking* about reading something into it. Really? This was Dan—Mr Two-Week Relationship himself. Even if that arm resting on her shoulders right now meant something—which it didn't—it would only ever be that.

Nothing meant anything to Dan Morgan except his work. He'd made that crystal clear this evening. And she wasn't in the market for anything that could be de-scribed as a fling. What would be the point? She'd had that with Alistair. What she wanted was not to be some throwaway bit of arm candy but to feel special, to come first, and she wasn't going to get that from Dan.

A hot kiss followed by a night sharing a room with him… The stuff of her dreams a few months ago. And now she had it, it was all for show. How par for the course of her life. They'd been alone together *loads* of times and he'd never had any intention of making a move. Pretend Emma got the hot kiss and the envious glances from female wedding guests over her gorgeous male companion. Real Emma got the awkwardness of bunking in with a work colleague.

She wriggled away from his arm and fumbled in her bag for the room key.

It had taken *months* to get over her stupid crush on him and to reinstate it now would be madness. She was just flustered, that was all, over a stupid fake kiss and a bit of a personal conversation. It didn't mean *anything*.

CHAPTER SEVEN

WHEN HAD HE last shared a bedroom with someone for a reason that had nothing to do with sex? Dan couldn't actually remember. It must have been Maggie. Way back when he was still at college and anything had seemed possible.

Had he now become so accustomed to room-sharing being about sex that his body simply expected it as part of the deal? Was that why he felt so damned on edge as he waited for Emma to change in the bathroom? Every nerve in his body was wound into a tense knot.

The air of awkwardness from earlier was back. But now there seemed a new, deeper edge to it. It was more than just the logistics of sharing a small space with someone you only knew on a work basis. His growing attraction to her was heightened by his new understanding of her. A few feet away from him in the velvet-soft darkness she would be there, lying in that bed, with her long, slender limbs and her silky dark hair.

His body matched his racing mind with a rigid, hot tension the like of which was going to make sleep an impossibility.

His pulse jolted as the bathroom door clattered open and she crossed the room to the bed, not looking at him.

Her dress was now lying over one arm, her hair loose and gleaming in the soft glow of the table lamp next to the bed. She was wearing a sleep vest and shorts which showed off the most impossibly perfect pair of long, slender legs.

He made an enormous effort not to stare at them as his mind insisted on wondering what other glorious secrets she might be hiding under her sensible work dresses and wide-leg trousers. He stared hard out of the window. His preoccupation became slightly less fake as he noticed movement in the grounds.

'Is that your brother down there?'

He immediately regretted mentioning it because she tossed the dress over the back of a chair and crossed the room to join him at the window, padding across the deep carpet in bare feet. What he *really* needed right now, with his entire body wound up like a coiled spring, was her standing next to him in her flimsy shorts and vest combo. Without her heels she just about reached his shoulder...

'Where?'

He pointed and she craned closer to him to see the lily pond bench. A figure was sitting and staring at the ground contemplatively, a bottle of champagne in one hand and a glass in the other. Her sudden nearness let Dan pick up the faint trace of vanilla perfume still clinging to her hair and his stomach gave a slow and delicious flip in response.

'It's Adam, all right,' she said. 'Even in silhouette that quiff is unmistakable. He's probably taking a break from negotiating family. Can't say I blame him.'

The soft breeze drifting in through the open window

ruffled her hair lightly. She turned away from the view and smiled up at Dan.

'Don't snore,' she said, her eyes teasing.

'I *don't* snore.'

She was close enough that in one swift tug she could be in his arms. He swallowed hard, his throat paper-dry.

Oblivious, she narrowed her eyes at him, considering.

'How do you know?'

'I've never had any complaints,' he said. Her lips, scrubbed of lip gloss, were a soft pale pink in the muted light. His eyes were drawn to them.

'That doesn't mean you don't snore,' she said. 'It just means no one's wanted to put you off them by telling you.'

'Whereas you…?'

'Will have no compunction whatsoever about lobbing a pillow at you.' She pressed an emphatic finger against his chest that made a wave of heat pulse through his veins. 'I'm not afraid to tell you what I think.'

'I know.'

For some reason the novelty of that was alluring. It occurred to him that the willingness to please of his usual girlfriends was something else besides easy and no-fuss. It was also very bland. When had he last felt on his toes with a woman?

He'd become slowly more aware of her looks this evening: the fragility of her skinny frame, her dark-hair-pale-skin combo—such a contrast to his usual choice—and now there was her liveliness, her cheek, sucking him in all the more.

For the first time he picked up on her physical similarities to Maggie. She was taller and slimmer, but the smooth dark hair was the same. Was that what this was about? Was that why she seemed to have slipped through his careful filter? Was that why it had been so easy to keep her at a distance and categorise her as a work colleague? Because his knee-jerk avoidance of any thought of attraction to a girl who might remind him of Maggie had gone on so long it had become automatic?

But he hadn't had the complication of being at such close quarters with her back then. Nuances and habits were laid bare now. The fun-loving, cheeky side of her was so much more obvious outside the work environment, where everything needed to be serious and professional. This weekend he'd begun to see what lay beneath. And it drew him in as no woman had. Not since Maggie had walked away.

She was smiling cheekily up at him, her brown eyes wide, and he marvelled again at how softly pretty she was when you took the time to look past her stiff outer layer. Her face was tilted up to his, at the perfect angle for him to kiss her. The warm, sweet scent of her hair filled his senses, and without taking time to think he lifted a hand to touch her cheek—just to see if it felt as satiny as it looked.

That one tiny connection with her gave his pulse an immediate leap and hot desire rushed through him. And in that fleeting moment he knew he had no chance.

Knowing he was acting off-plan now—and not just off-plan for this weekend but for his whole damned philosophy on life—was suddenly not enough to stop him. His mental filters weren't working. She'd already got past them. This was physical now, and there was nothing he could do about it.

Her eyes widened as he let his fingers trace further, around to the soft skin at the nape of her neck, beneath the fall of her hair. All thought of consequences gone, he lowered his mouth towards the silk of that tantalisingly full lower lip. He pulled her closer, melded her body hard against his, felt the contours of her long, slender limbs through the thin cotton of the shorts and vest she wore.

Sparks of hot longing fizzed in his abdomen as he let his hand slide lower, to find the soft cream of those long, slender thighs. Desire flooded through him, deeper than he was used to, steeped in the familiarity of her, the laughs they'd had together, their newfound closeness. This was not his usual throwaway date. He'd stepped outside the norm. The very novelty of that seemed to hike up his want for her to a new level.

A squeak of shock caught in Emma's throat as his thumb stroked along her jawline, his fingers tangling in her hair.

She hadn't imagined the shift in balance between them after all. She hadn't been seeing things that weren't there.

Despite all the flirting and the signs, the new feeling of intimacy as they started to get to know each other beyond the barriers of their previous life, she now realised that she'd never truly believed he could ever be interested in her. Not in *that* way. She'd quit any delusions about that months ago as she'd observed his repetitive dating habits, certain that unless she happened to morph overnight into a pouting curvy blonde, boring old plain Emma Burney simply wouldn't do it for him.

Her pulse had upped its pace so acutely that she felt light-headed. As his lips met hers she could taste a faint twist of champagne on them, warming her mouth as his tongue slipped softly against hers. Hot sparks began to tingle their way through her limbs to simmer hotly between her legs.

How many times had she dreamed of this moment in the dim and distant past when they'd first met? Every nerve-ending was tinglingly aware of him. She was drowning, every sense in her body filled with him. The lingering spicy notes of his aftershave made her senses reel. She let her fingers sink into his hair, its thick, soft texture exactly as she'd imagined it so many times.

The desire that had bubbled beneath the surface of her consciousness until she had abandoned all hope of it ever being reciprocated made a heady comeback, and she grabbed at the last thread of sense before it slipped away.

It was utterly, sublimely delicious, but none of it really counted because he was ending their agreement.

She latched on to that thought. Was that what all this had been about? The warmth of his newfound support and interest in her had delighted her, but she'd assumed it was simply down to friendship. His kiss was something she'd dreamed of, but if he'd wanted to snog her because of *her* he'd had *months* to do it.

All those months waiting for him to notice her, taking extra care with her hair and make-up when she knew she was going to see him, dropping everything to fit in his last-minute work dates. Months when he'd barely noticed she was alive. Months of opportunity, time alone together, work dinners out. None of it had been enough because he'd needed her for work then.

It had taken *this* for him to make a move on her. The fact that he was ending their agreement and had no need for her any more. Dan only slept with dispensable women. And now she was dispensable.

None of this had anything to do with real feelings for her.

With a monumental effort she stopped her arms from entwining around his neck and groped for his hands, grabbing them at the wrists and disentangling herself from his embrace. The sensation of loss as she took a step back made her suck in a sharp breath and she steeled herself against it. She was *not* going to be sucked into another bad decision because of some stupid age-old crush. She was in full control here.

'Why now?' she panted at him.

His eyes seemed a darker blue than ever, a light frown of confusion touching his forehead. She could hear that his breath had deepened.

He reached for her.

'What do you mean, why now?'

She took another step back, away from his hands, because if she found herself in those arms again she wasn't sure her resolve would stand up.

'We've known each other for months,' she said. 'And in all that time you've never looked twice my way. No matter what I did. No matter how many times I swung business deals for you or put myself out on your behalf. No matter how I tried. And then you decide we're going to go our separate ways, and out of the blue suddenly I'm fair game? Well, I'm not interested.'

She took a slow step back, shaking her head, avoiding his eyes, looking everywhere except at his face. Everything about her told him a very different story. Her shortness of breath, the flushed cheeks, the hard points of her nipples beneath the thin fabric of her vest.

His mind zeroed in on her words. *'No matter what I did.'* The meaning of that slammed into his brain and turned it to mush. Their agreement had always been about more than platonic convenience for her and he'd never even noticed. His stupid work tunnel vision had neglected to pick up on that point. The surge of excitement it now evoked shocked him to the core, telling him his belief that he was in control here was seriously misplaced.

'I'm not going to be your alternative choice because there's no handy blonde available and you're stuck sharing a room with me,' she said.

Clearly, to her, he was the same old work-obsessed confirmed bachelor.

'This has nothing to do with that.'

She gazed up at him, wariness in her wide brown eyes, and then they both jumped at a sudden flurry of knocks on the bedroom door.

She took a couple of fast paces away from him, her fingers rubbing slowly over her lips as if echoing his kiss. Another surge of desire flooded through him at the sight. She cut her eyes away from his.

Another mad cacophony of knocks sliced through the tension.

She made an exasperated noise and turned away from him towards the door, one hand pushing her hair back from her face in a gesture of fluster.

'Who the hell is that?'

'Emma, ignore it,' he said. 'We need to sort this out. You've got it wrong.'

The knocking graduated to a muffled banging of the kind a fist might make, and she shook her head lightly at him and moved towards the door again.

He glanced down at himself. In a sudden flash of clarity it occurred to him that the visitor might feasibly be Emma's mother, and his arousal would be obvious to her in the space of one look. He glanced at the door to the *en-suite* bathroom, thinking vaguely that he might take refuge in there for a couple of minutes while Emma got rid of whoever it was and then they could pick up where they'd left off.

He was on his way across the room when she opened the door and Adam, who had clearly been leaning on it, stumbled into the room, performed a twisty lurching pirouette and threw up into the nearest pot plant.

Oh, just bloody *perfect!*

'For Pete's sake, help me get him to the bathroom!'

Emma had managed to pull Adam to his extremely unsteady feet and struggled to hold him upright as he lurched about. Dan rushed in and took over, throwing one of her brother's arms around his neck and heaving him into the bathroom before he could collapse again. She followed them in.

'The wedding's off!' Adam groaned, slumping over the sink. His always-perfect hair hung in a dishevelled mess and his face was a sickly shade of green.

'What the hell's happened?' she said.

He lifted his head and pointed an emphatic jabbing finger at her as he swayed drunkenly.

'I'm a has-been, darling,' he drawled. 'It's all over. It's all gone.'

His knees gave way unexpectedly and Dan made a lunge to catch him before he hit the white-tiled floor.

'He's absolutely wasted,' Emma said, staring down at him. 'What the hell do I do?'

'Call down to Room Service,' Dan said. 'Black coffee. He needs to sober up.'

She left the pair of them in the bathroom and went to use the phone, her mind reeling. She'd never seen Adam lose his cool before. He had no worries that she knew of. His life was only ever full of things to celebrate. As she replaced the receiver there was the sound of gushing water from the bathroom and a piercing shriek of shock. Dan had obviously stuck him in the shower. She grinned in spite of her worry. Whatever she had to cope with now, at least Adam might be more lucid.

Adam emerged from the bathroom, still hideously pale, but his shocked eyes were now wide and staring. Water dripped from his face and his hair and he was clutching a towel and madly rubbing it at his front.

Dan followed him, his hands spread apologetically. 'Look, I'm sorry,' he said. 'I know cold water's a bit of a shock to the system, but it's great for sobering you up and I couldn't think what else to do.'

'Cold?' Adam wailed. 'It's not the bloody *cold!*' He cast horrified hands downwards at his sopping wet purple suit. 'What the hell have you done? This jacket's *designer!*'

CHAPTER EIGHT

DAN TURNED OVER for the fiftieth time on the sofa, knees bunched up because the damn thing was too short for him. Unfortunately that wasn't the only reason why sleep was totally elusive. The way Emma had felt in his arms had been far too delicious, far too enticing, for him to simply brush it out of his mind. Add in to that the way she'd put an end to it without having time to give a proper explanation and every nerve in his body was on full-scale alert, his arousal refusing to stand down even in her absence.

And, as interruptions went, needy family crises just about ticked his worst possible box. His stomach lurched between desire for her and the more rational desire to run a mile. It was bad enough to be in the middle of a huge family event when the last thing you wanted to be reminded of was the fact that you couldn't actually *do* family. He'd thought he was holding his own on that front pretty well, but now family complications were seeping in at every turn and he couldn't think of anything worse…

Somewhere in the small hours, after he'd finally given up on her returning to the room—not that it had made any change to his sleepless state—there was a soft click as the door opened. The benefit of his eyes being used to the velvet darkness meant he could watch the silhouette of her every move, while she had to feel her stumbling way from one piece of furniture to the next. Had he ever been more wide awake?

She muffled a yelp as she tripped over a chair and he took pity on her and reached to turn on the table lamp. She blinked at him in the muted golden light. She wore a sweater over her sleep shorts and vest that wasn't long enough to hide her gorgeous legs. His pulse immediately picked up where it had left off a couple of hours ago.

He heard her sigh as she clocked that he was still awake. He watched her run a hand through her already dishevelled hair as she sat down hard on the bed. Her face was a pale oval and there were dark shadows of tiredness beneath her eyes.

'You're still up,' she said.

He sat up on the sofa, the sheet bunched around his waist.

'I wasn't sure you were coming back tonight,' he said.

'Neither was I,' she said. 'I think Adam's drained the hotel's supply of black coffee.'

'He's sobered up, then?'

She nodded.

'He's sobered up. I thought that stuff about calling off the wedding was just cold feet—the usual night-before thing, down to him having drunk too much champagne. But there's more to it than that.'

She held his gaze for a moment.

'He's in financial trouble, Dan,' she said.

Worry etched her face and tugged at his heart.

'He's going under unless he can come up with a plan pretty damn quick.'

'For Pete's sake, what's he gone and done now? Spent a huge wad on a purple Bentley?'

She didn't smile.

He sat up straighter.

'Didn't you tell me his pictures sell for five figures?' he said, scratching his head and trying to think clearly. Tiredness was kicking in now. He had absolutely no desire to discuss Adam's spending habits at two in the morning.

'One of his pictures was supposed to. A month or so ago. Adam borrowed a wodge of cash on the back of it and then the sale fell through. He's been so in vogue recently that even *he* believed the hype. Instead of being productive he's been spending money he doesn't have like water. A new swanky flat here, a shedload of designer furniture there... And now things have reached breaking point. He only found out this afternoon.'

'Can't Ernie bail him out? I thought his family were swimming in cash.'

She frowned at him.

'That's exactly why he doesn't want to *tell* Ernie. He doesn't want him to think he's marrying him for a bail-out. And, more than that, he doesn't want Ernie to think he's a failure. You can't imagine what that means to Adam—he never fails at anything. *Ever.* He's refusing to change his mind about calling off the wedding. It was all I could do to make him promise not to do anything until the morning. I need to think of a way to persuade him by then.'

Dan looked at the worry darkening her face and saw a flash of hope in her eyes as she fixed them on his.

'What he really needs is some sound business advice,' she said, with a pointed tone to her voice that really wasn't necessary. 'From someone who knows what they're doing.'

She wanted him to step in. The unspoken request hung in the air as clearly as if she'd shouted it.

Cold clarity immediately took over his brain with the automatic response that had been honed and conditioned in him over the course of the last ten years.

Not his problem.

He didn't *do* family problems. That was actually the one big advantage of not having a family—not getting sucked into other people's dramas, not having anyone rely on him for help. He'd thought he'd done a pretty good job of distancing himself from the blasts from the past that the whole family wedding ambience kept lobbing his way this weekend, but this was a step too far.

'You want *me* to talk to him?' He could hear the note of frosty defensiveness in his own voice. 'I'm not convinced that would be a good idea. It's his private business—nothing to do with me. He needs to discuss it with Ernie. Isn't that the whole point of marriage—shared problems and all that?'

He dropped his eyes from hers so he wouldn't see the disappointment seeping into them. He ran a hand awkwardly through his hair.

'There isn't going to *be* a marriage unless someone gets him back on track,' she hissed.

'What makes you think that someone should be *me*? I don't think Adam would thank you for involving a stranger in his personal problems. This isn't down to me,' he said.

'A stranger?'

He glanced up and caught her gaze again. Bitter disappointment lurked there. Deep in his stomach a spike of regret kicked in unexpectedly at the idea of letting her down. He steeled himself against it. He shouldn't care about this.

She paused a beat too long, during which he held his position and didn't give in, and then she exploded.

'Fine. Absolutely fine,' she snapped, leaping to her feet.

Had she really thought he would step up to the plate? Why the *hell* had she assumed that? Because he'd kissed her? After months of zero romantic interest he'd kissed her. OK, so she'd thought there had been something more than their usual work relationship growing between them this last day or so, but clearly she'd imagined that. Her first instincts had been spot on and she'd been totally right to stop him in his tracks.

Her mistake had been in hoping that what was between them was in any way about more than the kiss and what he'd obviously intended to follow that kiss up with if Adam hadn't interrupted them spectacularly.

'You didn't even ask me what was wrong with Adam,' she said dully. Her head ached tiredly and she rested her hand against her scalp, lacing her fingers through her hair to pull the roots back from her face, trying to clear her thoughts. 'I thought you were waiting up for me all this time to make sure I was OK, to be supportive, but you weren't actually wondering for one second what the problem was. If I hadn't just told you, you would never have asked me about Adam, would you?'

She glanced down at her fingers.

'That's not what you were waiting up for at all, is it? You just wanted to pick up where we left off earlier. You thought I'd sort Adam out, get him over his hissy fit, and then we'd have the rest of the night to make it into that bed.'

She nodded across the room at the four-poster.

For a moment she got no response and she raised her eyebrows at him expectantly. See if he could talk his way out of this. Or if he would even be bothered to try.

'This has nothing to do with what happened earlier,' he said, not meeting her eyes. 'I just think Adam is big enough to sort out his own problems. I don't get why you need to get sucked into this. His overspending isn't down to you.'

She stared at him, incredulous at his lack of concern.

'Because that's what families do,' she said. 'You know, I always thought nothing could ever touch Adam. He's led a charmed life. As if everything he ever touches is sprinkled with happy dust. When I was a kid I sometimes used to wish for just one time when he would stuff up, show everyone that he wasn't perfect.'

She paused briefly, thinking of how upset Adam was now. There was no joy in that for her. She wasn't a stupid kid any more.

'For once I'm not the one who's screwed up, but I have no good feeling about that. What good would it do if my parents knew what had happened? I just want him to go back to his usual crazy self.'

She made a conscious effort to curb her voice. It was so late now the hotel was pin-drop quiet. Every word she spoke felt amplified in the silence.

'Of course you do,' he said. 'You're comfortable in his shadow, so you're hardly about to want that shadow to get smaller, are you?'

She stared at him.

'Just what the hell is *that* supposed to mean?' She

wanted to shout it. Her voice felt shaky on her tongue. She kept her tone measured with great difficulty.

He shrugged.

'It's safer, isn't it? Believing that you're always going to be inferior? Means you don't have to put yourself out there. You rely on Adam being the star that he is in every possible way because it's an excuse for you to take the safe option.'

'That's not true.'

'Isn't it? Look at our plus-one agreement. I know what *I* was getting out of it—easy networking, work contacts. But what about you? Your dates were all about presenting a front to your family, because that way you didn't have to put yourself there in reality. With me you couldn't fail.'

For a moment she had trouble comprehending what he meant because it came as such a shock. A sharp, hot lurch hit her in the stomach. She shoved away the thought that this was what it felt like to have someone touch a nerve. Refusing to engage in one-upmanship with Adam was a way of avoiding grief from her over-interested parents, *not* a way to embrace the safe option because she was afraid of failure.

Dan saw the dark, defensive anger flush her face and wondered for a moment if he'd gone too far. She'd made him feel such a lightweight for not pitching in instantly to help Adam—who, frankly, was responsible for his own cock-up. Discomfort at the situation had stopped him holding back, and second thoughts seeped in a moment too late.

Her hands flew to her hips, her eyes flashed in anger

and her previous attempts to speak in a low voice went totally out of the window.

'You're twisting things!' she yelled. 'I don't know where the hell you get off, preaching to me about family bloody values. Your concern gene is mutated. All this has been about—all anything has *ever* been about for you—is getting someone into bed. In this case, in the absence of any willing curvy blondes, that happens to be me. Well, I'm not interested in being one of your dispensable little-black-book girlies. I don't need you as a boyfriend—not even as a fake one. If this wedding goes ahead—which, the way it looks right now, is unlikely—I'll go it alone. I don't need you. So first thing in the morning you can get back to your sad workaholic singleton life in London.'

He'd never seen her lose her temper. Her voice shook with the force of it and she stood at her full height, her eyes wide and her cheeks flushed. Even in his amazement at her overreaction—which told him he'd not only touched a nerve but had held on to it and twisted it hard—the most visceral part of him zeroed in on how utterly beautiful she looked in that animated moment.

Then admiration fell flat as she turned her back on him, stalked into the bathroom and slammed the door so hard he was surprised the hotel didn't collapse into rubble around them.

Not the delicious uninhibited night of passion he'd expected when he'd kissed her a few hours earlier. Admittedly at the time his mind hadn't been working ahead by more than a few minutes. He certainly hadn't thought about the consequences—it had been very easy to discount those. Any possible repercussions had seemed very far away when the silk of her skin had been beneath his fingers.

If he'd been lying in a regular bed he would have been ramrod-straight. Instead he was cramped into a hunch with his knees up. His body was one big throb of pent-up sexual energy. Every muscle was tightly coiled up with it. And did he really think he could pass the whole night like this?

She'd spent an hour in the bathroom before she'd re-emerged into the darkened room and stalked past him into bed. No attempt to make conversation. Now a silver shaft of moonlight filtered through a chink in the curtains and fell on her bare shoulder as she lay with her back to him. The long legs were drawn up; she was curled beneath the sheet.

For an endless length of time he had felt sure, despite her silence, that she was awake. Her angry vibe had been palpable. Tension still filled the room. He shifted again, in a vain attempt to get comfortable, and wondered what exactly he was bothering with all this for.

He should be looking on Adam's rubbish timing as a very fortuitous wake-up call, shouldn't he? He'd been completely focused on the overwhelming physical pull of her. If he'd stopped for a second to analyse it he would have assumed it would be a one-night stand. After all, he'd made it clear that their agreement had run its course, and that had removed any benefit of keeping things platonic between them. He'd been thinking quick weekend fling.

Hadn't he?

If his interest in her was purely physical, dispensable, then why did her furious criticism of him gnaw at his insides like this? He had no obligation to her or her family, and yet somehow she'd managed to instil guilt because he didn't want to get involved in Adam's undoubtedly crazy problems.

He didn't *do* guilt. That was one of the main benefits of keeping his relationships shallow. He and Emma didn't even *have* a relationship and he couldn't bloody sleep. He had no idea how she'd managed to do this to him.

There was a part of him that was halfway back to London in his head already, keen to do exactly as she had suggested.

She shifted gently in her sleep and he sat up on the sofa, throwing back the crumpled sheet. He could see the smooth pool of her dark hair on the pillow. The quality of the light in the room had changed almost imperceptibly and he glanced at the luminous face of his watch. Dawn would be kicking in before he knew it. He could be back in his Docklands flat in an easy couple of hours if he left now. No need to battle London traffic if he left this early. Why the hell was he even still here?

You want to help. You want this involvement with her and her family.

He absolutely *did not*.

Every sensible instinct told him to get some serious distance from this situation but he rationalised furiously. A brief chat with Adam—and a brief chat was all it *would* be, too—might be the perfect way to take control of this situation. He wasn't about to quietly slink back to London on her say-so, leaving her with the upper hand.

He ignored the inner voice whispering that he didn't like being labelled as selfish, because labels were to him completely irrelevant. Results mattered. Successes.

Not good or bad opinions. Even if they happened to be *her* opinions.

Help Adam out and Emma would be in his debt. The fact that after that kiss she felt very much like unfinished business was beside the point. He was not about to fall for her. He was in total control here. When they got back to London he would end their agreement, as planned, in full possession of the moral high ground. It wasn't as if she wasn't expecting him to. He'd made it clear this was their last outing together. There would be no need to see her again after that. It would be over.

There was a chink in the curtains that let the sunlight in.

It took a moment for her brain to process the fact that the bedroom window of her flat in Putney looked out onto a tiny enclosed yard which the sun penetrated for roughly ten minutes somewhere around noon. Additional details seeped into her consciousness. This bed was hard, where hers was soft, and was that *birdsong* she could hear? Where was the roar of rush-hour traffic?

This was *not* her flat in Putney.

Reality rushed in. Luxury country house hotel. Adam's mad-as-a-box-of-frogs wedding. Disastrous room-share with her crush of the year.

She sat bolt upright and stars swam in front of her eyes at the unexpected movement. She turned instantly to look at the sofa. Every bone in her body ached with tension and her eyes felt gritty when she blinked. She could have sworn she'd been awake all night. Yet that couldn't be so. Last seen lying on the sofa as she climbed back into bed at two-thirty and turned her back on him in fury, at some point Dan had managed to get up and exit the room without her noticing.

She checked the time and that was enough to get her out of bed in a split second. How the hell had she managed to sleep in? Her stomach kicked into churning with a sudden sense of urgency. She needed to get up, check on Adam and find out if the wedding was going ahead or not.

The thought of dealing with the fallout if his world imploded filled her with dread. Adam would be in the doghouse and the spotlight would be right back on her life—her failure to keep a man, her failure to produce grandchildren. Her mind stuttered on that thought with a sharp stab of shame. Surely her only concern should be for Adam, for how she could best help him sort out the mess that was his life, how she could support him through the stress. The thought of the effect it might have on *her* shouldn't even be entering her mind.

Dan's accusation from the previous night rose darkly in her mind. Could he have a point about her living in Adam's shadow because it was safer there?

She crossed the room swiftly to the *en-suite* bathroom, knowing from the silence that Dan wasn't there but sticking her head around the door anyway to check.

Nothing.

She glanced at the hotel information brochure on top of the bureau. Breakfast had been running for at least an hour already—maybe he'd gone down to the dining room. The possibility that he'd upped and left lurked at the very edge of her consciousness but she delayed any consideration of it. And then, as she turned, her eyes took in the antique desk and her heart gave a miserable lurch that she refused to acknowledge.

His holdall wasn't in the room. And, worse, nor were

his laptop and all the associated office stuff which basically provided his identity. All of it was gone.

She threw on jeans and a T-shirt and speed-walked down
the deep-carpeted hall to the honeymoon suite. Ernie had
spent the previous night at his parents' home and had
planned to get ready there, so Adam should still be alone.

He opened the door on her first knock and stood aside
to let her in before crossing the room back to the full-
length mirror. He was wearing an ivory crushed velvet
slim-cut suit with gold piping and super pointy shoes
that even *she* would think twice about squashing her toes
into. He looked her up and down, an eyebrow cocked.

'I do hope you're not wearing that,' he said, waving
a hand at her jeans-and-old-T-shirt combo. 'This is a
classy event.'

'Of course I'm not wearing this,' she snapped.

There was something incredibly exasperating about
the way he was acting, as if the events of the previous night had never happened when they'd caused her
a stress-fest of monumental proportions.

'I didn't see the point in putting on a swanky wedding outfit and doing my hair when the likelihood of it
going ahead was somewhere around fifty-fifty. At least
it was when I left you in the small hours.'

She sat down on the enormous bed. Everything in
the honeymoon suite was supersized, albeit in a country
hotel kind of a way. The four posts were taller, the swags
of fabric bedecking them were bigger and sweepier, and
through the door of the *en suite* she could see an enormous sunken bath.

'Oh, that!'

Adam flapped a dismissive hand at her and turned

back to his reflection in the mirror. He looked a little tired and drawn but otherwise remarkably like his usual upbeat self. She caught sight of her own reflection behind him. She looked an exhausted wreck. How bloody unfair.

'That's all sorted now.'

She stared at him in disbelief.

'What about last night's meltdown?' His lack of reaction combined with her tiredness made her temper strain to breaking point. 'You puked in my plant, for Pete's sake! You had a total emotional meltdown. Your life was *over*.'

'Oh, that,' he said again, glancing back at her.

At least he had the good grace to look sheepish now.

'Sorry about that, sweetie. Glass of champagne too many. Still, there were compensations. In fact some might say it had elements of stag night perfection.'

He grinned at her mystified expression.

'Sharing a shower room with the gorgeous Dan, for example,' he said mischievously, spraying a toothbrush with hairspray and smoothing his already perfect quiff into place. 'Even if he did ruin my suit.' He tapped the side of his nose with one finger in a your-secret's-safe-with-me gesture. 'Lucky old you. I know you thought you hit the jackpot with Alistair Woods, but I've always thought Dan was in a league of his own. Nice work.' He winked at her and turned back to the top of the bureau, which was groaning under the weight of male grooming products. 'I never did think Lycra cycle wear was a good look—didn't like to mention it.'

He lavishly sprayed a five-foot-high cloud of oriental spiced aftershave into the room beside him and stepped into it.

Emma pinched her nose to stifle a sneeze. She shook her head in automatic denial.

'It's not like that. We're just work friends.'

He cackled mad laughter.

'Sure you are! That's why he's just given me an *enormous* business loan with zero interest and his personal phone number so I can tap him for strategic advice whenever I need it.' He winked. 'Either that or maybe he's got the hots for *me*. Maybe you've got competition, sweetie.'

She stared at him in disbelief and he obviously mistook incredulity for angry possessiveness.

'I'm joking!' He held his hands up and laughed. 'For Pete's sake, where's your sense of humour?'

'When?' she said, as if in a dream. 'When did he do all this? His stuff's gone from the room. I can't find him anywhere.' She paused. 'We had a bit of a disagreement.'

Adam shook his head.

'He'll be back. He turned up here around dawn, woke me up, ordered a gallon of black coffee and forced me to come clean about my debts.' He coloured a little. 'It wasn't pretty. Then he talked me through a business plan for the next three years and touted unbelievable terms for a loan. I thought he'd want a cut of everything I make for life at the very least, and I would have agreed to it, too. Frankly, I would have put up my *granny* as security to dig me out of this hole. But no.' He shook his head wonderingly. 'He is *so* into you.' He pointed the toothbrush at her.

Her brain was spinning, trying to process what all this meant.

'Where is he now, then? He didn't come back to the room.'

Adam shrugged. 'Around, I think. He was going to make a few calls, draw up some papers and get the ball rolling. I'm sure he'll show up once it's all organised, sweetie. He's probably in the lobby soaking up the free Wi-Fi.'

Or en route back to the city and deliberately avoiding her. Her heart gave a half plummet at the thought and she gritted her teeth. She tugged her fingers through her hair, as if she could somehow smooth some sense into her muddled brain.

She'd told him to go back to London and instead he'd stayed to put together a bail-out package for Adam. Her heart turned over meltingly and she desperately tried to rein it in, to come up with an alternative explanation to the one that was slamming into her brain.

He'd done this for her.

He'd done it to prove her wrong about him.

She cringed inwardly as she remembered the awful things she'd said to him in the throes of her enormous meltdown tantrum. What possible other explanation could there be? It was way above and beyond Dan's normal remit. Dan didn't step in to fix other people's crises. Ever. Since he kept the world at arm's length it was usually impossible to get close enough to his shoulder to cry on it.

He'd stepped outside the box. And what the hell was she meant to make of that?

CHAPTER NINE

Dan ran a hand through his hair distractedly as his phone kicked in for the third time in the last ten minutes. Each of the calls had been from Emma. For the third time he pressed 'call reject' on the dashboard and fixed his expression on the road. The motorway would still be pretty clear this time of the morning, but he'd hit traffic when he reached London. It was a Saturday so would be marginally better.

Dealing with Adam had taken a good deal longer than he'd thought it would. Still, it was done now. Loan organised, cash transfer organised, soul sold. Point made. The wedding would go ahead without a hitch and he would return to his work in London. The ridiculous plus-one agreement would be discharged exactly as he'd planned. They would move forward separately, but Emma would go with the knowledge that she'd been wrong about him.

Sad workaholic singleton.

Was that really what he boiled down to? His mind gnawed at it relentlessly and, try as he might, he couldn't shake the feeling that the reason it bothered him so much was because *she'd* said it. He, who didn't give a toss about how he came across to people so long as the job got done, *cared* what she thought of him.

A miserable, dark churning was kicking into his stomach with every mile he drove further away.

Emma pelted back up the stairs for the third time, having performed a whirlwind circuit of all the public rooms and lounges in the hotel, her heart sinking lower by the second. The marquee was teeming with hotel staff transforming it from plain tent into what was, by the look of it, to be some kind of yellow-themed fairy grotto, all under the supervision of a pristinely dressed wedding coordinator with a clipboard and a voice like a sergeant major.

There wasn't another guest in sight, she hadn't showered, washed her hair or applied a dab of make-up, and she only had an hour or so left to get ready before pre-wedding cocktails and nibbles were served. Her mother was probably already wearing her mother-of-the-bride outfit and preparing herself for an afternoon of wedding critique. Wherever Dan had disappeared to, catching up with him and sorting things out would have to go maddeningly on hold now that the wedding was going ahead as planned.

Maybe he'd come back while she was getting dressed…

She showered and changed with minutes to spare and there was still no sign of him.

Maybe he had no intention of coming back at all while she was there. She had told him he was selfish for not helping out a friend, that he cared about no one but himself. Without him here there was only one conclusion. This wasn't about any regard for *her*—it was about making a point, showing her she was wrong about him and then exiting her life with the moral high ground.

The finished marquee turned out to be a yellow flower explosion. Huge floral arrangements stood on plinths in every spare space. Yellow silk bunting decked the roof, and the chairs were wrapped in huge yellow bows, standing in twin rows separated by a wide aisle covered with a thick-pile yellow carpet. At the very front a perfectly dressed white table was decked in yellow flowers.

She was one of the last people to take her seat, earning a glare from her mother, who was perched in the front row rubbernecking at the other guests. Her furious face was topped by an enormous salmon-pink feather hat which clashed eye-wateringly with the mad overuse of yellow.

In a sudden burst of exasperated defiance Emma stood straight up again. She could just nip outside and try his phone again. And maybe while she was there check the car park. At least that would be conclusive.

She sidestepped out of her row and turned back down the aisle to the door. She had to get hold of him. She wasn't about to let this go now—wedding or no wedding. She was stopped in her tracks by a deafening funked-up version of the 'Bridal March' as Adam and Ernie blocked the door in front of her. They were both wearing dark glasses, probably in defence against the major overuse of yellow. Ernie's small niece walked at their feet, lobbing yellow rose petals. The eyes of everyone in the room bored into her back and she had no choice but to slink back to her seat.

What was she thinking? She might as well face facts.

The wedding was under way. And he was clearly not coming.

The wave of sadness that realisation evoked took her breath away and made her throat constrict. The assumption that he'd helped Adam for her, because he *cared* about her, seemed unlikely now that he hadn't hung around to soak up her gratitude. The surge of excitement she'd felt when Adam had told her what had happened took a nosedive into stomach-churning disappointment. She would have to resign herself to coping with the ceremony and its aftermath by herself.

It was an odd novelty to be stressed about something else for a change, instead of the usual prospect of mad parental behaviour. The thought of being without him beat all her other problems into submission. Nothing seemed to bother her now. Her parents could do their worst, and probably would.

And then, just as she mentally gave up on Dan and tried to steel herself to get through the day without losing her sanity, her stomach gave an unexpected and disorientating flip as he walked into the marquee.

He strode casually down the aisle behind Adam and Ernie, crushing the trail of yellow rose petals under his feet, and slid into the seat next to her as if he was just a couple of minutes late instead of having gone AWOL for the last twelve hours. Any possible annoyance with him was immediately sidelined by her heart, which went into full thundering mode. To hide it, she immediately faked irritation.

She spoke from the corner of her mouth as Adam launched into his personally written over-emotional vows. Ernie was gazing at him adoringly.

'You're late,' she whispered.

He stared straight ahead. In his dark suit and crisp white shirt he looked ready for cocktails at some trendy London wine bar. A yellow carnation had been pinned to his lapel by one of the super-efficient attendants. There was a hint of stubble lining his jaw and one tiny sign that he'd cut it fine—the spikes of his hair were still slightly damp from the shower.

'I'm not. I'm bang on time.'

'I thought you'd gone back to London.'

This time he looked her way and gave her a half smile that made her stomach go soft.

'Just because you told me to? You don't get rid of me that easily.'

Her stomach gave a slow and delicious flip. What the hell did *that* mean? That he wanted to stay or that he was making a point?

The service progressed at the front of the room and she barely heard a word of it. Her mind continued to whirl while cheers rang out around them and a shower of yellow confetti fluttered over Adam and Ernie as they raised triumphant hands above their heads. She hardly took in any of it. All she wanted was to drag Dan somewhere quiet to talk.

Nerves twisted inside her as she followed the rest of the guests back up the yellow-ribbon-lined aisle and into the hotel's conservatory for drinks while the marquee was reset for dinner. A string quartet kicked into action at one side of the room as waiting staff with trays of canapés began to mingle with the guests. Dan nodded around, smiling and winking at people, working the fake plus-one wedding guest image to a tee, and suddenly she could stand it no longer.

She grabbed him by the elbow and tugged him to a quiet corner of the room.

'Where *were* you all morning, then?' she said. 'You don't get off that easily.'

She waited for him to regale her with how he'd single-handedly solved Adam's problems and then sit back to watch her eat her words.

Instead he shrugged easily and took a sip of his champagne.

'Around. I'm an early riser. You were dead to the world, snoring away.'

He grinned broadly as she aimed an exasperated slap at his shoulder.

'I do *not* snore.'

So he was clearly not immediately going to volunteer what he'd done. What was the point of actually *doing* it, then, if it hadn't been to impress her?

She ran her hand through her hair, trying to think straight. She was so confused.

Dan watched her over the rim of his glass, trying to maintain a relaxed air of mingling wedding guest when all he wanted to do was stare at her. She looked prettier than ever in a silver-grey silk dress that set off her creamy complexion. Her hair was lying in soft waves, one side held back from her face by a sparkly clip. His desire for her was as strong as it had been the previous night. Nothing had changed. Had he really thought it would?

She held his gaze boldly and he heard her take a deep breath.

'You helped Adam,' she said. 'I know about the loan. I thought you didn't want to get sucked into family stuff.'

He deliberately didn't meet her eyes and kept his tone light.

'Yeah, well, I wasn't thinking straight when you first suggested it,' he said. 'Maybe I just wasn't crazy on Adam's timing.'

He watched the blush rise on her cheeks at his reference to the previous night and heat began to pool deep in his abdomen.

'Well, if you think I'll just hop into bed with you now, because you stepped up to the plate with Adam, you're wrong,' she said.

If only that were the limit of his need for her.

'If I'd wanted to go to bed with someone I wouldn't have wasted half the night counselling Adam. I would have been down in the lobby chatting up the receptionist.'

If he needed any reminder that he was in over his head here, there it was. This was *not* just about getting her into bed.

He'd actually done far more than he'd intended when he'd left her sleeping in the small hours. The plan to just give Adam some kind of rousing pep talk had gone out of the window when he'd realised the monumental size of the mess he was in. Within five minutes it had become clear that a couple of websites and the number of a debt helpline were simply not going to cut the mustard, and the temptation had never been stronger to simply bow out of the situation and leave all of them to it while he went right back to his safe and organised life in London.

But all he'd been able to think about was Emma floundering the next morning, trying to pick up the pieces, and he simply hadn't been able to do it to her.

And what that decision meant filled him with far

more trepidation than practically writing out a blank check to her lunatic brother.

He had feelings for her. Beyond anything he'd felt since Maggie. And even she now seemed to be taking on a vagueness in his mind that she hadn't had before—as if the edges of her memory were being softened by the reality of the present.

'To prove a point, then,' she said, narrowing her eyes. 'You can't stand being wrong and I touched a nerve.'

He cocked an eyebrow.

'With your "sad workaholic singleton" comment, you mean? I think I've had a few worse insults than that over the years.'

'Then what? Why would you do that about-face if it wasn't so you could have the last word?'

The cynical tilt of her chin finally tipped him into irritation.

'I notice you haven't asked me if I just did it out of the goodness of my heart. It hasn't occurred to you that I might just want to *help.*'

'Of course it hasn't. Because there's always an ulterior motive with you. Normally it's to do with work. Or possibly sex.'

'Emma, are you so used to being second best that you have to find some negative reason when the truth is staring you in the face? Why is it that you can't possibly contemplate that I might have just done the whole bloody thing for *you?*' he blurted in exasperation. 'You're maddening, your family are insane, you snore and your luggage habits are scary. But for some reason I'd rather commit myself financially to your mad brother and stay here with you instead of going back to London and my nice, peaceful, "sad workaholic singleton" life. Do you think I don't want to run for the hills? Truth is, I can't. I've realised there's nowhere I'd rather be than here.' He paused for breath. 'With you.'

She was staring at him.

His pulse vaulted into action as he met her wide brown eyes. He could see the light flush on her cheekbones. All the unrequited tension of the night before sceped back through his body. All around them the socialising carried on, and the urge raced through him to ignore the lot of them, grab her by the hand and tug her upstairs—let this crazy charade go on without them.

He closed the gap between them and lifted a hand to her cheek. The softness of her skin was tantalising beneath his fingers.

'Dinner is served.'

The Master of Ceremonies' curt tones cut through the background buzz of chatter and snapped him out of it.

'Do stop dawdling, darling,' Emma's mother called as she swept past them in her ghastly coral ensemble, undoubtedly en route to the top table.

Oh, for Pete's sake…

By the time the meal was over the presence of Adam's entire social circle was beginning to seriously annoy Emma. It was extremely difficult to have an in-depth personal conversation while seated at a table of eight overenthusiastic art groupies.

Dinner finished with, the marquee was cleared of the tables in the centre to reveal a glossy dance floor. Strings of fairy lights and candelabra supplied a twinkly, magical ambience. You couldn't move without tripping over a champagne waiter. And this after the most sumptuous four-course meal she'd ever been too strung-out to eat. Clearly there had been no expense spared. She wondered just how big Dan's loan to Adam was. If this was the level of his spending habits he'd still be paying it off when he was drawing his pension.

'I mean, really—no speeches? No best man. No bridesmaids. No tradition whatsoever! I just want to *know*—and I'm sure I'm not alone in this—' her mother glanced around for confirmation '—what happens about the name-change? Who takes whose name?'

She looked expectantly at Adam, standing nearby, who shifted from foot to foot.

'Mum, it's no different to any other wedding. You can take or not take whatever name you please,' Emma said, pasting on a smile to counteract any offence that might be caused. 'You're living in the past.'

'I don't agree. I don't see why Adam should change his name.'

'I'm not,' Adam said. 'And neither is Ernie.'

Her mother rounded on Ernie, who took an automatic defensive step backwards.

'Why not?' she demanded. 'Is our family name not good enough?'

'Mum, please…' Emma said.

Ernie held his hands up.

'It's perfectly fine, Emma. It's nothing to do with family names.' He looked kindly at her mother. 'I'd walk over hot coals for him, darling, but I cannot possibly be known as Ernie Burney.'

Adam took his arm and they moved away. Her mother gaped for a moment, and then took refuge in her usual critical safe bet in order to save face.

'Of course if *you* could only find a man who would commit there wouldn't be any of this lunacy,' she snapped at Emma. 'We could have a proper wedding with all the trimmings.'

The band chose that moment to launch into full-on swing music, mercifully making it impossible to hear any further argument, and the compère took to the glossy parquet floor.

'Ladies and gentlemen, I give you…the groom and groom.'

Her mother's mouth puckered and then disappeared as a pool of light flicked on in the centre to reveal Adam and Ernie striking a pose. A kitsch disco track kicked into action and they threw themselves into a clearly pre-rehearsed dance routine.

Dan stared in amazement as Adam danced past them, finger stabbing the air above his head, back to his full quota of sweeping flamboyant enthusiasm. Ernie skidded across the parquet on his knees, snapping his fingers above his head. A circle of guests began to form at the edges of the dance floor, clapping along. The room worked itself into a crescendo of rhythmic toe-tapping. It was bedlam.

'And…the parents of the happy couple…'

Ernie's father, completely unaware of what he was letting himself in for, held out a hand to Emma's mother and began propelling her around the floor. Emma watched her mother's stiff and obvious fluster with a grin.

'She can't complain. She did want a bit more tradition after all,' she said.

'And…family and friends…please take the floor…'

Dan held his hand out, a smile crinkling his eyes. She stared at him, her heart skipping into action.

'I don't dance,' she said, shaking her head.

He totally ignored her. Before she could wriggle free

he'd caught her fingers in his own and tugged her against him, curling his free hand around her waist.

'Just hang on, then,' he said.

The jaunty music demanded a lot more balance and rhythm than a swaying slow dance, and Emma silently cursed Adam for his disco obsession.

Dan turned out to be an excellent dancer. He propelled her smoothly around the floor in perfect time to the music and she somehow managed to hold on to him instead of falling over. Then at last the music mercifully slowed and embarrassment slowly gave way to consciousness of him. She could feel the hard muscle of his thighs moving against her own. Sparks jumped from her fingers as he laced them through his. His heartbeat pressed against hers.

'Why now, then?' she said, looking up at him, a light frown shadowing her face. 'You haven't answered that question. You had *months* to make a move on me if you were interested. Months of work dates back in London. Why now? Why here? Because you'd made it clear our agreement was over? Is that it? You were pretty keen to draw a line under our relationship when this weekend finished, so did that make me fair game?'

'If I'd known you were interested maybe I would have made a move before,' he said, knowing perfectly well he'd never have allowed himself to do so.

She made an exasperated sound.

'That's crap. I'm *so* not your type.'

'In actual fact you're *exactly* my type. And that's why I never made a move. I met you in your work role and you were so bloody good at it I wasn't about to ruin that by sleeping with you. I needed you too much.'

She pulled away from him a little as she processed what that might mean.

'And now you don't need me any more, sleeping with me is suddenly back on the agenda? Is that it?'

'That's not it at all. This weekend is the first I've spent with anyone at such close quarters without sex being the only thing on the agenda. And it isn't a piece of cake, I'll be honest with you. Nothing about you is easy. You're a pain to share a room with, and your family are more bonkers than I realised, but for the first time in I don't know how long work isn't the first thing I'm thinking about.'

She looked up at him and met his eyes, his expression clear and genuine.

'When I talked to Adam I realised there would be a massive fallout if the wedding didn't go ahead. I could imagine the embarrassment, the fuss, having to send the guests away. It wasn't about Adam. He's got himself into trouble and he should dig himself out of it. It might even be character-building. When I couldn't walk away I realised that the person I was really doing it for was you. And that's when I knew that, whatever I felt about you, platonic work colleague didn't really cover it any more.'

He carried on talking, thinking vaguely that they seemed to have lost time with the jaunty beat of the music. Other guests began to whirl past them.

She stopped dancing. He attempted a couple more steps before giving up and joining her. The thing about dancing was that you needed your partner at least to *attempt* to engage—otherwise it was akin to dragging a sack of potatoes around the floor at speed. Trepidation spiked in his stomach at the look of disbelief on her face, telling him that his feelings for her had climbed way further than he'd thought. He'd been kind of banking on a smile at the very least.

'Say that again.'

'Emma, we're in the middle of the bloody dance floor. Let's go and sit down, get a drink.'

'I don't want a drink. Say that again.'

'I couldn't give a toss about Adam getting into trouble?'

She punched his shoulder.

'Not that bit.'

He saw the mock-exasperated smile on her lips, saw it climb to her eyes.

'Platonic work colleague didn't cover it any more?'

The smile melted away. She was looking up at him, brown eyes wide, soft lips lightly parted, and the madly circling dance floor around them disappeared from his consciousness.

'Yes. That bit.'

He tightened his grip around her waist and slid his fingers into her hair, stroking his thumb along her jawline as he tilted her lips to meet his.

Emma's heart was thundering as if they'd done another disco turn instead of swaying languorously around the dance floor.

The Dan she'd known for a year and long given up on would never have helped Adam out for nothing in return—would never have taken the time to explain his feelings to her. And he would never have turned back having driven halfway to London—not when he'd made his point before he left. She'd bucked his little-black-book no-strings trend. He'd put her first.

Sweet excitement began to swirl in her stomach as

her mind focused on the feel of his body hard against hers and she breathed in the scent of spicy aftershave and warm skin as he kissed and kissed and kissed her.

At last she opened her eyes to see the *déjà-vu* disapproving stare of her mother across the room. Necking on the dance floor, this time, instead of in corridors—how common. Except that this time she found she really couldn't give a *damn*.

She laced her hand through his and tugged at his arm. 'Let's go upstairs.'

CHAPTER TEN

She followed him into the hotel room, buying a bit more time and space for her skittering nerves by leaning gently back against the door until it clicked shut. The party carried on in the marquee below them and music and faint laughter drifted in through the window, open a crack. The closed curtains fluttered lightly in the night breeze.

Delicious anticipation fluttered in her stomach as he turned back to her in the soft amber glow of the table lamp and tugged her into his arms, his mouth groping for hers, finding it, sucking gently on her lower lip and caressing it softly with his tongue.

His fingers slipped beneath the fall of her hair to find the zip of her dress and he pulled it slowly down in one smooth motion, sliding the fluttering sleeves from her shoulders, his mouth tracing the blade of her collarbone with tiny kisses. He smoothed her dress lower, until it fell from her body into a gleaming puddle of silk on the floor. And then her mind followed his hands as they explored her body, as he unhooked her bra, cast it aside and cupped her breasts softly in his palms. Her nipples were pinched lightly between his fingers, sending dizzying flutters down her spine where they intensified hotly between her legs.

Then came brief unsteadiness as he slid his hands firmly beneath her thighs and lifted her against him. She could feel his rigid arousal press against her as she curled her legs around his waist and he carried her the few paces across the room to the antique desk. He held her tightly against him and she leaned sideways as he swept her belongings carelessly onto the floor. Body lotion and hairbrush fell with meaningless thuds onto the deep-pile carpet, and then there was cool, smooth wood against her skin as he put her down on the desk in just her panties.

She'd had a few boyfriends, yes. In the dim and distant past she'd done the rounds, albeit in a minor way, at university. None of it had felt like this. And if during the last year she'd let herself imagine what it might feel like to be with him it had never touched this reality. His every touch made her heart leap and her stomach flutter. His touch was expert, but there was nothing by rote about this. He seemed in tune with her every need and desire, as if he could read her mind.

His hands found her thighs again, parting them softly, and then he was tracing kisses down her neck, his mouth sliding lower until he closed his lips over her nipple, teasing it softly with his tongue. Heat simmered in her stomach and pooled meltingly between her thighs as he sank to his knees and traced his mouth lightly over the flat of her stomach. She sucked in a sharp breath as his lips sank lower still and the heat of his breath warmed her through the lace of her panties. She gasped as his fingers teased the thin fabric aside and his tongue slipped against the very core of her.

Her hands found his hair and clutched at it as he stroked and teased until she ached for him to go further, and then delicious pleasure flooded her veins as he slid two fingers inside her in one slow and smooth movement. She moaned softly as he found his rhythm, moving his fingers steadily as his tongue lazily circled the nub of her, moving with her, until she cried her ecstasy at the ceiling and he moved both hands beneath her, holding her against his mouth, wringing every last second of satisfaction out of her.

Anonymity was gone. That inconsequential, easy gratification wasn't there. Because for once this wasn't about quick fun, satisfaction. Dispensable satisfaction.

This was about her. Wanting to please *her*. And that was a real novelty that knocked his senses sprawling.

The light change in her breath as he ran his fingertips over the softness of her thighs, the way she gasped and clutched at his hair as he moved them higher—all those little gestures delighted him and turned him on all the more.

Dan got to his feet in the hollow between her parted legs and pulled her close. She curled her arms around him, tugging him against her, her fast, short breaths warm against his lips. Her evident excitement, such a foil to her usual carefully controlled attitude, thrilled him to the core, and in the all-encompassing heat of his arousal he marvelled at the surge of excitement pleasing her elicited.

He had been going through the motions all this time. His dates, his easy flings... Plenty of them, but all a simple good time means to an end. The cost of that had been the detached quality about them that meant pleasure had failed to touch him below the physical surface. The combination of his visceral hot need for Emma, his delight at her eagerness to please him and his own desire to please her took him way beyond that level. There was nothing run of the mill about this.

The thought crept through his mind, tinged with fear at the deeper meaning of it, but he moved on regardless, powerless to stop.

He lifted her, his hands sliding across the cool satiny skin of her lower back, the sweet vanilla scent of her hair dizzying his senses, and crushed his mouth hard against hers. His desire for her was rising inside him like a cresting wave, driving him forward. Her legs wrapped around his waist as he carried her the few paces from desk to four-poster and eased her down gently onto the softness of the quilted bedspread.

And now he moved with intimate slowness, the better to savour every second, to explore. She slid gentle hands over his back and sparks of arousal jumped and flickered in his abdomen as her fingers found his hard length and stroked with deliciously maddening softness. A guttural moan escaped his lips as he tangled a hand in the silk of her hair and crushed his mouth against hers, easing her lips apart with his tongue.

Before he could be consumed by the deliciousness of it he caught her hand and moved away briefly to find a condom. And then control was his again as he moved against her, and her gasp thrilled him as he eased slowly into her. As she raised her hips with a soft moan, urging him on, sliding her hands around him to push him deeper into her, greedy for more, his spirits soared. And only as she clutched at his back and cried her pleasure against his neck did he finally let himself follow her over that delicious edge.

Bewildering *déjà vu* kicked in as Emma woke to bird-song and sunshine for the second time in a weekend. And then all thoughts of her surroundings disappeared as she came fully awake in one crushing instant of consciousness. She turned her head slowly on the pillow.

Not a hallucination brought on by wedding stress and too much champagne.

Dan was in the bed next to her. And they'd spent the night exploring every inch of one another. Hell, her cheeks fired just at the thought of what they'd done and she pressed her face against the cool top sheet. Had that *really* been her? Super-cool, professional Emma? Brazen—that was what she was.

His dark hair was dishevelled even beyond its usual spikes by action and sleep, and there was a light shadow of stubble now defining his jaw. She lifted a hand to her dry mouth as her gaze ranged down the defined muscles of his torso to the sheet that lay haphazardly over his hips. He was the stuff of dreams.

But the cold light of day was streaming in right through that window. She'd joined the ranks of Dan's little-black-book girls. How long did he usually leave it before he did his backing off? A day? Two?

She held her breath and without sitting up began wriggling inch by slow inch towards the edge of the bed, not really thinking much further at this point than getting some clothes on. They might have spent half the night screwing, but that didn't mean he'd have the chance to ogle her cellulite in daylight.

She was right on the edge of the bed and just thinking

about how to manoeuvre her feet onto the floor when he took a deep, relaxed breath and opened his eyes.

She froze like a rabbit in headlights.

'You look surprised,' he said, stretching easily.

He gave her that slow, laconic grin that never failed to make her stomach do flip-flops. Clearly she had the *look* of a rabbit in headlights, too.

'Is it such a disappointment to wake up next to me?'

She clutched the top of the sheet a modest few inches above nipple height and tried to move her bum cheeks back fully onto the bed so he wouldn't realise she'd been trying to make an exit.

'I wasn't sure I would,' she said. 'I half expected you to make a swift exit under cover of darkness. Didn't you tell me that was your usual modus operandi? Not to make it through to breakfast?'

He pulled himself up onto one elbow and smiled down at her. The benefit of having hair that naturally spiked was that he actually looked *better* first thing in the morning. How typical. She could just imagine the fright wig on her own head after the active night they'd spent.

'Emma, nothing about this is my usual modus operandi.'

His blue eyes held her own and her stomach gave a slow and toe-curling flip as the delectable things he'd done to her last night danced through her mind. He reached a hand out to stroke her cheek softly and a surge of happiness began to bubble through her. He was right. None of this fitted with him acting to type. Yet still it was hard to let herself trust him.

'I know you too well,' she said. 'That's the thing. None of your usual lines will work on me.'

'I wasn't aware I'd used any,' he said.

He had a point. He'd bailed her brother out, he hadn't washed his hands of her and disappeared to London after she'd called him selfish, he'd carried himself brilliantly through her brother's crazy wedding and he was still here at breakfast time. She let her guard slip.

Self-doubt. Any other reaction from her would be a surprise, wouldn't it?

Just looking at her lying next to him, all long limbs and messy hair and uncertainty, made heat begin to simmer again deep inside him. The night they'd spent replayed in his mind on a loop—the way she'd slowly put her trust in him, shedding her inhibitions, giving as much as taking. He wanted to smooth every kink of doubt out of her, convince her that this was far more than the throwaway night she clearly thought it might be.

He reached across and pulled her into his arms, fitting her long, slender body against his own, breathing in the faint sweet vanilla scent that still clung to her hair. His mouth found hers and he parted her lips hungrily with his tongue and kissed her deeply.

Desire rippled through her, peaking at her nipples and pooling between her legs as he gently turned her over, his mouth at her shoulder.

In her dreams of all those months ago he had been skilled. In reality he was melt-to-the-floor perfect. How did he know how to make her feel that sublime? Where to touch her? How hard to stroke? How softly to caress?

He lay behind her now, her pleasure his sole focus. One hand was circling her waist, his fingers easing slowly between her thighs, softly parting them to expose the core of her. She felt his moan of satisfaction against her neck as he discovered how wet she was. His thumb found her most sensitive spot and circled it with tantalising slowness. His fingers slid lower, teasing until she ached with emptiness and desire.

And then he was turning her expertly, one hand pressed flat beneath her stomach, the other cradling her breasts as he moved behind her. A moment of delicious anticipation as he paused to grab a condom, then she felt him press against her. And then he was thrusting smoothly deep inside her, filling her deliciously, his free hand teasing her nipples to rock-hard points, his mouth at her neck. As she cried out in uncontrolled pleasure he moaned his own ecstasy against the smooth contours of her back, not slowing or changing pace until he knew she was satisfied.

Afterwards, she lay in his arms, the warm length of his torso against her back, his soft breath against her hair. His hand circled her body, lightly cupping her breast, caressing it. They fitted together perfectly, as if they were meant to be together. For the first time she let herself tentatively believe that they might be. He'd made love to her again instead of making a sharp exit. He was still here with her. Yet still there were things that needed to be said.

'I didn't say thank you, did I?' she said softly. When he didn't answer she turned her head slightly, to catch his expression at her shoulder. 'For restoring Adam's shadow for me.'

She felt him tense briefly, then he tugged gently at her shoulder until she turned over in his arms and lay facing him. His mouth was inches from her own and his gaze was holding hers steadily.

He looked at her resigned expression and mentally kicked himself.

'I didn't mean that,' he said. 'It was a crappy thing to say. I know how difficult your family can be.' He paused as if groping for the right words. 'It wasn't a personal dig at you. It was more about reacting to your telling me where to get off.'

'You always have to have the last word,' she said quietly. 'I've noticed that about you. Why is that? Why is it so hard for you to accept anyone else's agenda? People *do* have them, you know—it's not just *you* living in a bubble.'

Was that how she really saw him? Was he really that blind to other people's feelings?

'It wasn't intentional,' he said. 'I'm sorry if it seemed that way to you. It was...' He groped for a way to explain that wouldn't sound totally crap. 'I like staying in control,' he said at last. 'Being the one that makes all the decisions. Perhaps it's become a bit of a habit.' He paused and added, 'A defence mechanism.'

The same one he'd used so successfully since childhood.

'If the only person you look out for is yourself, you can't be hurt.'

'I don't understand.'

He looked at the ceiling, at the blank white expanse of it.

'There was someone once,' he said. 'I'm not talking about one of the girls I see now. They're just dates. Nothing more to it than that. There was someone else a long time ago.'

He didn't look at her. It felt easier, not doing that.

'Maggie and I were housemates at college,' he said.

'There were six of us. Couple of girls, four blokes, each of us renting a room and sharing a kitchen and bathroom. You know the kind of thing. Student accommodation. For the first time I was living away from home.'

He remembered how liberating it had felt that his life was finally his own. An escape route.

'We were friends, Maggie and me, then one night after a party we ended up sleeping together. We kept it really casual, though. Both of us had big career plans. She was training to be a teacher. Primary school kids, you know?'

He glanced at Emma and she nodded acknowledgment, not interrupting. That was a good thing. If he stopped talking about this now he might never start again.

'And she lived up north, had a big family there, and she was going to be moving back once she'd finished her course. It wasn't serious. It was never *going* to be serious.' He laughed. 'Hell, I'd just got *away* from home life, finally tasted a bit of freedom. I wasn't about to get myself tied down to someone before I'd even finished my first year.'

She looked puzzled.

'But you did? You must have for her to have made such a big impact on you. What happened?'

He paused, gathering his thoughts. Who had he told about the baby? Anyone at all? He stormed ahead before he could think twice.

'Maggie got pregnant,' he said simply.

He felt the change in her posture as she shifted in his arms. She lifted herself on one elbow to look at him. He steeled himself to glance at her and read the response in her face, ready for the questions that he was sure would follow.

She said nothing. Her eyes were filled with gentleness but she didn't speak, didn't pry. She was letting him talk on his own terms.

'And that changed everything,' he said.

He took a sharp breath as he recalled the memory. It came back to him easily, in such perfect clarity that it made a mockery of his conviction that he'd done such a great job of putting it behind him.

'At first I was horrified. I thought it was the last thing I could possibly want. Maggie had strong views. She was going to keep the baby whether I was involved or not.' He sighed. 'She made it sound like she was offering me my freedom, but looking back I think to her I was dispensable even at the outset.'

'And were you? Involved, I mean?'

He could see the puzzlement in her eyes. She was wondering if he had a secret family stashed away somewhere.

'Once I got used to the shock I was more and more delighted. The longer it went on the more I bought into it. With every day that passed I had a clearer idea of what the future would be like. I was going to be the best bloody husband and father the world had ever seen.'

'You've been married?'

He gave a rueful smile and shook his head.

'It was my one and only brush with it, but, no, it never happened. I wanted it to be as different to my experience of family as I could make it. Proper commitment, hands-on parents with a strong, healthy relationship.' He paused. 'I probably envisaged a white picket fence somewhere. And a dog. Sunday roasts. All the stereotypes. I was right in there with them.' He took a breath. 'And then it all disappeared overnight because we lost the baby.'

The wrenching, churning ache deep in his chest made a suffocating comeback. Dulled a little at the edges over time, like an old wound, but still there, still heavy.

She was sitting up now, reaching for his hands, her eyes filled with sadness.

'Oh, bloody hell, Dan. I'm so sorry.'

He waved a dismissive hand at her, shaking his head, swallowing hard to rid his throat of the aching constriction.

'It was a long time ago,' he said.

In terms of years, at least.

'I'm over it.'

'I never imagined you being remotely interested in kids or family,' she said. 'I mean, it isn't just the way you keep your relationships so short or the fact you never see your own parents. You're the most un-child-friendly person I've ever known. You have a penthouse flat with a balcony and it's full of glass furniture and white upholstery. Your car is a two-seater.'

'Why would I need a family home or a Volvo?' he said. 'I have absolutely no intention of going down that road again. I gave it my best shot and it didn't work out.'

A worried frown played about her face and he gave her a reassuring *I'm-over-it* smile.

'That's why I didn't step straight up to the plate when Adam needed a helping hand. That's why I made it into the car before I realised I couldn't leave for London. I was trying to play things the way I always do. I don't get involved with people. I like keeping things simple.'

'At arm's length.'

'Exactly. Arm's length. After Maggie I decided relationships weren't for me. Family wasn't for me. I threw myself into work instead. After all, it had always worked at digging me out in the past. And it worked again.' He shrugged. 'But maybe it's become a bit of a habit. I never wanted to come across as selfish or unkind when I said you liked your comfort zone. It was a retaliation, nothing more.'

He pulled her back down from her elbow into a cuddle. Her head nestled beneath his chin. She shook her head slowly against his chest.

'Maybe it *was* just a retaliation but actually you might have had a point,' she said quietly.

He pulled away enough to give her a questioning look and she offered him a tiny smile.

'A *small* point,' she qualified. 'Did you ever know I had a crush on you for months, like some stupid schoolgirl?'

That flash of clarity kicked in again, the same as he'd felt the night before, as if something he wasn't seeing had been pointed out to him. A wood instead of a mass of trees, maybe.

'You did?'

'Why am I not surprised that you never noticed?' She sighed and rolled her eyes. 'I think maybe part of the reason I was so struck on you was because of what you're like. I knew you'd never look twice at me. I didn't fit your remit.'

'My *remit?*' He grinned and tugged her closer.

She snuggled into his arm. 'Blonde, bubbly, curvaceous. That's your type.'

'Dispensable, simplistic, inconsequential,' he said.

'Those were the real qualities I was aiming for. None of which apply to you.'

'That's exactly my point. I got to know you over months, I saw the kind of girls you went for and I knew none of your relationships lasted. I knew you'd never be interested in me and that made dreaming about the prospect from afar a very nice, safe thing to do.'

She held a hand up as if it was all suddenly clear to her.

'Plus it was a great reason not to get involved with anyone else, and it gave me the perfect way to fob off criticism from my parents when they asked about my life. So there you are, you see. When you said I was happy living in Adam's shadow, staying under my parents' radar, you kind of had a point. My choices were all about keeping an easy life.'

'You must have hidden it well,' he said, scanning his mind back over the last twelve months. Little signs jumped out at him now that he had that hindsight—the way she'd always been available for any work engagement, no matter how short the notice, the effort she'd always made with her appearance. He'd assumed those were things she did for everyone. Because that was what he'd *wanted* to assume. The alternative hadn't been allowed on his radar.

'Then again, I'm not sure I would have noticed unless you'd smashed me over the head with it,' he conceded. 'I had you filed very comfortably under "Work Colleague". That was what I needed you to be. I never intended things between us to be more than that.'

'Our plus-one agreement.'

He didn't respond, although the ensuing silence was heavy with the unspoken question. What would happen now with their ludicrous arrangement? He'd told her it would be over when they got this weekend out of the way and went back to their London lives. With every moment he spent with her, sticking to that decision and riding it out felt more and more difficult.

CHAPTER ELEVEN

'YOU WANT TO try and get to breakfast?' he asked.

Emma felt the light brush of his kiss against her shoulder. Even after the night they'd spent, followed by the delicious intimacy of this morning, his touch thrilled her.

She wriggled against him. Her arms fitted around his neck as if they were meant to be there. She smoothed the dense spikes of his hair through her fingers.

'Let me think,' she said, smiling into his eyes. 'Would I rather sit opposite my parents and watch my father drool over a full English while my mother force-feeds him muesli, or would I rather stay here with you?'

He laughed and pulled her tighter.

'Adam's married now. I think he's grown-up enough to manage without me watching his back through one little breakfast.' She dropped her eyes briefly. 'And I think you've done enough for him. We can catch him before he goes.'

Was it just that? Or was part of it that she didn't want to leave this gorgeous little bubble where he was hers for fear that it might burst? After wanting him for so long, all the while convinced nothing would ever come of it, to actually have her crush requited made it seem all the sweeter.

Needling doubt lurked at the edge of her consciousness despite the gorgeous night they'd spent and the way he'd opened up about his past. She knew Dan—knew the way he played relationships. Despite his reassurances there was no getting away from the fact that pretty soon after you made it into Dan's bed you made it just as quickly out of it, never to be heard of again. Was this like some holiday romance? Would the magic be theirs as long as they didn't leave? What would happen when they got back to London?

She'd noticed that her mention of the old plus-one agreement hadn't been picked up by him. His intention to cut all ties with her after this weekend gnawed at the edge of her consciousness as she tried to push it away.

Adam and Ernie stood at the hotel doorway, waving madly. Those who had made it down to breakfast clustered in the lobby. Emma had dragged Dan downstairs with moments to spare and eased her way through the group of smiling friends and relatives, her hand entwined in his.

Emma's mother dabbed a tear from the corner of her eye.

'Well, it wasn't the most traditional set-up,' she sniffed, 'but still…it's been a lovely weekend.'

She kissed Adam's cheek and then leaned in to do the same to Ernie.

'Tradition?' Ernie said. 'I think we can stretch to a bit of that before we go.'

He grabbed at a bunch of yellow lilies standing in a huge vase on the side table near the door, turned his back on the gathered crowd of guests and lobbed them high in the air over his head to the sound of claps and squeals, showering the guests with drops of water. As the flowers plummeted, twisting and turning, faces turned to watch their progress.

Dan shot out a hand and caught them on autopilot, to prevent them from smacking him over the head.

He stared down stupidly at the bunch of flowers in his hand as cheers and mad clapping rang out all around them. Even Emma's mother was smiling.

'You're next!' Adam hollered from the doorway. 'Great catch, sweetie!'

Dan glanced at Emma and saw the look of delight on her face. Her eyes shone. Her smile lit up her face. She radiated happiness.

Shock flooded into the pit of his stomach.

You're next!

Was he? Was that where this led?

He'd had a game plan way back in London, before they'd even set foot in the West Country. A plan to be a last-time-pays-for-all fake boyfriend stand-in for Emma and then go back to London. Back to work. Back to what *worked*. And somehow he'd been caught up in the moment, had lost sight of what was important to him.

He'd ended up standing here with flowers in his hands to the sound of excited applause because the path ahead of him led down the aisle. Maybe not now, maybe not even in the next few years, but *that* was the destination.

If they made it that far.

That was the risk. A risk he'd vowed never to take again after the months of despair that had plagued him when Maggie left.

This was way off-plan. Yet the thought of losing Emma now made his heart plummet and misery churn in his stomach.

He followed the rest of the group outside to watch Adam and Ernie pile into a yellow Rolls-Royce. Maybe he could find another way forward. A way to keep her that still minimised risk. A compromise.

She'd been right.

There really was more between them than one of his casual flings. They'd been back from the wedding for nearly a week now and he was a different man. He was in touch with her daily, and with every phone call and text she felt more secure. Flowers arrived from him at her workplace, eliciting envious stares and buzzing interest from her colleagues. He hadn't so much as mentioned their old plus-one agreement, but that was because it was obsolete—right? Past history. OK, so she wasn't expecting him to propose…let's not get ahead of ourselves—although a girl could dream. But she'd been the one to change his behaviour. He really *was* different with her. They were a couple now—not just work contacts.

Dan didn't *do* flowers and phone calls. He did swift exits and dumping by text. And now she was seeing him tonight and her stomach was one big ball of excitement and anticipation. She couldn't wait.

The doorbell. On time.

She checked her appearance one last time. A new dress, a less austere one than usual, with a floaty, feminine skirt. Deep pink instead of her usual black or grey choice of going-out outfit. Because going out with Dan was about pleasure now, not business. About getting to know each other instead of working the situation for every career advantage they could get out of it.

She opened the front door and excitement at seeing him brought an instant smile to her face—one she couldn't have held back. He stood on the doorstep, leaning against the jamb, his crisp blue shirt deepening the tones of his eyes as he smiled at her, a perfectly cut business suit and silk tie sharpening the look.

Not the same relaxed designer look he'd had at the wedding weekend. Her mind stuttered briefly. *Business suit.*

From nowhere cautionary unease jabbed her in the ribs and a wave of disorientating *déjà vu* swept over her. She could have rewound to a couple of months before Adam's wedding, before Alistair had put a stop to their agreement, and Dan would have looked exactly like this when she'd opened the door for one of their business engagements.

He slid an arm around her waist and kissed her softly on the mouth, starting up all the latent sparks from the weekend.

She pulled herself up short.

Jumping at shadows—that was what she was doing. She was so used to being doomed to failure when she put herself out there that now she was pre-empting problems before they even happened. She'd ruin things herself if she wasn't careful. Already he had a puzzled expression on his face—no doubt because her first reaction on seeing him since their gorgeous weekend at the wedding was to hesitate.

He'd called her. He'd sent flowers. He'd texted. And now she was spooked because of the *suit* he wore? She really needed to go to work on her own insecurities if she was going to move forward with her life.

'Where are we going, then?' she asked when he started the car.

'Dinner first,' he said easily, putting it in gear and

moving smoothly into the early-evening traffic. 'I've got a table booked at La Maison.'

Another jab of unease.

'La Maison?'

It was Dan's choice of venue for work dinners. She'd been there with him too many times to count, always as his stand-in date, always with a work objective in mind. Maybe it would be a new contact to impress, perhaps a sweetener before he put in a tender for services. Whatever it happened to be, she'd been there to help smooth the path.

He glanced across at her.

'For starters, yes. If that's OK with you? Then maybe later we could go on somewhere else? End up at my place?'

'Of course.'

She smiled brightly at him and pressed her palms together in her lap. They were damp.

He parked the car and escorted her into the restaurant. The usual subtle piano music played in the background, and the usual perfectly dressed dark wood tables and soft lighting provided the perfect ambience for discussion, which had always been the point of coming here.

His usual table. She felt Dan's hand rest gently on her hip as he guided her between the tables towards it.

Usual restaurant. Usual table.

It didn't mean anything, did it? The restaurant was a good one after all.

Usual quick run-through of background?

'Roger Lewis and Barry Trent,' he said in a low voice at her shoulder. 'Medium-sized business providing bespoke travel packages specifically aimed at the over-fifties. Looking for advice on growing their business to the next level.' He gave her shoulder a squeeze. 'Could be in the market for a change in legal services, too—you could be in there!'

As they arrived at the table she turned to stare at him and he actually *winked* at her. It felt as if her heart was being squeezed in a vice.

'Table for four,' she said dully, stating the obvious.

He looked at her as if she might be mad. As if there was nothing spot-the-deliberate-mistake about this at all.

'Of course it is,' he said. 'Just a bit of business to discuss and then the evening's ours. They'll be along in a minute.'

The waiter pulled a chair out for her and fussed over her as she sat down hard, her mind reeling. Dan gave him the nod and he poured them each a glass of champagne, replacing the bottle in the ice bucket to one side of the table.

Her throat felt as if it might be closing up and she swallowed hard. She clasped her hands together on the table to stop them shaking.

'I thought we were going on a date,' she said, making her tone as neutral as she could manage when what she wanted to do was grab him by the shoulders and shake him. 'Just you and me. But this is basically the same old set-up, Dan.'

She waved a hand at the extra two table settings, at the surrounding quiet tastefulness of the restaurant.

'Is that it, then? Now we're back in London it's back to the same old routine? Were you actually going to discuss that with me, or did you just assume I'd go along with it?'

He reached for her hands but she removed them to her lap.

'I don't know what you mean,' he said.

'What this looks like to me is the same old plus-one agreement,' she said, forcing the words out, voicing her worst fears. 'Just with sex thrown in.'

He grimaced and leaned across the table to touch her cheek.

'This is *not* the same old plus-one agreement,' he said, 'and I really wish we'd never given the damn thing a name. It makes it sound like we signed something official when all we really did was get into a routine over time. Because it worked so well for *both* of us.'

A routine? She pressed her lips together hard and pushed a hand through her hair as anger began to course through her. It felt suddenly uncomfortably hot in here. She hadn't missed the emphasis there on the word *both*. No way was she letting him lump her in with this as if it were some joint bloody venture.

When he next spoke it felt as if he'd tipped the contents of the ice bucket over her head.

'But if we *have* to call it that,' he continued, holding out a hand, 'for what it's worth I don't think we should be too hasty about changing how we relate to each other when it comes to work. Why end something that's worked so well for us just because you and I have got closer? What do you think about varying it a little? Adding in a few amendments?'

His tone was jokey—teasing, even. As if he were proposing something exciting. As if she ought to be taking his arm off in her eagerness to say yes.

'Different rules this time—it'll be fun. We can still do work engagements together, give it everything we've got just like we always have, but without the need to limit it. There'll be no need to *pretend* we're a couple any more—no need to go our separate ways at the end of the night.'

He wanted to carry on seeing her but without any full-on legitimacy. Work would continue to come first with him, just the way it always had. He would expect her to carry on acting as his plus-one, smoothing the way for his business prowess at charity dinners and the like. The difference would be that this time she would get to share his bed, as well.

Well, *lucky, lucky* her.

All the pent-up excitement that had built this week as she'd looked forward to seeing him again had quit bubbling and dissipated like flat champagne. The flavour would still be there—the tang of white grape and the sharp aroma reminiscent of the effervescent drink it once was—but when you got right down to it, it was past its best. What you were really getting was the dregs.

And one thing she knew without a shadow of a doubt was that she was not going to be the dregs. Not for anyone.

Not even for him.

She stood up, a veil of calm slipping over her. She'd wanted him to be hers so much she'd believed she'd give anything to keep him.

But when it came to it she found that her self-respect just wasn't up for grabs.

He looked up at her, his expression confused, as she picked up her handbag and lifted her wrap from the back of her chair, making it obvious this wasn't just a visit to the ladies' room. She was leaving.

'Where are you going?'

'Home,' she said, not looking at him.

She pushed her chair back into place. Sick disappointment burned in her throat, blocking it. She wasn't sure she could stop it transforming into tears if she looked at him. She absolutely was *not* going to cry. No way.

He stood up immediately, his hand on her elbow.

'Why? What's wrong? Are you ill?'

The look of concern in his eyes touched her heart and she almost faltered. But this was just too bloody reminiscent of the last guy she'd met for dinner, thinking she was on her way to a happy ending. Dan was just like Alistair after all.

'No, Dan,' she said. 'I'm not ill. I'm stupid. Stupid for thinking there might actually be more between us than *work.*'

She made a move to leave and he grabbed her by the hand.

'Hey, we can talk about this. That's what this is about? You're annoyed because I factored a work dinner into our date night?' He shrugged. 'I'm sorry. Maybe I should have talked to you about it first. I just didn't think you'd mind. Before last weekend you were all for carrying on with the agreement, and you'd gone back to work instead of taking that sabbatical, so I just assumed you'd be all for it.'

'That was before the weekend,' she said.

She looked down at her hand, encased in his.

'This isn't what I want. Some half-arsed excuse for a relationship. I thought you understood that. I don't want some relationship where we both have our own agenda and factor the other person in wherever they happen to fit. You know where that kind of relationship ends up?' She didn't wait for his answer. 'It ends up with separate bedrooms and separate interests and separate bloody lives. If we can't even get that right now, what hope do we have? I want you and me to be the priority—not an afterthought to whatever work ambitions we might happen to have.'

'It never bothered you before,' he pointed out.

'Because it was all I *had* before,' she said. 'It was the only way I could have some level of relationship with you. But I want more than that now. And after last weekend I thought you wanted that, too.'

Two business-suited middle-aged men were being ushered between the tables towards them. The over-fifties leisure break people, she assumed.

'Don't go,' he said. 'Let's get this business discussion out of the way and then we can talk this through properly.'

She gave a wry laugh and flung her hands up.

'That's the problem, you see. Right there. You *still* think I might actually sit down and put your work meeting first—before we get to talk about what's happening between us. I'm not doing it. Whatever this is for you—plus-one bloody agreement, quick fling, friends with benefits—it's over.'

She'd raised her voice and some of the diners seated nearby rubbernecked to stare at them. She didn't give a damn. She had no intention of ever visiting this restaurant again. In fact, the way she felt right now, she might not go out socially again. Possibly ever. Maybe she'd embrace her inner workaholic and make senior partnership by thirty-five. A new goal. One that was attainable. One that relied solely on her and so wasn't doomed to failure.

She walked away from the table.

He moved after her as she passed the two businessmen, one with his hand outstretched. She heard Dan apologise briefly before he ran after her. He caught her near the door, took her arm, turned her to face him.

'You're dumping me?' A grin lifted the corner of his mouth.

Her heart twisted agonisingly in her chest.

'Yes,' she said.

'What? No champagne-throwing?' he joked, as if he still couldn't believe she was making such a fuss.

She didn't smile. It felt as if her veins were full of ice water.

'That was a *fake* break-up, Dan,' she said. 'All for show. This is the real thing.'

She walked out of the restaurant without looking back.

CHAPTER TWELVE

DAN STARED AT the city skyline from the balcony of his flat. Grey today, misted in drizzle. The fine rain was the kind that coated and his hair and skin were slowly soaking; the boards were slick beneath his feet.

So she'd dumped him.

No one dumped him. *Ever.* And now she'd done it twice in the space of a couple of months.

The confused feeling of a loss of control which had buried him the first time, back at the art gallery, kicked right back into action. Had that really only been a month or two ago? It felt like years.

He wasn't going to make the same mistake again—grappling for control of the situation and leaving himself open to a second body blow.

Except it really hadn't been just a body blow, had it?

Let it go.

In the first defiant moments after she'd left him to sort out the embarrassment in the restaurant that had felt doable. He didn't need this kind of chaos in his life. That had been the whole point of keeping relationships distant. He'd had a lucky escape.

In the ensuing days it had become more and more difficult to keep himself convinced of that. It wasn't as

if he'd let her have an access-all-areas pass to his life
after all. Their paths crossed at work functions, they
communicated via e-mail and the occasional phone call.
Businesslike. At arm's length. She'd visited his flat on
two or three occasions—never when it was just the two
of them. So it wasn't as if her absence left a gaping hole
in his life where she'd previously been. How could you
miss something that you never had?

He knew that was possible better than anyone.

Somewhere in the depths of his consciousness he understood that what he was missing was the way she'd
made him feel—the way she'd altered his take on life.

He'd spent so long making sure no one became important to him, but she'd somehow managed to get past
that barrier. She'd done it so quietly that he hadn't realised how much he needed her until she was gone, so
perfect had his conviction been that he had everything
under control.

It had seemed like the perfect solution—the perfect
way to keep things at the comfortable distance he'd
thought he needed. Why not just reinstate the old social
agreement? Keep their relationship grounded in something that was tried and tested? Keep some areas of his
life untouched rather than investing his entire soul in
something that might fail?

And in his stupid arrogance he'd just expected her to
go along with his every whim, just to accept that their
relationship had a work slant to it. Especially after her
revelation about her age-old crush on him. She'd taken
whatever he'd thrown her way for the last year, never
asking for anything in return, and he saw now that he'd
just taken that for granted.

If anything he admired her all the more for finally

standing up for what she wanted. She'd wanted out because she wasn't prepared to settle for second best. After years of playing second fiddle to Adam and then being trounced by that moron Alistair Woods she'd been ready to risk everything to be with him and he'd failed her. He'd been too afraid to reciprocate.

The flat that she'd barely visited now felt empty where it had always felt relaxing. So far removed from any family vibe, he'd been able to look around him and know he'd built a new life—one that was successful, one that couldn't collapse under emotional rubble. The prospect of living here now felt empty. He'd had a taste of a different life. He'd tried to keep it in check. But apparently a taste was all that was needed to suck him totally in.

He was in love with her. And it was too late now to guard against loss because the damage was done. He'd screwed up.

He glanced around the balcony—hot tub with its cover on in the corner, railings with a sheer drop below. What had she said—his life was child-unfriendly? It was. Deliberately so. Only now he began to question whether he still wanted that. Whether he ever truly had.

He moved back inside and slid the double doors shut. The flat was totally silent and devoid of character. No mess. No clutter.

He could let this go. See if he couldn't put it behind him. Hell, work had done the trick before—it might do it again. Perhaps if he ceased eating and sleeping and all other essential functions, doubled the effort with his business, he could crush her from his mind.

Or he could take a risk.

He glanced around him again. What, really, did he have to lose?

* * *

'...and Adam and Ernie are heading back from Mauritius. Adam's already got a ton of interest in his new planned collection of pictures and there's talk of them being immortalised on table mats and coasters. Can you imagine?' Her mother paused a moment to let the enormity of that fact sink in. 'That's the kind of mass appeal he has.'

Emma held the phone briefly away from her ear. Dan should have held out for a share in Adam's business in return for helping him. He could have made a mint. Then again, it would have been another tie, another responsibility, another link to a family he wanted to keep at a distance. Of course he wouldn't have wanted that.

She gritted her teeth hard and forced Dan out of her mind, to which he seemed to return at the slightest opportunity.

She put the phone back to her ear.

'What about you? Any news?' her mother was saying. 'Is that Dan showing any signs of making an honest woman of you?' She gave the briefest of pauses, clearly believing the answer was a foregone conclusion of a no. 'Thought not. Work, then?'

How many times had Emma had varying versions of this same conversation? Made the right noises just to avoid interest and interference, just to keep her comfort zone comfortable? She never had any new successes to hold up to her mother's scrutiny, but she never had any epic failures, either. Comfortable, uncomplicated middle ground. And where exactly had it got her?

She opened her mouth to give her mother some stock fob-off—something that would buy her another couple of months below the radar before she had to repeat this whole stupid fake conversation all over again. Probably it would be something about her legal career boring enough to have her mother fast-forwarding onto her next gossip morsel before she could scrutinise Emma's life beyond the surface. It had worked like a dream these last few years.

For the first time in millions of conversations she hesitated.

She was the most miserable she could ever remember being and the hideous pain was sharpened to gut-wrenching level because she'd known that brief spell of sublime perfection before Dan had reverted to type. In actual fact there had been no reversion. He'd never left type. It had all been a façade.

Was there *any* aspect of her life left that was real or of value?

'Dan and I aren't together,' she blurted, then clapped a hand over her own mouth in shock at her own words. 'We never were.'

Except for a week or two when I thought I was the stand-out one who could change him.

'We work together and we had an agreement to stand in as each other's dates at parties and dinners.'

For the first time ever there was stunned silence on the end of the phone and Emma had the oddest sensation in her stomach. A surge of off-the-wall indignant defiance. She picked it up and ran with it.

She really had been wallowing in the role of Adam's underachieving sibling all these years, kidding herself about how hard that was, when in reality it had been the easy option. Pigeonholing herself as failure meant she had absolutely nothing to live up to.

She didn't need to define herself by her childhood inadequacies—she had known that for years—but knowing it really wasn't enough. The real issue was whether or not she'd truly bought into that. Or had a part of her remained that sweaty-palmed kid on the stage in spite of the passing years?

For the first time she took a breath and really did buy into it. Just how much of her inadequacy was she responsible for? Who had put Adam on a gilded pedestal and kept him there? Guilty as charged. It had been easier to live in his shadow than to prove herself in her own right.

Had it in some way been easier to accept the categorisation of herself as the clumsy one? The underachiever? The let-down? The singleton? No relationships for her, because that would lead to rejection. Just oodles of work, because that was the one thing she could feel good at, because it depended only on her. Had it been easier to blame her family for her failures instead of living an actual functional, healthy life?

'I'm taking a sabbatical from work,' she said. 'I'm going travelling.'

All that excitement she'd had about going away with Alistair, about escaping her dreary old life where everything was safe and secure and devoid of risk, made a cautious comeback. When she'd finished with him she'd finished with all of that, too. But now that Adam's wedding was over and the train wreck that was her friendship, relationship, romance with Dan was finished—she wasn't even sure what the bloody hell to call it—what exactly was there to keep her here? Why the hell did she need Alistair on her arm to have an adventure of her own?

She had absolutely no idea what she wanted in life any more, so why not take the time to find out?

* * *

She slid her bag from her shoulder and sat down at a pavement café overlooking the harbour. She ordered coffee and watched the bustle of tourists passing by, queuing for boat trips, browsing the local shops, fishing. The sun warmed her shoulders in the simple linen dress she wore. Just time for a coffee before her own boat trip departed—a day cruise around the island.

She looked up as someone snagged the seat opposite her with their foot, and her heart leapt as they pulled it out and sat down.

She must be seeing things. Maybe that was what happened when you missed someone enough—no matter how stupid and pointless missing them might be.

He took his sunglasses off and smiled at her, and she knew instantly that for all her telling herself she was way over him her thundering heart had the real measure of things.

'How did you find me?' she said.

He motioned to the waiter, ordered coffee.

'I had to ask your mother.'

Damn, he'd been serious about tracking her down, then.

'And how did that work for you?' She kept her voice carefully neutral.

'Well, it was no picnic, I can tell you.'

'She doesn't know where I'm staying,' she said. 'I've been picking up accommodation as I go along, depending where I want to go next.'

'I know. Didn't sound like you. What—no agenda? No travel itinerary?'

She grinned at that. At how well he knew her.

'My life's been one massive agenda these last few

years—all about what impression I want to give to this
person or that person. I needed a change. My mistake
was waiting for someone else to come along and insti-
gate that instead of biting the bullet myself.'

'She told me you'd been e-mailing her, and she knew
you'd booked a boat trip from here today. She just didn't
know what time.'

She stared at him.

'You mean you've been hanging around here all day
on the off-chance I'd show up?'

He shrugged.

'It was a good chance, according to your mother.' He
paused. 'It was the best shot I had.'

Bubbles of excitement were beginning to slip into her
bloodstream. She gritted her teeth and took a sip of her
strong coffee. Nothing had changed. Nothing would. He
might have jetted out to see her but it was still the same
Dan sitting opposite her. He probably just wanted the
last word, as usual. He earned a fortune. A plane trip to
the Balearics was hardly going to break the bank. She
wasn't going to get sucked back into this—not now.

'It wasn't particularly easy to persuade her to help
me, actually,' he added. 'Since you told her our relationship was fake.'

She looked sideways at him, one eye squinting against
the sun.

'It was, Dan,' she said.

He leaned forward, his elbows on the table, and for
the first time she saw how strained he looked.

'Don't say that.'

'Why did you come here?' she said. 'To make some
kind of a point? To finish things between us on your
terms? Go ahead and have your say, if that's what you

need for closure. Get yourself the upper hand. I've got a boat to catch. I've got plans.'

She moved her hands to her sides and sat on them to maintain some distance between them.

'I know that's how I've behaved in the past.' He held his hands up. 'I hated it when you met Alistair and pulled out of our stupid agreement. I've spent years making sure *I'm* in charge in every relationship I have. I've built a life on controlling everything around me. When you just dumped the whole thing without a moment's thought I just couldn't let it slide. I manipulated the situation until it worked in my favour—agreed to bring the agreement back just so that *I* could be the one to pull out of it. I thought I'd totally nailed why it bothered me so damn much. I thought it was about calling the shots. But really I think you've always meant more to me than I realised.'

He paused, held her gaze.

'I didn't track you down so I could make some kind of a point. I came to apologise and to try and explain.'

Her stomach was doing mad acrobatics and she moved one of her hands from underneath her legs and pressed it hard.

'Go on,' she said.

'I told you how things were with Maggie,' he said. 'The thing is, it wasn't just a break-up with Maggie— something that's tough but that you reconcile in time. There was this underlying feeling I've never been able to shake—that there was my one chance and I lost it. I never had that sense of belonging when I was growing up, and when Maggie got pregnant it felt like a gift. It was my opportunity to have a family and I would have done whatever it took to protect that.'

He sighed.

'Of course what it really boiled down to was an idea. I had this whole idealistic future mapped out in my head. Birthdays, holidays, where we were going to live. My family was going to want for nothing. I think Maggie understood the two of us better. If I'm honest, when she walked away, I think losing that whole dream future I'd been cultivating hurt a hell of a lot more than losing Maggie. I knew it, too, you see. It wasn't really working between us. If she hadn't got pregnant we might have carried on seeing each other for a few more months, then we would have gone our separate ways—wherever our work ambitions led us. We were fun. We were no-strings. It was never meant to be anything serious. Her pregnancy changed all of that. A baby on the way is one hell of a big string attached. Maggie didn't want me to look out for her. After we lost the baby it became very clear that for her any future we had together was gone. There was no alternative future—not for Maggie. She found it easier to cut all ties than to stick it out with me. And I knew that she was right. Because family hasn't exactly been my finest hour, has it?'

She held his gaze. She couldn't stop her hand this time as she reached across the table and touched his arm lightly.

'None of that means you're some kind of failure. It just means you haven't given yourself a proper chance.'

'I had absolutely no desire to give family a proper chance. Not when it ended up like that. It just seemed easier to accept that I'm not a family guy. And there were compensations.'

He gave her a wry smile. She smiled back.

'You mean your little black book of girlies?'

'I thought if I was going to cut myself off from family

life I might as well make the most of what the bachelor lifestyle has to offer. Don't get the idea that I've wallowed in misery for the last ten years or so, because I haven't. I've had a brilliant time. It's only very recently that…' He trailed off.

'What?'

He looked at her then and the look in his eyes made her heart flip over.

'That it began to feel…I don't know…hollow. Nothing seemed to give me the buzz that it used to. I kept trying to up the stakes—pitching for tougher contracts, brainstorming new business ideas. Dating just lost its appeal. I felt like I was doing the rounds—the same old thing, the same old conversations. I couldn't work out what it was I needed to fix that. And then you met Alistair.'

She glanced along the harbourside. The queue for her boat trip was gradually diminishing as people stepped into the boat. She should wrap this up…crack on with her plans.

But hearing him out suddenly felt like the most important thing in the world. She told herself it didn't mean her resolve was weakening, and for Pete's sake there were other boat trips.

'I don't think I'd considered you in that way before. I hadn't let myself. I'd conditioned myself to centre everything in my life on work. But suddenly you had all these big plans—you were buzzing with happiness, you were taking a risk—and I was stuck there on the same old treadmill. I didn't like it. I think I was fed up with my own life. But it's been so long. I've really typecast myself as bachelor playboy. I thought that was who I am. I didn't think I could be anyone else.'

She covered his hand with hers and squeezed it.

A sympathy squeeze. Not a leaping-into-your-arms-is-imminent squeeze. The hope that had begun to grow in his heart when she hadn't simply left the table at the get-go faltered.

'Alistair did me a favour,' she said. 'Until I met him I think I could quite easily have carried on in that same old rut I was in, pretty much indefinitely. Thinking one day you might come to your senses and show some interest in me—'

'Emma…' he cut in urgently.

She shook her head and held up a hand to stop him.

'The crazy thing about that was that I *knew* exactly what you were like. I'd seen it first-hand for months. Different women, same old short-term thing… You never changed for any of them. I used to think they were mad—couldn't they *see* what you were like? Didn't they *know* it was a recipe for disaster, getting involved with you? And then I went right ahead and did exactly the same thing.'

'It wasn't the same. You and I are different. *I'm* different.'

She was shaking her head.

'We don't want the same things, Dan. We're fundamentally mismatched. If I've managed to salvage one thing from the stupid mess with Alistair it's that I know I want to be with someone who puts our relationship first, above anything else. Above some stupid dream of a film career.' She paused. 'Above a crazy work ethic.'

'I want us to be together.'

'Back at the wedding…what you said about me and Adam…' She looked down at her fingers. 'You told me I *liked* living in Adam's shadow. That I was wallowing in always being the one who didn't measure up. And you were right. Knowing I'd be perceived as a failure was the perfect excuse for not trying things, for staying safe. All this time—right back since school, where it felt like nothing I did was right—I've been living in Adam's shadow, and somewhere along the way I learned to prefer it. It made everything easier. Doomed not to measure up, so why bother trying?'

'But you've done brilliantly at work. You're sought after. You do a great job.'

She shook her head, a rueful smile touching her lips.

'The one area I knew I could succeed at, yes. That was a safe bet, too. I made sure I picked a job that doesn't depend on other people's perception of you for success. And something as far removed from Adam's work as possible. I don't even think it was a conscious decision—it was more of an instinctive self-preservation thing that I've been cultivating since I was a stupid, oversensitive teenager.'

She looked up at him then and the look in her eyes wrenched at his heart.

'I even deluded myself, Dan,' she said. 'I thought the single most essential thing, if I was to find someone, was for them to put me first for once. That was my bloody dating criteria, for Pete's sake! Being important to someone. Anyone.'

She threw a hand up.

'Alistair would've done. An idiot like him! If he'd carried on treating me like a princess I'd probably still be there with him, feeling smug and telling myself I was happy with that self-centred moron. I was missing the point completely. The person I really want to be important to is myself. *I* never thought I was worthwhile, but it was easier to put that on other people. I thought I could get self-esteem by keeping away from my parents, moving to London, fobbing them off with a fake life of the sort I thought I should have. But all along that was part of the problem. I liked my fake life better than my real one, too. I never really wanted to be me.'

'I want you to be you,' he said. 'There's not one single thing I'd change about you. Not even your obsessive overpacking for one weekend, which fills me with horror at what you might be like to actually *live* with—how much *stuff* you might bring into my life. I've never wanted anything more. I was scared. Too scared to give our relationship everything I've got because I didn't want to risk losing it. My track record sucks. I couldn't afford to buy into it completely because I couldn't bear to lose you.'

He reached a hand out and tucked a stray lock of her hair behind her ear. She reached for his hand, caught it and held it against her face. But her eyes were tortured, as if she were determined to stick to her decision regardless of how much it hurt.

'What about kids?' she said quietly, and his heart turned over softly. 'What about your glass furniture and your bachelor pad and your determination never to have a family of your own? Because that stuff *matters,* Dan. I'm only just starting to find myself here, but what if I want to have kids in the future? Are you going to run for the horizon?'

A smile touched his lips at that, but her face was deadly serious. Inside his spirits soared.

'I never thought I'd have another chance at family,' he said. 'I know I've built a life that reflects that, but it's all window dressing—all peripheral stuff that I've built up to convince myself as much as anyone else that I'm living the bachelor dream. Truth is, the bachelor dream is pretty bloody lonely. I want to be with you—whatever that involves.'

The thought of a future with her by his side, the possibility of a family of his own with her, filled him with such bittersweet happiness that his throat constricted and he blinked hard and tried to swallow it away.

'So what are you suggesting?' she said, her eyes narrowing. 'Another crack at the plus-one agreement, just with a few more terms and conditions? Maybe with me living in?'

He shook his head, looked into her eyes in the hope that he could convince her.

'The agreement is dissolved,' he said. 'It's over—just like it should have been after that weekend. Months before that, even. I was just looking for a way to keep seeing you that held something back.' He paused. 'But by doing that I've undervalued you. I didn't know until I lost you that I'd taken that risk already. Trying to keep some distance couldn't change that. I love you, Emma. I'm *in* love with you.'

Silence as she looked into his eyes, except for the faint sound as she caught her breath. The guarded expression didn't lift.

'That's all very well, but you've got your business to think of. I'm going travelling. I'm doing something for *me* for a change. I want my life to go in a different direction. I don't want to end up some bitter, twisted woman trying to live my kids' lives for them because I've done such a crap job at living my own life that I'm totally dissatisfied with it. You can't just expect me to throw in the towel on all my plans because you've decided you want to give our relationship a proper go. Not after everything that's happened.'

'I don't expect you to back out of all your plans. I'll come with you.'

She laughed out loud at that and he realised just how entrenched his work ethic had seemed to the outside world.

She shook her head. 'That's never going to work and we both know it. What would happen to your business? You can't even leave it alone for a weekend without carting your laptop and your damn mobile office with you. You're the biggest work control freak in the universe.'

She stood up then and his heart dropped through his chest.

'I'll do delegation for you!' he blurted.

'You'll what?'

She looked back at him, her nose wrinkled, amusement lifting the corner of her mouth.

'I'll delegate. For you, I'll delegate. Give me a few weeks to promote someone to manager and do a handover and then I'll fly out and join you. Doesn't matter where you are—you choose the itinerary. We'll have a sabbatical together.'

A moment passed during which he was convinced he'd lost her, that there was nothing he could do or say that would persuade her.

He stood up next to her, took her hand in his, tugged her back down onto the seat beside him. The fact that she went willingly he took as a positive sign. At least she wasn't running for the boat without hearing him out.

'Please, Emma,' he said. 'I know how it sounds. I know I haven't got a great track record when it comes to taking time off work. But this is different. This isn't just some holiday. This is *you*. You're more important to me than the business. You're more important to me than anything.'

She looked down at his hand in hers, tentative happiness spreading slowly through her. He was ready to put her first. And she knew how much that must cost him after what had happened to him in the past. He'd spent the last decade not letting anyone or anything become important to him.

She laced her fingers through his, finally letting herself believe, and offered him a smile and a nod.

'You realise that if you take me, you take my family, too?' she said, and then he was kneeling in front of her.

'Your mother can organise the wedding,' he said, taking both her hands in his.

* * * * *

A sneaky peek at next month...

MODERN™
tempted

**FRESH, CONTEMPORARY ROMANCES TO TEMPT
ALL LOVERS OF GREAT STORIES**

My wish list for next month's titles...

In stores from 21st March 2014:

❏ One Night with Her Ex – Lucy King

❏ Flirting with the Forbidden – Joss Wood

In stores from 4th April 2014:

❏ The Secret Ingredient – Nina Harrington

❏ Her Client from Hell – Louisa George

Available at WHSmith, Tesco, Asda, Eason, Amazon and Apple

Just can't wait?

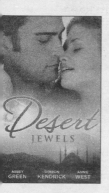

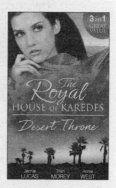

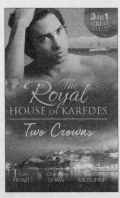
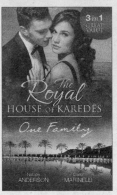
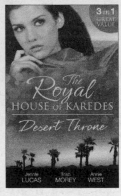

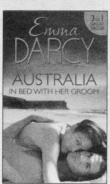

Discover more romance at

www.millsandboon.co.uk

- ❤ WIN great prizes in our exclusive competitions
- ❤ BUY new titles before they hit the shops
- ❤ BROWSE new books and REVIEW your favourites
- ❤ SAVE on new books with the Mills & Boon® Bookclub™
- ❤ DISCOVER new authors

PLUS, to chat about your favourite reads, get the latest news and find special offers:

- Find us on facebook.com/millsandboon
- Follow us on twitter.com/millsandboonuk
- ❤ Sign up to our newsletter at millsandboon.co.uk